PRAISE FO

"A rollicking page-turner, *North Country* captured my heart and imagination from the very first page. Sarah Branson's storytelling shines with rich, narrative prose and heart-pounding pacing. She crafted a story of resilience and empowerment that kept me on the edge of my seat, turning the pages late into the night."

—HEIDI MCINTYRE, AUTHOR OF *SEA MAGIC*

"Sarah Branson weaves together a high-octane adventure with deeply resonant themes of emotional growth, the search for belonging, and the pursuit of truth. I was drawn, in different ways, to each of the four main characters' personal journeys of self-discovery and transformation. Loved this read that kept me hooked from start to end!"

—SHAIL RAJAN, AUTHOR OF *THE SUMMER BREEZE* SERIES

"Sarah Branson's latest novel, *North County,* returns Kat Wallace to another heart- stopping sci-fi adventure. Imagine a steampunk world laced with pirates and special interests. This is no world for a woman to navigate —but Kat does so with zest. Readers and book clubs seeking strong can't-put-it-down sci-fi reading will find *North Country* filled with insights and vibrant encounters powered by likable, realistic women."

—DIANE DONOVAN, SENIOR EDITOR, MIDWEST BOOK REVIEW

"Kat Wallace is in charge. But that doesn't mean she's in control. This ensemble piece moves thrillingly fast, yet Branson captures the subtleties of character and interactions between women with care. I could not put the book down. Kat has grown into a woman of emotional maturity, decisive and compassionate. I strongly recommend this book!"

—ANNIE BALLARD, AUTHOR OF *THE SISTERS OF STELLA MARE* SERIES

"One mission, four women, four life-changing outcomes. Kat Wallace leads her pirates deep into the frozen North Country to face bigots, guns, biffo thugs, and torturous Chinese agents. Sarah Branson writes with insightful depth about women entangled in complex and dangerous relationships. Another stellar swashbuckling novel about the pirates of New Earth."

—STEVEN SAVANNA, AUTHOR OF THE *HOTEL EXOTICA* FUTURE CRIME SERIES

"*North Country* is a vivid adventure read with a social pulse. It ignites the pirate in us all who wants to throw off inhibitions and go after what we want in life. This book is both loads of fun and inspiring!"

– PAULETTE STOUT, MULTI-AWARD-WINNING AUTHOR AND PODCASTER

PRAISE FOR SARAH BRANSON'S PIRATES OF NEW EARTH SERIES

A Merry Life

> "Kat Wallace is one of the best heroines you'll find in contemporary sci-fi. We recognize Kat's flaws but admire her emotional depth and strength of character as well as her burning desire to do what's right."
>
> — DAVID ARETHA, AWARD-WINNING AUTHOR AND BOOK EDITOR

> "A fantastically fast-paced page-turner, with a dark streak. Sarah Branson plunges readers into the action and doesn't let us catch our breath until the very last page. You won't be able to put it down!"
>
> — DEBBY APPLEGATE, AUTHOR OF *MADAM: THE BIOGRAPHY OF POLLY ADLER*

> "Swashbuckling, vengeance and heart - all wrapped up in one heck of a strong woman."
>
> —SALLY ALTASS, AUTHOR OF *THE WITCH LAWS* AND REEDSY.COM REVIEWER

"*A Merry Life* starts as an adventure tale but quickly becomes something richer. Kat Wallace gains far more than her freedom when she flees to the New Earth pirate nation Bosch. Watching Kat develop from hot-headed revenge seeker to a competent, mature, powerful woman is deeply satisfying."

— R. L. OLVITT, AUTHOR OF *THE FEATHERED SERPENT*

Navigating the Storm

"Without a doubt, this series (and this book) is one of my favorite reads of the year. If you like pirates and sci-fi, Sarah Branson has masterfully combined the two, and you should absolutely check this series out."

–MELISSA LORINGER, BOOKSTAGRAMER @HEREFORTHEPLOTTWIST

"I absolutely adored *A Merry Life*. If possible, *Navigating the Storm* is even better than the first instalment in Kat's tale. Branson isn't afraid to rip your heart out or to make you laugh."

—SALLY ALTASS, AUTHOR OF *THE WITCH LAWS* AND REEDSY.COM REVIEWER

"This is an incredibly impactful, emotional, entertaining, funny, heart-tugging book."

—MARTHA BULLEN, BOOK PUBLISHING COACH AND OWNER OF BULLEN PUBLISHING SERVICES

"*Navigating the Storm* is not your typical pirate book. Rather, it is a blend of science fiction with steampunk and cyberpunk interlaced with realistic human emotions and experiences set in the twenty-fourth century. Action is high paced and riveting."

—CINDY VALLAR, EDITOR, *PIRATES & PRIVATEERS*

Burn the Ship

"*Burn the Ship* is as action-packed and entertaining as the first two books in the series, but in the third novel we see Kat growing as a person. The *Pirates of New Earth* novels are fast-paced, engaging, other world creative, and leave you cheering for Kat at every turn."

— JACQUELINE BOULDEN, AUTHOR OF *HER PAST CAN'T WAIT*

"In *Burn the Ship,* we watch as Kat comes into her own as a leader and a woman.

At its core, this is a pirate story, so that means lots of swagger, swashbuckling and narrow escapes. With Branson at the helm, it also means glimpses inside the home and family Kat has lovingly built – and will go to any lengths to defend."

–MARY ANN SABO, OWNER AND RINGMASTER, SABO PR

"This is Kat's third outing, and each book has gotten better and better. Branson writes her heart and soul into these astonishing novels, bringing the reader joy and heartbreak in equal measure. [Kat is] the most imperfect heroine that I've ever had the pleasure to read, and it's what makes her so compelling. Bravo, Sarah."

–SALLY ALTASS, THE INDIE BOOK NOOK AND AUTHOR OF *THE WITCH LAWS*

Blow the Man Down

"Sweet New Earth—the *Pirates* series culminates in spectacular fashion! This story is more riveting than anything you can watch on Netflix tonight."

— DAVID ARETHA, AWARD-WINNING AUTHOR

"Don't mess with Kat Wallace! This action-packed novel will keep you on the edge of your seat as Kat strikes back when her family is threatened. *Blow the Man Down* is a fast and captivating read, and a must-read for fans of action, adventure, and romance."

— BRITTANY COFFMAN, KAT AFICIONADO AND MIDWIFE, AGLOW MIDWIFERY

"*Blow the Man Down* caps Sarah Branson's wonderful, exciting *Pirates of New Earth* series perfectly. The deeply dimensioned characters leap off the page, the action is nonstop, and the thrilling ending more than satisfies. A real crowd-pleaser. I'm sorry the series had to end!"

— ANDREA VANRYKEN, AUTHOR AND EDITOR

"Sarah Branson creates just the right blend of action and discovery that keeps Kat growing, evolving, and challenged to do and be more. Together, the books create a world both realistic and thoroughly absorbing. Women will find Kat's dilemmas emotionally compelling. Book clubs will find many discussion points sparked by the series."

— D. DONOVAN, SENIOR REVIEWER, *MIDWEST BOOK REVIEW*

"*Blow The Man Down* dishes out the divine retribution and karmic justice that we've been patiently waiting for. Accentuated with signature Branson shock value, it's impossible to step away from this book once the first pages are opened. The only remaining question is 'what does Kat do next?'"

— IRIS HERMANN, WORDSMITHING FARMER

NORTH COUNTRY

A KAT WALLACE ADVENTURE

SARAH BRANSON

Enjoy the adventure!
Sarah E Branson

SOONER STARTED PRESS

North Country
A Kat Wallace Adventure

For more information, visit www.sarahbranson.com

Edited by Rebecca Maizel, David Aretha
and Andrea Vanryken
Cover design by The Book Designers:
Ian Koviak and Alan Dino Hebel

ISBN (paperback): 978-1-957774-18-3
ISBN (ebook): 978-1-957774-19-0

Printed in the United States of America

For Dilara, may you grow strong with the love that surrounds you and may you take your place among the strong women of the planet.

Stepping onto a brand-new path is difficult, but not more difficult than remaining in a situation, which is not nurturing to the whole woman.

MAYA ANGELOU

North Country
Dobarr
Arania
Fairneau
Toronto
Tabonne
Bosch
New Detroit
Haida
Ohlone Bay
State of Eternia
Truvale
New Lisbo
Bellcoast
New Caribbean
Mynia
Parida
Seething Swamp
Dakal
District I Banking, Financial, Theater
Distract II Light Industry, Business
District III Mining (Clay & Glitter)
District IV Harbor
District V Mining, Manufacturing (Bricks & Glitter) also a developing artist community
District VI Agricultural (Grains, Livestock)
District VII Agricultural (Vineyards, Orchards)

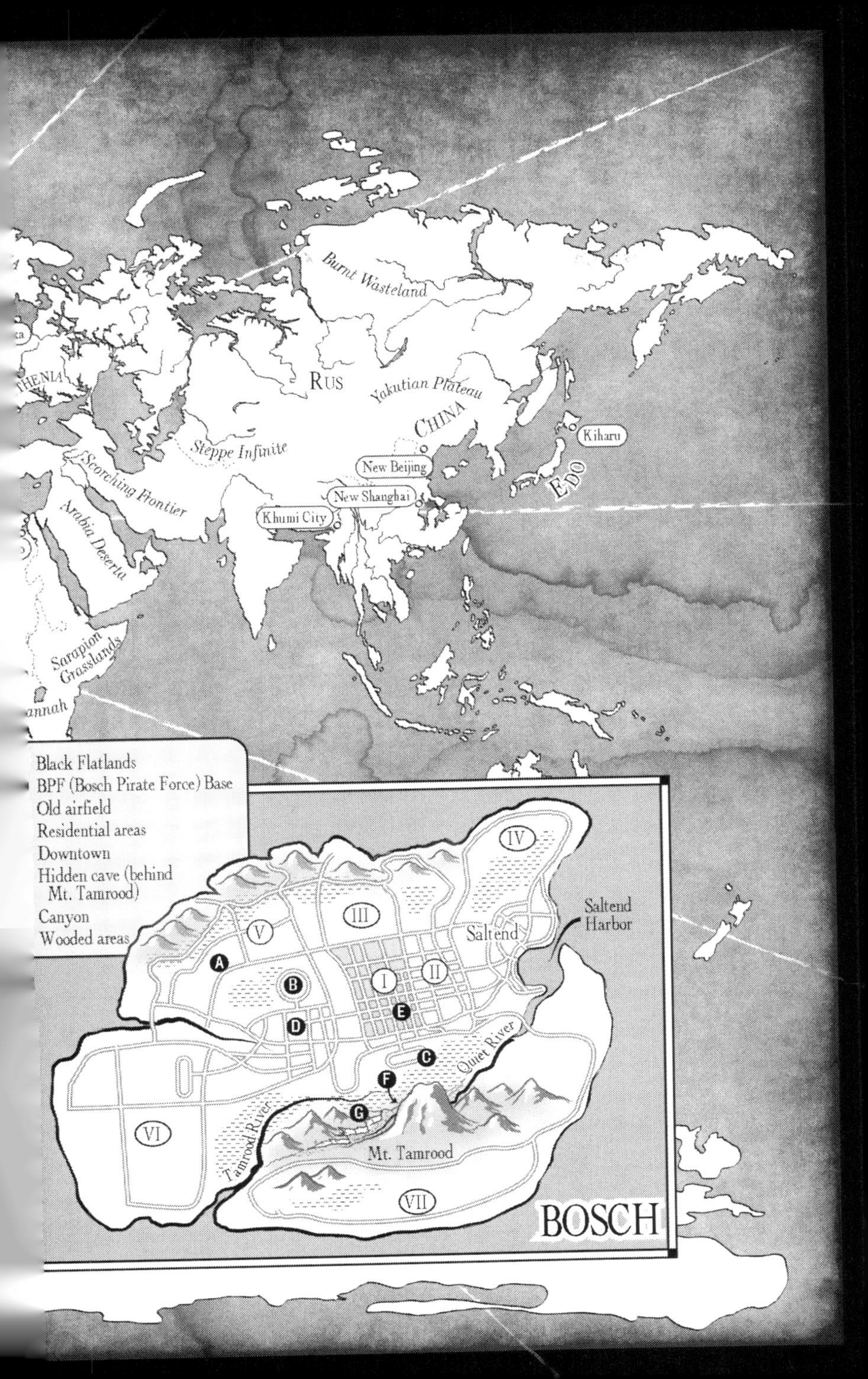

Burnt Wasteland
RUS
Yakutian Plateau
CHINA
Kiharu
EDO
Steppe Infinite
New Beijing
New Shanghai
Khumi City
Scorching Frontier
Arabia Deserta
Sarapion Grasslands
Black Flatlands
BPF (Bosch Pirate Force) Base
Old airfield
Residential areas
Downtown
Hidden cave (behind Mt. Tamrood)
Canyon
Wooded areas
Saltend Harbor
Saltend
Quiet River
Tamrood River
Mt. Tamrood
BOSCH

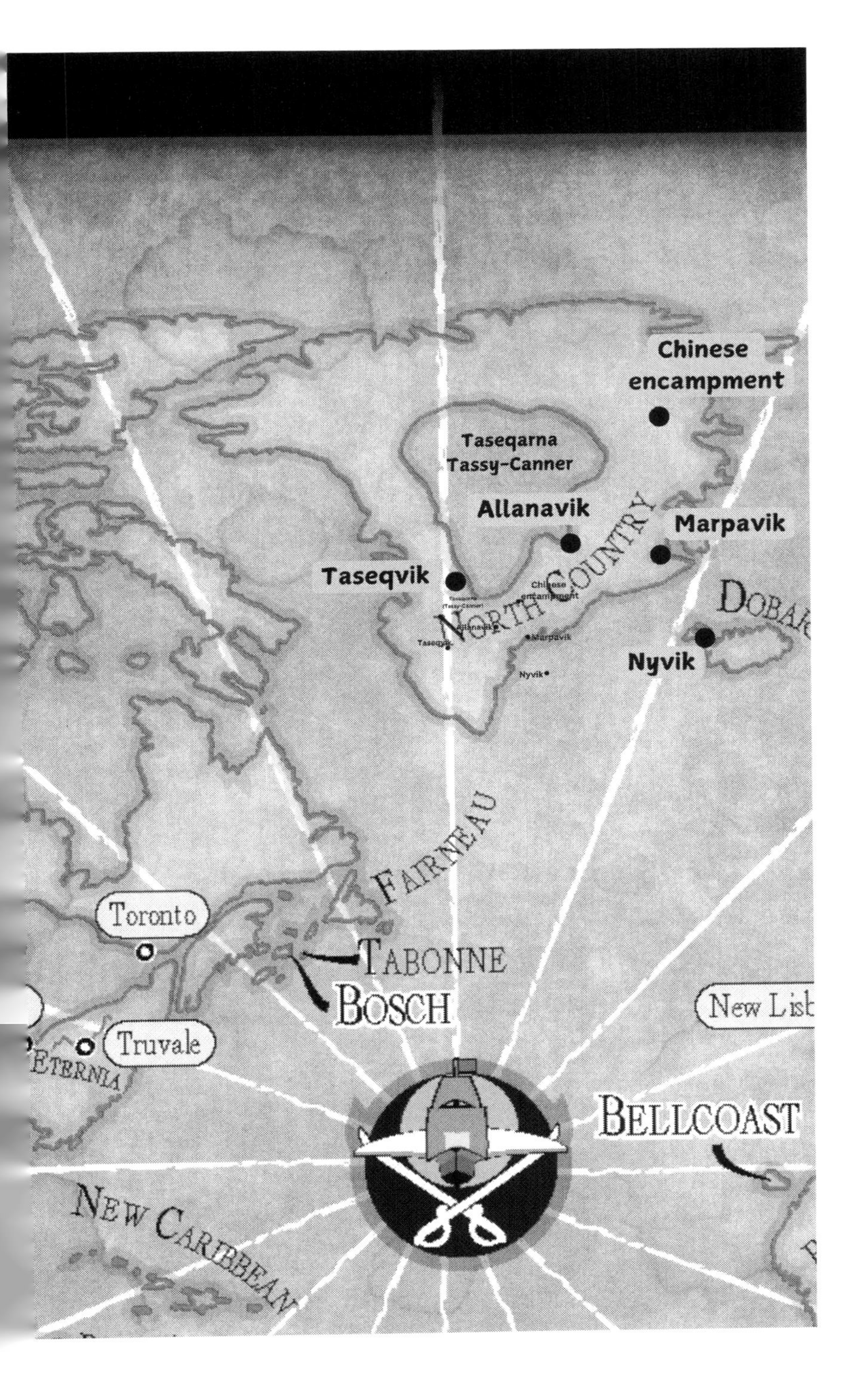

Chinese encampment
Taseqarna
Tassy-Canner
Allanavik
Marpavik
Taseqvik
NORTH COUNTRY
Nyvik
FAIRNEAU
Toronto
TABONNE
BOSCH
New Lisb
Truvale
ETERNIA
BELLCOAST
NEW CARIBBEAN

CONTENTS

DAY FOUR

PROLOGUE

North Country, December 2371

Cole Wallace tromped through early December snow, the storm swirling about him, creating a fog of icy bits that stung his cheeks and lodged in the many creases and wrinkles of his exposed face. His hands were shoved deep into his pockets and his head was bent down against the chill, cutting wind. *Can't be much farther,* he thought, though lately the three-kilometer trek from his place to The Burntback seemed to stretch a little more every week.

"I'm too fuckin' old for this," the old man murmured to himself. The older he got the more he despised the cold, and this year's winter was particularly rough. Fall had lingered into October, but then the first snowstorm hit the village of Allanavik with all the might and main of a blizzard, and afterward, the storms kept rolling in one after another every week, some lasting more than a day. The winter of 2371 was going to be one for the history books. Not that they had much use for those up here anymore, not since the militia shut the secondary school down and burned any objectionable books.

Marge…or was it Maude? She'd been living with him for a month, but he still wasn't positive—didn't much matter, though, as long as she kept his place decently clean, got a couple meals on the table each day, and spread her legs whenever he could manage to get it hard. Hell, she could be named Hortense for all he cared. But anyhow, the other day at breakfast, his most recent woman had said the storms were sent by the Christian god, the one that damned new preacher had embraced.

"It be like this because you and the other pagan men keep up with all the whiskey and the Glitter. He's angry and is gonna freeze us all if you don't repent and come with me to church."

"Is that so? Well, as I understand it, whiskey and Glitter ain't peculiar to these parts. You think he be freezing the whole of New Earth, or just us up here in the North Country?"

"Don't matter about what happens to foreigners. God'll deal with them how he sees fit. But preacher says we gotta get right if we want the weather to moderate." Marge/Maude had stamped her foot and put her hands on her hips as she said this.

It was somewhat exciting to see her all riled up and red in the face as she confronted him. Of course, he set her straight for talking to him like that, just as a man was meant to do, with a firm backhand that spun her into the table, scattering dishes and left-over biscuits and reindeer sausage. As she picked herself up from the floor, sobbing, he snorted a laugh. He stuck his fingers in the blueberry jam that now was oozing towards the edge of the table then reached out and smeared it across her face, criss-crossing the red mark his hand had made. "Well, now, don't you look like some of those Bluies that Preacher Burns is always sucking up to? Go show him your colors—see if he takes a slut like you into his house. Now stop thinking and start cleaning. I'm headed out to split wood before your god sends us another storm."

He grinned as he thought about the exchange and then shut his mouth quickly as the whirling pellets of snow hit his gums where his teeth were missing. Glancing up, the ghostly silhouette of a building took form through the monochromatic blur, and Cole blew out a thankful breath that swirled in a cloud around him. He had reached his destination.

A billow of warmth engulfed him as he opened the door and stomped the snow from his boots in the anteroom. Cole looked up and raised a hand to Ruben, the bartender, who tilted his head in response as he continued to wipe the glasses with a towel that likely put on as much dirt as it removed. Cole hung his coat up and moved into the seedy tavern. It was one of his favorite places. The place where he was king. They even called him Old King Cole from some ancient kid rhyme. It was a good palace. It smelled of woodsmoke and beer and there was a fresh scent of cut wood from the new sawdust Ruben had sprinkled over the floor before opening. There were several tables set up in the big open area, all filled with men laughing raucously, playing White Bear or poker, some just drinking whiskey and talking. A roaring fire was in the fireplace that took up most of the far wall, and rickety stools lined the dilapidated, wooden bar. Only one was occupied. A sturdy man with a long, wild beard, easily twenty years younger than Cole, sat at the far end, away from all the merriment and as far from Ruben as possible, a half-empty bottle of whiskey in front of him.

Cole's lips curled into a vile smirk as he called, "Hey, shit-bag, got any news for us?"

Cole's barb was rewarded as a roll of laughter came from several of the men from the tables. The bearded man, however, didn't even look Cole's way. Snorting his own laugh, Cole headed toward his table and his throne.

Cole was midway through his third beer when the kid showed up. Tall and gangly, with a shock of strawberry blond hair that made Cole think fondly of the days when he still had more than a few stray wisps on his head, he looked around Burntback with anxious eyes. Fuck, you could always tell the newbies. A raised hand by the King of Burntback visibly calmed the rookie, and he made his way over to the largest table where several men sat, Cole in his cobbled-together royal seat.

"You got my package, kid?" Cole asked without preamble.

The kid bobbed his head. "Yessir, Mr. Wallace."

"Hand it over then." Cole kept his voice even, but he could feel the itch in his brain as he thought about having that first chunk of Glitter. A couple mouthfuls and he wouldn't care if the snows lasted until June.

"Here's the thing." A sheen of sweat appeared on the kid's brow as he spoke. "Gaylord says this be the last. You gotta make another payment to get more. And the price's gone up."

Cole felt his anger crawl from his belly into his throat. "Gone up? Why the fuck has it gone up? You think I don't know how that piece-of-shit Gaylord doctors his product with fillers?" He slammed his palms on the table, almost upsetting a couple of the many beer glasses that littered it.

The kid took a step back. "I just be told what to say, Mr. Wallace." He stretched out a hand holding a small package wrapped in brown paper and tied with butcher string. "I don't deal with marker exchange." The sheen had become a full lather.

Cole grabbed the packet. "Well, dammit, I ain't got nothing left to sell. And we had an agreement that I got lifetime privilege after the last. I am Old Fucking King Cole! You tell Gaylord I expect him to hold to his word." His eyes were hot with fury. As he raged, some spittle landed on the errand boy.

"Yessir. I mean, your majesty. I'll tell him…" The kid was backing out of the tavern faster than a flash fire. In his haste, another small parcel fell, unheeded, from his coat. Cole waited until Ruben had signaled that the delivery boy was out the door, then he gestured to the bundle with his chin and slapped the arm of the man on his left. "Get that."

With a scrape of his chair, the man stood, retrieved the bonus Glitter, and handed it to Cole. Cole opened it with a laugh. "Looks like it's my lucky day." He offered the drug to the men at his table. "Not too much. It's mine." Each tore off a small piece of the deep brown, peaty-smelling, glittery square before tossing it into their mouths and chewing, finally washing it down with a slurp of beer.

Cole took his own larger piece, pausing to admire the threads of sparkling gold and silver that ran through it, before he too tossed it far back in his mouth where his few remaining teeth lay. As he chewed, he repeated in a grumble, "Had an agreement." He swallowed and huffed out his frustration. Glitter would float his irritation away soon, but for now he needed an outlet. His eyes flicked about the old tavern and settled on the bearded man at the bar. Cole's old eyes weren't as good as they had been but could see the whiskey bottle was close to empty and the man was sagging. Perfect.

He called, "Hey, shit-bag, we can't call you radio-man no more, can we?" He shoved his throne back and stood with a grunt. The man hadn't responded. He'd fix that.

"What's the matter, shit-bag? Cat got your tongue? Be that why that pretty school marm dumped you? Couldn't keep her happy?" Cole held up the first two fingers of his left hand in a V-shape, displaying nails that were long and dirty, with pale beds capped with brown bands. He made a nasty motion with his tongue at the base of the V and cackled. "Of course, the only women who want that are sluts and queers. Which I guess is right down your alley."

The man at the bar still made no comment.

Cole got closer until he could almost breathe down the big man's back. He hissed, "You be bad luck, you know. Anybody who fucked death carries the stench of it forever. It just be hard to smell on you over your shit-bag." The man shifted slightly on his stool, and Cole added one more stab, "But you be bad luck even before you took that shot. It was your fault they took her. You should've left well enough alone. She would've earned me good markers. You could've visited her here at Burntback. We know she'd spread her legs for you. Hell, I might have even given you a discount." Cole was about to spit on the man when suddenly he reared off the stool, spun, and lifted Cole by his shirt, shoving him up against the bar.

The man's blue eyes had narrowed, and the hatred in them made Cole's own eyes widen with panic. Finally, the man spoke, low and dangerous, carefully enunciating each word in his deep voice, "Don't speak of her. You got no right. I ain't forgot none of it. Never will." He slowly set the shorter man down onto his feet, keeping one hand on Cole's shirt. The man reached out and picked up his coat, releasing Cole long enough to slip it on. He took a step toward the door and then turned to thrust a finger at Cole's fear-blanched face. "You and me, Cole Wallace—we got unfinished business."

PREPARATION

CHAPTER 1

Kat, January 11

"No weapons in the negotiation room." A tall, broad-shouldered man with short, dark hair sprouting both from his head and his nose and wearing the uniform of the Visswani Royal Guard, a small principality located just east of New Cairo, barks out the order as Teddy and I start into the small, windowless chamber. I tighten my grip on my AR-86 and freeze mid-step, shifting my eyes to my master commander.

Teddy stands, his right hand in his pocket, his left draped loosely on top of his rifle, and tips his head ever so slightly as he looks at the guard. I survey his dark brown face; the familiar furrows and folds carved there over the years crease as he grins, the toothpick he had picked up after his meal with our host hanging carelessly in the corner of his mouth. His broad shoulders are still at ease, which I find reassuring, then he gives me one sharp glance that heightens my senses as he answers, "Ah. You expect us to ride in bare? Then I assume our Visswani negotiators will also be unarmed?"

The guard answers stiffly, "I will collect all arms and hold them on the weapons table." He glances at me and shifts uncomfortably, likely over the thought of disarming me. Teddy always briefs me on the customs and expectations when we go on missions together, which is more and more often now since I graduated from the Bosch Pirate Force and finally got my pilot's credentials. Most of our missions have been fairly straightforward as Teddy has worked to teach me the nuances of Glitter negotiation. It certainly seems simple enough. Bosch is, as far as we know, the only source of Glitter, the sparkling drug that makes all the problems of life simply disappear for a time, on the planet. We supply the Glitter to groups wishing to distribute it, and those groups pay us handsomely. It is the basis of the Bosch economy. But there can be mishaps and misunderstandings when such large sums of markers exchange hands, and that is why Teddy is training me himself. This is my first time at a virgin negotiation. Bosch has not done business with the Visswani before, so Teddy has been lecturing me on what he views as the essentials throughout the entire flight and even while home last night.

"If you want to be the best, you might as well learn from the best," he says—almost every single time we head out together. I roll my eyes and scoff because that's what Papa expects me to do, but I know he is the best and I am grateful for his tutelage.

As I flew us here, the lecture topic covered Visswani customs.

"These folk are traditional, with a capital 'T.' And they're patriarchal. Women aren't seen in the business environment," Teddy instructs. "That means someone like you… I mean, a person of your… Well, you know what I'm saying."

"You mean someone with tits and a twat?" I tease, knowing that this sort of talk makes my papa scandalized.

He frowns and gives a cough. "Now, Kat, there's no need to be so crude." He looks askance at me.

I start to laugh, but then say, "Crude, is it? What exactly did you expect when you enlisted me in your pirate army where people with, ah…my sort of components are outnumbered by folk with your appendages fifteen to one?"

Now Papa shakes his index finger in my face. "How many

times do I have to tell you, I don't like you calling it an army. It's the Bosch Pirate Force."

"Ah." I give him my best sassy look. "That would explain the initials on my tattoo then." I gesture at the figure of a ship that sails against the moon with the crossed daggers below and the initials "BPF" emblazoned on the inside of my left lower arm, just north of the puckered, circled "T" of my thrall brand. I let my eyes twinkle at this man, whom I would go to the ends of New Earth for.

He catches the tease and I see him suppress his grin. He covers it with a grunt. "Yeah, well, anyway, the point is you can use this sort of intel to your advantage."

And, of course, he has been proven absolutely correct. The Visswani don't think of me as a threat. In fact, they have treated me as if I am some odd curio that the old man keeps in his pocket. And so, for today, I am. I'll happily surrender my AR, but Teddy's glance tells me that caution and vigilance are necessary.

Teddy runs a hand over his head. His hair is a mass of tight curls, black underneath but overlaid with white as if a coal pile had been covered by a heavy dusting of snow. He smacks his lips slightly, continuing to play his part—a somewhat doddery old man. I chuckle inwardly at this ruse because although he is approaching his seventh decade on New Earth, he is well-muscled, an expert at hand-to-hand combat with a mind as nimble and discerning as any young pirate.

"Now, Kat, dear, give the gentleman your rifle for safekeeping." Teddy drawls the words a bit as he hands his identical AR over to the guards.

I follow instructions and divest myself of my rifle. "Yes, sir, Master Commander, sir." I say this formally and with a straight face and watch as the ghost of a smile crosses my adopted papa's lips. He turns and walks into the negotiation room, me at his heels, the Visswani guard close behind.

The room is completely white—walls, ceiling, floor, and furnishings. Three men wearing white tunics and pants sit on a long, white, padded bench that curves around a white table that holds a silver pot and four elegant cups—I'm guessing I won't be offered any refreshment in this room. I wasn't offered any earlier either. *A girl could get pretty hungry and thirsty living here.* I'll deal with my own needs when we are back on board our vessel and headed home heavy with markers.

Against the far wall sits a long table fitted with a glass-like box on its surface. Inside are three long rifles similar to what the guards carry here, but these look less ceremonial and more business-like. Hairy Nose Guard walks over and pulls out a set of keys, unlocks the box, and lays our weapons inside, locking them in securely. He then pivots and almost marches back out the door, shutting it behind him. A very quiet click catches my ear as a lock is engaged. I don't turn my head but simply file the information away. I can tell by the tiniest cock of Teddy's head that he heard it as well.

"Master Commander, please come and sit. We are honored that the leader of the Bosch nation has graced us with his presence." One of the Visswani motions to the bench while another pours a bright green liquid into the four cups. Teddy acknowledges the compliment and takes a seat, graciously accepting the offered beverage, though I don't see him lift it to his lips just yet.

I walk to the edge of the bench and position myself where I can see all four men. I stand at attention and listen to the conversation about me that does not include me.

"Women are not allowed at business in Visswani," Man Number One states in a flat, preemptory way.

Teddy chuckles. "This is my daughter, Kat Wallace. She is new to the Force, and I am training her up."

The men in white look curiously at me and then back at Teddy. I echo Teddy's chuckle in my head, though I keep my expression neutral. Their confusion is understandable; after all, I don't look a thing like Teddy. While he is just a hair taller than I am, I am as pale as he is dark; my eyes are a blue-green, and his, and Mama's, are a deep brown. And at twenty-one years old, I have no white in my dark blonde, loose curls, which I keep short, but not as short as Papa's.

"Daughter?" Man Number Two inquires.

"Daughter," Teddy reiterates. He gives no further information. "At ease, Kat." His voice is soft, but it contains all the authority to brook no argument.

I step into an at-ease position. This allows me to put my hands behind me, which allows me to easily access the pair of pistols I have strapped to my back under my uniform. The pistols that I did not offer up to the guard.

The three Visswani murmur together in their own language. While I am not fluent, I can pick out the essentials. I'm a woman; they don't want me here; they have a job to do; I won't be a problem. One seems to think I may bring bad luck, but he is overruled. Man One says to Teddy, "Well, then. We are happy to negotiate with you, Master Commander Bosch. Your…daughter…may stay and listen but cannot participate."

"Fine, fine, fine." Teddy waves the comment away as if it means nothing. "This green stuff is quite tasty. What is it called again?"

"It is called Amnaru. It is the traditional business drink for Visswani men." The respondent casts a glance at me to be certain I hear the implication that I am not to be offered any of the libation. As if I care; I have access to Teddy's whiskey stash at home.

My master commander dips his head equably and takes a drink. "Ahhh, quite delicious. I think I detect some licorice flavor, perhaps?" Then without waiting for an answer he cuts to the matter at hand. "Let's talk Glitter price."

And with that, the negotiation dance begins, filled with parries and thrusts, extreme suggestions, and casual allusions to walking away, pleasant chatter, and serious questions. The patter is generally the same at each mission, and while I am listening, my mind is also reviewing other matters. I have recently become intrigued with extractions, a mission where a specialized Bosch Pirate Force (BPF) member goes in and liberates a person or item and then returns that person or item to the paying customer. I plan to have Teddy teach me those skills as well. My mind then drifts off into a discussion Mama and I had about dating and making friends, two things I have not been successful at since I arrived in Bosch close to a year ago. I close my eyes for a moment, trying to remember the three suggestions she made to help me improve in these areas when raised voices and sudden movement bring me back to the now. I am stunned by the sight that I open my eyes to.

One of the men in white is standing and shouting, and another has rounded behind Teddy and is holding a broad hunting knife to his throat. The third sits on the bench, relaxed and smiling. He speaks. "Sit down, Oriel. Master Commander, we will take the Glitter, your airship, and your daughter. You are worse than a fool —you are an old fool. Your daughter, if that is indeed what she is to you, can be an exotic pleasure to one of our royals, or she can be sold as a thrall. It matters not to us. No one on that island of yours will know why you did not return. Your body will never be located. We do not negotiate with pirates." He gives a flick of his wrist. "Kill him."

Something happens in my brain and in my body. Time slows down; emotion slips away and leaves me with razor-sharp senses. I feel myself pull my pistols and don't even pause to assess the threat as *Kill him* rings in my brain. Before I can even form a thought, I raise my hands and three shots ring out. The man with the knife tips to the side, the blade clattering to the floor and blood spatters staining Teddy's head, the back of the couch, and the pristine floor. The standing man looks down at his front, watching the growing crimson rose blossom on his elegant white tunic, then he crumples. The man on the bench sits momentarily still, a round red hole in his forehead echoed by the roundness of his mouth, which is curved in surprise, before he topples forward onto the table, spilling his Amnaru so the green flows to meet the puddle of red. I glance at my hands and see the pistols, then glance over and see Teddy staring at me and the men dead on the floor. I turn and shoot again, this time at the glass box, which shatters, sending glass shards in all directions.

Teddy runs to the table, holding up a hand to me, and, while kicking away some vicious fragments, grabs not only our ARs but also the Visswani weapons. He tosses my AR and one extra firearm to me. We make for the door, where I shoot the lock out while Teddy kicks it open. Hairy Nose has turned from his station and is fumbling with his weapons as he tries to respond to this unexpected event. I drop him.

"Time to go home, girl, fast," Papa orders. Before obeying, I look intentionally back into the negotiation room. The pure white is gone. Bright red and shades of pink stemming from three men's blood and brains stipple and dapple the bench, the floor, and even the walls. Good riddance. We take off for the nearest exit as an alarm is raised in the Visswani palace.

Almost seven minutes pass as we make our way through the halls and grounds to our vessel. There is no talk except for the occasional "This way" and "Heads up!" As we board, Teddy says, "You fly. I'll shoot." He mans the left gun as I take us up, high, fast, and away from the red and white room on Visswani.

After about twenty minutes in flight, he slips into the navigator seat next to me. His eyes are on me as I look straight ahead, engrossed in the joy and business of flight. "So, Kat. Thanks for my life."

My lips quiver and tears start to blur my vision.

Teddy's strong hand is on my shoulder, squeezing. "So, was that your first?"

This question disrupts the emotions that are building inside of me like a wave as I try to understand what he is asking. "First?"

"First kill. Are those the first people you've killed?"

The question makes me realize that I actually killed three, no four—Hairy Nose is likely dead as well—people. I pause, considering, and then answer, "Yes, sir."

The hand stays on my shoulder, firm and grounding. "The first time's real hard. It's okay to cry."

Turning my face toward Papa, I wrinkle my brow. "They are the first I have killed but not the first I wanted to kill." As I say this, the truth of my statement and the reality of what has occurred grips me, and I feel a small split in my brain. A memory flashes through my head of the first time that primal want flared in me—I am little and sobbing in a dusty, decrepit woodshed, hearing grunts and feeling pain deep inside. The image fades as quickly as it formed, and I look at Teddy. "I'm not crying over them. I was terrified that they might hurt you, and I could never allow anyone to do that, Papa. And besides, I will never go back to being a thrall."

Teddy looks at me and narrows his eyes, but a grin grows on his face, and he gives an actual laugh before he leans over to kiss me on my cheek. "That was damn fine shooting in there, Kat Wallace, and damn fine work getting us out safe. You've got a gift, which we will discuss. Later. For now, let's go home."

"MC? MC? Kat?" Betsy's voice pulls me out of my long-ago memory.

"Hmmm? Umm, sorry, Bets…" I turn from the French doors of the balcony off my third-floor office in Bosch Hall where I had been looking out at the green at Teddy's memorial statue. The "green" is now mostly brown as winter is coming swiftly; the sky is gray and heavy with the cold rain that was predicted. It is a marked contrast to the greenery and sunshine in the picture I hold, taken that day of Papa and me, twenty-one years ago. The one he kept close to his heart until the day he died and that I now keep close to mine.

Master Sergeant Fred was a junior ground crewman then and had just embarked on his photography hobby. He pulled his camera out when we landed and disembarked. "You two look like you've had an adventure. Shall I commemorate it with a photo?"

Papa and I looked at each other and laughed, then posed, our arms slung over each other's shoulders, each mugging for the camera. I realize now that if I look closely, I can see a small trickle of blood from a tiny cut on Teddy's neck.

Betsy looks at the picture in my hand and beams. "Oh, my, I remember that day. You two came in looking like butter wouldn't melt in your mouths. That's when I knew there had been a situation."

I grin. "Yeah, Papa had a tendency to gloss over some of the dicier events we engaged in."

"Oh, yes. But he couldn't pull anything past me." Betsy's laugh tinkles like bells.

I can't help but laugh as well. "None of us can, Bets."

"Well, I don't know about that. I did want to let you know, though, that Grey is outside and wants to see you."

My mood perks up at the idea that my daughter has come to see me. "Really? Now this a treat."

Betsy looks at me and crinkles the skin between her brows. How old is Betsy anyway? I have never dared to ask. I just take her out to lunch at her favorite spot in District 1 every year around the third week of September. She sighs. "Well, Kat, she's not alone. She has some schoolmates with her."

A sigh slips from my lips. Schoolmates—that means that boy she's been dating and the group of militant teenagers that he seems to attract. "It's that damn anti-Glitter group, isn't it?"

Betsy reframes. "They seem very…passionate."

"Of course they're passionate. They are sixteen and seventeen. Everything is black and white to them, and they are convinced that they absolutely know best."

"Well, I can tell them you are busy." Betsy begins to prepare her executive assistant evasion dance.

Another sigh. "No. I'll see them." I struggle to button the last two buttons on my vest, a task that of late requires that I blow a deep breath out and tighten everything.

Betsy watches. "Oh, dear. Shall I have the base tailor come in and re-adjust your uniform?"

Re-adjust. A euphemism that clearly means let out and make larger. "It's the damn desk job, Bets. I am not as active as I was before."

Betsy's eyes are sympathetic. "I understand. You've also had a time of it the last few months."

A little gasp escapes me as she references the topic I have carefully avoided confronting. "I s'pose so." I tug and wiggle as I fasten my master commander vest around my large, soft, and very empty midsection. "Let me go pee, and then you can show the idealists in."

Betsy reaches out and cups my face with one warm palm. "I'm just so glad you are still with us, Kat. Certainly Bosch needs you, but I would have been lost without my friend."

Now I feel tears threaten, and with that physical release, my rougher emotions manifest. Lately the two most common ones are Grief and Shame. Grief rises up in my head like a wraith, all dressed in deep purple robes and wearing a somber expression. They start to shake their head and come forward. Shame steps next to them, tall and thin with sharp features and a hook nose perfect for looking down over. *I cannot entertain any of you at the moment.* I shove them back and take a deep inhale, replying in a shaky voice, "You can't get rid of me so easily."

"And we are all thankful for that. I know your Matthieu is." Betsy turns toward the door. "I'll show Grey's group in in five minutes." She pauses and turns back to me. "Also, happy birthday, dear."

"Thanks, Bets." I wait until her back is turned to swipe the tears off my face. It is my birthday, but is it a happy one?

Flossie, January 11

The heat is a-risin', fire's in the sky,
But baby, when I'm with you, I'm feelin' so high.

Flossie Porter had her music cranked this morning as she stepped into the shower. She noticed a small crackle in the sound and pushed the door ajar, swiped her hands dry, and adjusted the wiring system she had fashioned so she could have shower music. She paused, tilting her head to listen, and then nodded, returning to the water to wash her hair as she sang,

We're survivin', baby, just you and me,
Through the storms and the flames, endlessly.

Using one of the half dozen skimpy washcloths that were standard issue in the barracks, she scrubbed her soft body. Dropping it to the floor of the small square shower, she pushed off the faucet with her toes as she bumped open the door with her hip and grabbed the rough towel from its hook with her hand all in one smooth motion. The efficiency of the move gave her a tingle of delight. She rubbed the dingy, worn towel across her body, then, frowning at its sandpaper-like texture, moved to blotting herself dry. A wistful remembrance of the large, thick, soft towels of her youth came to her. There wasn't much she missed about the affluence of her old, privileged life, but the towel factor.... *Who are you kidding, Floss? All the sumptuous towels in the world don't make up for having to grow up with an abusive dick of a father and a sad, drunken mother.*

With this thought in her head, she swung the thin, damp towel in a circle above her head and swayed her shoulders and hips to the smooth beat of "Surviving."

With the world fallin' down, love's all we need,
In your arms, I find what keeps me free.

Monday mornings, with their usual dreary assignment meetings, had taken a definite upturn for Flossie the past few months, ever since her master sergeant, Diamond Miata, had shifted from beauty-to-be-worshipped-from-afar to team member to actual friend. Flossie spent an inordinate amount of time since then spinning fantasies in her head about Diamond.

Now she artfully snapped the towel over the door of the shower and took a moment to run a hairbrush through her straight, fine hair. She leaned forward, peering into the small bathroom mirror, and eyed her pale face. Maybe some makeup today? Almost immediately she heard her father's voice in her head, dripping disdain. "Really, Farris, I don't think accentuating your unattractive parts is going to help."

"Fuck you, Mr. Vice President," Flossie answered the voice. "I happen to think I have very nice eyes. And lips." She ran her fingers over her full mouth. "And my name's not Farris anymore. And you're dead, so you can fuck right off." Flossie always liked reminding her father's voice of his deceased status whenever the niggling insults floated to the surface.

She had gone with friends to the shops in the elegant section of District One over the weekend and spent some of her hard-earned markers on some swanky cosmetics. Opening the container of Flame Red gloss, she applied an ample layer, then puckered up in the mirror and imagined kissing Diamond.

As she swiped on a bit of mascara, the music switched to one of the newer pop songs she had put on her Monday morning playlist, "My Temperature's Soaring," and Flossie sang along.

> The sun's too close, it's burnin' up the ground,
> But I'm on fire, can't cool this feeling down.
> Skies are red, rivers dried to dust,
> But when you're near, baby, it's more than just lust.

Flossie pulled on her Bosch Pirate Force uniform and looked in the mirror once more. She frowned. The makeup was too much, she decided. Her inner voice scolded, *Listen, girl, you may be smart and a tech whiz, but you are as plain as paper. Dressing it up won't change that. Don't try to be something you're not.* She grabbed the cloth from the floor of the shower and rubbed it over her eyes and mouth. Turning around, she looked again in the mirror. *That looks more like you.* She dropped the cloth, smeared with black and red, into the sink as she headed out to start her week, going to see the woman she adored.

Diamond, January 11

"Ronny…Ronny…listen, I have been bailing you out for half your life. When in the hell are you going to learn to take care of yourself? You're only five years younger than me," Master Sergeant Diamond Miata, tall, dark, and lanky, with her comm to her ear, had a distinct tone of impatience in her voice as she strode across the Bosch Pirate Force green through a soaking Monday morning drizzle on her way to the weekly assignment meeting at Bosch Intelligence. Several troopers, mostly men, but also several women, greeted her, their eyes filled with hope, enthusiasm, and desire, as the woman who was known to keep a dating waitlist passed them by. Diamond sighed. Everybody wanted something from her, not just her brother, Ronny. She knew she was expected to toss her beaded braids, showing off the diamonds she wore, and offer the supplicants a glowing smile, and usually, she enjoyed the attention. But lately her status as the "most beautiful trooper on base" felt like a heavy garment she had to wear every single day. Why couldn't she just go to work, run her missions, and maybe put away a few extra markers towards her retirement dream?

She used to dream big. There was a time, early in her recruitment, when she thought she'd be able to stack away enough markers to build a place on the beach out in Saltend like some of the officers had. She had envisioned it supplied with all the comforts, including someone to share it with. But that dream got pared back in the decade and a half that had passed. First there had been all that glorious attention she got when she arrived on base as she evolved from pretty Joselyn Miata, just another kid from District Four trying to get ahead, to Diamond Miata, the stunning, talented, and oh-so in demand pirate. It was a heady transformation, and one that required the purchase of thirteen diamonds studs over the course of several years and some rather painful piercings, but being Diamond felt right to her. Or at least it had for fifteen years.

But the diamonds weren't the reason the markers hadn't stacked up in quite the way Diamond had hoped. Her mother, who had never been great with personal economy, had essentially quit working a couple years after Diamond started getting paychecks from the Force and sending a little bit, and then a little bit more, home to help out. She didn't mind helping her family out, but the full weight of being responsible for her own mother and two of her three adult brothers drained her. "Listen, Ronny, I'll figure something out. But no more wagers until this debt is cleared up. I gotta go. I have to get to work. You should try it sometime." She didn't wait for the flippant response she knew was forming on her brother's lips as she clicked the comm off and pocketed it.

She showed her ID at the entrance to the Intelligence building and made her way to the room, knowing she was a few minutes late. She was in no mood to make an entrance and feel the weight of attention and admiration on her. Instead, she inched the door open, slipped in without a sound and peered about, looking for a place to sit.

In the back corner, she saw a plain young woman with a soft round face fiddling with a device for a moment and then handing it to a corporal who sat a table ahead of her. The corporal looked at the device and brightened with an appreciative look, giving a thumbs up.

The young woman returned the gesture, then her eyes saw Diamond and she raised her hand and patted the chair next to her. Diamond felt some of her frustration fade as a flush of warm gladness spread through her pushing up the corners of her mouth in a warm smile. The woman flushed slightly as Diamond made her way to the proffered seat.

"Thanks, Flossie," she murmured and saw her friend beam at the expression of gratitude. Flossie was so guileless. Her friendship was the most genuine and uncomplicated relationship that Diamond had experienced since childhood. If she was honest with herself, which she was most of the time, she did not have many actual friends. Sure, she was admired, even respected, but never really befriended. People always wanted something from her. Some wanted to sleep with her, others just wanted to be in her circle of influence. And then there were the ones that were jealous of her. Sometimes the same person shifted among all three categories.

But Flossie was different. She was several years younger than Diamond, and Diamond enjoyed being perceived as a mentor, but what she never said out loud to Flossie or anyone else was that her friend was whip-smart: smarter than Diamond. This had been discovered about six months earlier when both women were assigned to a team and a mission.

Diamond recalled that on that first assignment, she had been all too ready to disregard the bland-looking woman partnered with her. After all, there was nothing outstanding about the woman's looks. She was average or even slightly below in every way. Even her hair was, as Flossie had self-described it, the color of an aging mushroom.

The turning point of Diamond's view of Sergeant Flossie Porter had come when no one, including the senior officers of the team, could make sense of the intelligence Diamond had collected in the field. That was when the young, exceptionally unexceptional Sergeant Porter spent three minutes looking at it, tilted her head once or twice, and pieced the information together like a child working a puzzle. Diamond was then quick to realize how advantageous and valuable this ordinary-looking but brilliant colleague would be.

So, Diamond had figured she could make use of Flossie. What she hadn't counted on was the development of an unfeigned friendship. "Thanks, Floss. Not even nine bells on a Monday and already it's been a week," she grumbled. Flossie was so easy to talk to and she listened, really listened, to Diamond.

She crinkled her brow in sympathy, "Ugh, that's no good. Let me know how I can help."

Diamond's felt some of the tight tension in her shoulders drop off with Flossie's words. As she started to answer she noted the reverent look on her friend's face. There was no artifice to this woman, Diamond knew that Flossie had developed a crush on her, but she also knew her friend's low self-esteem would never allow herself to push beyond the bounds of friendship, and that suited Diamond just fine. Diamond had even mentioned her initial disparaging thoughts to Flossie after they had been friends for a few weeks and was surprised when the sergeant had simply said, "Makes sense. I'm not much to look at. I used to hate that, but now it's sort of my secret weapon. Someone once said I was like everyone's old, maiden aunt they could trust with all their secrets. Those are the same folks who get tongue-tied talking to someone as drop-dead gorgeous as you." Diamond had laughed and could see the truth in her friend's statement. She had been surprised by how much she appreciated the matter-of-fact compliment from the young woman.

Now, the master sergeant glanced at her teammate and replied in a low voice, "It's my brother. He's got himself in a fix again. And he and Mom are inundating me with messages reminding me of my *duty* to family." She glanced up to the front of the large, windowless conference room. The beige paint was peeling a bit near the far wall where Colonel Greene stood droning on. She gave a small, tight tilt of her head in his direction in an attempt to get Flossie to focus less on her and more on the CO. *Let's not draw negative attention.* Diamond was quite cognizant that if she was going to move ahead in the Force, she needed to make an impression on those in charge. Her luxurious beach house dream was now scaled back to one that involved opening a gym in District Two and having a nice apartment nearby with a holiday to District Four once or twice a year. But to make that dream happen she had to focus her energies on Diamond not Diamond's constantly needy family.

"It's fine." Flossie whispered back, "We already have our assignments for the week. Greene won't care. So, which one is it? Ronny, Max, or Kyron? You're not going to have to sell another diamond, are you?" Flossie always commented on Diamond's sparkling jewelry, though she never wore any adornments.

Diamond scoffed quietly, "Same old story. It's Ronny—again—and, no, not if I can help it this time." She had sold one jewel last year after her ne'er-do-well Ronny had gotten himself in debt to some of the guys from the old neighborhood. Ronny liked to gamble, but winning did not seem to be part of his plans, no more than holding down a job was. "I'm going to need to come up with some markers for him, though." She hit the table with her fist, far more softly that she wanted to and puffed out a disgusted breath.

Flossie went quiet and sat staring at the floor for several minutes. Diamond was careful not to disturb her. She had learned that when her friend took on that glazed expression, wheels were turning in her brain getting ready to churn out some amazing ideas. After another few minutes, Diamond's patience was rewarded. "What if we picked up one of the premium off-island assignments? Those can be pretty lucrative."

Diamond brightened at this suggestion. "Good idea, but... we'd need a decent pilot." Neither Diamond nor Flossie were qualified BPF pilots. Diamond could certainly maneuver a vessel from point A to B, but she could not do anything fancy in the air, and the Pilots' Coalition was clear as to who was allowed as the pilot of record for missions. Flossie avoided flying, and the two times Diamond flew with her, she saw that she actually got airsick. "And a good pilot will cut into the profits."

A voice from the front of the room interrupted the conversation. "Master Sergeant, Sergeant, am I being too loud up here for the two of you?" Diamond looked up and saw Colonel Greene staring at them both. She rapidly dropped her device into her lap and glanced at Flossie who had flushed a deep red. Truthfully, she felt the warmth of a flush as well but was pleased it didn't show as easily on her face.

"No, sir. I mean, apologies, sir." Diamond sat up, and folded her hands in front of her, attempting to look sincere and apologetic at the same time. Fucking officers—as bad as schoolteachers when she was a kid. Someday maybe she'd be the one giving disapproving looks and making the rabble shut their mouths. But for now, she thought about Flossie's idea. She needed to make serious markers. Ronny was deep in debt—again. And if that didn't let everyone know what an idiot he was, he also told his bookies where he had gotten his markers to pay them last time. And now, those hoodlums he owed markers to wanted to meet with Diamond. She could go into the meeting with a weapon, and she wouldn't miss, but killing a Bosch citizen would mean banishment for life off-island, which was not on her list of things to accomplish; so another option was necessary, and cashing in on some profitable missions could be the ticket.

Carisa, January 11

Carisa Morton stood in her office on tiptoes, one hand gripping the middle shelf of the tall wooden bookcase and the other stretched to its limit toward a large leather-bound book on the top shelf.

"Hey, careful there, Morton. Let me get that." The deep voice came up behind her, and a broad, brown hand grasped the book her fingers had been tickling.

Carisa dropped back off her toes and rocked slightly as she struggled to regain her balance. Her department chair, Nate Cain, put a hand on her shoulder for the briefest second to steady her. She pressed her lips together, aggravated that her condition merited any notice. "Thanks, Nate. I shouldn't have shelved it so high." In a move that spoke of habit, she tugged her sweater sleeve down over her old thrall brand, her fingers grazing the familiar raised T inside a circle. She wasn't ashamed of it, but she knew it made Nate uncomfortable. Carisa could hear her therapist, Nanette, asking, "And why do you think you are responsible for everyone else's comfort?" Carisa sighed inwardly, *Old habits die hard, Nanette.*

Nate was a good chair, easy to talk to and upfront. But just like everyone else, he had become a bit over-attentive since her diagnosis went public. Just regular attention made Carisa feel unsettled and unworthy—an issue often at the crux of her sessions with her therapist, Nannette. Now all this extra attention made her want to both dig a hole and hide and, more recently, explode in anger and frustration.

A deep laugh rumbled out of her boss. "Well, for someone as little as you, everything is 'too high,' am I right?" Nate teased.

Carisa wanted to roll her eyes at this all-too-typical jape, but she was actively working on her eye muscles to improve her double vision, so she just shook her head. "Really, Nate? Short jokes?" On an island filled with tall, fit descendants of pirates who were mostly dark-haired and brown- and black-skinned, Carisa's petite, Nordic form was notable.

"Ah, I work with what the audience gives me." He chuckled as he began leafing through the book in his hand as Carisa took her seat behind her desk. "Norse mythology, huh?" He set the tome on the stack on the right side of the desk. Carisa glanced at it. The design on the front was almost like a snowflake but with eight trident-looking arms extending from a circle center with three crosshatches on each arm. Its form was haunting, and Carisa wanted to delve into the book to discover why it sparked memories for her. She hoped her fatigue would allow her a few hours to do so.

"Yep, it's for my comparative mythology class this semester. We're looking at Norse, Yoruba, and Olmec traditions this time."

"Mmm-hmm, I see that." Nate idly perused the titles in the stack, before moving on to the pile of vintage texts on the left-hand side of the desk. Carisa cringed inwardly; she had meant to put those in her bag to take home before anyone saw them. She watched as Nate's eyebrow came up for a moment. "Not exactly your usual fare, Morton." He began to read the titles aloud: "*Neuroimmunology, Demyelinating Diseases and Treatments in the 21st Century, Multiple Sclerosis—A Practical Manual…*"

Carisa reached over and scooped the texts up, depositing them in the oversized canvas tote she had brought with her today just for these books. "Those aren't for work."

Nate grinned. "Good, I didn't want to think I was losing you to the biology department." Then his face turned serious. "But, multiple sclerosis? What's that? I thought your diagnosis was UN?"

"Oh, it is. But 'Unraveling Nerves' or 'UN' is more of a colloquial name. It's actually called DMSAID, or demyelinating and sclerotic autoimmune disorder. And it used to be called multiple sclerosis during Old Earth times." Carisa looked thoughtful. "I kinda figured taking a look at what they were doing with MS before everything collapsed might garner something useful."

"You do love your research. But really, Carisa, the docs will take care of the UN, and the rest of us will take care of you. You don't need to worry." Nate's face was warm and sincere as he said this.

What if I don't want *to be taken care of?* Carisa felt a tiny flame of heat in her chest that she pressed down. *He's just being nice,* she reminded herself. "Thanks, Nate. I know you always have my back."

"And your top shelves," he said as he moved out her open door. "Don't go climbing around. Call me if you need something. Remember, you have a responsibility to avoid getting hurt." He pointed at her and winked.

For some reason this statement grated at Carisa, but she used her most pleasant smile. "Thanks, Nate. I will."

CHAPTER 2

Diamond, January 11

The chill rain had abated, and the two women strolled slowly back to the large office on the second floor where Flossie had her own cubicle, complete with a very cutting-edge computing device, three screens, and a bookcase that held work material, along with several novels, poetry books, and a mess of Old Earth communication devices that Flossie liked to collect. Diamond, as a field trooper, did not have an office, so Flossie's space had become hers by extension. She flopped down in the chair beside the desk.

A middle-aged officer stuck his head into the office. "Hey, Porter. Thanks for cleaning up my computer. It runs so much faster now."

"Sure thing, Captain. Anytime," Flossie answered.

Diamond scowled slightly, a bit surprised at the twinge of jealousy she felt. "Why is he bothering you with that instead of tech support?"

Flossie rolled her shoulders. "Tech support always has a long wait, and he needed it to work. Only took me a minute."

"Still," Diamond grumbled, "I don't like him using you like that. Isn't that just like an officer? Use the little people. I tell you, Flossie, if I could just make a big enough score, I would post up on some tropical island with a lover and let the world roll by. Now let's see that list." She leaned forward.

Flossie pulled up the premium assignment list, filtering it both for intelligence work and by marker sign notations, a rough indicator of its profitability. "Okay, let's see what the options are…" For several minutes, the two women poured over the offerings, discounting some immediately and marking others for consideration.

"What's that one with the asterisk? It's got four marker signs…" Diamond pointed at the screen nearest her.

"Mmm—it does look profitable, but it's actually a combo intelligence/extraction mission… You might be able to swing permission, but not me—I never get into the field. Greene keeps me in the building as his pet codebreaker." Flossie's voice held a tone that seemed to blend irritation, resignation, and pride.

Diamond waved her off. "Look, I got some sway with the colonel. I can advocate for you. Nothing ventured, nothing gained. Four marker marks, that's really unusual."

"Or really dangerous," Flossie observed.

"Hey, there's a reason I won the Force sharpshooting award. I can keep us safe. And I've run a couple extractions early in my career. C'mon, let's see the details."

Flossie clicked the link and Diamond leaned in as both women began to read.

"Holy shit, Di. It's in the North Country. No wonder they are paying so much. That place is at the ass end of nowhere. And it's probably snow-covered this time of year."

"Floss, for that kind of markers, I'd dress up as Father Christmas and ride a reindeer into the snow. Look at that—it's just a smash and grab of some scientist and his gear—hostiles with weapons very unlikely, it says. C'mon, let's give it a go." Diamond gave Flossie her best pleading look and was delighted to hear her friend sigh.

"Fine." Flossie gave a shake of her head, but her face gave

away its hopefulness. "We'll make an appointment and see what Colonel Red says."

The use of Cal Greene's informal nickname made Diamond giggle. This mission was it. She could feel it. There would be enough markers to get Ronny out of trouble and enrolled in a trade program, with maybe a bit left over to replace the diamond she had cashed in a few months earlier. North Country. A bunch of backwater yokels. Sounded like easy markers to her.

Flossie, January 13

"He's going to say no to me." Flossie moaned for a third time as she and Diamond advanced toward Colonel Greene's office for their ten-bell appointment. Flossie couldn't believe she was doing this. It was astounding to her the lengths she would go to make Diamond happy.

Diamond grinned. "That's why we're going together, Floss. He hasn't said no to me for years." She gave a suggestive wink.

Flossie had been part of the Bosch Pirate Force for over five years, ever since fleeing her father's house in Truevale and changing her name to sign up. Going from the estate in Truevale to the barracks in Bosch had been one of the hardest things she had ever done. And for the most part she liked it. She liked being part of the Intelligence department and solving codes. The people at work seemed to actually like her. She even had a group of co-workers she went out on weekends with. But then she met Diamond, and suddenly all Flossie's extra time was spent thinking of and planning to see her. She sort of missed seeing her friends, but getting a wink from Diamond made it all worthwhile.

"'Kay, I guess," Flossie murmured. The closer they got to the corner office on the third floor, the more her stomach roiled and tightened until she felt as if she would vomit. What had she been thinking? She was perfectly happy in her cubicle, pulling data together from various sources and playing connect the dots until the true picture of the intelligence became clear. And she was damn good at it. Why go off and do something out of her reach? Better to stay safe doing what she knew. Then she glanced over at Diamond, who strode confidently next to her chattering about how many markers and how much fun the mission would be, her long braids gently swaying as she moved, causing the beads that decorated her hair to sparkle in the overhead light. How could any one human be so brilliant and amazing in so many ways? She looked over at Flossie, and her face blossomed in an expression of pure joy. The young sergeant almost lost her footing. Flossie took a deep breath in and searched for her resolve. A mission with Diamond was worth everything to her.

"Okay, when we get in there, let me do the talking at first," Diamond reiterated as they stood in front of the office door.

Flossie agreed. "Roger that. I'm way too nervous to speak, so that'll be easy."

Diamond reached over and laid a strong hand on Flossie's shoulder, creating a shiver through Flossie that almost came out as a groan of pleasure. "Hey, no need to be nervous. We are in this together."

Any misgivings Flossie had melted away. "Okay then." She placed her hand on top of Diamond's and gave it a squeeze. "Together." *If only.*

Flossie, January 13

Colonel Greene leaned back in his chair, hands clasped and resting on his midsection, as he peered at the two women. "Miata, I certainly can endorse your participation in a mission of this substance, but Porter? Why in the world would you want to hie yourself off to the frozen north? Your skills are better used here."

Diamond began, "Well, sir, Sergeant Porter can..."

"I was addressing the sergeant, Miata," the colonel interrupted in a cool voice.

Flossie had yet to speak in the meeting beyond the initial greetings. She stood staring, her mouth slightly agape, at the colonel, whom she ordinarily could speak with quite comfortably. "Umm." Why did she want to go? *I want to be with Diamond. It's all I want in this world.* No, this was not the time nor the place for truth-telling. "I…" She watched as the corners of Colonel Greene's mouth started to twitch as he suppressed a less-than-officer-like expression. He was about to deny her request; she could tell by his mannerisms. She had to think fast and come up with a plausible reason. She blurted out, "Because I've been stuck in my rank for over a year longer than anyone else I graduated with, sir. And you and I both know it's because I joined the BI immediately after graduation, per your request, instead of getting the field experience the other troopers got while exploring various specialties. Without some kind of field experience, I can't move up in rank. This mission would give me that experience."

Colonel Greene sat up and leaned forward. He looked as surprised by Flossie's pronouncement as Flossie felt. Even Diamond looked impressed and gave Flossie the smallest of encouraging nods, which almost made Flossie melt with joy.

The colonel's expression shifted to contemplative as he opened Flossie's file on his desk. He rifled through a few papers, pausing at one or two, then flipped the file shut. "You scored highly in shooting as a recruit and it appears you have kept up with that at the range. Is that correct, Porter?"

"Yes, sir." She didn't add that she had never shot at anything that actually moved.

"And your trainer commented that your fight techniques are strong," he continued.

Again, Flossie did not add any details to her CO's observation. He didn't ask about her sparring, which she was lousy at, so no need to comment. *Just agree, Floss.* "Yes, sir."

The colonel stood and walked to one of the large windows in

his office. He stood with his back toward the two women for a minute. And then another minute. Then he turned. "This mission is not a particularly dangerous one, nor is there a significant time constraint, but it is sensitive. The early reports indicate that the Chinese have a scientific research base, and they have a Dr. Aung there doing research on climate control. The hiring party is the Federal Alliance. Which is unsurprising given their ongoing competition with the Chinese. The FA would like to have Dr. Aung and his research for themselves. The doctor should be glad to go, given that he originally lived in Khumi City and was taken from there, by all accounts, unwillingly. We will, as a corollary humanitarian mission, send in a team to extract his family in order to reunite them. Aung's retrieval is an easy enough extraction, complicated only by the fact it is in the North Country. I recommend that before you both embark on this mission, you gain some knowledge about the area."

"Wait." Flossie's voice trembled with excitement. "Do you mean I can go?"

Again, she saw the corners of the colonel's mouth twitch. "Yes, Porter. You can go. But let's have you start with utilizing your excellent research skills to prepare properly."

"Thank you, sir. I mean, yes, sir. I'll find some information immediately, sir." Flossie's words tumbled out on top of each other.

Now the colonel did allow a smile. "Excellent. Let me know if you run into any problems. Let's set up a review for this same time next week with a tentative mission execution date of..." Colonel Greene paused as he scrolled the calendar on his device. "...February...sixth, no, seventh." Flossie quickly marked her calendar on her comm and saw Diamond doing the same. The colonel continued, "Any questions? No? Then you are dismissed."

Flossie was delighted but refused to look at Diamond for fear of breaking into an ecstatic laugh. The two women turned and headed for the door.

"Oh, and Corporal Porter...?" Colonel Greene's voice caused Flossie to turn. "Well done stating your case."

Flossie turned and said as professionally as possible, "Yes, sir. Thank you, sir."

CHAPTER 3

Kat, January 27

I am sitting in silence with five other women, two of whom I know from base and the other three I may have seen around the area. Physically, we are all comfortable as the room has a cozy couch and several squishy armchairs, but you could cut the tension with… I reach down to finger my dagger I keep strapped to my right thigh.

I tried to tell her.

I've been seeing Ruth, whom I refer to as RTT—Ruth-the-Therapist—for going on eight years now, mostly because, well, it turns out that I have, as Ruth so diplomatically puts it, issues and baggage. Boy Howdy. When I first started coming to see her, I was under the impression that pirates don't do therapy and feelings, but given that there were a half dozen therapists at the base clinic eight years ago when I met Ruth and now there are twice that many on base and at least another six or eight working in private practice off base, there must be quite a few pirates sorting out their shit.

That said, folks don't usually broadcast their plunderings into the depths of their psyche, so when Ruth suggested something she called "group therapy" with other ex-thralls, I was a firm, clear *hell no*.

I also told Ruth it seemed like double-dipping to charge for regular sessions and then again for a group. That's when she made the crack, "You know, Kat, the way you fully personify each of your feelings, every session with you is a group session…"

She wasn't wrong, and I couldn't help but laugh, but I then pointed out, "There's no way a group of Bosch women wants to hear lurid details about their master commander's post-traumatic musings about her time as a thrall, nor would they want to share theirs with me. The NDAs alone would scare them off."

"Kat, everything in session is fully confidential—you know that," Ruth replied all serious. "And, the women I'm thinking of were not born in Bosch. Including you."

This statement irritated me, even though it was true and provoked some heavy side-eye from me. I gave a peevish response. "I was reborn here. Almost everything else before doesn't count."

"And there's the classic Katian denial."

I am certainly not in denial about human trafficking, which developed as New Earth rose from Old Earth's ashes, driven, as usual, by the powerful under the guise of needing workers. It became an entrenched problem as the sale of humans became a major economic trade on the planet. People became rich selling other people. Those not making a profit from it simply shrugged and rationalized it as a regrettable but necessary part of life. Of course, those folks had never been thralls themselves. I had. Five years earlier, when I became a general in the Force, I implemented the Burn the Ship anti-trafficking program, which systematically freed hundreds of enslaved people and took down some of the largest cartels. A small number of the trafficked people we freed, women in particular, elected to stay in Bosch. These are the people Ruth wants me to "go to group" with.

I was still saying no as I left my session, even as she laughed and said, "I'll take it up with a higher authority." Given my position as the leader of Bosch, I figured she was being metaphysical. I hadn't banked on her going to Betsy.

Betsy, my loyal assistant, maneuvered me over and then dropped me off here under the guise of "Let's go for a stroll since the rains have let up." Once I figured out her intention, I protested that there was no way I was going to bare my soul in front of a bunch of other ex-thralls. She just looked at me in that friendly way she has and asked, "Do I need to let Miriam know you aren't behaving?"

I'm forty-three years old as of two weeks ago and here my executive assistant tries to threaten to tell on me to my adopted mama. Honestly.

It worked like a charm, of course, and I went inside. But now that I am in the room, it does not seem to be going as smoothly as Ruth had hoped. I knew there would be landmines in this group —that's one of the reasons I didn't want to participate. But now, I'm here and I need to be prepared to either skirt them or disarm them.

We have introduced ourselves by first name only. I recognize Sunniva, whom I met during the raid that freed her five years earlier, and Isa, who was also freed on one of the first missions. The other three are Jaylene, a university student studying design; Gyeong-Hui, a clerk at Battle Variety in the City; and Rachel, who, surprise to me, also works on base over at BI. When I introduced myself as "Kat who works at Bosch Hall," Sunniva snorted quietly. The rest just stared at me and shifted in their seats, glancing at one another and around the room—anywhere but at me.

I sneak a look at Ruth. Her dark hair is in its standard sleek coif, held back with one of her many clips. Today it's a gold dolphin one. Her appearance is anything but frazzled, but her eyes are slightly narrowed and there's a tiny crease between her brows that signals her discomfort at how this group thing has begun.

I decide to set the ball rolling. "How many of you didn't want to come today?" Ruth's eyes widen as I ask this and I say to her and the other women, "Well shit, I didn't want to be here." My hand rests on my hidden dagger and calms me.

Isa speaks next. "Why not? You think you're too good to talk with the rest of us?"

"What? No. I..." I am stammering, "I don't think..."

"Then why didn't you want to come?" Rachel follows up with her question.

Gyeong-Hui says in a very quiet voice, "What do you keep fingering on your leg?"

At this Sunniva laughs. "I know."

I try to signal her to hush. I never have shared with Ruth that I am armed at all times, including in sessions with her, but Sunniva presses on, "You have your dagger on you, don't you?"

I'm not going to lie. "Of course I do."

"Let's see it." Jaylene's voice is low and eager.

I sigh. I can't imagine Ruth will be happy about this. But I said I didn't want to come. Slipping my hand into the hidden pocket, I pull the eight-inch, bone-handled knife Teddy gave me over fifteen years ago from its place on my thigh. Each woman, except Ruth, leans forward the smallest bit. Sunniva, tall and blonde with a thick Nordic accent, laughs. "That's a little toy." She reaches into her boot and pulls out an impressive and vicious-looking twelve-inch hunting knife with a wide fully tanged blade that has saw-like serrations on one side. It is a weird anomaly that everything in New Earth is measured on the metric system, except certain types of weaponry, including knives. Sunniva and I are brandishing our weapons and there's an electricity flowing through the group as we lock eyes as if we are going to battle.

I hear one woman whisper, "Who do you think would win?"

"Against the old woman?" This is Isa's voice, guaranteed, "Sunniva, of course."

I want to take exception to the "old woman" comment, but suddenly Ruth's voice booms, "Kat Wallace, Sunniva Nilsson! Put those weapons down immediately!"

Sunniva and I grimace at each other, and I mouth, "We're in trouble," to which she nods. *And I was just starting to have fun,* I sulk to myself. We both set our blades down and hang our heads like recalcitrant children.

Ruth is in high scold mode. "I am shocked that the two of you would bring weapons into a therapeutic environment. You both owe the rest of this group an apology."

There is a pause as she waits for one of us to begin, but words don't seem to be coming to me or Sunniva.

"Well, maybe not one to me." Isa stands and removes a pistol and a switchblade from somewhere under her heavy sweater. She checks the safety and casually sets them on the table as well.

"Uh, I have this." Rachel places a telescopic baton on the table that I'm pretty sure has a hidden blade concealed in its length.

Jaylene produces a taser and then removes her necklace, which is actually a fascinating and lethal metal whip.

Gyeong-Hui hesitates, and then, with a sigh, unveils a tiny pink handgun from her side pocket.

A giggle begins to spread among the group members as I reach back and remove the matching pistols that belonged to Teddy's father from their place in my back holsters. I am giggling along with them as I too check their safeties before I lay them lovingly on the table.

Ruth is speechless. She sits in her very civilized leather chair and looks at the array of small ordnance on her elegant coffee table. I feel as though I am responsible for this armament reveal and I hate seeing her shocked by it. I consider the issues they represent. "So I guess this is a prompt right here. Regular people —people who haven't been enslaved—don't carry all this shit all day long. Why do we?"

The question quiets the group, though a few small chuckles remain. For the next three-quarters of a bell, one after another of us speaks about what we need to feel safe and how our weaponry gives us a sense of control. Jaylene and Gyeong-Hui admit they have never used any weaponry since coming to Bosch but having something close feels important.

Rachel tips her head to the side. "My work doesn't require weapons, but I feel more confident with my baton on me.

"My job does require I am armed, but I have not used any weapons on anyone on Bosch," Sunniva declares.

Isa simply says, "I just like having them. I feel more powerful."

I think back to when I arrived. "It's true, my first opportunity to handle a personal weapon occurred the day I came to Bosch, and it made me feel…safe…" I look to Isa. "And yes, powerful, which was such a novel feeling. It seemed to me that if the bastards came for me again, I'd might actually stand a fighting chance."

Isa asks in a friendly way, "What bastards?"

You know, that's the thing with landmines. You just don't see them until your foot is on top of them. "The bastards who came and stole me from up North and killed my partner and baby boy." I have told my story enough that I can say this without tears anymore.

Rachel is frowning, "Stole? Like randomly?"

"I don't think so," Isa states in a flat tone, clearly skeptical of my story. "All the enslaved I have spoken to have all been sold into the trade."

Sunniva adds, "That's my story to a great extent. I was taken as trade for my ex-lover's debt."

"My uncle sold me." Jaylene recites this as matter-of-factly as if she was telling the time.

"It was my oldest brother," Gyeong-Hui states.

"My own mother sold me," Rachel says with contempt. "She needed markers to feed the younger kids."

Now Isa drills down in my inquisition. "Didn't you ask the people you were trafficked with how they became thralls?"

"I…I didn't spend much time in a coffle. I was delivered

almost immediately to Bellcoast and Abernathy." My voice has dropped to a murmur.

Now Jaylene squeaks, "Bellcoast? That place sounded horrible. And Abernathy? The senator and vice president? He was your enslaver? I've heard stories..."

"They are likely all true." My voice is grim. "He was the swollen hemorrhoid on the asshole of the world."

Sunniva nods. She had her own run-in with Abernathy. "You went straight there. Probably because he bought you from someone. Men will do almost anything if enough markers are involved."

I go quiet, reflecting. Ending human trafficking on New Earth has been my focus since my escape. But no matter my involvement, it seems I still have more to learn about this horrible trade. Of course, I had heard that families sometimes sold members into enslavement to pay debts or just to garner some extra markers, but those were isolated incidents. At least, I thought they were. But all these women in the room share a version of the same story. My focus for the past several years has been on getting thralls free and destroying those that traffic humans, not on the circumstances that led to enslavement. This is a gap in my understanding that I will fix. I shake my head a bit. I know what my history is, so I repeat, "No, I was taken. No one sold me from home."

Isa looks at me, her eyes doubtful, her lips pursed, her voice dubious. "And there was no one at home who may have profited from you 'being taken'?"

I stare at her and it's as if I can hear a distinct *Boom* as a landmine explodes, clearing the area and allowing me to see the landscape as it actually is. A heavy boulder now sits in the pit of my stomach, and as the realization becomes unmistakable, my fury melts it into a mass of bubbling lava. It was Dad. It was my own fucking dad.

There's more discussion of trauma responses and such during the rest of the session. But I hear little of it and have little to add. I am distracted by the heat in my middle and I long to reach out and gather my weapons for battle. The clock chimes and Ruth says, "It is time to close our session now. You have all been willing to share some feelings of vulnerability as well as some personal history. Take some time over the next week to process the new information both on your own and in individual sessions. I can assure you; I will be processing the fact my clients come to their sessions carrying such an assemblage of weaponry." Another chuckle makes its way through the group, skipping me, though this time Ruth joins in before continuing, "But I do accept each of your needs for them. Perhaps we can work on meeting this need in a different way during these sessions."

The other five women stand, a low buzz of chatter among them. I rise as if my legs are made of wood and mutter my own goodbyes to the women. I can't say I enjoyed this session, but I think I want to come back next week. Finally, I reach for my blade and pistols, but a hand on my shoulder stops me. It's Ruth.

"Kat, could you come upstairs for a moment? I have some questions." Ruth's eyes reflect concern. It looks like after eight years she's good at reading my body language.

We make our way to the small room upstairs where we have our individual sessions. I have re-holstered my pistols, but Ruth sits in her chair with my bone-handled knife, turning it in her hands. "It certainly is a quality piece," Ruth allows.

"Papa had it made for me," I say offhand. "He sent it to me after the night I first saw Abernathy. I had seen him at a fancy banquet when my now big girl was just a baby. It was after I escaped, but before the trial. I had tied a steak knife to my leg during the dinner. Mama and Takai…"

"So, this must have been early in your relationship with Takai? Before his infidelities were revealed?"

"Oh, well before that. We were still practically new lovers. He hadn't even convinced me that marriage was a reasonable idea. Which it plainly wasn't, now that I have the clarity of hindsight."

"So, what were his and your mama's perspective on your makeshift weapon?"

"Well, they were both a little shocked when I showed them, but Papa looked at it and said, 'Well thought out.' About a week later a box arrived for me in Edo with that knife and a thigh sheath. The note read, *Now, you have a proper fucking knife. Papa.* It's gotten me out of a few tight spots before."

Ruth wrinkles her brow and looks at the knife. "You've used this? On people?"

Somehow knowing her disquietude is active calms mine. I give her a matter-of-fact answer. "Well, yes, among other things. It's great for cutting rope too."

Ruth sets the knife down on her side table and shifts away from it as if it has magically turned into a poisonous snake. She frowns at it and then peers at me. "Kat, we haven't really spoken about this before, but I think it is an important topic for you to consider: how many people have you killed?"

This question actually pulls my focus from the wrath and ruminations I carried up from downstairs. The first answer that pops into my head is *not enough,* but over the years, I have learned to hold my tongue to allow a second, more appropriate, thought to appear. Somewhere in my brain I watch as Present-Kat receives some hearty congratulations from Past-Kat for this moment of growth. The only problem is, no second answer readily appears. "Ummm..." *Who loses count of how many people they've killed?*

"You don't have to share the answer with me," Ruth says quickly, "But I have counseled many troopers over the years and have come to recognize the burden that taking a human life represents. So, I want you to consider your answer and consider what burden you carry.

"You often refer to your soul as being 'tattered' and 'fucked.' I wonder if your tendency toward violent behavior and those descriptions might be related in your mind."

Caution steps up at this statement, arms crossed, eyes narrowed, a skeptical expression on its narrow face. It holds a memory close to its chest. I know which one it is—The Quiet Assignments. My head bobs a bit to assure RTT I have heard her. "Mmm. I guess I can consider that." Caution settles back, careful to keep its back to a wall.

Ruth settles in her chair, her body relaxed. She knows when I have closed a conversation. She shifts the topic, "Something happened downstairs. While we don't have time for a full session right now, I wanted to give you some space to talk about whatever it was."

Kneeling in the soft armchair I have come to think of as mine, my back to Ruth, I look out the window at the creek. Nature and especially moving water always has the power to calm me and help me focus my thoughts. It allows me to harness the fury in me and stabilize it. Still turned away, I give voice to my ruminations. "Ruth, my dad loved his whiskey and his Glitter when he could piece together enough markers to buy some. He was terrible with markers, constantly in debt." I watch, captivated, as a fox approaches the creek for a drink. "I think..." A deep breath in steadies me. "I think my dad sold me to the traffickers." There it is. I said it out loud. The fox slips into the underbrush and I feel tears sting my eyes, "Could he have really done such a horrible thing? I mean he was always a mean bastard, did awful things to me, but to sell me into enslavement?"

After a slight pause, Ruth's voice comes to me, strong and even. "There's a lot to unpack in those questions. Do you want to start by talking about your dad?"

I shut my eyes tightly for a moment. Most of the time, I don't even want to think about Dad, much less talk about him. But now...I turn around and look at Ruth's calm face as I settle into my chair. "Sure."

❋

Kat, January 27

The air is winter chill as I walk home from therapy, and I keep a brisk pace both to stay warm and to help me process all the thoughts running through my crowded mind. Ruth had said there was no point in postulating about whether Dad had sold me because it was simply something that couldn't be known, and I should focus on working through the traumas I knew he had inflicted upon me. So, our abbreviated session was filled with me recalling some of the more spectacular beatings in the first ten years of my life and the unpleasant fondling that had gone on as far back as I could remember. As usual, Ruth sent me off with a homework assignment. This one was to keep a small notebook close to write down any memories of Dad that would come up in the next week. "Write them down and then close the notebook, Kat. We can work through them together. I don't want you dwelling on them alone. They are too raw and could be triggering."

Triggering is right. I can feel my twitch slightly every time I think of that bastard. All this talk about my dad has left me feeling soiled, and I calm myself with plans for a deep, soaking bath after the kids are in bed.

I have to lift the gate slightly when I arrive home. That's a repair for spring. I smile as I look at our little white house. Grey's cat, Jerome, is curled up on his bed on the window seat, his jet black fur a counterpoint to the cream colored fabric. I reach my beautiful, cobalt-blue front door, and open it just a crack. The warmth of the house flows out and around my bare hands and face, and with it, Matty's rich baritone singing along with a popular song that Grey has had on repeat for the past few weeks. Dishes are clinking and our little Rini's bright voice alternates between the chunks of lyrics she knows and some made-up phrases that must sound right to her.

"I'm home!" I call, now fully inside. Rummy, the red gold dog, roused as the door opened and now is waggling enthusiastically next me, looking for scritches and attention. An enticing smell of garlic, onions, and olive oil wafts to me, and I can hear the big kids singing along to the tune in the kitchen. Matty is swaying in time as he sets the table. Rini twirls about, casting napkins on the dining room chairs as if she is a fairy queen offering a boon. She turns toward my voice and shouts, "Mama!" as she barrels to me.

I catch my four-and-three-quarter-year-old up and swing her into the air, giving her several kisses before wiggling out of my coat and settling her on my hip. She plays with my curls and traces the scar on my neck with her little finger.

Matty turns and beams. "There's my love."

"I your love, Daddy!" my little brown bird chimes, her face a mask of indignation.

Her tall, handsome father bends down, and his brown eyes sparkle in his copper-colored face, which sports his own scar that runs down his left cheek. We joke he got it to complement the long-healed wound that runs across my neck. "Well, yes, you are, but so is Mama. That's how we got you."

I lean in to give him a kiss, which sends our daughter into paroxysms of giggles. We linger just a bit with our lips, and when we part, our eyes make promises that I give voice to. "More of that later," I whisper.

"So much more," Matty breathes, playfully running his hand up the side of my neck to caress my cheek. It makes me pull in a shaky breath, which in turn creates a very self-satisfied look on my colonel's face as he returns to setting the table.

I move into the kitchen, where my older children are involved in dinner preparations. I take a moment to admire the three best things that came out of my dozen years with their philandering father. And while Takai and I now have established a fairly amicable co-parenting relationship, he remains my one and only husband and my one and only ex. I never want to go through that pain again, and Matty and I are happy waking each morning knowing that we have chosen each other. Lately, though, especially since our loss, he has been heavily hinting about ceremonies and commitment, but I am still terrified that it will create complacency and neglect.

Grey is pulling a pan of roasted vegetables out of the oven, creating a far more intense cloud of delicious fragrances than what I smelled at the door. Two roasted chickens sit on the stovetop, and Kik is tossing a salad with dressing. His twin, Mac, sits on one of the tall chairs on the far side of the center kitchen counter, his new comm in hand.

"Look at you all, hard at work." I make a sweeping gesture with my arm and finish with a point at Mac. "Well, most of you." I give him a cheeky grin.

"Hey, I chopped and washed all these veggies and greens," he protests as he hops down and reaches to take Rini out of my arms. She giggles furiously as he gives her a tickle. She wraps her still-chubby arms around his neck and snuggles into him.

I provide a quick kiss to my younger-by-twenty-minutes son. He looks so much like my youngest brother, Virgil, it shocks me sometimes. "Well done then and thank you."

The boys, at thirteen, are getting tall, both only about half a head shorter than me, and their voices… It's astonishing to hear them shift deeper at times, though not consistently, which annoys Mac when he is trying to sing. I feel like I had just gotten used to seeing Grey enter a room looking like a grown woman, when suddenly my little boys started becoming young men. I watch Rini in her brother's arms receiving tickles and raspberries on her neck and tummy as she howls with joyous laughter, and I feel awash with love. At least I still have one baby left. The joy that flowed in with the love ebbs double pace, and I feel tears threaten. No more babies. Not ever. Matty made that clear after everything that happened this fall. My hand drops to my belly, and I find I am still surprised it is not round and full of our little boy.

I feel a hand slip into mine and look up to see Kik gazing at me. "I love you, Mama." The way he says this is so forthright, and his eyes are so compassionate.

I squeeze his hand. "I love you. Thanks." He grins before

returning to his dinner task. "I'm going to go change," I announce. I give Kik's long black hair a loving tug and head upstairs for some cozy clothes and a good cry.

CHAPTER 4

Kat, January 27

"You running a mission this week?" I watch as my words make clouds in the icy air.

Matty grunts his answer, "Mmm-hmm."

"Glitter?" I almost whisper this. There is a growing anti-Glitter sentiment brewing in Bosch, spearheaded by young people both at the secondary school and university. To be honest, I'm pretty sure a good portion of the folk in the districts support the movement, but it's just not that simple.

"No, extraction. There may be some thralls to free as well," Matty replies.

We are bundled against the cold, walking along the trail in what we still think of as the *new* park near the house. The family that had owned the land decided to donate it as a green space with trails and a bit of play equipment for the area children close to four years ago. Matty and I started our evening walks when I was heavily pregnant with Miss Irina Mae. Now we slip out as often as possible after we get Rini to bed because the older kids stay up forever now, so this is our time to talk without the invaluable input of the teens.

The stars are glittering above us, but streaks of high clouds hide some as yet another front heads toward the island, bringing with it more torrential rain. The rains this year could have been devastating if not for the past work of our climate engineers, who have skillfully developed ways to collect the stormwater and aid in rerouting the runoff. But tonight, I don't want to talk about rain or thralls.

"Can I tell you something?" I know it is fully unnecessary to ask this of Matty, but I am nervous.

He chuckles. "Of course."

I stop walking and he looks at me, his eyebrows crinkled together. I pull a deep breath in. "Today Ruth asked me about how many people I had killed."

He blows out a sigh. "That's a big question. You and I both know it's hard for someone who hasn't been in a combat situation to understand..."

"Let's walk." I bite my lip and give his hand a slight tug as we return to our stroll pace, our gloved hands intertwined. Matty is quiet, waiting patiently for me to say what I need to. "You know the picture I have of Papa and me?"

"Yep."

"I told you about when it was taken, right?" I am hedging as I see Caution waving a warning finger. But I ignore the admonishment—I trust Matty, and I rely on his counsel to help me clarify my thoughts. And I want someone else to finally know this part of my history.

"You've told the story a couple times." His voice is steady. Now the universe and I have a grudging relationship, but since meeting Matty, I have, on occasion, sent a heartfelt thought—but not a prayer—of gratitude out in the general vicinity of the universe for the gift of this man who tolerates, and sometimes even celebrates, my foibles and flaws. Tonight, my talking around the issue that needs to be addressed is on display.

"Dinner was really good tonight." Even I roll my eyes at this pivot.

I can hear the grin on his face as he responds, "I'm glad you liked it, but Kat, you have something to say, and I am sure it isn't about chicken roast or the winter salad."

"No. It's not." I inhale the cold air deeply. "Okay...so, remember that photo taken after the mission where I had made my first kills?"

"I remember..." There is a tone I recognize in his voice; it prompts, *Get on with it, Kat.*

I blow out my next breath and imagine I am one of the dragons from the books Grey loves. "So, two days later, Teddy invited me to the cave to work on some of his special vessels and at lunch suggested we go for a walk. 'Bring your pistols,' he had said in that offhand way he had when he actually was being very deliberate. We walked and chatted, and then he pointed at an old stump about seventy-plus meters away.

"'See that rock on that stump?' he asked me. 'Shoot it.'

"I could see a lump on top, and I was used to doing whatever Papa asked, so I pulled a pistol and shot, shattering the stone.

"Papa just noted the action and kept walking. But every now and then he'd tell me to shoot something. The farther we walked, the more frequently he'd call, 'There. Shoot.'

"After about half a bell, we turned around. Papa stopped talking, but I was on high alert for rocks and snags that might need to be shot to pieces. When we got back to the cave, he motioned for me to sit. 'You have a calm, accurate shot, Kat. That's a skill that could be monetized if you wanted.'

"'Lotta folk need someone to shoot up their landscapes, Papa?' I asked him. I was teasing, of course, but I really wasn't sure where he was headed.

"'Very funny. I'm talking about people, girl,' he answered.

"I remember just staring at him for a bit before I said, 'I can't just kill somebody to make markers.'

"'No, no, of course not, but there is a market for the skills you have, and you could train it up and use it to take out some pretty bad folk,' he responded.

"'Like Abernathy?' I asked him then. My revenge against him was always at the forefront of my mind.

"'Not him. Not right away. But the skills can help get you ready.'

"I stood up then and walked to the edge of the clearing in front of the cave to consider the possibility."

"Did you have your thumbnail between your teeth?" Matty's voice is gentle.

This forces a small chuckle out of me. "Probably. You do know my tells."

"That I do. Go on, then."

"I went back to Papa and said, 'Okay, but I'll only do it for people I think are really bad.'"

Matty sighs deep in his chest and murmurs, "Oh, Teddy, really."

My knee-jerk defense of Papa comes quickly. "No, I wanted to. And he was really careful. He put some feelers out and got a deluge of requests. Apparently, there's a whole lot of people out there that want someone else dead but don't want to be the one to pull the trigger."

"I'll just bet," Matty sniffs. I now wonder whether I should be telling him this story. We have had a few arguments about Papa in our time together. While he admires our old master commander, he says he "takes exception" to the way Papa asked hard things of me. And, I guess, he isn't wrong, completely.

I decide to push on with the story. "Papa initially vetted them, tossing out all the 'please kill my ex-wife/husband or annoying neighbor' ones. Then he brought me ten requests. He handed them to me and said, 'Here. You can choose one, some, or none. Research them. Decide which ones, if any, you wish to do. Then let me know.'"

"And this, Matty, is where I learned the value of details. I researched the shit out of the subjects for about a week. Then I went back to him with four names and said, 'I'll do these.'

"I tell you, love, these were four awful people. They had done so many horrible things, that, in my opinion, they had broken the covenant that made them human—much like the traffickers. So, I had no issue eliminating them.

"I ran those four assignments. We called them 'The Quiet Assignments' because we never talked to anyone else about them and barely to each other. The first two with Teddy and the second two on my own. The missions took place over about six months. I was paid very, very well. After that, I'd take an assignment every few months if I felt it met my parameters." I pause and take a couple of breaths, and Matty leans in and kisses the side of my head before I continue. "A couple years later, I returned from one. It had been straightforward enough, but the man's wife had been in the vicinity, and the way she wailed out her agony as I dropped him tore at my heart." I don't mention that I still dream of that wail and that, in my worst nightmares, it comes from inside of me. "I went to Papa's office to give a report, and after I ran the specifics, I asked him if he thought what *I* was doing broke the covenant that made me human."

"Oh, no. Kat..." Matty stops in his tracks and pulls me close. I realize I am crying now. I swallow. "Papa just looked at me and said, 'No, girl. That could never happen' and then 'You're done.' So that was it. I never ran another Quiet Assignment mission, or as the dictionary likes to term them, assassinations." I burrow into his heavy coat as he holds me and rocks me back and forth a tiny bit.

He breathes in and out several times before saying in my hair, "My love, you are the most human person I know. Never, ever, doubt that. I am so sorry you've carried this alone for so long."

I take his reassurances and plaster them all over my brain like the music star posters on the walls in Grey's room, but Doubt comes behind me, pulling each one down. Determined, I keep my hands on one of my affirmation posters and stare Doubt down until they throw up their hands and fade. "Do you ever wonder about...? You know..." I snuffle a bit.

My very own Colonel Warner rumbles in my ear, "Anyone

who has had to take a life wonders, Kat. It's that wondering that reassures me that we have not lost our souls to the act."

Kat, January 29

The weekly meeting with the new quartermaster, Fatima Brewer, has left me feeling distinctly uncomfortable. I asked her to draw up three budget drafts for the coming fiscal year, each with a decreasing percentage of Glitter profits. None of them looked promising. My meeting with the anti-Glitter group the other day brought to light just how much a growing portion of Bosch's population is against our production, distribution, and sale of Glitter. Edmund, the young man in his second year at the City University that Grey is so enamored with, is the spokesperson for the group and, frankly, quite eloquent.

"Master Commander, you have to understand, the youth of Bosch do not desire to be the drug dealers of New Earth."

I had to admire how in one sentence he managed to dismiss the entire basis of Bosch's culture, its economic foothold on the planet, and call me old to boot. If he didn't piss me off so much, I'd likely admire him. I wonder briefly when I stopped being part of "the youth" of Bosch. Realistically—a helluva long time ago.

Now every thought, consideration, and discussion about Glitter stirs memories of my dad and his (usually drunken) complaints about the markers it cost him to get a square or two of the drug. "What the fuck is a man supposed to do if those thieves keep jacking the price up?" he'd snarl. Not that Bosch had anything to do with the price he was forced to pay. That was entirely on the local distributors. Nevertheless, as I arrive back at my office on the third floor of Bosch Hall, I slip through the inner door with a quick wave at Betsy, pull out the notebook Ruth has directed me to keep, and begin to jot down the bones of a particularly ugly memory of Dad and one of his schemes to generate markers for his habit. I frown as I try to recall how it came about, but I have kept the recollection so tamped down for so many years, the particulars leading up to the horror are vague. Doubt nudges, *What if Glitter didn't exist? Maybe it never would have happened.* I frown as I keep writing. *Hush,* I tell it. Knowing I'm on the ropes, Doubt goes in for a final blow, bringing Fury in as their second: *How many other girls have to do the things you did because of their dad's Glitter habit?*

I blow out a breath as the ire rises in me. *Oh, fuck.*

I stare at the page and my scribbles and think of Ruth's question. How the hell did I become a person who can't account for the people she has killed? I can't possibly be a monster. I have children whom I love and who love me. The most spectacular man on New Earth adores me and holds me each night. I have friends and family. Soulless killers don't have those things. *Or don't deserve them.* I frown at the voice in my head. Whose voice is that? *You always thought you were special, Kat Wallace. Didn't think you deserved the punishments you earned. Whether I took the belt to you or used you for my Friday fun, you'd look back at me with those defiant eyes. So, I had to double down on you. Defiant women come to no good end.*

I know the voice. *Fuck you, Dad.*

I haven't talked to anyone besides Ruth, not even Matty, about my suspicions that Dad could have sold me to the traders, but the issue continues to eat at me: while I walk to work in the chilly mornings, prep for my day at the office…even during lulls in meetings. Suspicion has now taken its place in the box seat near my right ear, whispering dozens of times a day, *I think he did it. You know he was capable of brutality.* Hell, I've thought about Dad more in the last week than in the past quarter century. A quarter century since I last saw him. This realization feeds back into the fact that *youth* is no longer a descriptor that I can apply to myself.

So, my non-youthful brain continues to fill with thoughts of Dad. Fucking Dad. If he had sold me off, then he was responsible for my partner, Zach, and our sweet little Sean being killed by the traffickers. I was so young then. A few tears start to well in my eyes. Thinking about Sean's long-ago loss prods memories of my more recent one, and my heart feels a rip in it, creating a wave of nausea. I am quick to remake my grief and hand it over to Fury to direct toward my dad. Ruth said there is no way to know the truth, but goddammit, I still want to know. There is a familiar click as the door to my office opens, and I quickly slip the notebook into the small side pocket of the elegant, fish leather bag Mama gave me years ago. With a brisk shake of my head, I return to the present and discover Betsy approaching my desk in her usual efficient fashion. *Work, Kat. Focus on work.* "What's next on the agenda?" I try to keep my voice steady, but it breaks the tiniest bit.

My sweet friend, loyal supporter, and right hand crinkles her brow. "Cal Greene is here with two BI troopers for an informational meeting, but I can reschedule them if you need a break. Do you, dear?"

"No, Bets," I close my eyes and take a deep breath in. "I don't need a break. Just need to stop wallowing."

She tips her head of dark, tight curls with no hint of gray in them to the side and looks directly into my eyes. Doubt and Fury pull back, knowing they are no match for this force of nature. "MC, grieving the loss of a pregnancy and a child is not wallowing. It is essential. I'm going to send down to the mess for a lunch that has a good portion of red meat in it. You need to build yourself back up after all that your body went through."

I know better than to argue, so I just ask, "What would I do without you?"

"Oh, you'll never have to find out." She pats my arm in a grandmotherly fashion. "I'll send Cal and the troopers in in three minutes. Is that enough time?"

"Yes, ma'am. I'm on the job," I reply as I put my hand over hers and give it a squeeze.

Three minutes later, I have performed all my necessary ablutions, remaking my expression into that of a calm master commander. The door opens and I rise to my feet. "Cal, how is my favorite beverage manager?" He laughs at the reference to his humble beginnings in the Force, working as what could be described as a squire to my adopted papa, Teddy Bosch, when he was the master commander.

"Life is treating me quite well, MC. Shall I get you a whiskey?" He points to the ornate bar off to the side in my office and gives me a wink.

Cal manages to pull a true laugh from me, and it is so appreciated that I am replete with delight. I stand and come toward him. He reaches out his hand for me to shake, and I pull the tall, red-haired, freckled man in for a hug. "It is always good to see you, Cal." I notice the two troopers standing somewhat hesitantly behind him.

Cal gestures at them with a sweeping motion of his arm. "And here are two of BI's finest, Master Sergeant Miata and Sergeant Porter."

"Trooper Miata. Trooper Porter." I nod at each woman. They salute me smartly, and I return the gesture, then say, "Come, sit," motioning to the three chair seats in front of my desk. "What can I do for you three snoops?"

Cal begins the introduction, explaining the mission to extract a scientist at the behest of the FA, one of our most loyal and lucrative clients. I listen until I hear him say, "The Chinese have established a base in the mountains bordering the central, inner region of the North Country. They've set up Dr. Aung there to conduct his experiments, which..."

The words *North Country* slip from my friend's lips, and the world stops spinning. It is so jarring; I am surprised no one else in the room notices. My hand goes to my desk to steady myself against this sudden alteration of motion. Cal is speaking but not loud enough to be heard over the voices of Caution, Doubt, and Fury in my head: *This is your chance... You said you'd never go back... There will never be such an opportunity... He's probably dead anyway. Everyone else is... If he's alive, he's probably even meaner... You could find out what happened after you were taken... Maybe you don't want to know what happened... You don't want to go there... What's to be gained?* Suddenly another voice booms through my head, silencing the rest. I know this voice. It is one I had intimately lived with for decades but that had all but disappeared after my enslaver's death: *It was him. He made you this way. He owes you.* And to the forefront stalks Revenge, sword in hand, dressed in black and gold armor, a horned helmet on their head. Their eyes redden as Fury touches their shoulder, gifting them with their wrath. I embrace them like the old friend they are, and the earth begins to move again. I glance around at the troopers and Cal.

"...so, I figured, since you had grown up there, you could give some concrete information to the troopers before they set off in early February," Cal finishes.

I blink several times, and there is an extended silence before I clear my throat and begin to debrief the troopers on the particulars of North Country culture, terrain, customs, and peculiarities. I tell them about its isolation and poverty, the patriarchal and xenophobic nature of its people. But as I talk, my mission-planning brain has been activated.

The universe and I had a falling out the day she let my son be murdered, but apparently a truce has been offered me in the form of this gift: a North Country assignment. A rush of clarity and relief I have not felt since the group session, maybe even before that, flows over me as I consider all I will need for this mission. We are in Q&A time now as first Miata, then Porter asks me about specific aspects of the old place. I'm delighted to answer them because, though they don't know it yet, these two troopers have provided an answer to all my questions. We're going with them, Revenge and me. We will return to the North Country. We will find my dad. I'll ask him whether it's true that he sold me to the traders. And then, either way, we will kill him. What's one more?

CHAPTER 5

Carisa, January 30

The vehicle was warm. Irritatingly warm–at least to Carisa who shifted uncomfortably in her seat. She took a deep breath in, tucked a lock of her blonde hair behind her ear, decided to ignore the pain radiating down her back and into her right leg, and simply looked out the window at the dull January day. The day fit her mood. Everything was gray. The trees stood holding their naked branches aloft, trunks a sad mottled gray. The undergrowth was stripped of foliage as well and now showed the tangled chaos that summer's glory and fall's colors had hidden. The road was a darker, ashier gray, and the sky was covered with a slate-gray blanket of clouds that drizzled a cold, slow rain. Carisa shut her right eye and then her left, and then opened both and kept up the pattern until her husband's voice in the driver's seat pulled her from her experimentation.

"Back still hurting?" Aaron asked, his brow knit with the worry that seemed to constantly be present on his handsome face ever since her diagnosis of UN (unraveling nerves) almost a year ago.

Carisa grimaced a bit. "Yeah, but not as bad as it was at the end of last month." She tried to sound pleased, but while less pain was good, she still pined for the innocent days when pain could be "fixed." *No sense depressing him too,* she thought. *Try to stick with positive news.* "And my eyesight seems better. The double vision is almost gone."

"That's great!" Aaron's face smoothed and relaxed, and there was that lilt to his voice that always made Carisa's heart feel lighter. Even now.

A small voice piped up from the back seat to ask, "That's great! Wait, what's great?" in exactly the same tone as his father's.

Carisa turned around in her seat, willed her face to not telegraph how much the move hurt, and let her eyes twinkle at her son, whose messy-blond hair framed his little boy face. "That my funny vision seems better, Arthur." She watched as his almost five-year-old brain considered this information.

A broad grin spread over Arthur's face. "That is great, Mama. Is your funny leg better, too?"

"No, darling, that isn't any better."

The expression faded from her child. So, she rushed to add, "But it isn't any worse, either."

Her son beamed at that. "I can help you, Mama. I can carry things."

She hated everything about this disease. Hated how her foot dropped, causing her to swing her right leg out when she walked, and how she sometimes couldn't balance. Hated the constant exhaustion she felt. Hated how her organizational ability that everyone used to exclaim about at work seemed to be slowly slipping away. But what she especially hated was that her children were going to grow up having to *look after* their mama when she should be the one doing the looking after. *He's just a little boy who loves you, Carisa,* she intoned to herself as she shifted the topic. "Do you know what you want to play with Rini today at Aunt Kat's and Uncle Matt's?"

Arthur grinned. "Yeah, we're gonna build a base in her room and play BPF."

"That sounds wonderful." Carisa reached her left hand out and peered into the carrier strapped next to Arthur, checking on her year-old daughter, Carly. The little girl had just the lightest, fluffy cap of blonde hair even now, and she had pulled her little hat off and dozed off with the pom at her lips.

Aaron asked his son, "So, who's going to be the pilot this time?"

"I am!" Arthur was clearly resolved on this point. "Rini says I can fly if she gets to be MC."

Aaron broke into a deep belly laugh. "Well, I'm sure her mother would be happy to cede that job to almost anyone, including a four-year-old."

Carisa couldn't help but laugh as well, partly because it was true, but mostly because Aaron's laugh tickled her and made her feel that everything would be fine, no matter what. She so wanted that to be true. *But it won't be. I won't be.*

Kat, January 30

With little Carly playing at my feet, I turn to Aaron as soon as Carisa leaves the room to check on the four-year-olds playing upstairs. "So, how is our girl? Really?" Carisa has been putting on a brave face since she walked in the door, and I want to know the truth.

My navigator-friend looks serious. "This relapse was tough on her, both physically and emotionally. You know how depressed she was right after she was diagnosed." And I do. I remember the days I went over to take care of Carly when all Carisa wanted to do was lie in bed and sleep or watch the Obi.

Aaron continues, "But she's coming out of the physical part now. Her pain is better. Her vision is better. She's back at work part-time..." He trails off and lifts his daughter into his lap, kissing the top of her head as she pulls at the buttons on his blue sweater.

"But?" Matty prompts our friend.

Aaron sighs and releases the now squirmy toddler back to the floor, where she goes straight to the barrier we have set up around the fireplace and mutters to herself. Her father distracts her with a bright red stuffed toy in the shape of a star with a little face, and she plops onto her bottom with it. "I don't know. Sometimes, she just seems so passive. But when I go to help her do something she'll snap at me And I get it, sorta. But she is still Carisa: smart, capable, funny. I just want her to remember how amazing she is. She is more than just her diagnosis." He rubs his face with both hands, and he blows out a breath. Matty, sitting near him, reaches out and gives his shoulder a squeeze.

I slap my knees with both hands and Carly startles and then giggles. "Well, then. She and I can go and do something fun together. Maybe that will help pull her from her funk. She still talking to Nanette, right?" Carisa started seeing Nanette even before I started up with Ruth.

"She is. Every week."

"*What* am I doing every week?" Carisa appears from the kitchen door, and Carly squeals, "Mama" and toddles toward her.

"Therapy," I say with a grin.

Carisa hoots a laugh. "I think Nanette would search the island for me if I didn't show up to her office for an appointment."

I consider that possibility. "Do therapists have their own houses and families or just their offices? Ruth never talks about anything personal of her own. She says, 'It's not part of a therapeutic relationship.'" This last part I voice in an over-the-top imitation of Ruth's smooth tone, which provokes a ripple of laughter. I mean, I know Ruth is married with grown children, but that's only because I've done my research.

Carisa admits, "Honestly, I only asked once, and Nanette said essentially the same thing. But…" Now she frowns. "…why are you three talking about *my* therapist?"

I take the hit. "That was me. You know how I worry." I watch as Carisa hitches her way over to the couch carrying Carly, her right leg swinging out with each step. "How about you and I go out and do something fun sometime?" I offer.

"Like what?" There is a skeptical intonation to the question.

"Whatever you want to do," I answer.

"How about skiing, or ice skating, or ballet dancing? No? Maybe we could go for a run together?" Carisa's voice is taking on an increasingly bitter tone. This was not the reaction I had hoped for.

"'Ris, I mean something we can do together. I didn't mean to…" I throw my hands up.

With a heavy sigh, 'Ris engages me. "Let's talk about something else," she proposes. "How about my doctoral work?" Speaking fast, she gives me no opportunity to shift the subject. "Right now, I am doing anthropological research into some Old Earth stuff—indigenous peoples, culture, religion, myth, that type of thing. You know, like seven hundred years ago—the 1600s. The connection is intriguing because some of the current and deeply rural New Earth people—for example, in the North Country—are so superstitious, and yet they have no passed-down culture that the indigenous people had. It's all sort of a mishmash." She stops, wearing a pleasant expression, and I can see she is attempting to deflect my concern. "Okay, that is me. Kat, how is work for you?"

"Work?" My brain rushes a bit. The woman talked me in a circle.

This could be the perfect time to tell Matty I plan to be gone for a few days on a mission. More people, less questions. "I have an opportunity to fly a mission for Bosch Intel."

Matty's head swivels. "What do you mean, flying a mission? Not in one of the new 2070s?"

This is a point of contention between us, and as he exchanges glances with Aaron, my ire rises. "No, not in one of your precious *new* fucking vessels." I catch myself and glance at Carly, who, fortunately, is busy flipping pages in one of her toddler books. I continue my tirade without the colorful language. "Which, may I point out, I could easily learn how to maneuver, probably quicker than either of you learned, *and* which *I* made the case to the quartermaster for funding the development of two years ago."

Matty puts a hand up. "Fine. You got them developed and you could learn. But to be clear, it took both of us…" He gestures between him and his navigator. "…over three months to really master the new controls."

"Hmph, slow learners, huh?" I figure I may as well use this issue to distract. That way my boring little mission in an old vessel won't provoke any disagreement. I don't like keeping things from Matty, but planning to kill my dad seems like a subject he might have big feelings on, and I don't need to hear those now.

Matty rolls his eyes at the "slow learners" comment. "So, what are you talking about?"

"Just flying a couple BI folk up so they can pull a Chinese scientist doing experiments for the FA. It's a simple in and out, though likely an overnight, maybe two." My voice is breezy, making it sound like a lark. Which it would be if I didn't have my own plans.

Matty, though, knows me well, so he is dubious as he replies, "Uh-huh. We all know simple can change pretty fast. Who is going, and where?"

"You know, you're not my father," I counter. *And be happy you aren't, given my past and future plans.*

One dark eyebrow rises on his handsome face. "That is not an answer."

I puff an annoyed breath out. "Fine. I'm flying Flossie Porter and Diamond Miata up to the North Country."

Now Aaron joins in. "That's where you're from."

"Yeah, so?" I keep my answer short. I hear the defensiveness in my tone. *Easy does it, Kat. Don't overplay your hand.* I don't want them to go on a deep dive into the meaning of the locale of my first mission in over five years.

Matty's eyes are narrowed in that way he has when he is sussing out a situation. I decide to get in front of it. "I just need to do something different. Teddy ran missions when he was MC, and when I heard about this, I figured it might be good…closure for me." I'm not lying; I'm just not telling the whole story.

There is a beat before Matty says, "Well, you certainly don't need my permission, nor my blessing. But it sounds like it could be fun. And maybe good for you."

Boy howdy, if I'm successful, will it be. "I think so."

He continues, "Want me to go with you?" The offer comes out of left field, and my eyes widen.

"No." I hear the abruptness in my voice and see the cloud of suspicion that had lifted start to settle back into his eyes. "The folks up there are all pretty pale—most of them are skin-bigots," I snort derisively. "I don't want you to deal with that." This is absolutely factual, though completely secondary to why I don't want him to come.

"You said Diamond was going. And they don't come much darker than her." The statement is presented casually, but I sense a minefield there that must be negotiated.

My hand starts to move my thumbnail toward my teeth. But I suppress my tell and direct the hand to my temple where I lean my head carelessly on my hand, elbow on the chair arm. "Diamond's been briefed, and she knows the kind of treatment she is likely to be subjected to from the locals. But I suspect the amount the FA is offering is too tempting to let that concern her. That's part of why I want to help. I negotiate the area so it doesn't become hostile." I am dropping all sorts of mission lingo.

I am waiting for the next volley from my lover, but instead Carisa speaks up. "Closure…" I could use…" She quiets but her expression is distant. "Primary sources from the North Country could bolster my research. And it's so close to Dobarri…." She trails off.

I am thrown by the non-sequitur, and I see the same reaction on Matty's and Aaron's faces. Carisa's far-away look refocuses on me. "I want to go with you. We can go to Dobarri after the mission."

Before I can explode into all the reasons this would be ridiculous, I hear hollering from upstairs, followed by four small feet trampling down the steps, voices raised in four-year-old annoyance. All four parents turn toward the coming onslaught, but I am able to get in a single-word question to Carisa: "Why?"

As a little boy steams toward her, and a small girl marches toward me, complaints at the ready, she says, "Because that's where I came from. I was a child there."

I look up, shocked at this unexpected revelation from an old friend. Aaron's and Matty's expressions reflect mine. So, this is news to all of us.

Carisa, January 30

Carisa had fallen asleep tucking Carly in, which wasn't an unusual occurrence, but when she woke with a start, she immediately blamed the UN. So tired, so often. Aaron had been in charge of settling Arthur and Rini, but she didn't hear his snores. No, she knew he was down with the adults, having a glass or two of Warner Reserve wine that Matt got from his family's vineyard and getting a chance to be an adult.

An adult that doesn't have to take care of you, she thought guiltily. Her guilty feeling morphed into annoyance, which bubbled inside of her. She had specifically asked for someone to wake her if she dozed off. But everyone was so damn solicitous since her diagnosis last year. "Oh, Carisa, sit down and rest." "Oh, Carisa, let me get that for you." "Oh, Carisa, don't take a chance on falling." Even her son, a little boy, intently carried bags into the house nowadays, saying things like, "I can do it for you, Mama." She had thought she had put her life in Dobarri behind her. But lately she had been thinking of her childhood. She wanted this opportunity. Kat would throw up roadblocks in the name of protecting her unless she laid the whole story out. As it was, her friend had always fretted like some mother hen—the diagnosis just made her double down.

She rolled silently away from where her little daughter slept and slowly crawled out of the room. Carisa grasped the base of the doorframe and, holding onto it, got her feet under her and stood for a moment to regain her balance. Then slowly, one halting step at a time, she made her way downstairs, pausing in the kitchen to pour herself a glass of seltzer water. From the front room, she heard Kat say, "She always said she didn't remember where she was born or grew up."

Carisa chuckled to herself and thought, *Well, there couldn't be a better intro than that...* She moved to the doorway and commented, "Well, now, Kat, you are the one who taught me that blocking something out was sometimes easier than actually remembering it." She lifted her glass in a salute to the three surprised faces and continued, "But truth time: I never really forgot. It was just easier to *choose* not to recall it at all." She moved into the front room, stepping and swinging her foot out methodically so as not to spill her drink, until she reached the sofa, where Aaron rose to help her. He took the glass and set it on the table behind the sofa. Then he wrapped her in his arms. She loved how she felt fully enveloped by this big man's embrace.

He whispered into her hair, loud enough for Kat and Matt to hear, "Well done with the drink." His voice radiated pride, and Carisa looked up at him with love and gratitude.

Then she sat with a slight grunt and ran her eyes around the room, pausing on the faces of her husband and friends. "I guess I owe you the story now that I have cracked it open."

Reaching back, she picked up her glass and looked deeply into it, as if the story was floating amongst the bubbles. "I was the only child to my parents, and the first eight years of my life, the bits I remember, I was like a princess to them." She giggled and then her face darkened. "We weren't rich, I don't think, but there were toys and pretty dresses." Carisa put her fingers to her throat as if feeling for something that lay just beyond memory. "Mother was absolutely beautiful. Classically Dobarri with long blonde hair and deep blue eyes the color of a summer morning. I never remember her being angry with me, even when I'd come inside in one of those pretty dresses covered in mud with tears in the hem and sleeves because I was climbing the willow tree in our backyard to feel the wind blow. She'd gently say, 'Carisa, maybe play clothes next time.' She helped me out of it and by the next day it was washed and mended.

"My father worked long hours, but I remember once going to his office. He let me color at his desk, and then walked me around the building introducing me to everyone and saying with pride, 'This is my little girl.'" She paused and looked up, not seeing the little house she sat in, but the world as it was then.

She frowned as she thought about the next part. "We all took ill the fall after I turned eight. I remember my mother's cool hand on my forehead, and my father tucking another blanket over me. Voices jabbered and went faster and faster and then slower and slower, and I was cold and then hot and then cold again. I don't know how long I was sick for, but when I opened my eyes and could see the room, it looked different. I called for Mother and Father, but it was my Aunt Elka, my father's younger sister, who came in and brought me broth. She said I was the lucky one. Mother and Father had died, and I was her responsibility now. I know I was only eight, but I still remember how she spat out the word *responsibility*. It made it sound like what she really meant: burden."

Aaron slipped his arm around Carisa as she said this, and Kat whispered, "Oh, 'Ris" in a pained voice.

Carisa inhaled and pushed on with the story. "For the next five years I took care of my little cousins, though Elka didn't treat me like family. She said I had 'a *responsibility*'—there was that word and that tone again—'to offset the cost of my upbringing by being useful.' So, I made sure I was useful. I took care of the children. I cleaned the house. I tried to do all the things my mother used to do for me. My dresses and toys and even my play clothes went to my cousins, and all my mother's jewelry went to Elka.

"When I turned thirteen, Elka sent me to one of her friends' houses to care for their children. And, honestly, for a little while it was better. I still worked hard, but at least I didn't have to see my childhood treasures just out of my reach. But within a year, as I was growing out of childhood and into womanhood, the father of the house noticed and pursued me, and before I knew it the mother of the house sent me packing back to Elka, who blamed me for leading the husband into temptation. I swore to her I had done nothing to encourage the behavior, but she did not believe me.

"She then sent me off to another household. This pattern repeated itself for the next three years until finally Elka came to me and said, 'You have a *responsibility* to help support yourself and to pay us back for all we have given you. You seem to be unwilling to behave like a modest young woman, flirting shamelessly as you must at my friends' homes, so you have no choice but to take yourself to the thrall market. I will send a letter with you explaining your skill with children and basic household tasks. The price they will pay me for you will more than pay me back. In fact, if you work hard and are diligent, I am sure you can earn your freedom. To show you how much I am devoted to the memory of your father, I will purchase a property for you with any markers left. Just think, a home of your own, if—rather, when—you return.'" She had such a condescending look as she said this.

"I was naïve enough to believe her word. The next market day, I walked willingly with her to the thrall booth. They told me it was my responsibility to help the family. It was the last time I ever saw her or Dobarri." Carisa sucked in a small sob. "I was so ashamed for so long that I allowed myself to be sent into enslavement. To be honest, I still feel shame telling you." She gave a mirthless laugh. "You know, I thought if I was quiet and did what was asked of me, I would earn my freedom. I didn't understand. How could I have?"

"You couldn't have, my sweet." Aaron's voice carried both agony and anger.

Matt commented, "Because you were a goddamn child, for New Earth's sake."

"I know that now. In my head, but in my heart… That's why I want to go back. I mean, visiting the North Country itself plays right into my dissertation and then Dobarri is right there, Kat." Carisa knew who she needed to convince. "I could visit my parents' memorial sites…and I could find Elka and show her, that no matter what she did to me…" Carisa felt a small flame ignite inside her. "…I did fucking survive…." Her voice was suddenly fierce, and Kat's head jerked up, surprised. Carisa understood her reaction. Unlike Kat, she rarely ever swore, so the expletive falling from her lips was enough to make her friend take notice.

"'Ris, listen. You can't possibly go on this mission. You aren't a member of the Force."

Carisa felt her heart sink as Kat said this and her brain buzzed as she tried to structure an argument. Then Kat continued, her voice soothing, as if she was cajoling a child who wanted iced cream. "How about Aaron and Matty and you and I go once spring comes?"

The cover to the Norse mythology book with its stave design flashed in Carisa's mind. *But why*? she wondered. No answer came but resolute determination flared in her. "Why? So, the three of you can pave the way and make it simple for poor, sick Carisa? No. You're the master commander. If you say I go, then I go. And dammit to all the old gods and new, I *am* going." She saw Kat's eyebrow rise, but her friend didn't argue.

She pushed on. "With this damned disease, by spring I may not be able to move in any purposeful way that will allow me to make a trip like this. This is the time. Now. Not later."

Carisa glanced over to her handsome husband. He looked as angry as she had ever seen him. She reached up and caressed his cheek with her hand. With a breath, she answered his arguments before he could make them. "Aaron, my love, I know you would walk through the fires of hell for me." Her husband nodded, even as he wiped the tears of pain and anger from his face. "So, I know you would do this for me. But, you see, you can't. It is my..." She laughed a scornful laugh. "...*responsibility* to retrieve my own past. Kat, I don't want to debate this. I'm going with you, and I will not take no for an answer."

DAY ONE

CHAPTER 6

Kat, February 8 0500, Mission morning, five bells.

In the dim of pre-dawn, I roll away from Matty with a kiss that he sleepily returns by reaching out to pull me back to him. I reluctantly dodge his grasp and slip out from under the warm quilts to pull on my extraction gear. I reimplemented my old workout program for the past couple of weeks in anticipation of this mission, but I haven't worn this garb for a few years now, and it feels uncomfortably close around the middle, causing me to pull at it and puff air out of my nose in annoyance. I check my pistols and settle them in their holsters on my back before sliding my blade into its place on my thigh. Last night I did an inventory of my black sling bag that holds a variety of tools and equipment that can come in handy. Matty refers to it as my "Mary Poppins bag" ever since he read the old P.L. Travers book to Rini. I grab the bag and pad out of the room as quietly as a mouse, but before the door closes Matty rumbles, "Stay safe and stay alive. I love you."

I grin at the old trooper saying. "I love you. I'll be home before you can miss me."

A deep sigh escapes his lips as he rolls over in bed and pulls up the covers, murmuring, "It's already too late for that."

Smiling at how loved I am, I make my way downstairs and put on a pot of water to brew a strong cup of coffee. Pouring it up into a small flask made for journeys, I grab an apple and two of the cookies Mac made yesterday. Not exactly the breakfast my old trainer would recommend, but it will do for today.

I head out to my small vehicle, messaging Carisa that I am on my way. Her story of being sold by her family has further rooted my need to confront my dad. But I can't help but worry about the wisdom of bringing her along on this mission. Over the past two weeks, I have tried, multiple times, to talk her out of her plan, once putting on my master commander voice and telling her I was ordering her to stay in Bosch. She laughed that tinkling laugh she has and said, "Oh, Kat, too bad for you I'm not a pirate in the Force. You can't order me to do a damn thing." Frankly, I'm torn between being annoyed at and loving this new cussing Carisa.

The late-winter rains have blown past, leaving a deep chill in their wake, but also leaving clear skies that now sparkle with millions of stars. Orion twinkles at me, so I give a wave to the star in his belt that Papa and I decided was his before he died. (Was killed? Even after all these years I am uncertain which verb to use.)

Carisa hobbles out to the vehicle, accompanied by Aaron. He tosses her small hand luggage in the boot and wraps his wife in his arms, and they share a whispered exchange that ends with a lovely kiss. He opens the door for 'Ris, and she gets in, somewhat ungracefully, but more smoothly than she was able to last month, so I take that as a win. He closes the door and comes around to my side. The set of his mouth and the tightness in his jaw tell me just how worried he is about this journey. Our gazes connect and I promise, "I will be sure she returns as good or better than when she left. Promise." He says nothing, just grunts and jabs an index finger at me to emphasize that I must keep that promise.

As we pull away, I ask once more, "You sure you want to do this, 'Ris?"

"I've never been more sure of anything. There are a few things

I need to say to Elka if she's alive, and I want one last look at where Mother and Father are. It seems fitting that my one big, final adventure should be with you."

I chuckle. "Don't be so sure this is the last adventure. Once you get a taste of it, it's addictive."

I hear her chuckle in response as she murmurs, "We'll see." Then her voice gets serious. "So, Kat, you said you were going on this trip for closure. Why now? You flew all over the place for years when you ran missions on the regular. You could've gone back anytime. But whenever I've heard the North Country mentioned around you, you pretty much rage about how you are never going back."

My friend has put her finger squarely on a major inconsistency in my story. Silence fills the vehicle for a minute as my brain searches for ways to avoid what is the simplest course—honesty. I don't want to lie to Carisa, so I opt for most, but not all, of the truth, "Once I got to Bosch, I never really looked back. Life growing up in the North was pretty shitty, and for the longest time after I was enslaved and then free. I locked the memory of my partner and my baby away so deeply, even I couldn't find them. Once I remembered them and their deaths, I needed to grieve as if they had just occurred. But I didn't have time to do that. The anti-trafficking project needed my focus, and it wasn't long after I remembered that Matty and I got together, I was prepping to take over the MC position, and then there was the awful Abernathy summer."

I look sidewise at my friend. I haven't told anyone, not even Ruth, what I'm about to say. "So, I kinda told myself that maybe I was wrong, maybe I was just taken, and Zach and Sean haven't been dead for twenty-five years. That instead, they lived together on the farm where we used to all live. Of course, in my fantasy, they missed me terribly but moved on and had happy lives. I don't know. Maybe the fantasy is rooted in survivor's guilt. Because, after all, I did move on and my life is happy, mostly. Going back would have meant facing up to the fantasy I had created and knowing that, for them, there wasn't even mostly happy—just nothing."

"Oh, Kat..." Carisa reaches out and squeezes my knee.

"I know it's make-believe, but it helped then, and it even helps now. But recently, some things have come up, and, well, I have to set the fantasy aside because I need to see my dad." I feel the Fury wake, and I am unsurprised to see Revenge in their bed. My voice hardens. "Him and me..." I stare out the front window as we approach the base. "...we got unfinished business."

Kat, February 8 0600

Hangars are one of my favorite places. Always humming and bustling with energy, they hold the promise of potential adventure. I greet several troopers who are visibly surprised to see their master commander wandering in so early.

Using my I'm-in-charge walk, I stride over to the assignment board and replace Captain Burgess's name with my own. I sent out a notification to the captain that the roster was changed late last night. He'll likely be happy to sleep in a bit. I note it is a skeleton crew, with troopers Miata and Porter listed as the gunners—sure, why not? It's unlikely we'll need to use the vessel weaponry, and if we do, Diamond has a reputation for being a great shot. A Sergeant Reeves is listed as the flight engineer. No navigator, though. Of course, I used to run my extractions solo back in the day, so fewer people is just fine with me.

The supervisor of the day directs me to where my vessel is. It's an older model, a Whydah-62, which sits on the apron with ground crew buzzing about it, readying it for flight. I take a moment to do a walk around, running my hands over its sleek, matte surface, fingering the etching on the side. It's an outline of an old-style pirate ship outfitted with wings that adorns all Bosch vessels. My eyes close for a moment as I connect with the vessel's spirit. Yes, I know it is a machine, but we pilots are a superstitious bunch, and we want to know that the vessel we take to the air will be a loyal companion. We want it to know we respect its power. My eyes open and I pat the Whydah before heading back to the bench near the door where I left Carisa.

I gather Carisa's bag and mine and we head for the ramp. Carisa is obviously working very hard to keep her hitch to a minimum, and I am impressed by the pace she is keeping. Moment of truth as we step into the vessel. Three women are deep in a discussion at the flight engineer's station, and they look over their shoulders to glance at who has come aboard. There is a beat and then, with the recognition that I have come to accept as part of my position, they each pivot, salute, and stand at attention. I see Flossie's eyes go big as she takes in Carisa's presence. I think briefly of the coterie that the two of them and I make up—both Carisa and I were enslaved and tormented by Rob Abernathy, who also was such a shit father that his daughter, Flossie, fled his home and enlisted.

"As you were, troopers." I give a salute in return and watch the unit members relax slightly. "I'll be piloting Mission 6412. This is Carisa Morton for those of you that don't know. She is coming along as an observer to collect information about the North Country for the university." I sometimes amaze myself with the not-really-lies, more-like-stretched-truths that I can come up with on the spur of the moment. "We are adding on a stop in Dobarri for the return trip, a diversion of what looks to be only about five hours. However…" And here I grin because I know what the response will be. "…Nyvik is pretty cosmopolitan, and if all y'all want to overnight there after a successful mission here, I imagine that could be arranged."

Sergeant Reeves, a slight woman with light cocoa-colored skin and short, spiked, dark hair, gives a small whoop, and my other two troopers laugh and give a thumbs-up. It's good for morale to have troopers get off island and play a bit.

I continue, "Troopers Miata and Porter, you are the team responsible for the implementation of M6412. I will not be cutting into the actual mission. It is your assignment and your markers. I have, however, taken a look at the intelligence file on the mission, and I'm a little dismayed at the maps for the areas beyond the Chinese encampment—I get the feeling they were carved on stone tablets back during the Climate Wars. How come we have nothing more recent than the old FA surveyor's map from 2360? That was a dozen years ago, and while the mountains, rivers, and lake won't have altered, the damn villages are sure to have. Where's the recent drone data?"

Sergeant Porter speaks up. "We sent drones, ma'am, and they were able to get images of the mission site, but when they came around the central lake and the villages, the recordings were all disrupted once they went low enough to do any mapping, and the drones themselves went offline."

I sigh. "Say what you will about North Country folk, the men do know how to hunt. I'd imagine your drones were taken out by shot." All three troopers frown, but Reeves looks particularly offended that some item of Bosch engineering would be treated thus. I chuckle at the image my brain creates of some mountain man bringing home a brace of drones for his wife to cook up.

"My plan is to land us near the village of Allanavik. It is about a three- to four-bell hike for the two of you to the mission coordinates."

Diamond Miata speaks up. "Why not land closer to the coordinates?"

It's a good question. "Ideally, we would. But the foothill area would be tight for landing this vessel and even on the old maps, it is marked as cropland, which means no cover and people. And we don't want to have the farm folk gathering around the Whydah."

"Makes sense." Miata elbows Flossie Porter. "Looks like we have a walk in front of us."

I continue, "So this is an area I am familiar with, having grown up on the far side of its outskirts. We can leave the lake and travel about six kilometers east northeast and create a base for your mission in the outbuildings of a farm I used to know." I turn my hands up in a who-knows gesture. "If it is even still there. Not many other options, given the dearth of recent information. But I've gone into missions with less before, so improvisation will be the watchword of the day. In the unlikely event that we run into civilians, I will help you negotiate the plethora of weird North Country customs, behaviors, and superstitions to allow you to focus on your mission." *And that will allow me to focus on mine,* I think as I toy with the snap that holds my knife steady in its holster.

There are several things I don't like about being the MC, meetings and budgets being at the forefront of that list, but the fact that I can just lay something out like I just did, and no one argues, is a pretty sweet perk. I look at my unit and start to grin as I note this. "So, looks like we are an all-female crew—I can't tell you how delighted that makes me. While Captain Burgess is undoubtedly a fine pilot and a fine person, we get to have a mission sans stinky boys." At this statement the other women glance around at each other, and all begin to laugh.

I continue, "Now, of course, I jest with my 'stinky-boy' statement. I respect and honor all the members of the Force—male, female, and middle. Though I do have two early teen boys and, well, they can be pretty stinky. Also, while we are on the topic of men and boys, remember what I said in my office: The communities of the North Country are very patriarchal and paternalistic. Women out and about without men might create suspicion, so while the plan is to avoid contact with the locals..." Revenge, with their gleaming armor, is romancing Fury, coiling their russet curls with one finger. They glance up and remind me, *Mostly.* They can be a pushy one. "...if we do encounter folk, follow my lead if any men question us. Is that clear?"

Four women nod, affirming their understanding.

"Reeves, you will have the responsibility of the Whydah while we are off-vessel. From all the reports in your file, you are an excellent FE, and this vessel is well-known to you. Do you need anything from us?"

"No, ma'am. But I'll happily buy everyone a drink in Dobarri after," Reeves replies.

"You are on, Reeves." And with a clap of my hands, I call out, "Let's get this party started. Start your final checks."

Now the vessel returns to a hum of work conversation as we all take our places. Carisa moves to the jump seat, and I see Flossie intercept her. Those two share a history as Flossie is the daughter of the late Rob Abernathy, one-time vice president of the Federal Alliance, past kingpin of New Earth trafficking, and the sadistic bastard who enslaved and tortured Carisa and me, along with many others. Flossie immigrated to Bosch several years ago, changed her name, enlisted in the Force, and does not acknowledge her past history and past relationship with the man, except with Carisa, who had cared for her as a child and who she still clearly adores.

"Okay, unit." I call, "Flight time is a sweet three bells. Imma gonna land in Tassy-Canner and taxi it all in from there. It'll be deep dark still, so be ready."

The vessel goes quiet, and I look over my shoulder to be sure I'm not suddenly alone. All four women stare at me as if I have stripped naked and set my hair afire. Sergeant Reeves speaks up, using a voice that might be helpful for coaxing scared kittens out from under a porch, or perhaps calming a raving-mad master commander. "Uh...*Tassy-Canner*, ma'am?"

It takes just a moment for me to realize I have dropped into my North Country patois. Funny how fast it happened. I swallow and use my normal, Bosch tone. "Sorry, little throwback there. But that's what you're going hear in the North. I mean to land in the big lake in the center of the island. The native folk referred to it as the Ocean Lake or Taseqarna because you couldn't see across it. Tassy-Canner is the pronunciation the non-native folk who live there give it. And the deep dark is what we call the winter nights that last way beyond twelve bells." Now I envision shifting back into my North Country speech, saying, *Hellas waitin' on you, arsehole,* as I dump Dad's body into the center of Tassy, and it brings me joy. I press my finger to my ear as final instructions come from the tower. In perfect Bosch, I say, "We are cleared for take-off. Please buckle up. Let's get this done." And with that I turn the Whydah to the runway as I head for, what was long ago, home.

CHAPTER 7

Diamond February 8, In flight

Diamond leaned back in the comfortable seat at the left gunner's station, feeling anything but comfortable. She punched numbers into her comm's calculator one more time. The MC showing up in the pilot's position was not part of the plan– guaranteed she'd want a far bigger share of the mission markers than what she had budgeted for Burgess. That's how the heavy vests got ahead. Sticking it to the enlisted. She had been so sure this mission was the solution. A knot grew in her belly as disappointment mingled with irritation. With a premium pilot pay off the top, now the basic payout for this mission wouldn't be enough to clear Ronny's new debts, pay the percentage his "friends" had required of her and get her diamond back. Not to mention there would be nothing for the nest egg she was nurturing. Dammit. Her mind went to the Officers Training School option. More markers, sure, and definitely more power, but, shit, she didn't want to be an officer. They were all assholes. She slapped the small device onto her thigh and let out an exasperated sigh. She was never going to get ahead, that was clear. She leaned her head back and shut her eyes.

"Comm bringing up some big feelings there, Miata?" The

MC's voice broke into her rumination. "The way you slapped it made me think Colonel Warner's face might be on it."

At this, Diamond sat up like someone had lit a fire beneath her. "Oh, ma'am, I would never… I mean, I did, but I don't… I…" Even to herself she sounded like a babbling idiot. She looked at the master commander of the whole of the Bosch Pirate Force with apprehension and saw a wide grin on the woman's face. Damn Matt Warner to the glitter mines, he actually told the MC they had dated and that she had punched him.

Before she could create a reasonable response, the MC said, "We've never really spoken, Miata. Your visit to me with Cal and Flossie was more an abbreviated lecture on my part than a conversation." Now she gave a tip of her head toward the navigator's chair. "Come sit next to me. We can talk. Still got a couple bells before we're solidly up north."

Diamond took in this officer who was the first woman to serve as master commander in Bosch's history. What must it be like to be the person in charge of an entire nation, not just the best military force on New Earth? The woman was somewhat of a hero with most of the troopers, especially the female ones. The story was that it was her influence that opened the Force up to women. But that was probably just a myth. No one person could wield that much influence. Still, when Kat Wallace had been a general, Diamond was as much a fangirl as the next trooper.

Up close, the woman looked like any number of ordinary, middle-aged Bosch women. The MC was very pale in contrast to most of the Force. She did have nice eyes, sort of a green-blue shade. Not unattractive, if you liked that sort, though she clearly had not missed meals lately as her black extraction garb stretched snugly across her belly. Just based on appearance, she was nothing remarkable. However, her reputation as a savvy negotiator, an extractor extraordinaire, and the driven leader of the Burn the Ship anti-trafficking initiative was legendary not just within the Force. Even the world news had at times lauded the MC's accomplishments. She was reputed to be open and easy to talk with, as well as a willing listener. She also was rumored to have invested her markers so well that she would never have to worry about cash flow. That was something Diamond was interested in learning about.

But this wealthy scion also lived with and had a child with the one man on base who younger-Diamond had thought could be her equal. He was also the one man who had been foolish enough to spurn Diamond, in public no less, and had received a well-deserved, mighty blow from her right hook for it. Granted it was years ago, but Diamond did not forget even a minor slight, much less what amounted to public humiliation. It was evident the master commander knew the story as well.

Couples in long term relationships fascinated Diamond. She and Flossie would analyze the ones they knew, attempting to parse out what it was that allowed those couples to last. She never could get any of her romances to continue beyond a few months. Most of them followed a standard arc: a few weeks of romantic excitement that gave way first to broad silences in conversation when Diamond described her ambitions for her life that morphed into eyerolls that spawned disagreements that grew into arguments and the inevitable "This isn't working," conversation. Rinse and repeat.

It was a mystery to Diamond how a man as wickedly attractive and charming as Matthieu Warner was willing to settle for someone this ordinary. She imagined the proximity to power was a heady aphrodisiac. And the access to markers didn't hurt either. The master sergeant pasted on a pleasant yet respectful expression and made her way to the right-hand seat of the cockpit for what was sure to be an awkward and probably dull conversation.

"So, Diamond… May I call you Diamond?"

"Uh, sure," Diamond stammered, then coughed a little to cover her nervousness.

The MC continued, "You are welcome to call me Kat during this mission. I'm not exactly serving in a master commander capacity here. So, what's frustrating you so much that you are slapping your comm?" Her commander's voice was steady and friendly, but Diamond still worried a trap might spring.

Best to be upfront. "Ma'am, uh, Master Commander Wallace… I feel I should apologize…"

Now the MC looked at her with narrowed eyes, though there was humor about her lips. "Wait, you aren't going to apologize for smacking Matty way back when, are you? That is one of my favorite Diamond Miata stories. And you and I both know he deserved it."

Diamond relaxed the tiniest bit, her lips curving up. "Well, *I* certainly thought he did. I mean, when I am out with someone, I expect them to focus on me. I don't like being second to anyone, and for a drunk…"

"But handsome," the MC chimed in with a gleam of mirth in her tone.

Sergeant Miata paused; it was true, but she would only admit to it grudgingly. "Well, I suppose… For a drunk– but handsome– man to decide to announce to a gym full of my peers and colleagues that he preferred some woman on a motorcycle, whose face you can't even see, in an old video over me was beyond anything I had ever dealt with. So, I hit him and then I left, mostly so I wouldn't hit him again." She was surprised at how annoyed the story still made her feel even ten years later, and how satisfying it was to remember landing the blow. Ah, the rashness of youth.

To her surprise, warm laughter rolled from the master commander. "What a complete dick move that was, even for Matty, who has lots of asshole/dick moves." As her laughter subsided, she commented, "Though I am glad he pulled it. There's no way I could have competed with you."

This comment surprised Diamond and she let her guard drop a fraction of a centimeter. The master commander was not wrong. When it came to looks and possibly skills there was no competition between the two of them. But it would do her career no good to observe that the MC had simply been fortunate to be taken in by the old master commander emeritus and it was this power position that allowed her to attract the likes of Matt Warner. She decided diplomacy was best and observed, "Given that the woman in the video is you, I'd say you had his heart before he ever knew you." She was pleased to see a satisfied expression cross the pilot's face, accompanied by a sigh.

"Well, my heart is all his, so it works out." The MC pushed a couple of buttons and peered over at the navigational computer. "So, now that that's out of the way, tell me what is your comm did to piss you off."

So, with an undercurrent of hope that perhaps some of the famous Kat Wallace influence might flow her way, maybe even accompanied by a few markers, Diamond began to explain the financial fix her brother was in again. "That's why Flossie and I wanted this mission. The pay should have cleared the debts, but he's gone and run up more before I can even take care of the old ones."

Now the MC frowned. "What about his SI? Can't he cover it with that?"

The SI, or Standard Income, was paid to each adult citizen of Bosch after they reached seventeen years old. It was essentially a profit sharing of Glitter monies. Each child born or adopted in Bosch received a payout at birth and then a nominal but increasing sum was paid to their account each year until they reached majority. Then they received their yearly SI. Those who enlisted in the BPF had their SI invested until they left the Force, relying instead on their Force paychecks. It was an elegant system established to guarantee each citizen an income that could meet the necessities of living, though it was not without its loopholes. Diamond sighed. "Well, my mother squandered all us kids' childhood SIs and still has access to Ronny's and probably Max's—he's my middle brother. Only Kyron and I have transferred our accounts to where she can't touch 'em. And the Force controls mine for now."

The MC's expression had shifted to one of clear contempt. "You know that's a fucking crime. You could report her."

Diamond knew she was right. "I know, but she is my mom." What did this woman know about dealing with crappy parents? She was the adopted child of the most prestigious of master commanders, Teddy Bosch, and his powerhouse wife, Miriam.

"Yeah, I hear you. Still. That kind of shit is something my dad would do for sure." The commander let out a disgusted breath.

"*Your* dad? Teddy Bosch? The late Master Commander Emeritus, ma'am?" Diamond was stunned. This information did not ring true to the stories of the dead man's unimpeachable reputation.

"Oh, Sweet New Earth, no, not Teddy. Teddy would never. I mean, Papa had his faults, but he was a good, kind, savvy man. Also, call me Kat." Diamond's current master commander grinned as she said this, but then her lips twisted into a sneer. "I mean my North Country dad. He was, and probably still is, as crooked as a rail fence and mean as a snapping turtle. But I need to talk to him, so I've brought my bite-proof gloves, and I'll watch my back."

Diamond was glad that her image of Teddy Bosch remained pristine. "Okay, then, that makes more sense." The conversation lapsed briefly as she considered this piece of information. "How long has it been since you've seen your dad?"

The MC snorted a scornful laugh. "Twenty-five years. It's been twenty-five years, a fucking quarter century since I was taken…" She paused. "Yeah, taken from the North Country."

"How do you know if he's even still alive?" Diamond had read through Flossie's research and knew life was pretty tough where they were headed.

Kat Wallace's face took on a closed look as she said, "Two reasons: one—I'm pretty sure he's too spiteful to die on his own, and two—because the universe, one of the bigger assholes I've encountered, owes me. It won't step in front of what I need to do."

Flossie, February 8, In flight

Flossie sat at her post at the right gun, eyes closed, rocking back and forth ever so slightly as she took deep breaths in and out through her nose. She did not want to have to rush to the small head to vomit. Of course, if she did, there would be precious little to come up as she had halted any food intake after a late breakfast the day before. She would have taken the medicine that curbed the in-flight nausea, but it tended to put her to sleep, and she wanted to be ready for the mission when they landed. She glanced at the timepiece on her wrist. Three more hours. *Bells, Flossie,* she reminded herself. She'd been in Bosch for five years, but she still mostly thought in her native tongue, the language of Eternia, which had become the standard language throughout the countries of the Federal Alliance. Bosch was, fortunately, pretty similar in construction and shared many words with standard FA, but still, she slipped up on occasion.

She was startled as a voice behind her said, "Here. I found a stash of ginger fizz. It'll help." She looked over her shoulder. Carisa stood with a cup of amber liquid releasing bubbles into the air.

"Thanks. But I'm nervous about drinking it. My stomach doesn't do well on flights." Flossie bit her lip and cast an anxious look at the cup.

Carisa said softly, "I know. Remember when I flew with you and your brother to Toronto? You must have been about ten, and it was a rough trip for you."

A wan expression crossed Flossie's lips. "I do remember. Not much has changed, has it?"

Carisa gave a short laugh. "Well, neither of us has to live under your father's tyranny any longer. I have a husband and two beautiful babies. I have graduated with my bachelor's and master's in Old Earth history and am working on my doctorate in Old Earth mythologies, and on top of all that I have this horrid disease. You are enlisted as a pirate, and you solve puzzles and break code, and we both have found ourselves a home in Bosch. So, tummy issues aside, I think quite a bit has changed."

Flossie guiltily pulled her shoulders up and sank into herself. *Why do I always say the wrong thing?* She cursed herself for doing anything to remind this lovely woman about that awful UN disease. In the back of her mind came a whisper: *I wouldn't be surprised if the vice president caused it with all the beatings he doled out to Carisa during the years she was a thrall in our house.* "Vice President" was the name she used for her father. It seemed to have the right amount of distance and disdain. She still despised him even in death. She accepted the cup of ginger fizz and took a tiny sip. "I'm sorry, Carisa. I didn't mean... You are right. A lot has changed. I remember you used to always talk about someday learning everything about the past. It's great that you finally are doing that. I'm glad you have a home and a family even if you have..." She trailed off, not wanting to name the disease. Suddenly she blurted out, "But Bosch doesn't feel like home to me. More like an extended stay at summer camp."

Carisa looked at her with kind eyes. "It took a few years for me to feel it was home as well. You still live on base, right? That could be part of it."

"I guess..." Flossie shrugged. "But I like my quarters. It's a space that feels like my own." She took another sip and was surprised and pleased at how much it helped her stomach and her mood. "Thanks for this. I feel a bit better."

"Happy to help. Okay, I'm going to go take a rest now. UN leaves me tired even after a decent night's sleep."

Flossie watched her slowly walk away, her right leg swinging out slightly. She glanced over to the helm where Diamond sat talking with the MC. She could tell by the tense set of Diamond's shoulders that her friend was nervous. But she still looked beautiful. Flossie sighed a bit as she took the opportunity to stare at this woman who had bewitched her with her perfect face, perfect body, and perfect self. A sigh escaped her lips. She was glad to be

Diamond's friend and, given her own looks, she knew that even the title of *friend* was an awful lot for a goddess like Di to bestow on her.

But Flossie had grown up being used to scraps of attention and affection. It was how the world worked. Her father had taught her that. He might have been a horrible man, but he wasn't wrong—the attractive ones reaped the harvest of position, wealth, and companionship, leaving the rest of the masses to scrabble about for what was left over. She could hear her father's voice: *Be satisfied with what you have. It's more than you deserve.*

Certainly, Bosch was better than most places Flossie had been, but the same rules applied the world over. She liked the Force and her job well enough, but she often wondered whether she was essential to this enterprise. Her dream was to make a difference, but for now, she had to remain reasonably content just to be in Diamond's sphere of attention. It was all she deserved.

Carisa, February 8 1030

"I didn't come on this trip to be tucked up in the vessel all safe and sound like some broken toy with sentimental value!" Carisa slapped her hands on her thighs in fury as she spat the words out at her friend.

Kat's eyes, on the other hand, went wide and her hands came up in a defensive posture. "Whoa! You know I promised Aaron nothing would happen to you." Her face, peering out from the hood of her parka, was tight and resolved.

"And so, letting me come along was just window dressing?" Carisa felt the familiar bubble of anger that had become omnipresent in her life since her diagnosis started to rise to the surface. She jabbed her index finger toward her own chest. "*I* get to decide what is right for me. *I* get to decide if something is *too much*. *I* get to be in charge of *me*. Not, you, Kat Wallace!"

Kat closed her eyes and blew out a breath. "You know this is the only thing we ever argue about." Her face had relaxed a bit, telling Carisa that she had made the inroads necessary to win the argument. A bit more was needed, though.

"You mean we only argue when you try to control my life? If I had listened to you, I wouldn't have Aaron or the kids, remember?"

The woman Carisa considered to be her best friend sighed and gave a small laugh. "I remember. Of course, it helps that you remind at least twice a year."

Now Carisa let her anger back off as she stood a little taller. The fact that she was at least a head shorter than the rest of the women on the vessel suddenly didn't matter. In Carisa's mind winning this argument gifted her with stature. And she knew she had won. With a flick of her hair, she picked up her heavy coat from the deck, where she had thrown it several minutes before when Kat had told her she was to "stay put until we finish the mission," and slipped it on. She maintained eye contact with Kat as she buttoned up, as if to dare her to try to put another road-block in her way. She figured this was her one shot for adventure before the UN took her down for good, and she was damned if she was going to spend it staring at the inside of a Whydah.

She glanced around the vessel she sought to escape. The other three women had definitely taken a step back as the argument had escalated. Flossie and that tall woman, Diamond, were already well bundled in North Country outfits designed so they wouldn't "stand out" with the locals. A moment earlier they had been ready to step out into the "deep dark" as Kat called it, and both now looked as if they wanted to fade into the vessel walls. The engineer, Reeves, was puttering at her station, eyes darting from one woman to the other as she glanced up at the spectacle. Now, Kat shook her head a little and pushed the button to open the ramp. A wave of icy cold came flowing in, and Carisa wanted to gasp but tamped the impulse down. *I won't give anyone a reason to think I can't manage… I sure hope I can.*

"Okay, then. Reeves, the Whydah is yours. Let's keep in mind, as far as we know there are no signal towers here, so our personal comms won't talk with one another. We have some ear comms based on radio waves that we can use to communicate over short distances. Is that clear?" Carisa and the troopers all nod in understanding. "Okay, then. Let's go, team. Everybody keeps up. There's to be no stragglers." Kat no longer sounded like the bossy older sibling she had earlier, but it was clear she still wasn't happy about Carisa's choice to accompany them. *She'll get over it,* Carisa thought. Besides, she had said this was a simple mission, virtually no risk. "I'm ready. Let's get this done." She grinned cheekily at her friend as she recited Kat's standard announcement before most events.

The expected grin came from Kat. "Sweet New Earth, you want to be in charge too?"

Carisa flipped up her hood as she lumbered down the ramp behind the two BI agents in her heavy, waterproof boots. "Maybe." And she was gratified to hear a warm chuckle as the master commander followed behind out into the snowy depths of the North Country.

CHAPTER 8

Kat, February 8 1100

The four of us tramp along for three-quarters of a bell through the snow from where the Whydah is parked and camouflaged, following the old, wooded, water path. Our footsteps are muffled and our voices silent in the dim dawn. The cold stings my cheeks, and in my gloves, I pull my fingers from their assigned places to rub against my warm palms. The horizon, when the trees are clear enough to be seen, has the thin, chill, morning light of winter filtering about the soaring, craggy mountains that jut up and keep the villages near the lake isolated from the coastal folk and, let's be honest, almost everyone else.

A deep inhale pulls the icy air inside of my nose, where it stings, but I can catch a hint of wood and coal smoke in the air. The fragrance brings a host of memories with it, and I'm actually surprised that not all of them are bad. Grandma Rina's voice rings in my little girl ears: "Stick to the trails, my little Kitten, and always fill both your water jugs to the same level. It makes balancing them easier." This recently unearthed memory lifts my spirits, and I shake my head a little as less pleasant ones try to push to the front to gain my attention. I focus on putting one foot in front of the other, which is work, as through the night the snow has blown onto the path, and it almost feels like we are breaking a new trail.

We reach a small crossroad clearing that, while snow-covered, still shows the ruts from hand wagons having been pulled along over the years. I pull out the old compass that Teddy left me after he died and check our bearings. "Based on my memory and those old maps, we have about another bell-plus to reach the farm location." My breath blows out in puffs of steam.

"Why didn't the settlers build the village closer to the lake? Seems like a long way to trek for water before they dug wells." Carisa has her academic inquiry voice on.

With a chuckle, I challenge her, "Oh, I think you know. Given what I've said about their superstitious nature..."

"A lake monster?" Carisa sounds giddy. "Oh, that is the stuff of great mythology."

Sergeant Porter looks back, her brows creased. "Not a *real* monster, though, right?"

I grin and give the North Country answer. "Well, I ain't never saw it myself, but I got a cousin who had a friend whose uncle was 'et up by it." Flossie Porter looks horrified, and I laugh. "There's two kinds of folk here in this village and the surrounds, Porter, the superstitious ones and the ones savvy enough to exploit the superstitious. Is there something big in Tassy? Maybe. Is it a monster? Doubtful? Will the story keep your kids from going too close to the lake? Absolutely. Will it guarantee a quiet meeting place for less than legitimate endeavors? Yes, ma'am, it will."

Carisa is still staring back toward where the lake lies. "The Myths of the North Country." She says wistfully, "I'd like to write that book."

"Sounds like a fine idea. More of the research can happen on our next trip here." *Which will be just this side of absolutely never*, I quip to myself. "For now, we should come to where the road veers off toward the farm location in another couple kilometers. Once we have established a base." I point at the two BI troopers. "The two of you can head to the mountain. Carisa and I will continue our own fact-finding efforts." I wink at my blonde friend as we start back on our journey through the snow.

Kat, February 8 1130

"So, this would have been nice to know about," I hiss under my breath. "I thought BI was my detail organization." The comment is directed at no one in particular, but it garners two distinct responses.

Sergeant Porter looks almost miserable as she whispers, "I'm sorry, ma'am."

While Master Sergeant Miata says, "If only Bosch had better drones."

I don't spare either an answer. We spied the sudden appearance of buildings just as we came out of the tree line. Apparently, twenty-five years has allowed Allanavik, the village I used to call home, to expand its borders. And talk about modernization, at least by North Country standards: There are old-school wooden poles carrying wires lining the main part of the road. The wires run to almost every building we see. Electricity? Doubtful. I'm not sure where they'd generate it. It could be for those old, wired comms that Old Earth had back in the twentieth century. Whatever they do, they don't serve to improve the appearance of the place—it's still not much to look at.

From our vantage point behind a large log pile a few hundred meters distant from the far edge of town, I can see a collection of low buildings. They are ramshackle and thrown together with wood that looks as if it has been scavenged from homes and businesses that have collapsed over the years. Thin plumes of both wood and coal smoke waft up from the chimneys and float away in the slowly brightening light of the day. Most of these are likely inhabited by town families that have skills beyond farming—the storekeepers, schoolteachers, medics, and such. Even so, I can see the fenced-in humps of snow where the vegetable and herb gardens will be planted in the spring, and most places have two outbuildings: one that holds tools, and the other is simply an outhouse. There are a few, though, that are distinctly built more sturdily. These are painted bright colors—one is a brilliant blue, one is sunshine yellow, and another is as red as an apple. The red one has a sign protruding out from above the door that sports the figure of a bottle and a glass. Gotta love the universal sign of a tavern.

Diamond stomps her feet as we pause. "Gotta keep moving to stay warm," she says as she marches in place.

"That wind down off the mountain is fierce," Flossie adds.

I chuckle to myself and resist calling them tender Southerners, a derogatory moniker popular in the North applied to just about all outsiders.

"It is cold up here," Carisa comments. Now I feel my concern ratchet up. I search her face to be sure it is still pink. I hear Aaron saying, *Make sure she eats, and no extremes. It might cause a flare.* Dammit. This wasn't how I wanted things to play out, but I won't be responsible for causing her more pain.

Gazing at the village extension that stretches in front of me, biting at my lower lip, I consider the options. The farm is still a few kilometers away, and the cold is penetrating. I'm not even positive there will be shelter there beyond the tent I carry. Damn, I hate not having all the details. My eyes settle on the red tavern. There are probably not many men in there at this hour. A story could be created to allow us a quick dip into it to get warm. It'll be fine and maybe I can score some intel about Dad.

"Okay, listen, we will go in there and warm up." I gesture to the red building without turning to see my little assembly. "Folk here are suspicious of...well, of just about everything. So, when we get in there, let me do the talking and, most importantly, stay together." I turn now and address Master Sergeant Miata, pulling her hat down to cover her sparkling, imprudent earrings. "Miata, you, especially, will get some looks."

She gives a careless gesture. "Nothing I'm not used to, MC."

I appreciate her confidence, but this ain't Bosch. "Troop, it won't be the good kind. Remember I told you most of the folk here aren't used to anyone who looks different, and there's a fair share of skin-bigots as well."

"I guess in all these layers of North Country clothes, my skin will stand out. It's not usually what people notice first." Diamond replies with the kind of nonchalant laugh reserved for only the most beautiful people. I know because I live with her male counterpart and have heard that laugh on more than one occasion. She thinks this will be a lark. She is in for a surprise.

"Just keep your temper and go along with what I say. No weapons," I advise all three women. "Oh, and don't call me MC. In fact, don't even call me Kat. I'll be…Rosie." I grin at the name. I glance at Carisa, who is trying very hard not to look cold, but her lips, which are now moving from purple to blue, are a dead giveaway. "Let's go get warmed up."

Kat, February 8 1145

We wipe our boots on the faded rug made with braided fabric scraps and shake and brush the snow off our coats before stepping from the foyer into the tavern proper. It's a pretty nice place, definitely on the new side; reminds me a bit of Ray's back in Bosch. The walls and floor are all rough wood, with heavy beams on the ceiling. Stools, most occupied, surround several tables, and two or three men sit on barrels at the bar. The floor is littered with sawdust and nutshells that crunch under our boots and release a fragrance that stirs a memory and causes my stomach to turn. I breathe out through my nose as if to cast the flashback aside. *Wrong bar, wrong time.* The place was buzzing with conversation from the early drinkers when we first walked in but went quiet as the locals turned to see four strange women arrive. My delight at having this be a woman-only mission wanes a bit. Women don't go wandering into taverns on their own without a man in Allanavik. At least they didn't twenty-five years ago, and given the somewhat ominous silence, I don't think they do now either.

I herd my little group closer to the bar and start to order something to warm us up. The bartender, dressed in a somewhat clean homespun shirt and dark pants with an apron wrapped around his moderate paunch, is tall and middle-aged with dark stubble on both his head and his chin. His gray eyes survey me and my friends, and before I can speak, he asks, "Where are your menfolk?"

I hear Diamond give a quiet scoff behind me, but I ignore her. Instead, I look right at the man and lie through my teeth. "They just a bit behind us. Should be catching up soon."

Stubble-Head looks slightly mollified both by the answer and my North Country patois, but has a follow-up. "You folks aren't from around here." It isn't a question. "Hunting party?"

"Yep," I answer but add nothing. Keep the lie as simple as possible.

Now his eyes rest squarely on Diamond. He gestures with his head. "She yours?"

Fuck. He is assuming Diamond is a servant or even a thrall, simply based on her coloring. This is not the place to make a moral stance, though, so I just say, "She with us."

He gives a disinterested tilt of his head. I take his quiet for belief in my story and quickly lay a few markers on the bar. "We be chilled. Might we get a bit of soup to warm us? And some tea? Maybe some whiskeys for our men?" The markers are whisked quickly away and with a grunt and jut of his chin, Stubble-Head directs us to a standing table next to the fireplace against the far wall. I'd rather be closer to the door, but this will be warmer, and at least I can see the whole joint this way. With his acceptance of our markers, the rest of the clientele assumes we are harmless and return to chasing their lunchtime buzz as they talk shit about their neighbors, and likely us.

Kat, February 8 Noon

I sit at the table looking from my hand of the three White Bear cards, one Gatherer, and one Healer, to the hefty pot and the four bearded faces of the men I am playing against. Joining the game may have been…strike that…*was* an error in judgment brought on by my audacity. Good to know some things don't change as I age.

We had deflected three separate attempts by men to engage with us as we consumed our soup, bread, and tea. I snuck a sip or two of the whiskey that still waits patiently for our imaginary menfolk who have yet to arrive. My team got the message about female status here not just from me, but also from the first Romeo who came up to the table and rested his elbow casually on it so he could lean into Carisa's space. To our credit none of us laughed when his elbow slipped the first time, requiring him to jerk himself back into place and reposition as he so romantically inquired, "So, who do you belong to? And do you think I could take him in a fight for you?"

Carisa had paused for a moment, undoubtedly weighing the words she wished to use versus the words that would keep the peace. She kept her expression neutral and replied, "My *husband* is called Aaron, and no, you couldn't."

The man stepped back, clearly disgruntled at such a direct rejection, and threw out, "You know maybe if you smiled more, people might think you were pretty," before slinking off to his table to complain about women, especially foreign women.

When he sat, I snorted as I reflected, "Well, this is a far better experience than the last time I was in an Allanavik tavern."

"What happened the last time, MC?" Flossie had asked.

"No ranks, Flossie. These folk don't need to know that much about us. My name is Rosie," I cautioned in a low voice.

She put a hand to her mouth as I said this, and her eyes showed regret. "Oh, shit, sorry. I forgot."

I lifted a hand briefly from the table to reassure her. "No harm done this time. But be careful."

"I will be," she whispered.

Bitterness and Fury came forward in my mind to sit together on the floor at Revenge's feet, watching the memory with distaste as I spun the tale. "When I was sixteen, my dad dragged me to the old tavern close to our place. He had discovered I had a boyfriend and was determined to make me sorry for it. He said I shouldn't give away what he could get markers for." I ground my foot on the floor to release the scent of wood and nut permeated with beer and let myself feel the anger that had percolated for years. I sneered, "So he announced my availability to the men in the tavern—and proceeded to do just that."

My compatriots look at me with round, shocked eyes but say nothing. I continue, "It's no wonder I waited this long to come back. I intended never to return, but I got some questions for the old fucker."

Before any of us could say anything else, the next suitor appeared. That one and the next man were not quite as unpleasant as the first and, in fact, seemed amiable enough when we pointed out the glasses of whiskey waiting for our make-believe male protectors. The third one even commented, "Well, when they get here, have them join us for a round of cards. We're playing White Bear."

A wave of memory came to me at the mention of the game, and I couldn't resist. "White Bear, huh. Winter-betting rules?"

The young man looked surprised. "Yep. You know the game?"

"I do. I spent my early times here, from nursling to urchin and a bit beyond. Still, it's been years. But I know the game. Don't suppose you fellows would deal a woman in? For old times' sake?"

He rubbed his chin and gave me a dubious look. "Well…" He drew the word out as he considered. "…I s'pose I can ask the table. It'll cost you markers to play. Will your man allow it?"

I actually batted my eyes and said conspiratorially, "I have a few of my own put aside from my butter and egg sales." Hey, I really wanted to play.

This comment positioned me perfectly as a foolish wife with markers to be relieved of. And so here I sit, having carefully lost 80 percent of what I said I had and now preparing to regain it all back, along with the markers from these amateurs.

I lay down my Gatherer and draw up two cards. Two White Bears. "Well, isn't that something?" I say casually, as I lay my hand down, saying, "White Out."

There are groans from around the table as I scoop up my winnings and tuck them away. I leave a few markers in front of me for the next hand and am humming quietly to myself when the man to my left says, "I been looking at you, Ms. Rosie. You look like a Wallace. You any relation to the Wallaces of Allanavik?"

I keep my game face on and in as offhand a way as possible say, "Yeah, distantly. Know where I can find any kin?"

There's a grumble around the table at this, and the red-bearded man who got me in the game says, "Old King Cole lives at the far end of town. He don't come all the way out here—just holds court at the dive on the other end of town."

My brain pauses to process this. Old King Cole. I had forgotten that nickname he loved so much—Cole Wallace, my dear old dad, is indeed still alive. For now, at least. I am so absorbed in this realization, I don't notice the group of six armed men all wearing the same white and gray camouflage kit come in from the cold and approach the bar. They pause to speak to Stubble-Head. When I do notice them, they have turned en masse and are following his finger as he points to where my friends stand at our table.

"Well, shit." Big North Country guys in ersatz uniforms coming over toward my team is not good. It is clear we have overstayed our welcome, and it's my fault. Hopefully, we can get out of this with just some finessing. I do not want to draw on these people. At least not until the snoops have finished their mission, and I've finished mine. I gather my markers and stuff them in my pockets. "Deal me out of this hand, boys. I've got a situation."

CHAPTER 9

Flossie, February 8 Noon

Flossie's eyes widened as six large men quietly approached, then stationed themselves in a circle around their table. She wanted to look for the MC, but was afraid of giving away too much, so instead, she carefully studied the men. They were all fairly tall and well-muscled. Each was dressed in mottled gray and white with a thin band of blue around the collar, carrying a firearm that Flossie didn't recognize, and each wore a serious expression as they eyed her, Diamond, and Carisa. All sported beards in a range of lengths. Four had varying shades of blond hair, one had red hair almost the color of the colonel back in Bosch, and one man had dark brown hair and a lighter brown beard and mustache. One of the blond men had a puckered facial scar on his right cheek, just down from his eye, while the red-haired man's face was covered with freckles. And they all smelled —not bad, but of a mixture of smoke and sweat and something else Flossie couldn't quite put a finger on.

It was the dark-haired one who spoke first. "I thought there were four of you."

"There are." The voice came from directly behind two of the

blonds, and Flossie was amused to see both men flinch ever so slightly from surprise as they quickly pivoted about to find the MC staring up at them with an expression that clearly expected compliance.

The dark-haired man turned as well, but neither his actions nor his expression showed surprise or concern. Instead, he looked her up and down, narrowing his eyes a tiny bit. "And there you are." He gestured to the space the MC had occupied at the table before she had gone off to play cards. "Join your friends." Flossie watched as her leader ignored the direction and felt both pride and a tiny bit of fear at the woman's cool confidence. She would love to feel that way in any circumstance.

Now, the MC used her North Country speech and asked, "What be your business with us? We are just a hunting party waiting for our menfolk."

One of the blonds, a burly man with curled hair cut short, gave a snort. "You be waiting? Not so. We tracked your trail back a ways, and there ain't no evidence of man-boots or of prey." Now he leered a little at the MC. "Women on their own, without a man, needs be careful. Never know what lurks around the corner."

The MC seemed unperturbed by the leer and the poorly veiled threat. "Maybe your tracking skills be poor. Maybe you be looking in the wrong spot. We traveled from Taseqvik on the far side of the lake. Our men probably went to the boats with their kills."

The dark man stepped forward, and the burly blond took a half-step back. "Taseqvik? That's a long hunt." Again, he narrowed his eyes and studied first the MC, then each woman in turn.

"You and the little one, there..." He pointed at Carisa. "...you two look like Northerners, but them two..." Now he gestured at Flossie and Diamond. "They ain't from here. The dark one especially."

Flossie heard Diamond give a little growl. The MC spoke up and pointed at Flossie. "She's a far cousin, here for a visit. And you're right, family moved South couple generations ago. But she's still kin."

The dark man raised his eyebrows. "A visit? In the deep dark time? Don't seem real likely, now, do it?"

"Folk in the South don't hunt like we do. Her grands wanted her to take a deer." MC stated the lie with conviction.

"Why not in fall? And what about her?" The leader of the men indicated Diamond. "Dark one ain't no kin of yours, though…"

Flossie felt her protective nature rise. She wasn't going to let these men hurt her Diamond. She stammered, "Di…anne is a friend of mine. From school. Uni. We are on winter break. That's why we came now." Flossie looked at Diamond to gauge her reaction to the sudden name change. Diamond's face was unreadable.

At this the dark-haired man finally grinned as he said to his group, "School, huh? Uni? Is this what's happening in the South? Fancy schools let in all kinds?" He snorted with derision. "Didn't your mama ever tell you that book-learning ain't good for women?" He leaned toward Flossie, eyes wide as he pointed to his temples. "Makes their heads get crazy and shrivels up their woman parts. That happened to you two yet?" Several of the men chortled at this as Flossie pulled back and shook her head, unsure of how to respond.

The MC stepped between Dark-Hair and Flossie. "I asked, what be your business. So, what be it?"

The dark-haired man raised his chin in pride and gestured to his men. "We are part of the Allanavik Militia. We look out for our own. This is my unit. I'm Captain Slade Myers. And what do you go by?"

The MC did not even hesitate. "I'm Rosie. Rosie Warner. Since when does Allanavik have a militia?"

Dark-Hair smirked. "Not that I owe any of you women any explanation, Rosie, but since foreigners, like those China folk, started to arrive. Haven't they made it over to your side of the lake?"

Flossie's ears perked up at the mention of the Chinese. The scientific base they were headed to had been established by the Chinese, and they were the ones who had placed Dr. Aung there to test his climate control project. It certainly sounded like the locals knew about and didn't much like the Chinese incursion.

Captain Myers continued, "Sergeant Darreau ain't wrong. It's too dangerous for women to travel on their own. So, until we locate your menfolk, we be keeping you safe. And if it turns out you don't have menfolk..." He grinned. "Well, then we have gained property." He gestured to a door on the far right of the bar. "Troy has generously lent us a room for you women to keep safe in. Byrne, I want you to talk with the folk in here and in town. Pollard, go recheck the trail and see how far you track it back." He went to grasp the MC's upper arm to direct her toward the door.

She side-stepped him and gave him a sharp look, her eyes narrowed in a way that Flossie would never want directed at her. She growled, "You are making a mistake doing this. I want you to let us walk out of here."

The captain of the militia gave the master commander of Bosch, whom he knew as Rosie Warner, a condescending smirk. "It's my mistake to make, ma'am. I'll be sure to apologize to your man *if* and when he ever claims you." He placed his hand on his rifle and gave the MC a nudge with it as he pointed to the door. "This way?"

The MC set her jaw and gave a short nod to the other three women before she strode off toward the indicated door. Flossie watched as the woman halted halfway, pivoted, and returned to Carisa's side, walking slowly as her friend hitched her way across the bar room floor.

Myers waited until all four women passed him, then he took up the rear guard, raised his hand to the bartender, and said, "Thanks for the tip, Troy," as he herded the Bosch landing party into a small room with two beds, two chairs, no windows, and one locked door.

Diamond, February 8 Noon 30

Diamond stood against the rough, far wall of the small room, one hand tucked inside her parka resting on her weapon. Her mood was spiraling father and farther down a deep well of aggravation. The idiots didn't even check them for weapons before they ushered them all to this room—fucking amateurs. Sweat beaded on her forehead and dripped down the back of her neck. She kept her eyes on the dark-haired man in conversation with the MC. She really wanted to shoot him. The MC walked to the door with the militia's leader, her face tight. She put her hand on the door as the captain went to shut it on his way out, and a rifle barrel appeared in her face. Diamond grasped the grip of her gun, but then relaxed her grip as the master commander's hands came up, and the door shut. When the lock clicked, she let out her breath in a whoosh and hustled to strip off the heavy coat; the blue knit hat she had kept pulled down around her ears, hiding the diamond studs there; and the woolen sweater she wore underneath.

"Damn! Finally. I was about to melt into a puddle," she complained. "I didn't think they were ever going to leave." She took off her holster and pistol, and removed her black extraction top, leaving only her base layer stretched across her breasts and shoulders. Lifting her braids from the back of her neck, she used the top to sop up the sweat that had accumulated there. "MC, why didn't we just shoot those assholes?"

The MC looked over, narrowed her eyes, and lifted her hand, putting up fingers as she enumerated her reasons. "One, because despite all evidence to the contrary, this is not the Old West of the United States in the 1800s, and we do not solve our problems with a shoot-out. Two, because any weapon fire will undoubtedly compromise your mission, and three, because being a misogynistic asshole merits a swift kick, not a death sentence. Are we clear, Miata?"

Diamond stood up a bit straighter and tamped her frustration down with a deep breath in through her nose. "Yes, ma'am. Clear." The Force required she remain courteous in her words and actions, but it didn't mean she couldn't finish the statement in her head. *Clear you don't have the edge necessary to run these missions.* It wasn't as if Diamond went around killing locals when she went on mission. In fact, she never had killed, but she had taken hostiles down with one shot before. Her specialty was to wing them in the shoulder of the hand they shot with, exploding the joint. Once a shooter was foolish enough to demonstrate he was ambidextrous; she made sure he was non-dexterous after that.

"Good." The MC's voice carried no anger, and she gave Diamond an amiable look.

Diamond forced the edges of her mouth up in return and looked around the room.

The civilian, Carisa, was lying on one of the narrow beds, almost asleep. Flossie sat close to her in a straight-back chair with caning on the back that bore several frayed holes. Her friend was gently rubbing the leg of that gimpy little blonde, so very solicitous. Diamond felt a stab of resentment. On base, the sergeant was always falling over herself to indulge Diamond's interests, so it was exasperating that Flossie now seemed more concerned about some half-crippled housewife. *After all,* Diamond thought sulkily, *I'm the one who's been insulted, treated like an inferior, and made to stand sweating uncomfortably while the ridiculous MC took far too long to send the men out of the room. Flossie is my friend. How does she even know this civilian? I've never heard of her.* She puffed a snort of pique. *I'm the one that deserves a little attention, not her.*

Her instinct in the tavern had been to draw her weapon and simply shoot those North Country oafs who leered and humiliated her. But if the BPF had done nothing else, it had taught her discipline. She knew how to follow orders. She had a mission to complete that would make her marker and family troubles dwindle. The opportunity to even the score with the yokels would present itself after that. However, right now, she wanted her friend back. "Hey, Floss, let's talk about the mission." She pulled a map of the area from the inside pocket of her parka, unfolded it carefully, and spread it on the other bed, bringing one of the four wall lanterns nearer to illuminate it.

Flossie looked up as Diamond called to her, then rose and nestled a blanket over the civilian before coming over to stand next to the tall, black woman. The MC walked over as well and peered at the map, "So, Miata—or maybe I should stick to calling you Dianne." MC grinned at Flossie who flushed. "You see what I mean about the folk here? These fuckers can't see beyond skin. They can barely see beyond their own noses. You'll need to be careful."

Diamond looked at her commanding officer. "You really grew up here?"

The MC appeared a bit abashed. "Yep."

Diamond found this intriguing, and a bit hard to believe. Ordinarily, she wouldn't have such free access to the MC, so she figured she might as well ask whatever questions she could. "So, you didn't see anyone but people with pale-skinned faces until you got to Bosch?"

The enigmatic woman gestured in a circle. "I didn't see anyone who didn't live in about an eight-kilometer radius before I was taken as a thrall. The first darker people I ever saw were two women and a teen boy in the coffle when I was first trafficked, and then there were several that came through when I was Abernathy's thrall at Bellcoast. But there they were treated as subordinate to the pale thralls. Bosch was the first place I lived where there were more brown and black faces than pale ones. And the first place where everyone was free and treated equally."

Flossie added, "Truvale has people of all shades. But there are still some skin-bigots there. The vice… I mean, my father was one."

"That he was." The MC agreed with gusto.

Diamond looked from the MC to her friend. What was all that about? The only family Flossie ever mentioned was her brother who was some sort of starving artist in Truvale. When Diamond had asked about her parents, Floss had said she was no longer in contact with them. But this... "Wait, how do you know her father?" The question evoked a surprising reaction: Flossie's face became even more pale and took on a panicked look as she stood frozen in place.

The MC's face, however, stayed neutral, and her body relaxed as she said, "I make it a point to know as much as I can about all my troopers, Master Sergeant." Diamond accepted the answer but observed the color rushing back to Flossie's cheeks, the return of her steady breath, and the relaxed drop of her shoulders. There was more to the story than what the MC had stated. Diamond filed away the topic for later. Intelligence this juicy had to come out. And she knew she could get Flossie to spill it to her. Later.

Carisa, February 8 1400

Carisa woke with a start on her left side; her eyes felt dry, so she blinked several times and squeezed her eyes open and closed to stir up some tears. She stretched out her right arm and held her index finger out, focusing on it as she brought it slowly closer to her face. The double vision she had been experiencing had now dwindled to only being an issue when she first woke up, and her eye exercises seemed to help. She wondered for a moment where the kids were, before remembering that she was not in her bed at home next to Aaron. She sat up and looked around.

Flossie lay on the floor on top of a pile of coats, softly snoring, while in the other bed, Diamond was stretched out, feet hanging over the edge of the bed, knees bent ever so slightly, and one arm draped luxuriously above her head. *Does she always look like a goddess? Even when she sleeps?* Carisa wondered as she wiped the little crusts from the corner of her eyes and mouth and smoothed her hair. She turned her head. Kat sat in the straight-back chair, slumped down a little with her feet resting on the end of the bed

Carisa sat in. Her hands were clasped behind her head, elbows out, and her eyes were closed.

Carisa considered her oldest friend. From the time they had met as thralls in Bellcoast, Kat had proclaimed herself Carisa's protector. That was what motivated her friend to rescue her from Abernathy almost a decade ago, so she should be grateful. Certainly, the woman inspired love, friendship, and loyalty in Carisa, but currently, she also inspired irritation and annoyance. It had been her overprotective nature toward Carisa that led her to take the unit into the tavern in the first place.

As Carisa began to move her legs in the bed to wake the muscles up and remind them they had a job to do, Kat murmured, "We all figured you had the right idea to rest so we can be ready to get out of here when the sun goes down."

Carisa thought it was charitable to assume it was her idea to rest, not the damn UN forcing her to. Now she looked around the room and frowned. "How are we getting out? There're no windows, and the only door is locked from the outside. Even for you, that would be a trick."

Kat stood up and came to the bed. "I happen to have a few tricks with me. But for now, I'm going to stretch out." She flopped down, her head next to the smaller woman's feet and her own feet under the pillow. Carisa chuckled, scooted around, and lifted her old friend's foot to massage it. As she did, she thought about her own decision to come North. Not for the first time she worried that this whole thing might have been a mistake. *You should just stay at home where it's safe, Carisa. Aaron and everyone else will take care of you. Your body has betrayed you, so why push yourself?* Well, it was too late to turn around and go home. She was here, and she hoped she would be able to keep up with these troopers and not endanger their mission or their lives. Kat gave a little happy groan and then went quiet.

After a few minutes of fretting, Carisa hauled herself out of the bed and found a chamber pot shoved underneath the bedframe. She cautiously removed the lid and sighed with relief at finding it clean and empty. She wiggled out of her pants and peed, shaking herself off a bit before pulling up her underwear and pants and recapping the pot. Then she moved slowly about the drab room, finally settling in the far chair. She pulled her comm out and started to send a message to Aaron as she had promised, only to find there was no signal. She got up and walked around the room again, holding the comm up at intervals to see whether any signal manifested. As she did, she heard the other women start to stir.

Flossie murmured, "Whatcha doing?" as she sat up and stretched her back, eliciting an audible cracking sound.

Before Carisa could answer, Kat spoke, "Won't work. Remember? No towers around here. Except over on the coast in the big fishing village of Marpavik. And by big, I mean there's just a hair more than five hundred people living there…so don't get your hopes up for a North Country city. Our ear comms are the only option, and those are just for direct, local transmissions among ourselves. So keep them charged and remember that their signal can be blocked by obstacles."

Carisa groaned. "But I promised Aaron I'd check in. If I don't, he'll grab Matt and they'll bring one of those new glitzy Adventure-2070s vessels to…" And here she used her *very dramatic voice*. "…save the day."

At this Kat laughed. "Those boys and their new toys. You'd think they invented flying the way they talk about the 2070s." She popped up and began to rummage through the coat pile, pulling out a device that was just a bit larger than the personal comms they all had. Carisa was intrigued with the device and also envious with the speed and grace in her friend's movements. Kat held it up. "As you BI folk know, we actually have a satellite group we can connect to now, thanks to our scientific exchange program with the FA. And this is a present Cal gave me before we left: a SatComm."

Carisa looked at Flossie and Diamond; both were looking impressed. "I'm not in BI. Explain."

"It's a comm that can link up to satellites that orbit New Earth and beam the message down to a comm tower, so you, my dear, sweet friend, can send a message to worry wart Aaron and let him know all is well." She brandished the device elaborately as she handed it to Carisa.

"So, I shouldn't mention that we are being held hostage in a locked room," Carisa asked.

Kat waved the comment away. "Ah, that's just a minor inconvenience that will be rectified within the hour."

Carisa narrowed her eyes at her friend, but laughed as she typed in: "A-okay in the North Country. Much love to you and the kids," as a message. Kat leaned over her shoulder and showed her which button to push to send the message and then took the device back.

"Okay, gather 'round." Kat slapped her hands together and dragged her chair over next to Carisa's as Flossie and Diamond came over and sat cross-legged on the floor. "We all should use the pot before we get ready to leave."

"Check." Carisa raised her hand.

"Nice work. Always ahead of the curve, you academics," Kat teased. She bit her lip and looked at Carisa, seriously. "Listen, I was wrong to ask you to stay behind simply because I didn't know the lay of the land." Carisa looked pleased. She always liked it when Kat admitted a mistake, mostly because she knew it was a challenge for her friend.

"However," Kat continued, "we now know there are men with guns that want to take control of us here. So, I would..." She took a deep breath in. "...greatly appreciate it if you would return to the vessel and update Reeves on our situation." Carisa started to object, but Kat pushed on. "Your mission is in Dobarri, and I will not stand in your way to implement it as you see fit. But, here, our BI mates have specific mission specs to meet. And I...well, I have business as well."

Carisa was silent for a few moments and then stood and moved in front of Kat, squatting to look up at the leader of Bosch's worried face. She willed the rest of the world away as she saw the room narrow to hold just the two of them. "Kat, I think my return to the vessel is a good idea. My mobility, or the unpredictability of it, could put any or all of you in danger. I think my observations here are complete." She glanced over at the other two women. "I'll wait for my Dobarri mission until you and the troopers return. Reeves and I can keep the Whydah safe."

She watched as Kat's face relaxed, and then she reached out and gathered her friend's hands in her own. Carisa owed this woman, who was like a sister to her, so much, even though they often argued, usually about Kat's attempts to boss and overprotect her. Now, she had to speak her mind. "The story you told about the other tavern today…" She watched as Kat's eyes narrowed. "There's that and I believe there's more that you are holding onto that your horrible father did to you over the years. I know you, Kat. I know how revenge drives you. You're planning to kill him." Kat's face shifted into one of a damaged and bruised child as she opened her mouth to answer. Carisa stayed the response with, "You don't need to deny nor affirm it to me. You, Kat Wallace, are strong. The strongest woman I know. And you will do as you think best. Whatever you do, I will always be your confidante and friend. But I say this out of love for you: Please, Kat, consider what killing him might do to *you*. He doesn't matter anymore. But you, my sweet hero, you matter so much to me and countless others."

There was silence as Carisa sat back on her heels. Kat's eyes were misty. Carisa decided to combine a very real physical issue with a way to break the tension. "And I can't get up from here, Kat. Give me a hand?" At this Kat chuckled, swiped at her eyes, and lifted the tiny woman to her feet, giving her a small, affectionate squeeze as she did. Carisa returned the gesture, then made her way to her seat and settled in to hear the rest of the plan.

The master commander took a deep breath and sat up. Carisa watched, astonished, as the wounded child was transformed into a savvy and confident pirate leader who looked out at the troops that were hers to command.

Kat cleared her throat. "So, Diamond, you and I are going to start a fight. And hopefully finish it. Porter, I know you are good on the bag, so I know you can get a punch or two in, if needs be. But your main task is to get Carisa to the vessel. We've got the new infrared night vision glasses, and I'll supply both of you with one for the woods, as well as a set of ear comms for you, Flossie. Diamond and I will keep the boys in gray and white busy and out of our way." She pulled out a small map and indicated a spot on it. "There used to be a farm about two kilometers northeast of here. If there are outbuildings still standing, we can lodge there. Otherwise, there's a huge rock about five hundred meters back from the road that we can use as a checkpoint."

Diamond was in her element. "I can handle four of the militia if you can manage to keep two busy, MC, but there's one large issue you haven't addressed. We are locked in a room with no windows. How are we getting outside?"

The MC answered, "First, the population of Allanavik is not well educated. Not unintelligent, mind you, but education beyond learning to read, write, and do basic figures is seen as non-essential and even dangerous. Second, women are seen as lesser here. If you didn't believe me when I told you that back on Bosch, today's events should have driven the message home." Carisa wasn't sure what these facts had to do with escaping the room, but she waited as patiently as possible and was glad that Flossie and Diamond also wore perplexed expressions. Kat went on, "But we women are also seen as mysterious creatures whose bodies do strange and frightening things in order to bring forth life." Her voice caught a little at the last three words, and Carisa reached out and squeezed her knee, evoking confused looks from the younger BI troopers.

In an effort to help her friend cover her emotions, Carisa reeled off, "Sounds like a typical patriarchal cultural response to denigrate the mother goddess figure by othering women."

The two troopers stared at her as Kat glanced over gratefully. "Oh, sorry," Carisa remarked. "Doctoral work thinking."

Kat shook herself a bit, put her hand on top of Carisa's, and squeezed back. "So, we shall combine these two points, because those strange things we do have created some remarkable superstitions in an uneducated populace that we shall make use of." Then she looked at each woman. "We all are about to have our bleeding cycles."

CHAPTER 10

Kat, February 8 1800

"Hey!" I pound on the inside of the door and yell. "Hey, somebody! We need help!" The door rattles and I hear a key in the lock. The room is dim as we have extinguished all but one of the lanterns.

Captain Myers and the man he referred to as Pollard opened the door. I stumble out into the brighter main tavern room, my three compatriots pushing out after me. Our hands are covered in blood. Blood streaks across our faces.

Myers looks shocked. "What happened, ladies? Be you injured?"

To create this plan, I had to reach far down in my memories for the one where Grandma Rina walks twelve-, almost thirteen-year-old me out through the late December snow to the far back of her property, just where the clearing skirts the trees. A blazing firepit stands there with a large cast iron pot—a literal cauldron—hung from a tripod over it, steam rising into the air.

"Come now, sweet girl. My little Kitten has become a Kat and must learn the ways of women." She carries her gathering basket covered with a towel in one hand and a quilt under her other arm.

I offer to help but she shakes her head. "You will carry it back as I pass the wisdom on to you."

We arrive at the fire. "Turn around, child." She slowly loosens my braid and draws a hairbrush from the basket, brushing the tangles from my waist-length dark blonde hair. Then she bids me to do the same with hers, the soft gray locks moving like water in my hands.

She scrapes away the snow from near the fire. "Now we undress, so the moon goddess may see us in our true form." I glance up at the crescent moon and hesitate. "Don't worry, my darling, you are lovely and will find favor with her."

I strip away my old, patched dress, my winter undershirt, the half-shirt that covers my still-new-to-me breasts, my shoes, and my stockings. I fold each piece and carefully hand them to my grandmother. She clucks with sympathy at the bruises that lay across my back and thighs. I pause again at the undershorts where I have pinned the pad as my mother told me to. She had cautioned me to avoid the chicken house and let my brothers collect the eggs as a bleeding woman could put the hens off their laying. The same was true for the milk house, though we didn't have a cow, and those that did were getting precious little milk this time of year anyway.

Grandma Rina prompts me, "It's alright. The moon and the earth know it is your bleeding time." I slip them off and remove the blood-marked pad. Rina takes my undershorts. "You hold the pad. The blood has power."

"What kind of power?" I whisper, eyes wide as I stare at the red smear.

"It is the river of life. And tonight, you will learn to navigate it." She pulls off her dress over her head in a single motion, and I am pleasantly scandalized to find she is wearing no clothes beneath it.

She takes up her gathering basket, sets her feet, and lifts it high above her head. "You do the same with your pad, Kat."

I obey, holding my pad high and looking up at it and the starry sky.

Grandma Rina calls out in a voice far stronger than I have ever heard her use, "Oh Goddess of the Moon and Sky, Goddess of the Earth and Waters, I present you with my granddaughter, Katrina Wallace. Name of my name and flesh from my flesh. She has reached her womanly time, and I ask that you show her that she is now one with the universe." She then begins to sing in the old tongue of the people who first inhabited the North Country. As her voice rises and falls using words strange to my ears, the sky begins to dance with roiling bands of green and red, pink and purple curling and arching through the heavens. I am of the North, so I have seen the night lights before, but never so vivid and brilliant. They seem to be drawing a picture just for me, and I start to laugh with joy. Grandma Rina drops her arms, scoops me into a warm hug, and laughs as well.

"Now, then, my sweet girl, name the herbs you know," she says as she begins to toss handfuls into the boiling cauldron.

I have had similar quizzes before, but not involving women's herbs. Still, I recognize many of them. "That's silphium. That's wild carrot. I don't know those two. That's smart weed. Those are thistles. I'm not sure about the rest," I recite as I squint in the firelight into the basket.

"You are learning well. Now, throw your pad in and give the potion its power."

I do so and the mixture bubbles furiously.

The colored lights in the sky are subsiding and Grandma Rina wraps the quilt around us both, and we sit together on the log. "What is the potion for, Grandma?"

"You will drink a cup each morning. It will allow you to choose when you wish to accept a child into your body. Most girls don't start drinking it until later and don't use their own blood." She frowns, and I see tears in her eyes because she knew. "But a grandmother must do as she can to protect her special granddaughter. And you are special. And I will do what I can to protect you. You will start with it now, and we will conjure more each month during your bleeding time."

"How am I special?" I sound far younger than my twelve years.

"Because you now know the power of your body, of your mind, and of your heart. Never doubt it, Kat. The universe gave you life at your birth, and now it gives you light as you step into adulthood."

Now, with an inward murmur of thanks to Grandma Rina, I look at Captain Myers and ask for the universe to guide me now. "You fool! You closed four women into a room with no natural light for hours. It happened! Our bleeding times all began together. We must have the light of the stars and the moon if we are to survive!" I hear the moans and wails of my team behind me. Carisa even stumbles forward, smearing a bloody hand onto the white of Myers' uniform.

He steps back, horrified. "Go, get outside. Don't touch anything!" Ah, the superstition has not abated even all these years later. As we tumble toward the door, I see Troy looking aghast. I veer to the bar and keen, "Your beer will turn, and your milk will curdle. You have angered the old goddesses." He goes as white as a sheet and falls back, knocking his cheap whiskey bottles to the floor with a crash.

Once I see the four of us safely outside, Diamond and I turn back to back. I throw a kick to the nearest man and then rush up to another, planting an elbow firmly on his cheekbone, where a satisfying crack is heard. The fools don't have their weapons on them, so much the better for us.

I step back, feel Diamond's back, and we slowly wheel, bestowing knees, fists, elbows, and kicks to men who are afraid to touch us lest their cocks dry up and fall off. I can't believe how simple this is. I hear Diamond land a hard punch to someone's midsection and feel her twist her body hard; this is followed by a grunt and a thud. A few counterpunches have grazed me, but none have done serious damage. I want to look to be sure Carisa and Flossie are well away, but my instructor from long ago, Tommy Gallagher, broke me of that by punching me in the face every time I got distracted. So, the Diamond of the BPF and I keep up the battle, until suddenly there is no one left to fight. Six men are on the ground, and while there are a few civilian onlookers, no one seems inclined to have a go with us.

"Let's go!" I say to Master Sergeant Miata as I grab our outerwear from where Carisa dumped them.

"You don't have to tell me twice." She is breathing heavily.

We start to run, and I hear her gasp, "Look!" Her finger points to the sky, where green and red, purple and pink ribbons of color dance.

Diamond, February 8 1830

Diamond was not one to run from a fight but would not dispute the direction of the Force's leader. So, she jogged along the rough path that the master commander referred to as a road. This place was so backward and crude, and not just the infrastructure but in the people's thinking as well. Though that aspect had worked to their advantage, allowing them to get free of their captors—well, superstition and a good rear hook. Diamond glanced to her right at the woman who ran alongside her. She was surprised at how well the MC had done in the fight. Her reputation was well founded. The woman was at least ten years older than her, but she'd taken down three men and even threw a kick at one of Diamond's who had tried to get up after she dropped him. What a bunch of jackasses.

It was a mystery to her how in the hell the master commander became such a leader—and a wealthy leader at that—growing up here—the ass end of nowhere. It gave Diamond hope for herself.

She could see this mission playing out to get her things she hadn't dared dream of. Not just markers, but power and influence. A little flattery and some of the patented Diamond Miata charm, and she'd have the MC eating out of her hand. She started to imagine her rise in the Force. Maybe she'd even be the first non-com master commander. That beach house might actually be back on the table.

"Sweet New Earth." The MC interrupted her thoughts with her low exclamation. She had stopped and was staring at a long, tall, sturdy wooden fence entwined with barbed wire.

"What's wrong?" Diamond asked.

The MC approached the fence. "Barbed wire? Since when do folk around here use barbed wire?" She didn't seem to be addressing Diamond, so no answer at all seemed prudent as Diamond had no idea on the fencing practices of the area.

The two women walked along the fence line until MC Wallace pointed to a huge, dark shadow a distance back off the road well beyond the barrier of wood and wire. "There's the rock I was thinking of. The farm entrance is just up a ways. If it's gated, we'll have to clip the wire in an inconspicuous spot to get in. I hate to do damage to the fence, but I hate doing damage to me more." She looked over her shoulder. "No pursuit. That's good. Though not too surprising." She grinned up at Diamond. "After all, we're just bleeding womenfolk."

Diamond couldn't help but chuckle. "It's good to be underestimated, sometimes."

"At times," the MC agreed. They walked on until they came to the gate, and the MC gave a low whistle. "Whoever took over the place isn't interested in having neighbors drop in."

A wide metal gate topped with loops of barbed wire with two sturdy locks stretched across the farm entrance. "I'm guessing this isn't normal for here," Diamond ventured.

"Nope, not normal. And look here." The MC was kicking at the ground.

Diamond could make out vehicle tracks. And as she did, she

realized she had not seen many vehicles. Maybe just one or two small ones near the tavern.

The MC was standing still looking at the tracks. "Truck tracks," she said slowly, then commented almost to herself, "Weird. Who's got a truck around here? Who owns this place now?"

"You've been here before?" Diamond asked.

"Well, the village isn't that big, so, yeah." The MC paused, listening.

Diamond listened as well. "Dogs?"

"Dogs," The MC reiterated. "Damn, I figured it would be abandoned, but it appears it is not. That can be good and bad. Good, because the barn likely hasn't been razed, and bad, because, well, people." The Bosch leader stood for a moment, her thumbnail slowly rubbing her front teeth. "Well, it's past evening chore time, so let's backtrack to that copse of trees. We can clip the wire there."

"And use the tree to boost over the fence. Great idea," Diamond added.

The MC beamed. "Exactly. Glad we think alike."

"What about the dogs?" Diamond kicked herself for not bringing a stunner from the BI supply department. She liked dogs but not the kind trained to chase her and sink their teeth into her flesh.

With a pat on her bag, the MC grinned. "I have something to take care of them."

"You have a stunner then?" the tall woman asked.

"Nope, something better." The MC scrabbled through her bag and pulled out a leakproof bag. "The best dog treats ever. Learned how to make them when my girl got her dog. Once I toss a few to a pup, they decide I'm their best friend for life. It's never failed me…yet." Her MC wore a devilish grin.

Diamond gave a small nervous laugh. "Hope this won't be the first time."

"Only one way to find out. To the trees." And with that MC Wallace set off.

As they made their way back to the small grove they had passed earlier, Diamond decided to implement her "befriend-the master-commander" plan. "How did you manage to get from this…" She swept her arm to encompass the entirety of the North Country. "…to being the leader of the strongest force on New Earth?" She heard the hyperbole as she spoke but hoped the MC would take it as a compliment to her leadership.

Now her leader laughed. "Troop, I'm pretty sure Lys Russell and Emperor Xiang would argue that the BPF is not the strongest force on the planet. And frankly, I would agree with them, the first over a bottle of wine, and the second only very reluctantly." She chuckled a bit. "But I would say our Force is the smartest and most nimble on the planet. And *that*, Lys would agree with. Xiang? Well, that dude plays his cards close, but the Chinese are pretty fucking nationalistic, to the point of jingoism, so even if he agreed, he'd never admit it."

Diamond's head spun. She knew the master commanders of Bosch were in charge and made decisions about not only the Pirate Force, but also the whole of Bosch, including the central city and the districts. The General's Table and the civilian council played their part, certainly, but she hadn't realized that this MC was on a first-name basis with the president of the Federal Alliance and actually knew the leader of China. So much power. So much influence. Just being near it gave her a sense of heady excitement.

The MC continued, "I got to where I am because I happened to hop onto Teddy Bosch's vessel when I escaped being a thrall. That got me to Bosch and got me a family and a teacher. The rest was hard work, one or two good choices in a sea of bad ones, and the love, friendship, and support of the best people on the planet—the Bosch."

Diamond blew out a disappointed sigh. "Oh well, I guess that counts me out. There's no chance that you're going to adopt me."

"Given that you did date my life partner, I'm pretty sure that would be weird." They had arrived at the trees, and the MC rifled through her bag and pulled out a multi-tool to clip the barbed wire. As she did, she asked, "Why do you say count you out? There's no reason you couldn't be master commander someday. Hell, if can I serve in that capacity, anyone can. It just takes a certain...willingness." She stuffed the tool back in her bag, and she and Diamond carefully pulled the spiky wires' ends away.

This statement pleased Diamond, who commented as she boosted herself up one of the trees, "I'd love to be the one wielding the power someday. I've spent far too much time being told what to do. I want to be the one doing the telling." She clambered over the fence and dropped to the ground.

The MC landed lightly next to her a moment later, "Let me tell you a secret about leading, Diamond Miata. And it's a secret only a select few can understand—at least at first."

Diamond felt excitement bubble up inside of her. A secret of the powerful and the rich. This could be her ticket to gaining everything that had been denied to her as a child and a youth. "Yes, ma'am?" she prompted eagerly.

"The farther up in leadership you progress, the less it is about you and what you want. Fuck, in fact, I hardly ever get my way. About anything. And yet, I still have to fill out the paperwork and fight for the budget to implement those things. In leadership, those you lead, not your personal wants and desires, must be at the forefront of every decision and choice you make." She threw up her hands, and Diamond could see her expression in the dim moonlight. She looked happy.

Diamond felt cheated. People in power *did* get their way. She saw it every day in the Force; she saw it back home in District Four... Hell, even here in the backwater world of the North. She frowned and was surprised to hear the master commander laugh quietly.

"I can tell by your expression you don't believe me. Can't blame you. I didn't believe it either until I was neck-deep in negotiating in favor of issues that, on any other day, I would have been arguing against." She sighed and began to walk forward. "Here's a couple dog treats. Let's get to the barn. I'm cold into my bones."

With a sigh, Diamond looked with distaste at the pungent-smelling clumps she had been handed, then turned and followed her master commander through the dark of night in the February snow to hide themselves in a barn that might or might not exist.

CHAPTER 11

Carisa, February 8 1830

Carisa kept her eye on Flossie as the two women slipped from building to building without a word. In silence, they made their way to the edge of town. The light that shone from windows and the occasional outside lantern made visibility sufficient. As they passed some of the run-down homes, she could smell the pleasant scent of onions being cooked in oil and of fish being fried for a family's dinner. It took her several minutes, but she now realized a smell that was missing. After living so long adjacent to the ocean in the port city of Nyvik in Dobarri, then in Bellcoast, and now in Bosch, Carisa could always smell the salt perfume of the sea. Here, it was absent, replaced by the deep green spice of cedar and fir. Carisa saw Flossie, pistol out, motion to her, and she ran to catch up. It pleased her that if she moved a bit faster and didn't think too much about where her foot went, her gait seemed to improve. She filed that small data point away to research later.

It took only a few minutes for them to reach the outskirts of town and slip into the forest. Here the light was far dimmer than in the village. Flossie stopped. "Let's put the IR vision goggles on. I don't want to trip and break my ankle."

Carisa admired what Flossie had become. As a thrall in

Flossie's family home, she had watched when, as a child, the girl had been misused and tyrannized by her father and ignored and neglected by her mother. It was nothing short of a miracle that she had grown into such a capable adult.

"Good idea. Once we are on what Kat called the water path, I will be able to make it back to the Whydah without issue, and you can join back up with Diamond and Kat." Carisa had seen the looks Flossie gave Diamond and knew that was where her young friend wanted to be. She was determined not to slow down these young, healthy women by asking one or another to make up for what she struggled to do.

Flossie looked unsure but then capitulated. "Okay. But let's get farther into the forest before we split up. I know the MC and Diamond can deal with the militia guys, but I want to be sure none of them came after us."

"Agreed."

They continued their trek, and Carisa found her body getting increasingly fatigued. And with that fatigue, her mood descended. Of course, her brain understood why she should return to the vessel. Hell, she was the one who brought it up. She was not a member of the BPF; she was a civilian, and Kat was responsible for the safety of everyone on board. Her heart, though, was another matter. One decade. Ten short years. She was forty-two years old and had only been free to make her own decisions for a short quarter of her life. Even the first couple of years, after Kat and her team had rescued her from Abernathy, she had spent half in shock and half learning how to make her own decisions. The thing about enslavement: It made the enslaved dependent on their owners. No need to contemplate what you wanted to do today, what you would wear or have for dinner—that choice was made by the owner or their overseer. But now she could choose, and yet was still having choices made for her. Out of love now, but made for her, nonetheless.

She needed distraction; she could feel her thoughts turning

dark. "So Flossie, everything I hear from Kat about your work at BI sounds like you are excelling. Are you happy?"

Flossie looked surprised. "The MC talks about me?"

"Of course she does." Carisa didn't know why this talented woman couldn't see herself as others did. "She says Colonel Greene lucked out when you came to Bosch."

"That's…" Flossie paused. "…really good to hear. Though I don't know if it's true."

"Sweetie, listen, when someone pays you a compliment, take it. Don't negate it. Just say thank you."

"Oh, sorry." The young woman's shoulders came up as she dropped her head.

Carisa touched her arm as they walked. "No need to apologize. I used to do the same thing. Until someone told me what I just told you." She was pleased to see Flossie's posture shift, and her face relax. "Now tell me about this friend you are on mission with. You seem to like her quite well."

It was a shy voice that said, "Diamond is my friend. I… I am really glad to be on this mission with her."

"I am sure she is glad to have you on her team as well. I hope it all goes the way you wish."

They arrived at the crossroads, where the water path veered deeper into the forest a few moments later, and paused, surprised to see someone else there. A young boy, no more than ten, dressed in a threadbare coat and gloves with holes at the tips of his fingers, had a hand cart full of stones that had tipped over. One of the wheels was stuck in a snowbank and lay at an awkward angle. He was alternating between digging at the snow around the wheel with his poorly gloved hands and struggling to right the cart without unloading its heavy cargo.

Carisa started to move to help him, but Flossie put a hand on her arm. "You go ahead to the vessel and get warm. I'll help the boy out. I don't want you lifting heavy stones in the dark and the cold."

After considering putting up an argument, Carisa waved to

the boy and gave her friend a kiss on the cheek. "You're a good person, Flossie. Always remember that," she said before turning to head back to wait for her adventure to begin.

Flossie, February 8 2000

Flossie's arms shook as she pushed the hand cart with its heavy rock load. The little boy, Colm, kept running ahead and then looping back to ask, "Are you sure you be okay, Flossie? Do you want me to push for a while?" And each time, Flossie shook her head. She was not going to let a child tackle a job that she found challenging. She groused in her head, *What kind of a parent sends their kid out in the dark and the snow and the cold to haul rocks? What kind of a place treats women and children this way?* She was cold, hungry, and exhausted. All she really wanted to do was find her Diamond, get the mission accomplished, and get as far away from this place as she could.

Colm was back, hat in his hand, hair flopping as he circled the cart. His loops reminded Flossie of a big loping dog on a hike. "We be almost there!" he hollered. "Can I help? You be so great to do this!"

"I'm good, Colm. You lead the way." While she longed to be done with this task, she couldn't help but grin at the boy's intensity and enthusiasm. They'd be at the boy's house soon, and, she reminded herself, it was fortunate that they were headed in the same direction as the farm where the MC and Diamond were billeted. She'd be at the barn the MC described in less than an hour.

"This be it!" the boy's treble voice called. Flossie could just make out a long pathway off the road. She squinted and saw a wavering light a distance away. With a deep breath and a small groan, she rotated the rickety cart, put her head down, and began pushing toward the light.

"Colm? Colm? Where be you?" The voice in the darkness made Flossie look up.

"I be here, Ma," Colm answered. Flossie paused and realized she hadn't thought this fully through. What if one of the militia lived here? Dammit! She was not going to get recaptured. She would not be the weak link. No, she would get the cart close to the house and slip into the woods before the person attached to the voice saw her. This would be the best course of action. The house was getting bigger. She was almost done.

"Here she be, Ma." Colm appeared on Flossie's left side as if out of nowhere, pulling on the arm of a woman in a knee-length dress. "Ma, this is Flossie. Flossie, this my ma, Eliza. See, Ma? She fixed the cart and loaded the rocks!"

Flossie stood frozen. *Should I run for it? She looks harmless enough…but…*

Eliza had a pleasant look on her face as she approached. "Flossie, be it? Oh, I can't thank you enough." Then she turned to her son, and while her words had a scold to them, her face stayed gentle. "And you, young man. I told you we could haul the first load together tomorrow. I be worried sick about you when I came home to an empty house. I brewed so much tea to offer to Hlin, begging her to keep you safe."

Colm hung his head. "I be sorry to worry you, Ma. But now we have a head start on rebuilding the chimney. Soon we can have a proper fire."

Eliza reached out and caressed her son's face. "That was sweet of you to think that way. But you know how to write—leave a note next time." She explained to Flossie, "A tree came down on the place in the last ice storm and collapsed the chimney. But thanks be, the chimney saved the roof! Now you let me push that cart the final way. You must be frozen, and I have plenty of hot tea."

Hot tea sounded heavenly to Flossie, but she paused. "I… I don't want to interrupt family time for you and your husband, ma'am."

Eliza shook her head. "It be just Colm and me at home. Please come, let me give you a proper thank you. And you needn't be so formal. Call me Eliza." And with that, the woman lifted the handles on the heavy cart, and the three began the short walk to the little house at the end of the path.

Flossie, February 8 2300

Full and warm, with cookies wrapped up in paper in her pocket to take to Diamond, Flossie strode with purpose toward the rendezvous point, following the directions and coordinates the MC had given her a few bells before. She felt a little guilty about lingering so long with the Edwards, but they had been so kind and their home so welcoming.

Eliza had bustled about in her small but neat kitchen, apologizing for keeping the door to the sitting room closed. "Until the fireplace be back up and useable, we just keep the cold in there and stay in the kitchen and our bedroom." She pointed to the floor where she had neatly rolled a rug to block any draft coming from the sitting room door. She added, "I'm afraid the table space is limited," motioning to the piles of books on half the rustic, wooden table. "Don't want Colm having to go into the cold for his schoolbooks, and I can't do without a good read before bed." She had laughed merrily as she said this. Flossie had thought, *Reading by candlelight? What these folks need is some electric lamps. I bet I could rig a couple up—there's certainly enough wind power here*. She had been about to say something when her brain shoved her. *You're only here for a day or so on an assigned mission. You can't get sidetracked.* So instead she just nodded, saying, "I like to read before bed as well."

With the tea, she served some tiny cookies that held a dollop of jam in the center. "It's my cloudberry jam from last summer." Flossie had never heard of cloudberries before, and she couldn't believe how delicious the rich, tart jam was on the sweet, sugary cookies. She could have eaten a dozen of them but stopped at three, cognizant that Eliza's and Colm's circumstances were limited.

When asked about herself, Flossie stuck to the story she had told to the militia. "I'm on break from university and visiting some distance kin." She had really hoped Eliza wouldn't ask too many follow-up questions about which village and where it was.

But she needn't have been concerned because at the mention of "university," Eliza practically gasped. "Oh, by Odin's beard, aren't you the fortunate one, strong enough to haul that ridiculously heavy cart of rocks Colm collected and smart enough to go to university. And such a pretty face as well." Eliza had sighed then. "What I wouldn't give to go to a university—so much to learn. You know, I used to be the schoolteacher here, before that blasted, excuse my language, militia shut down the secondary program." Her voice took on a disapproving tone. "Now, the girls be no longer allowed any schooling, and once the boys be able to read certain passages from the CNE Book of God and show they can write their name and do basic ciphering, they be told to go home and be a man. For pity's sake, most be younger than my Colm when they be told that."

Flossie had blushed furiously at the compliment. But Eliza's description of shutting down the schools distressed her. She couldn't imagine not being allowed to go to school. Sure, she had gotten teased and even bullied a few times while there, but she managed, and it was so wonderful to learn new things every day. She had told Eliza, "I like the work I do now, but I think I'd love to be a teacher. It's like you are doing something that really matters."

"I agree. It matters so very much." She looked down at the table and stirred her tea with a pensive look. "There was a time when my neighbor and I talked about setting up a secret school for the girls and the older boys," Eliza remarked.

"That be Mr. Z, right? The radio-man?" Colm piped up, looking mischievous. "He be sweet on Ma."

Eliza flushed and then frowned a bit at her son's comment, but Flossie could see sadness cross her face. "That's enough out of you, young man. Time for bed." Then she said to Flossie, "He used to be...but not anymore. I had my hopes, but neither the two of us nor the school was meant to be it appears."

Flossie decided that it was actually good fortune she had met Colm and Eliza. The icy weather and encounter with the militia had made her feel like the North Country was a bleak and ominous place, but there was at least one house where people laughed and talked about books and learning. She guessed there must be more. Eliza's description of the delight of a warm summer day out in the lush woods picking cloudberries conjured up an entirely different vision of the North Country. Flossie, with her coat collar turned up against the biting wind, just couldn't quite envision it because, for now, all she could see was snow, cold, and the tall wood and wire fence under a tree that surrounded the barn she was headed to sleep in.

DAY TWO

CHAPTER 12

Kat, February 9 0530

I look at my timepiece and see it is just shy of five and a half bells North Country time. This time of year, this far north, the sun isn't really up until about ten bells. So, it's pre-pre-dawn. Birdsong has yet to begin, but I do hear the chirps of two BI troopers whispering to each other. I may be projecting, but I'm guessing they think "the old woman" needs her sleep. The reality is I've been awake for hours just taking in this well-ordered, well-maintained, no-longer-mine barn.

The memories came to me in waves when Diamond and I first set foot in the door. I had gotten very cold on our trek here, and my first impression upon stepping in was one of sweet relief to be out of the deep dark with its icy fingers invading my body—slowing first my fingers, then my knees, then attempting to work its way to my very core. The cold here wants to paralyze its prey, and the only defense is to keep on moving. As I took deep breaths of the warm air and shook out my body, stomping my feet and fluttering my hands, I could feel myself begin to thaw, and as I did, the cut I had made on my arm, between my BPF tattoo and my thrall brand to cover us all with blood, began to throb. I pressed my palm to the gauze Carisa had wrapped around it and winced. *Just breathe through the pain, Kat,* I told myself, so I took a deep inhale through my nose. The scent of hay, cow, sheep, wheat, chicken, and the tiniest bit of manure flowed into my nostrils. My eyes had opened wide then. This farm was owned by someone wealthy by Northern standards. Looking around, I could see that the small barn I had known so intimately a quarter century earlier had been enlarged to accommodate two cows, five sheep, and an indoor chicken coop. I moved to inspect it and found that this rich man… (It could have been a woman, sure, but up here? What were the chances?) …had installed electric lights so the hens could lay all year round. Smart. *Wonder how it's powered?*

This was the farm where Zach brought me after that awful tavern night. After he had marched in and slapped every marker he had, and quite a few he had borrowed from family, on the table in front of my dad. After he had carried me, weeping, bruised, and used, to my grandmother who had soothed my body with her poultices and my mind and heart with her sleeping herbs. After, she had declared me healed, and he had promised to never allow Dad to hurt me again. But that was before we had conceived Sean, and before they were both murdered by the traders who took me and sold me into thralldom. This was the farm where I had my first taste of happiness, peace, and love. I felt the tears build, but swallowed them as I had no desire to share these memories with Master Sergeant Miata, who I am discovering is only interested in how to attain more markers and more power.

We had settled in to rest soon after arriving in the barn. I popped out my ear comms after my two conversations with my people last night, the first with Flossie, who checked in for more detailed coordinates and data on reaching the rendezvous point. I think she was a little taken aback when I told her where to find the dog treats. She had escorted Carisa to the crossroads and then sent her ahead to the vessel. Not ideal in my book, but I'm sure Flossie was unable to argue with Carisa. She also mentioned something about helping a kid she had met at the crossroads. The second comm was with Reeves, whom I assigned to be in charge of Carisa until my return. It was a good conversation with the flight engineer, and I stayed on long enough to hear Carisa arrive safely. *Take that, Aaron. I told you I'd look out for your girl.*

Flossie arrived late after the full dark, the barn door creaking open. I watched her come in and heard her call softly to Diamond, who murmured something from the loft. *Behave yourselves, kids.* I didn't go up there because I wanted to allow them privacy if needed, and because it's in the same place as it was twenty-five years ago. Too many memories—even good ones—can be overwhelming, at least for me. I posted up in the empty stall next to the cows. Their bodies radiated heat toward me. Zach and I had always talked about getting a cow someday. I'm glad whoever took over the farm has them.

I sit up and shake the sleep from my head. We had better make ourselves scarce before the land's owner comes in for morning chores. And all these memories fuel the fire in my belly to confront and punish Old King Cole.

"Hey, troopers. We need to get around and get on with our missions," I say in a low voice that still fills the space. The soft gray cow next to me turns her head toward my voice. I had whispered to her for a bit last night about the times I had been in this barn. I named her Twilight since her coat is the color of the sky after the sun has set. She lows out a soft moo in response to my call to my team.

I stand and lean over the squat stall wall and reach to scratch the cow around her ears. "What's up, Twilight? You planning on joining the Force? I must be honest. I don't think it's for you."

Flossie's voice floats down from the loft. "MC? Who are you talking to?"

"Twilight. She's my newest friend. Don't let the fact she is a cow make you think she can't be a friend." A thought occurs to me. "Hey, Twilight, any chance I could milk you?" The thought of warm, fresh milk makes my stomach realize that those assholes never fed us, and it growls in response. I do a quick search around me and find a pail and a stool. I approach Twilight, softly caressing her silky coat and murmuring reassurances. I reach under and find her udder is fairly full. "Impressive, girl. Given the time of year." I place my stool and pail and get down to the business of pushing, pulling, and squeezing. She stomps only the smallest amount and calms as I hum a little milking song pulled from my deep memory. It only takes a moment for my muscle memory to kick in, and the sound of milk hitting the sides of the pail and the smell of the sweet goodness tells me that breakfast will be served soon.

The soft thud of feet on a ladder alerts me to the arrival of the BI pair. "What the hell…?" Diamond says.

"Is that even safe? Won't the beast hurt you?" Flossie adds.

I chuckle as my head rests on Twilight's flank. "You city girls, you haven't lived until you have some milk fresh from the cow." I punctuate my statement by leaning down and directing a teat toward my face as I squeeze a stream of milk into my waiting mouth. I swallow. "Nectar of the goddess! Which I think would have to be Hathor." I continue my milking rhythm and am pleased to see the pail almost half full. I feel the tiniest bit guilty for stealing from the owners but decide that this is a perfect blend of pirate marauding and farmgirl skill.

I finish up and carry the bucket to the two women—one tall, dark, and lanky, and one pale, shorter, and softer—who stand looking suspiciously at my bucket. "Go on, take a drink," I urge. They both shake their heads and take a step back.

"No. Milk is supposed to be cold," Flossie comments.

I laugh and my North Country comes through. "You be looney. Milk come warm and sweet when the world is chill." I see both troopers' mouths drop, and they stare at me as if I have gone insane. So, I repeat myself in a way they will understand. "To translate: No way. Cold milk is old milk. This will warm you up before you go outside."

Diamond looks unconvinced but takes the proffered bucket and raises it to her lips, tipping it up. I watch as her throat moves as she swallows. She moves the bucket down, and her eyes are wide. As she passes it to Flossie, she wipes her upper lip. "It tastes so sweet!"

Flossie peers into the bucket and looks dubiously at her friend, who urges her on with vigor. Then she too takes a swallow, and then another. When she drops the bucket from her mouth, she is grinning. "That's the most amazing thing I have ever tasted! It's winter, but I can taste summer in it!"

"Well, don't hog it all," I comment. "I'm the one who did the work for it." I take the bucket and lift it to my mouth for a long drink. As I finish, I look over my shoulder. "Sorry, Twilight. You did most of the work. Credit, where credit is due."

After several more rounds of pass-the-bucket, the milk is gone, and we all need to relieve ourselves after a long night. "There should be an outhouse between the house and the barn. Just stay aware in case the farm owners come a-knocking."

Flossie leaves and returns quickly, and then Diamond heads out. I am stomping a bit to convince my bladder to exercise patience when the barn door opens, and Diamond walks in with her hands raised ever so slightly. I see the barrel of a hunting rifle behind her, and I reach for the pistols I keep strapped to my back. The rifle-holder steps into the barn and calls, "Come on out. I seen three sets of footprints. I don't be planning to shoot this girl, but trespassers ain't welcome here. Don't make me loose the dogs." The voice echoes in my ears and down through the years. I look at the bearded face, and my heart drops.

I yell, "Hold!" knowing Flossie likely has a bead on the man from her position in the loft. My pistols hang slack at my sides as I step out from the shadows. My voice trembles as I name the ghost. "Zach? Zach McKay?"

Kat, February 9 0600

I feel my knees buckle under me and the world spins backward. It can't be. Is everything I have known wrong? My emotions come forward, forming a circle around me as I sit helpless on the hay-strewn floor. Anger and Joy and Grief and Remorse, Love and Fear and Guilt and Hope all join hands, whispering amongst themselves. Fury and Revenge stand to the side, hands over their mouths as they watch in shock. I have broken before, but it was not like this. Then, my emotions were the enemy, each demanding they be heard; now they are united, throwing themselves in front of what is an impossible explosion of my reality. From a distance, I hear that voice again.

"No. No. That's impossible."

I see two feet in heavy boots flecked with snow and muck appear before me. Sturdy legs in thick homespun are attached to them and my eyes follow them up. I see working hands—rough with callouses on the thumbs and stains about the tips as if they've spent the winter working hides. Mine used to have stains like that. One of those hands holds an old rifle, loose and pointed to the ground. I pause to look down at my own hands—two pistols that I've had forever sit limply in my palms. I let them slip to the ground as I raise my hands, turning them over—no stains, no callouses.

I take a steadying breath and tip my head to look up—past the broad chest and shoulders clothed in a heavy barn coat, the edge of a tattered, green flannel shirt against a pale neck—to look at that face again. The beard—long, wild, and untrimmed—is darker than I recall, but also lighter as it is shot with gray. The mouth is full, though the lips are winter-dry and cracked in places. Hair hides most of the face, but there's an old scar on the cheek that I don't remember. A thick knit hat covers the top of his head, but an ample amount of light brown hair sticks out, tangled and shaggy. Then I look at the eyes. They are blue. How did I forget they were so blue? I recall other blue eyes I have gazed into. These are different. They are not the cruel, icy blue of my enslaver or the warm steel blue of a different lover, just as long gone. No, these are the rich color of the deep ocean around the New Caribbean as seen from far above. But I couldn't have known they were that color before. Because the last time I looked into them, I had never seen any ocean, much less flown a vessel over one. Now I let myself sink into the ocean of those eyes and watch as their shock and disbelief are erased by the tears that begin to fill them. They start to blur as my own eyes fill.

He drops to his knees and reaches out to touch my cheek. Not like the lover he once was, but tentatively, as if to assure himself I am real. I feel my own hand rise to do the same.

His lips move and the deep voice rumbles from his chest. "Kat? My Kat? You're alive? You've come home?"

I have my own question. "How, Zach? How is this happening?"

Suddenly, another thought floods my brain, pushing out all the others, and Hope, all dressed in white, comes and stands near me, hands clasped to her breasts, eyes wide. Maybe the fantasy I created isn't a fantasy. What if…? My hand drops to grasp his sleeve, and my voice is eager and intense. "Sean?"

A wave of pain washes over his face, and he slumps and squeezes his eyes shut. As he reopens them, I see deep sadness and what looks like shame. He shakes his head. "No, Kat. I'm so sorry. It should've been me. Not him. But he was just a baby. Kat, I barely survived the shot, and I was a grown man. Seany, well, he was just too little."

The picture his words paint in my mind is horrific. The agony of loss comes at me as fresh as it was twenty-five years before. Now I grasp the front of his dusty coat with both fists, and a keening wail rises from me as we wrap each other in our arms, rocking and sobbing on a barn floor, grieving our infant son who was murdered so very long ago.

CHAPTER 13

Kat, February 9 0730

"I just don't understand how you ladies got away. Those militia boys are brutal." Zach is providing a monologue on the state of the North Country as he stands at the stove, frying eggs.

The three of us "ladies" are seated around the kitchen table—my old kitchen table—sipping steaming tea from sturdy mugs. I am still stunned by the events of the morning, and so I am very quiet, my hands wrapped around my mug as I take in this kitchen where I once cooked. When I was here, a scant quarter century earlier, everything was spic and span.

Now I see grime on the windowsill, the floor, and around the sink and the pump. There are enough cobwebs in all the corners to qualify for a role in a haunted house. Shoved up against the walls and beneath the table are boxes and more boxes. Teddy would have described their contents as "a bunch a' crap." One seems to hold a variety of boots and shoes, one has rags, and one is filled with gears. Another holds tools that at one time had been in Zach's outdoor woodworking shop. Along with all the boxes, the floor holds other flotsam and jetsam: piles of clothes; pots, pans, and dishes; a few books; a heap of blankets with a dingy pillow on top; and even a globe. What in the hell? The Zach I remember, while not fastidious, certainly could pick up after himself. I glance around. The door to the sitting room is shut as is the door to the upstairs. If the room he brings us into looks like this, I shudder to think of what the closed-off rooms contain.

After helping with morning chores, we all came in from the barn, but not before I had to negotiate two rather contentious discussions; the first began when Zach asked me to come up to the house "for some tea."

"But them two..." And he actually gestured with his rifle. "While I appreciate the help this morning, it was a fair exchange for the night's shelter. But I don't know 'em. They need to leave the property now."

I frowned. "Don't be ridiculous. They aren't leaving."

"It's my place. I say who stays and who goes." His voice was adamant.

I could play chicken. "Fine. We all will leave then."

His voice took on a slightly desperate tone. "No, Kat. Wait. They can stay in the barn."

Not good enough. "No goddamn way, McKay. Yes, I am currently fucking astounded and gobsmacked, and yes, I want to talk more about how in the hell you are alive. But these are my... friends." I stalled at calling them my troopers. I figured me being alive and here was enough to start. The pirate leader part could be an aspect of a later discussion. "The three of us came together, and for now, we are staying together."

I'm not sure whether I made a good argument or he was just taken aback by my swearing. Either way, he grunted an assent, said, "Suit yourself," and headed for the house, walking with a slight limp.

Then as I signaled to Miata and Porter to come along, Miata approached me. "Permission to speak freely, MC?" She practically stood at attention.

Intrigued, I responded as her MC. "Proceed."

She pointed accusingly in the direction that Zach had gone. "That man threatened me and all of us with a loaded weapon. I do not think that it is prudent to place ourselves in his home, even if the two of you had some previous relationship. It opens us up to any number of compromising situations."

Okay, so she was disinclined to trust someone who had held her at gunpoint. Fair enough. I expect I would have felt the same. And we Bosch are egalitarian and value each and every voice. However, I don't love being accused of being "imprudent." I narrowed my eyes just slightly as I answered her. "Trooper Miata, I've asked that my title not be used on this mission. I would think a master sergeant in Intelligence could recall a simple order like that." I saw her eyes widen slightly. "And if I may remind you, we *are* technically trespassing, so in these parts, that was a measured response." Hell, a good portion of the old boys up here would've just shot her on sight, half of them because she was trespassing and half because she was dark-skinned. That part I kept to myself. "But if you are uncomfortable with coming to the house, where there is a fire and we can be fed, then by all means, make yourself comfortable here in the barn. Never mind that I just stood my ground to get you *into* the house." I lifted my eyebrows before motioning to Flossie. "Porter, let's go. Unless you too are nervous about the big, bad man with a gun."

I headed to the barn door and, within a moment, both troopers trailed behind like little ducklings.

Zach's voice pulls me back to the present moment. "Basically, every bully Allanavik has ever produced joined up with the militia to terrorize and intimidate in the name of safety. And most of 'em are using the new church teachings to justify their abuse."

Flossie asks, "What do you mean new church?" She's the one asking most of the questions. Diamond, on the other hand, has been as quiet as me, though I suspect it is more of a sulky quiet than mine is.

Zach begins to explain about the church. "It started when Preacher Burns showed up. His kin be from here, which gave him some credibility and, somehow, he had taken up with them CNEs."

"The Bluies?" I finally speak up, and my voice is incredulous. The CNE, or the Chosen of New Earth, are a group of religious fanatics who wear blue, hooded robes of varying hues depending on their position in the church. The whole lot are real pieces of work who advocate the separation of races, the keeping of thralls, and, of course, donating lots and lots of markers to their favorite charity: themselves. "What the hell are they doing up here? I thought they just stuck to places where they could insinuate themselves into rich politicians' pockets."

Zach looks at me. "Preacher Burns takes exception to the term 'Bluies,' though we've coined a few others as well, but yep. He brought folk around by linking the old gods to the CNE one. Now, I don't have much schooling, but…"

"More than me," I say automatically. It is an exchange we used to have back when the world was younger, and we looked to the future together.

He sets four plates of scrambled eggs and, according to him, the last of the toast on the table, before turning to the pantry. After digging in it for several minutes, he brings out a jar of jam. "Here…cloudberry. I seem to recall it was your favorite."

I lift the jar; it has a faded homemade label. "I haven't had cloudberry jam in decades, Zach, thanks." Then I consider the state of the kitchen. "Did, uh, you make it?"

"No. A neighbor did."

Flossie picks it up and looks intently at it. "Cloudberry…interesting." Diamond looks studiously uninterested.

"So those Blue-types have made themselves known even where you have been living, Kat Wallace. And where is that?" Zach's question is straightforward.

I don't want to run my full history with him while my troopers are here, so I give a straightforward answer. "Bosch."

"The pirate nation?" His blue eyes look into mine. "That's where you three escaped enslavement from?"

Diamond snorts with disdain as she soaks up her yolk with the last bit of her toast.

I shake my head. "No. No one keeps thralls on Bosch. In fact, we have been at the forefront of breaking the trade and freeing thralls from enslavement. Zach, Bosch is where I became free. It's my home."

Now Zach gives his own snort. "Your home is the North Country, Kat. You were born and raised here. I know a bit about Bosch. They are pirates—an unruly, raucous bunch of men who peddle Glitter throughout New Earth. You don't belong with them." He looks at me and his eyes narrow. "Have you taken up with one of the pirates? Is that why you call it home?"

Okay. I sigh inwardly. Moment of truth. "Zach, I am one of the pirates. As are these two troopers." I point to my companions. "We all serve in the Bosch Pirate Force."

Zach is silent for more than a minute, looking from me to Flossie to Diamond and back. Then he starts to chuckle. "Ah, Kat, you had me there for a minute. Women pirates. That's a good one."

In my head, Annoyance gestures with its thumb at Zach with an irritated expression. At the table, Diamond wears almost the same expression. Flossie, though, is smiling at him like an indulgent parent. I am about to answer when he asks, "For real now, is Bosch where you ladies are running from?"

Several deep breaths center me as I evaluate whether the statements I am about to make are prompted by a desire to help Zach understand who I am now and why we are here or are motivated by pridefulness and ego. I settle on a sixty/forty split in favor of understanding.

"Zach, let me introduce you fully to my troopers. This is Master Sergeant Diamond Miata. She works as a field agent for the Bosch Intelligence Department. Her expertise is in weaponry and tactical skills. You won't find a person, on Bosch or elsewhere, who is more skillful than her in sharpshooting or hand-to-hand combat."

His eyebrows go up, and he still wears a smirk. "Be that so? Well, I managed to trap her pretty quick this morning." He points at Diamond, who finally speaks, and there is venom in her response.

"I was taking a piss in a smelly, little, wooden house. Not much room for evasion." She shakes her braids, and the morning sunlight glints off the diamonds she is no longer trying to hide. "And you were fortunate that the m—I mean, Kat—recognized you, or I would have laid you out in the barn."

For a moment there, I was ready to test my hand-to-hand skills against Diamond's before she shifted from my title to my name. But as she finishes her tiny tirade, I realize why the master sergeant has been so quiet. Her pride has been scraped up at being captured twice in as many days.

Zach leans back in his chair. "Is that so? Pretty big talk for a young lady."

The chair scrapes on the floor as Diamond starts to rise with her dark eyes fixed on our host.

My hand goes up and gestures for her to keep her seat as I intervene. "It isn't big talk, Zach. She has the skills to back up every word. Just ask a few of those militia bullies she dropped." Diamond takes in an audible breath as she settles back in her seat. She gives me an appreciative look, but her eyes return to bore into Zach.

I continue, "And this young *lady* is Sergeant Flossie Porter, also of the Bosch Intelligence Department. She is one of the most brilliant recruits we have had in many years. She can break any code, and she has a talent with electronics that cannot be matched." This garners a look of pride from Flossie. "Hell, she could probably build a computing device out of the refuse you keep in these damnable boxes." Okay, my voice did raise a slight bit at the end there, but I think I kept my cool quite well. "Don't underestimate my troopers." I hear the pride in my voice as I finish.

Zach's eyes are narrowed in thought, and he wears an appraising look. I probably have revealed too much. He leans toward Flossie, and what he asks surprises me, "Electronics whiz, huh? Do you think you could fix a radio?"

Flossie, February 9 0830

"A radio? A real radio? Like from the Old Days? With mixers and oscillators? We trained with them, but I've never seen one still being used. Is it one-way or two-way? Are we talking tubes or crystals or integrated circuits? How big is it? How do you power it?" Flossie could feel her eyes get big as she let the questions pour out. She loved tinkering with old electronics.

Zach held a hand up. "You look at it and then you'll know more." He stood and motioned to the closed door on the right side of the kitchen. Flossie practically leaped from her seat.

The MC stood, the breakfast dishes stacked in her hands as she carried them to the overloaded sink. Her left eyebrow went up, "A radio? Times have surely changed in Allanavik if people have radios in their homes. When I was last here there were two in town. One at the general store and one in the front office of the secondary school."

"Times have changed." Zach agreed. "*People* don't have 'em. *I* do. The militia controls access to any outside news. All radios are now under their control."

Flossie looked concerned. "But won't you get in trouble with them if they find out you have one?"

The bearded man shook his head. "They know I got it. Them's the ones that came when I was gone from the place and busted it up. After that I reinforced the fence, and now, I always put the dogs on the property when I'm out…which, while we are the subject, how did you three get past the fence?"

Flossie glanced down to the floor. Granted he had held Diamond at gunpoint when they initially met, but since then this man had been very generous with his resources. Flossie felt badly they had damaged his property. The MC must have felt the same because she commented, "Don't worry about it, Zach. Anything we undid, we will repair better than we found."

He gave a skeptical grunt. "See that you do. Anyhow, it also helps that those militia boys be a superstitious lot and be afraid of me, having been brought back from the dead and all. Fact is, I expect one of the reasons they smashed my radio be to prevent me from talking to demons, spirits, and the old gods. Idiots." He looked at Flossie, his hair wild about his face, and said with a gruff bark, "Let's go, Sergeant Pirate Electronics Wizard."

Flossie's eyes sparkled with anticipation. "Aye-aye, sir. And you can just call me Flossie. It's easier."

"Flossie, then." The man's voice was still gruff, but Flossie thought she detected the ghost of a smile under all that hair before he turned and led her to the radio.

Flossie, February 9 0900

It was like one of those delightful, nested dreams Flossie had when she was a child, when she would be dancing through some beautiful field only to awaken inside a more magnificent dream. Tables lined the three doorless walls of the small, dim, interior room, which was really more of a large closet. Above each table were three long shelves, and on each were bits and bobs of electronics, including several empty outer cases of radios. Two of the tables were also covered with boxes of electronic detritus with the third holding a clear space, a chair next to it, and an electric light just off-center.

Zach walked in and fiddled with the light's cord, then switched it on, and the room fully came to life. "There. The parts in the boxes I scavenged when the militia destroyed as many radios as they could find a couple years back. I didn't need any of them until the militia busted up my radio last fall. And I ain't no electronic wizard."

Flossie sat down, picked up the crushed device, and carefully removed the damaged casing. Her expert eyes moved over the old analog device as she carefully moved the damaged sections. "Well, I doubt the power supply was damaged, but the main board looks like it's been through a war. See these capacitors? Some of them are bulging. I'll need to replace them. Same with any cracked or burnt resistors." She looked up at Zach. "Do you have a soldering iron? We can use it to remove the damaged components and to repair any cracked connections."

"I think I got one in one of the kitchen boxes. I'll check." The big man left the room.

This is almost like heaven for me, Flossie thought. As she sunk into the delightful task of examining each tiny section, her brain began to work a puzzle that she hadn't been aware lay before her. The word *radio* tickled something in the back of her mind. She certainly had heard it plenty of times today, but even the first time, it had a familiar ring. She knew better than to plumb for the answer. It would come.

Several minutes later Zach appeared. "Sorry it took so long. Kat said you and that dark girl…"

"Her name is Diamond. And while her skin is magnificent, there's so much more to her than just the word 'dark.' Do me a favor—call her Diamond?" Flossie said all of this matter-of-factly, without any ire.

Zach paused for only a moment. "That you and Diamond got some kind of a mission up on the mountain. I told her I'd take you in my truck to where the road ends in the foothills. Seems a fair trade if you get the radio working. Save you both a long, cold walk."

"Thanks." Flossie barely looked up.

"Here's the soldering iron. I'll leave you to it."

CHAPTER 14

Diamond, February 9 1030

Diamond rolled her eyes and wrinkled her nose as she looked out the dirty truck window at the white and brown landscape. The truck smelled of sweat, hay and cows. Probably all stemming from the dirty bearded farmer driving them north about twenty kilometers on the snow-covered dirt path the yokels here considered a road. The entire way Flossie had continued her chatter about the radio she had tinkered with back on the farm. Though the ride did save them a good three bells and trekking through the cold, still she couldn't wait to get out of this antique vehicle and get on with making the markers she had come here to accrue and then get out of this land that time forgot.

Diamond found herself wishing she had come on this mission solo. She could have been in and out in a matter of hours and back home collecting her markers. She grumbled to herself, *this is what happens when brass gets involved with their heavy vests.*

Honestly, everything about this whole goddamn trip galled Diamond. Having a crippled civilian tagging along had annoyed her from the moment they took off. At least that situation was managed. She resented the fact they didn't just shoot the assholes in white who locked them up, all because the MC had decreed a *no weaponry* clause since she was afraid of creating chaos. Diamond snorted to herself; a little chaos could be good. At least the fight was fun. Then the previous night the MC taunted her with a secret about becoming a leader. Of course, she ruined it by spouting off her stupid platitude about leaders not getting their way. Diamond squeezed her fist so tightly that her fingernails almost drew blood from her palms. The woman was gatekeeping. Diamond knew the routine. The powerful had no intention of sharing power, so they downplayed it. She shook her head the tiniest bit. Why had that damn MC even bothered to come on this trip.? If she wanted her shitty dad dead, all she had to do was send in a unit, and poof, he'd be gone. Maybe that was why she thought leaders didn't get their way. She didn't really know how to wield the power she had.

Then there was the uncomfortable night sleeping on scratchy hay in a broken-down barn loft. And to top it off, the whole morning had been absurd and offensive. From her morning pee being interrupted by a rifle barrel, to the ridiculous outburst of emotion in the barn between the MC and that man who continued to refer to them as *ladies,* to Flossie's fawning over the stupid primitive machine the man had. The last part was the worst. Diamond had spent the last fifteen years having people be jealous of her. She was not accustomed of feeling jealous. She knew that deep down, she admired how easily Flossie connected with the civilian, and the MC, and even the farmer, for Earth's sake, and they all acted as if they had some claim to her. Which they did not.

She toyed with some of her darker thoughts, first seeing the little blonde fall flat on her face, maybe in some mud, as she and Flossie laughed together, then imagined herself announcing to the force that their MC was a faithless bumpkin, happy to get all cozy with her old partner while pretending to be on BPF business. She pictured the arrogant woman shrinking in disgrace, while Matt Warner, humiliated and cuckolded, begged her to take him back. The force cheered Diamond and asked her to lead them. Sitting in the old truck, she could hear the cheers as she humbly accepted the position. The stink of farm brought her back to the present and she tried to imagine how to shame the farmer but could think of nothing worse than to be condemned to live in this awful wasteland full time.

Flossie was still prattling on about radios and tech, and Diamond felt resentment bubble inside her anew. She looked over expecting to see the dowdy little nobody who should be grateful for Diamond Miata's attentions. Instead, she saw a vibrant young woman, cheeks pink and face animated with excitement. The image made her catch her breath. Flossie Porter attractive? This was something Diamond had not considered, and it caused her to feel even more possessive of her friend.

The farmer interrupted Diamond's musings. "I'm gonna pull off up here a pace. You can get out and head northeast across the field until you get to the tree line. Follow the path into the forest about two kilometers, and then you'll start going up, and up. Hope you ladies don't mind scrambling, since from what you've told me, that camp is pretty far up the mountain." Diamond sighed. She had a compass and coordinates; she didn't need him telling her to turn left at the big tree.

Flossie, however, gushed, "Thank you so much, Zach. We really appreciate you bringing us this far."

The farmer brought the truck to a stop. "Pleasure's mine, Miss Porter, Miss Miata. You ladies be careful. Pirates or no, the mountain is unforgiving, and from what I hear, the Chinese ain't much better. Thanks for the attention to my radio, Miss Porter."

"I'll work on it some more when we get back. I might be able to help you build a transmitter for it with all those spare parts you have," Flossie said as she climbed out of the vehicle.

Diamond raised her hand. "See you. Thanks for the ride." Then because she just couldn't help it, added, "Hope you and the MC have a cozy time catching up." Her face held insolence as she stared at him. His eyebrows rose in response. She turned and stalked off across the field without looking back. "C'mon, Flossie. We have a mission to attend to."

A few moments later, Flossie caught up to her. "Are you okay? You seem pissed off."

"Oh, you think? This was supposed to be a mission for the two of us. To make some heavy markers and all. First you are late to the rendezvous because some local half-wit can't keep their cart in decent repair, and then this morning, when we should have been planning our mission strategy, you go off playing tech support to some dirt-grubber. You need to learn to stay focused on what's important, Flossie." It felt good to vent some of her frustration, and Flossie was an easy target on which to do it.

Her friend was quiet for a few moments, "I didn't think of it like that. I'm sorry, Di. I just felt bad for the kid last night; he couldn't have been more than ten, and he looked so distraught. Then his mother wanted to show her appreciation....and the old radio was a real distraction. I'll do better. My focus is you and this mission."

Diamond paused to check her compass and bestowed a forgiving expression on Flossie, who now looked fretful and uncomfortable having lost the vibrancy she had in the truck. Diamond paused, and felt a flush of shame in her cheeks and her gut as she wasn't sure which version of Flossie she liked better. "Well, okay. Let's just concentrate on what we need to do. We can talk strategy as we walk."

Diamond, February 9 1145

She didn't want to admit it, but that fucking farmer was right. The ascent up the mountain was steep and difficult. They had to move diagonally, switching back every few meters. She and Flossie had stripped off their parkas and tied them around their waists; even as the air grew colder, they grew warmer with exertion. Flossie was huffing and puffing. Diamond glanced back at her and saw she was red in the face. But she didn't complain, and didn't fall behind. This was a good lesson for her, the master sergeant thought. She could get in shape, or at least learn the kind of work that actually was required in the field.

As they trekked along, a past conversation occurred to Diamond. "So, Floss, you said you weren't in contact with your parents, but then you said your dad *was* a skin-bigot. Did he change, or is he dead?"

There was a moment of panting, then Flossie responded, "So dead."

"Oh, sorry." Diamond didn't really care, but she had been raised to show sympathy for people's losses. "But a skin-bigot? Did you not tell me that because I'm dark?"

Flossie paused and wiped the sweat from her forehead with a hand dirty from grasping onto rocks, leaving a smear on her face. "That never entered into it. I probably never mentioned it because, in the list of his awful qualities, that actually was one of his lesser ones. Bottom line, he was a real shit and I'm glad he's dead. So, no need to be sorry. I sure as hell am not."

Wow, Diamond thought, *and I thought I had issues about my folks.* "Is your mom dead too?"

"Hang on, I need a break." Flossie sat down on a rock and gulped for air. After a couple of minutes her breathing normalized, and Diamond stood as patiently as she could. "My mother was a drunk, a very refined one, but still a drunk, for most of my life. I can't really blame her. She had to deal with my father who we have already established was just this side of evil incarnate. After my father was removed from the planet, she dried out and, apparently, remarried and is pretty okay."

Diamond wrinkled her brow. "Apparently? You don't know?"

The ample sergeant looked troubled. "She and I are not…in contact. I left home before my dad fell and didn't tell anyone where I was going. She was in a rehab place at the time. She never came looking for me, though New Earth knows she had the resources. Granted, I had moved to Bosch and changed my name."

"What?" This was more intriguing than anything she could have imagined. The phrase *she had the resources* echoed in Diamond's ears. She had always thought Flossie had come from some lower-class neighborhood in Truevale and enlisted in the Force as a way to escape the cycle of poverty. But that comment made it sound like her friend had a bit of markers behind her. Very interesting. More information was needed.

"You changed your name? Like me? We are name change twins and I didn't know it. That's wild." She approached the woman on the rock, then reached out and put a hand on her cheek. "You poor thing. It must have been awful."

She watched as Flossie's emerald-green eyes softened. *This girl has got it bad.* Diamond decided to up the ante. Flossie was her friend, and she intended to lay claim to her. "Let me give you a hug." She crouched down and wrapped her arms around the younger woman, feeling the soft, round body melt into hers. In a moment, she felt a small rhythmic quiver begin. Flossie was crying. She had never had a friend who cried on her shoulder. A wave of emotion flowed from her chest to her stomach making her feel full and warm.

Diamond rubbed soft circles on the young woman's back and stroked her hair. "Oh, hon, you should have told me. That's what friends are for."

Flossie pulled back, snuffling. "I...just...wanted...to...forget."

"Well, just know that I'm here to listen if you need anything." She leaned forward and gave her a soft forehead kiss. "Are you ready to push on?" She kept her voice kind and gentle. Flossie wiped at her tear-streaked face and stood. "Okay then. Let's go, friend."

Diamond's brain whirred. There was more to her friend's story, she was sure of it. And she intended to find out what it was. The idea that her loyal friend had an intriguing secret gave Diamond a thrill of excitement. Her grandfather had taught her how to fish in one of the ponds in District Four. She knew how to set her line and be patient before reeling her quarry in. The conversation was paused for now, but she would return to this topic and, maybe, it might help her land a big one.

Kat, February 9 1030

The truck heads toward the road from the farm carrying two of my troopers and one of my ghosts now come to life. Turning from the window, I realize I am alone in the first house I ever was alone in. The realization makes my belly flop over. There are questions I have for Zach that I didn't want to pose in front of my troopers—chief among them being what happened after I was taken. The whole of the North Country has been frozen in place in my memories, and I am just now weirdly coming to terms that everyone here just moved on after I was gone. I want to know how Zach's survival unfolded, where my Seany is buried, and what happened to Grandma Rina and my siblings and friends.

I feel Anxiety poking and prodding at my belly, so I make my way to the outhouse to see if I can leave him in the pit. As I return, I pause at the rain barrel next to the house. There's a pump inside, but it's slow compared to filling a few buckets. I break the ice on the surface of the barrel and scoop up water into the bucket that sits next to it. I carry it to the kitchen where I ladle some into the kettle and set it on the stove to heat. When it whistles, I pour the boiling water into a basin, and add enough cold so it won't sear my skin off, and then proceed to wash up.

I start by washing up the sink full of soiled dishes. Now, I am no one's maid but sitting around with all this crap piled up in here makes me crazy. And I have an ulterior motive: I want to bathe. Once the dishes are clean, dried, and put away, I heat more water, scrub the counters, and then use some vinegar and water to clean the two kitchen windows until they sparkle. I wipe off the kitchen table, which had been decidedly sticky even before breakfast, and then sweep and mop the floor. Well, as best as I can with all the boxes piled up.

Finally, I heat another round of water and wash myself. First my hands and face, which after all my tasks turn the water quite gray. I toss it out and heat a fifth round of water. I pull off my sweater, then my extraction top, which handily has been constructed with built-in breast supports, and wash under my arms and under my breasts. I pull off the heavy hard pants and slide out of my tight-fitting extraction bottoms and underwear so I can wash between my legs and bottom. Standing naked in the block of sunshine that falls through the now clean kitchen window brings me the joyful memory of being seventeen and romping naked with Zach in a little house all our own. The world was so much simpler then.

A chill passes over me, so I pull open drawers until I find one that contains small kitchen towels. I grab one and pat myself dry. My clothes only marginally pass the sniff test, but I have no others, so I do with what I have and pull them back on, flipping my underwear inside out. As I retrieve the towel from where I dropped it on the floor, my heart feels a pang. It's embroidered on the end with the shape of the big rock and a "Z" and "K." I run my fingers over the threads I placed there several lifetimes ago. The edges are starting to fray. *So are yours, Kat Wallace,* I think ruefully.

Clean and refreshed, I contemplate my situation. While my body feels more in order, my emotions are still a jumble—Joy has pushed themself to the front, joining hands with Amazement. But Guilt and Anguish keep trying to shoulder their way in, and impatient Revenge keeps looking at their watch. Which is strange. Who wears a watch on top of armor? I leave them to their own devices and focus on what I need to do. What am I going to say to Zach when he returns? How do I manage this? Sweet New Earth, I wish I could talk to Matty. I let myself lean back on the counter and close my eyes. My eyes pop open as I remember. The SatComm.

Digging in my bag, I retrieve it. The sitting room is just to the left of the kitchen and would be far more comfortable. Unless it too is piled with boxes. I cringe at the thought. The door sticks slightly but releases with a small shake and shove. It is as if I've been transported through time as I stand in the middle of the floor and look around me in wonder. There are the two upholstered chairs Zach's grandparents gave us as housewarming gifts, shipped all the way from Dobarri. My hand runs over the stones of the fireplace hearth, recalling how the two of us picked each one carefully. The fire box is cold, and there is no ash, as if there has been no fire in it for a long time. After opening the damper, I set in some kindling and a few very dry logs and light it with one of the long matches. The flame hungrily eats through the kindling and soon a decent fire is crackling merrily. My eyes run over the mantel, the walls, and the shelves, which are filled with unfamiliar pictures and knick-knacks.

Plopping myself down crossed-legged on the braided rug that Zach's mother made, my fingers move across it, feeling the areas where it is starting to thin. It's pretty impressive it has lasted this long. It's also pretty dirty. I push the buttons on the fancy comm as Cal showed me to switch it from message to voice call and tap in my beloved's number.

"Yo, who's this?"

"Hey, big boy, wanna go sneak off and have crazy, wild sex under the moon?"

He chuckles. "Sorry, miss, while I am not married—though I'm hoping that may change—I am completely besotted with my partner. Also, you should know, she has a knife and a temper. Just saying."

I start to comment, but he continues. "Also, it's February. Crazy, wild sex under the moon needs to be implemented during the warmer months."

"Aaah, warmer, shwarmer. You southern folk don't know what cold is."

"My ass on frozen ground knows cold, miss. What else can I do for you since sex is currently off the table?"

I laugh. "I miss you so much, Matty Warner. I need your sage advice."

"Doesn't sage advice come from someone older? In which case I cannot help you."

"Fuck you, asshole." I'm a mere three years his senior.

"I think we have already established that we are not fucking any orifice currently."

"Rini must have slept well last night. You are full of vim and vigor."

"Well, she slept partially on top of me, with her hair in my face. But I am so used to you doing that that I found it quite restful."

This makes me laugh and I am overwhelmed with gratitude for my life.

Matty's voice modulates. "How are you, my love? What's going on?"

I blow a sigh through puffed cheeks. I don't know where to begin.

"Sounds big."

"It is. And I still haven't wrapped my head around it. Matty, Zach didn't die when the traders shot him. He's alive, and I'm sitting in the house where I lived with him for about a year and a half while he drives my BI troopers toward their mission site."

There's a pause. "He's alive?"

"He's alive."

Another pause and I know what he wants to ask, so I answer first. "No. Sean is dead."

"Oh, my love…"

I rub my face with my hand and slap my cheek gently to avoid crying. "This is really fresh intel. I only discovered it a few hours ago, so haven't had time for much follow-up."

There is a pause. Then Matty says, "You know, when I first met you, I remember thinking, I wonder what she'd have been like if she hadn't been a thrall. I thought without that staining your life, you would have been carefree. Carefree. That's the exact word I thought. But then when you told me about your family, I realized you never got to be that. Not even as a little girl. I guess *carefree* is really a summer child thing to wish for."

I feel tears spring to my eyes both for the sadness I hear in his voice and that I feel for that long-ago little girl who never once was carefree.

"I guess what I'm trying to say is you've told me the stories. Zach McKay defended you with his life—even if he didn't die. And he got you free of that horrendous tavern night when you were a kid—you were Grey's age for fuck's sake—and away from the fucking monster that dares to call himself your dad." The sadness in his voice escalates rapidly toward anger. He takes a breath that can be heard through the distances. When he speaks again his voice is calm, but there is still an intensity to it. "You tell Zach McKay for me he has my eternal gratitude for making sure the other half of my soul survived so I could find her."

It's funny how love can envelop you in its warm embrace even when you're alone. I close my eyes and feel Matty's strong arms around me; it centers me. "I'll tell him." My eyes flick about the room. "There are pictures of a couple of children in various stages of growth on his walls and his mantel. I hope they are his." I stand and peer at one. "This one sure looks like a younger version of him."

"Talk to him when he gets back. Ask him about them."

"It's not weird or intrusive?"

"Kat, you two just realized each other are alive after twenty-five years. There's bound to be a little weird."

He's right about that. I consider. "There will surely be some twists and turns as we reminisce."

"Well, just don't go too far down memory lane. I'd hate to have to fight a man I have just recently given my eternal gratitude to."

"The only lane I want to go down is that dead-end one near

the new park with you." I giggle like I'm twenty. Matty and I have had a few passionate trysts there. Since we have big kids who stay up until all hours, we do what we have to.

His warm laugh rolls through the thousands of kilometers that separate us. "I told you, gotta have warmer weather."

His laugh is infectious, so I chuckle along, and then say with all the wistfulness this place pulls from me, "I miss you."

"I miss you as well, my beautiful, brightwork girl." I can hear the love in his voice as he tells me, "Come home soon."

"I will. I love you so much."

"You are the love of my life, Kat Wallace. Give 'em hell up there, especially when you just happen to run into that shit that once was your father. Listen, baby… I know you have feelings with a capital 'F' about the old man, and I know Revenge has got to be right up front. You spent a whole chunk of your life letting it call the shots when it came to Abernathy. It can be an overpowering emotion. I have utter faith in you and your judgment. Just give some of those other emotions a chance to have their say and take care of my brightwork girl."

The warmth of his love permeates through me upon hearing his special endearment for me. His words reaffirm to me the depth of our connection. "Oh, Matty, you know me so well. I will try. Thank you. I love you. I'll let you know when we are headed home. Kisses to our babies."

"I'll pass them each one. I love you, Kat. I will be waiting."

And with that I click the SatComm off.

Carisa, February 9 1030

Carisa's eyes opened to light filtering into the Whydah through the thin shades pulled over the vessel windows. *How long has it been since I woke up because I was ready to wake up?* she wondered wistfully. *Fully two kids ago.* She felt more refreshed than she had felt in months, but there was also a hollowness in her belly as she thought of the usual start to her mornings with Carly's wispy hair tickling her chin and that sweet baby smell that still existed for a moment before she woke fully and became a busy, active toddler. She imagined Arthur stomping in at first light, probably holding some contraption he had built from his stick-on blocks, and climbing into the big bed, demanding, "Where's Mama?" from Aaron. She sighed. She adored her little family and would send them a message telling them just that as soon as she returned with the SatComm. Her hand searched under the cot she had slept on for her timepiece, bringing it up to check what bell it was, and was astonished, first to realize her double vision wasn't active this morning and second, that it was after ten bells.

Upon reflection, she actually wasn't surprised how long she had slept. After all, her body had been very fatigued when she arrived back at the vessel from the trek into town and then the hustling return trip in the dark, not to mention all the hijinks that had ensued in the shabby little village. And yet, she had still stayed up far too late laughing and getting to know Sergeant Zoya Reeves.

"But the only one who calls me Zoya is my stubborn-as-a-mule mother, who—and I'll only say this out of her earshot—I take after, both in looks and temperament. Hell, even Allanah calls me Reeves 90 percent of the time, and we've been together for almost two years," Reeves quipped as she took a sip of the red wine she had pulled out and opened after Carisa arrived.

Carisa didn't drink much anymore; it was enough of a pain in the ass to maintain her balance with the damn UN. Adding alcohol on top of it just compounded the issue, but she was happy to share a small glass with a new friend. The two women had made plans to explore the lake shore the next day. Reeves had a strict rule to never go farther than about a five-minute walk away from her vessel while on mission. "I'll stretch it to ten minutes if I have a clear sightline, but I like to stay close. Fortunately, the lake shore is right there, and I bet we could find some fossils. They're a hobby of mine. You work at the university, right? I love the prehistory museum over there."

Carisa had been cautious. "My gait is bad enough. Not sure about wandering over the rocks."

Reeves looked curious, then said, "Stand up and walk for me. Don't try and correct." So, Carisa had walked several steps across the deck and back. "Hold on," Reeves said as she opened a storage bin on the vessel side and began plundering in it, pulling out several flat pieces of metal. Within the hour, she had constructed an L-shaped brace. "Okay, see, this short end will go under your right foot, with the long end against your calf. Then we can fasten it on with a couple of these hook-and-loop cargo straps."

Carisa picked it up and turned it over a few times. "I don't know, Reeves. My physio says I just have to keep doing exercises, but not to expect much improvement."

"Yeah, well your fucking ray-of-sunshine physio isn't here, is he? What do you have to lose?" Reeves grinned.

Carisa thought that sounded reasonable. "You do have a point. Okay, put it on me!"

"Great!" Reeves knelt down and placed the brace on Carisa's right leg. The straps were extra long for cargo, so she had to wrap them a few times. "You can get shorter ones back in Bosch if this works. It's just a prototype."

Carisa slipped her shoe back on and repeated her walk. Her face brightened. "I don't have to swing my leg! I can clear the floor without my foot-drop." She grinned at Reeves. "Thank you! You are officially my newest hero!"

"Totally self-serving." Reeves ran her hand through her spiky dark hair. "I wanted someone to explore with tomorrow." She gave Carisa a friendly wink.

Now Carisa sat up and looked around. The vessel was empty, although the hammock Reeves had slept in was still up, not yet stowed. *Probably went to relieve herself in the fresh air,* Carisa thought as she looked over at the door that enclosed the cramped head and wrinkled her nose in disgust. Her own body was nudging her to find relief, so she pulled on her sweater, leggings, and socks. The brace Reeves had made for her the previous night lay next to her shoes, so she strapped it onto her right foot and slipped on her shoes and coat to step outside to pee.

Several minutes later, she pushed the button to reopen the ramp and come aboard. "Are you ready to go exploring, Reeves? I am loving this brace!" she called as she walked—slowly, but far more gracefully—up, only to find the Whydah, silent and empty. Odd. Perhaps Reeves had gone down to the lakeshore on her own. She grabbed her walking stick—she balked at calling it a cane—to help her maneuver the frosty rocks and then turned and headed back down the ramp to the lakeshore to catch up with her new friend.

Standing at the shore of Tassy-Canner, she realized why it was called the ocean lake. When she looked out across it, all she could see was blue water with large chunks of ice pushed up by the winds, creating frozen castles against the shore. Carissa tried to imagine what the lakeshore must look like in the heat of summer: trees, green and lush; a warm breeze blowing; and the water, cool and refreshing, lapping at her bare feet. But this morning's February lake breeze was brisk and chill, whispering around the tree line and carrying with it the pleasant scent of cedar, the musty smell of old leaves, and a vague, disagreeable, rotten-egg smell that made Carisa wrinkle her nose. In the cold, clear morning, she could see far down the shore; there was no Reeves. She looked to her left and her right. *I can certainly see farther than a five-minute walk,* she mulled as an ominous feeling settled in her belly. This was not good. Where the fuck was Reeves?

I can't even comm Kat to tell her my concerns. I could walk into the village, but I told her I'd stay at the vessel, and who knows where she and the rest of the team are, even? The weight of responsibility sat fully on her. Okay, what were the options? *I could just go back to the vessel and wait.* She considered this choice. Waiting was what she did best. She had waited for her parents to come home and for her

Aunt Elka to tell her she was released from family obligation. She had waited at the thrall market, hiding in the Bellcoast marketplace, hoping she would not be found. And she had waited in New Detroit for some sign that she would eventually be free. She shook her head at the thought. She was fucking done waiting.

Okay, Carisa, think: Where would she go to pee? You only have to search a five-minute radius. She bit at her lip as she tried to think which way the woman could have gone. *Just be systematic,* she told herself. *It's like looking for a mis-shelved book in the library or specific information in a research article. Start with one section, scan it carefully, and then move on.*

Carisa made her way back to the Whydah and went on board to grab her timepiece. She stopped for a moment to sketch out her plan in her notebook. She'd walk away from the vessel for six minutes in one direction, assuming she moved more slowly than Reeves, then cut over and walk back until she could see the airship, and then repeat. She looked at the image she had created. It looked like a flower that Arthur might draw, with the Whydah in the center and the pie-shaped petals radiating from it. She paused and considered the drawing, then tore out the page and wrote, *Zoya, I went looking for you, this is the pattern I'm walking. Hang the Bosch flag in the front window if you get back before me.* Carisa was glad to have thought of the note. It would prevent confusion and double-searching if Zoya showed up before Carisa had returned. As she started to leave the vessel, she looked at the blanket on her cot and picked it up, stuffing it inside her parka. If Reeves had been outside for long, she'd be pretty cold.

Okay, 'Ris, you've ruled out the lakeshore already, so let's start at the tree line. She checked her watch and began the search for the absent flight engineer.

CHAPTER 15

Carisa, February 9 1130

Carisa had finished two full petals of what she was now referring to as her flower search pattern by walking at a slight angle away from the Whydah for six minutes, turning left, walking for four minutes, and then turning left again and walking at an opposite angle back toward the vessel for six minutes or until it came into view, calling Reeves' name every few steps. Both times as she returned within sight range of the clearing where the Whydah was parked, she looked up, hoping to see the BPF flag with the flying pirate ship silhouetted against the full moon, daggers crossed below it, its red flag bright against the white background displayed in the window, but both times she only saw the buff-colored shades.

She turned for her third petal walk, as she was calling them. She was only about four minutes into the walk away when she came to the ridge. It wasn't obvious at first, because the tops of the cedars came up beyond that, pretending to be trees the same size as the ones to her left and right. In fact, the rocky edge of the drop-off was not obvious to her until she was just a meter or so from it. Fear struck at her. *If it were dark, I wouldn't have seen this.* She swallowed, afraid of what she might see over the edge. *She won't be there,* Carissa reassured herself. She took careful steps and peered down the steep ridge.

Zoya Reeves lay face-up, broken, and unmoving on the snow-covered rocks at the ridge's base. Carissa gasped in horror as she looked down. "Zoya! Zoya!… Reeves! Please be alive!" Carissa stared down at what looked to be about six meters, saw no response from the woman, and tried to suppress the panic that made her want to freeze in place.

What if she's dead? Carissa thought. She felt a pit in her stomach. *I'm gonna have to go down there and find out.* She tried calling out once more. "Zoya! Zoya Reeves!"

A tiny movement of the woman's head caught her eye, and Carisa saw her mouth opening and closing, though she could hear no sound. *She's alive!*

Moving back from the edge of the ridge, she looked around. *I can't go straight down the steep side,* she thought. *I have to go around.* She skirted the ridge, walking deeper into the forest until the ridge had dissipated into a small slope. She sat down and scooted herself down the slope; she wasn't going to chance falling. Two busted-up people were even worse than one. Then she turned and hiked along the ridge line that slowly began to tower over her.

She had to zigzag around some large boulders and piled snow, but she finally arrived where Sergeant Reeves lay. Carisa knelt next to the woman and called her name. "Reeves. Reeves, please still be alive." Reeves did not open her deep brown eyes but began to make the same motions with her mouth that Carisa had seen from above. Leaning close to the woman's lips, she could just make out an almost silent "help."

Carisa sat back on her knees. "I'm here, Reeves. I'll help you. But it's gonna take a minute. I probably need to go get reinforcements." As she said this, she knew that would be impossible. She had no working comm. Anyone in the village would likely turn her over to that damned militia, and the odds of her finding someone who would help and getting back here before Reeves froze was astronomical. *It's up to you, Carisa.* She thought to herself then, *What if I can't?* "Well, I have to try. I can't not try," she said to the snow-driven woods and the rocky earth where Reeves lay.

She took stock of the woman's injuries. Both her legs were bent at curious angles, and her right arm lay to the side, clearly broken. Her face was scraped up. Carisa was no medic, but she knew if bones were broken after a fall from that height, there was probably damage on the inside as well. The first order of business was to get her back to the vessel. Carisa had been thinking about a scenario like this as she had trekked the petal path. She remembered the reading from one class about the ancient people from the Central Continent who used to move across the plains while carrying their gear and even their children behind them in a rough sled. The name eluded her, but she remembered the picture.

She started to talk her plan through with Reeves. "Okay, I need two branches twice as long as my walking stick. But I don't have an ax or even a knife. Dammit. Maybe that's why Kat always carries that sling bag of hers, so she has what she needs in emergencies." Carisa stood up and took a deep breath while looking about her. She crossed her arms and grinned. "Hey, Reeves, I may not have Kat's sling bag, but I have a warm blanket." She pulled it from her parka and tucked it around and under the flight engineer, careful of the broken limbs. She spied Reeves' red knit hat in the snow and dusted it off, planning to put it back on her, but then changed her mind and switched hats with her. "There. My hat is warm and dry for you. And yours will warm up as I move around. Fair trade. I'm going to look for branches now."

It only took about ten minutes before she had found two suitable downed branches. Each looked to be about three meters in length and sturdy enough to support the load. She dragged them back to where Zoya lay, and after checking her friend's breathing, began breaking off the smaller branches to create two smooth-ish poles, then she took off her parka. It wasn't dangerously chill out, and her body actually functioned better in the cold than when it was hot. "Lucky for you, I like the cold," she commented as part of her ongoing patter to the either unconscious or semi-conscious woman. It felt better to talk to someone, even if they were unresponsive.

She shoved the branches in until they stuck far out of the parka sleeves. "Okay, I need them to cross at the top. Dammit. I was going to zip up the parka, but it's too wide at the base with the sticks crossed. But the article I read said it had to be this shape." She looked over at the blanket-covered woman. "Any ideas?" No response came from Reeves. Carisa looked at her. "Can I have your coat?"

Relieving Reeves of her parka was easy enough, although she moaned with pain when Carisa worked it off her broken arm. "This will do it." The small woman grinned as she zipped the coats together.

"Now the hard part for you, Reeves. I'm gonna have to put you on it. I'll be careful, but I'm pretty sure it's still going to hurt." Reeves' eyes were still shut, and her breathing was shallow, but she was still breathing, which Carisa took as a win. She rolled the injured woman onto her side, which evoked a sob of pain. "I know, Reeves. It hurts, but it's just for a little while. Hang in there," she reassured both Zoya and herself.

What the hell was it called in the article? she wondered as she tucked the sled as far under Reeves as she could before rolling her back onto the parkas. After a few repositionings, Carissa thought Zoya was situated well enough that she could pull the sled without dumping the unconscious woman into the snow. Then she looked at the twisted, broken legs. They were going to drag. Damn. Carisa sat on the ground, put her head on her knees, and felt tears begin. She was going to fail, and Reeves was going to die. She was a fool to think anyone could depend on her. She was wrapping her hands around her legs to roll into a ball of misery, when her fingers felt the metal of the foot-drop contraption Reeves made for her. Her head came up and she pulled her shoe off. "That brace you made for me is going to pay off, Reeves."

Several minutes later, Reeves was tucked between the parkas with a blanket wrapped under the sticks and around the crossbar that Carisa's walking stick provided. Her legs were supported, and the rest of the blanket was wrapped across them and fastened with the cargo straps. Carisa stood between the crossed branches and lifted with all her might; she was shocked at how easily the woman's weight came up behind her. "The terrain is rough, anyway, Reeves. My foot's misbehavior won't slow us down, I promise." Carisa took a step. The sled moved. She took another, and it moved again. "One step at a time, Reeves, right?" Carissa posited. "One step at a time."

Kat, February 9 Noon 30

The engine whine of the truck alerts me to Zach's return. I have occupied myself with cleaning, which seemed the most efficient use of my nervous energy. So far, I have pulled the downstairs rugs, hauled them to the clothesline, and beaten them to release what could be months or years of dust and dirt. Then I refreshed the starter from the back of the cool box to get a sponge rising for some fresh bread tomorrow. After that, I dusted, swept, and mopped, and damp-cleaned the upholstery in the sitting room. The place needed some greenery, so I went out to the tree line, cut a few holly branches with berries, and settled them in a vase on the kitchen table, slipping a lovely, crocheted doily I found in a drawer underneath. Once I had aired the house out for about an hour, I rebuilt the fire to warm the place. Finally, I sorted through the cool box and headed down into the basement root cellar to get what was necessary to make a pot of soup.

Zach comes in the door, stomping his boots on the mat. There's a grunt as he uses the boot jack to pull them off. I hear a step or two of his limping walk, then it stops almost immediately. I look over. "You okay?"

He is frowning as he sniffs the air. "What the hell did you do?

Be that soup I smell? Why be this door open?" He yanks the sitting room door closed and then immediately opens it again and peers in. His voice rises in volume and vehemence, "What be you doing in there? A fire in that room be a waste of resources. You have no right to come into my home and just start changing things, Kat. You said the North ain't your home. So, if you ain't fixing to stay, don't go digging through my private life. Do you understand?" He is practically roaring as he finishes.

I sigh. He has a right to all those feelings. But I have a task to do before I find my dad. "If the yelling at me helps, Zach McKay, then by all means, keep going. But while you are yelling, you sit your ass down in this chair so I can do something with that mess you have let get away from you on your head and face." I point at where I have placed a chair on top of an old, thin blanket, then I hold up a pair of scissors; a comb and mirror wait on the counter.

He snorts and grumbles, "Don't know why you'd bring the holly inside," as he walks over and sits heavily in the chair so Mission Reclaim Zach's Face can commence.

"Because it's pretty. Seems to me you've forgotten what pretty is, all hermitted up like you be in this kitchen." I slip into a bit of North Speak as I work a bit of water through the tangled forest I am about to tame.

"I ain't forgot." His voice has moderated, and he points to the table. "Where'd you find that doily?"

"In the third drawer of the breakfront. Which needs its runners oiled."

He nods. "I'll take care of it."

"Hold your head still. I don't want to lop off an ear."

Another snort. "Can't see as it would much matter. Goes with the rest of me."

This is my in to pose the question I have been itching to ask. "So what happened after…well, after you got shot? I mean, I heard it, and I saw you fall, but…"

"Don't like talkin' about it." The words are clipped with a clear finality.

I see I'm going to have to step up my negotiation game several notches with this one. I decide to start mild and with a comment, not a question. "Probably need to go to town this afternoon. Used the last of the flour on the sponge." I like my technique—acquiring food stuff: not too personal. Just practical, nonthreatening. I await a response.

"Becca made that doily."

This is a fascinating non-sequitur, so I pursue it. "Becca who?"

"Becca Martin…McKay. My wife. Well, I guess not no more. She got a wife of her own now."

I stare at the crown of his head for a moment. My jaw has dropped so far, I may have to go spelunking to find it. "Okay, there's a lot to unpack there. Are you telling me, you married Rebecca Martin? *My* Rebecca?" Rebecca was my first crush and the reason my dad pulled me from school early in my first year of secondary and sent me off to work.

Zach blows out a breath. "Same Becca. She used to call you *her* Kat."

I can't help but feel a little warm inside about that. But only for a moment. I need to follow this thread and get more intel. "And those kids in the pictures in the sitting room? Those are yours and Rebecca's?"

"Yep. Lily and Max."

My scissors are fighting their way through some hair mats that I hack off and drop to the floor. He must have more to say about his kids. I wait. And wait. Finally, I dig, "You, uh, want to add anything to that?"

"Like what?"

My patience, which generally runs about as thin as April ice, cracks, and I give a thick lock of hair a firm tug, which elicits a "Hey, that hurts!" Zach twists his head around to glare at me.

I move in front of him and lean in until I am inches from his face and pile on my I-just-might-kill-you look. "So does being stonewalled. I assure you, McKay, I have other techniques that can induce conversation that will hurt much more. So, spill the details,

Zach. Where are Lily and Max? Where's Rebecca? What happened? How'd the two of you get together? What 'wife of her own'? Why are you incapable of human conversation?"

His glare recedes, and he reaches up and strokes my cheek. "Nope. I ain't forgot pretty."

I feel the blood rush to my cheek where he touched it, and I straighten up quickly and step back behind the chair. "Tip your head forward so I can get to the back." He does. Then he answers.

"I don't have many folk I talk to these days. Guess I'm outta practice. Kids be practically grown now. Lily, she got Becca's red hair and a fair, few freckles that she hated, but I liked. She must be...twenty-one? Last I heard, she be in Paris, which be where Becca settled. Max be nineteen. He took after me in looks, poor kid. Born on your birthday if you want to know. Becca says he's at university in New Lisbon. We, Becca and me, sorta…gravitated together after...well, you know. Likely 'cause I was the closest thing to being with you. We got along, still do. But I really wasn't her type if you know what I mean."

I do know what he means. My scissors continue to snip away, creating form out of chaos. "Yep. Being gay or anything not what the folks up here consider *regular* can be real hard."

"More than hard these days, Kat. Dangerous. Especially with the Bluies and their following now. I wouldn't have really minded Becca having a friend or two if it meant she could have stayed. But she had a couple pretty close calls, so we arranged for her to leave."

"When?"

"Max was five, and Lily seven." Zach clears his throat. "I… Well, they were real good kids." Another throat clear and small snuffle from Zach, and I have to blink fast to keep my vision clear as tears pool. "We talked and figured they'd have more chances, you know, education and all—Becca be a real stickler about book learnin'—away from here."

"So, then they all moved to Paris?"

"Not right at first. They started in Nyvik over in Dobarri. I went over a few times, and Becca brought 'em to Marpavik over on the coast a few times. Then she got offered a job in Paris and met her wife, and the kids got bigger, and…" He takes a deep breath in and lets it out slowly. "I ain't seen them in a few years. Get letters sometimes, though."

I try to imagine my babies being so distant, and my heart hurts. He lost two families. No wonder he's a fucking mess. I stand back to look at his hair. "Looks a helluva lot better. Now the beard."

Not much conversation passes with the beard trim, but when I'm done, I survey my handiwork and am pretty pleased. "Could have done a better job if I had a razor. Maybe we can pick one up in town." I can really see the handsome young man I fell for when I was a girl. I hand him the small mirror. "What do you think?"

He scrutinizes his reflection from several angles. "Looks real good. Thanks."

"You are most welcome. Now I am going to heat some water, and you are going to bathe and put on some clean clothes. I will wash these piles…" I gesture around the kitchen. "…and you can hang them to freeze dry." I grin at him. "There will be no more dirty recluse living here. Savvy?"

"Savvy? That be a pirate word. Which reminds me, what does MC stand for? That some kind of a nickname?"

"Where'd you hear that?" As if I don't know.

"The dar… I mean, that Diamond girl. Whew, she don't like me much." He rubs his newly trimmed beard and shakes his head. "She called you MC before she went off with Flossie, so I was just wondering."

One of the things Teddy taught me while schooling me in the art of negotiation: You always need to bring something of equal or greater value to the table to bargain with. My current extraction and negotiation mission is to drag information out of a man who has become so taciturn, he threatens to transform into stone. Therefore, I must be willing to contribute worthy details as well. "I don't think you are the only one she doesn't much like. But it doesn't really matter. She'll still do as I order because MC stands for master commander. Zach, I am the master commander of Bosch." I feel my posture straighten as I announce this.

Now on New Earth, in the circles I move in, this pronouncement typically evokes respect, esteem, sometimes a little awe, sometimes a little fear... Often a few laudatory comments like, 'We here in [their nation's name] have heard exceptional things about your work,' or 'Impressive for one so young.' I particularly like that last one. But here in the North Country...

A simple one-shoulder shrug and a "Huh, so be that good? You like the team leader for them or something?"

I sweep up the shards of my exploded ego from around the room and reply, "Or something, yep." I choose an alternate set of details to offer up. "I have kids too."

Now Zach looks very pleased. "Well, thanks be to the Goddess. You were a wonderful mother to our Seany. Tell me about your kids."

So, I brew some tea, dish up the soup, and tell Zach about my daughter Grey, my twins Kik and Mac, and little Rini. Who, after all, are far more important than any title.

CHAPTER 16

Carisa, February 9 1300

Two things occurred to Carisa as she dragged Zoya Reeves through the woods beyond the edge of the ridge before turning back toward the Whydah. First, "It's a travois!" she practically shouted as the name of the contraption she pulled finally surfaced in her brain. And second, "Oh, fuck, Reeves. I'm going to have to fly you out of here." Aaron, a seasoned navigator and a talented pilot, had taught her to fly in a Whydah when they started dating, and she had taken off and landed a couple of smaller vessels as well, but she was definitely no expert.

"I mean, what other choice do we have, Reeves? This damn place has nothing like a hospital anywhere close, if at all. And I've been studying the maps of Nyvik for this trip. I know exactly where the hospital is there." She could have contacted Kat via Reeves' ear comms, and she had planned to do just that, but after a search of Zoya's person and clothing and the general area around where she fell, Carisa had come up empty-handed. She looked up as she trudged and saw a glint of silver from the Whydah's hull just ahead. Glancing back, she tried to discern whether Reeves' face was getting paler. There was no time to waste. A life depended on Carisa. She had to act. "It's you and me, Zoy. We're going to Dobarri."

Kat, February 9 1530

"Blood of the White Bear! What's going on?" Zach's voice boomed out as he returned to the general store after carrying the fifty-kilo sack of flour to his truck. "Jake Kepner, you get your hands off of her!"

I am in the corner of the store farthest from the door surrounded by what Zach had described as *woman's goods*—bolts of cloth, dishware, and cookware—squared off in front of two men; one brawny and bald man with a non-existent neck and an overly hairy one who is a bit sparer, but still with plenty of potential power in his punches. The hairy one must be Jake because just as he lunges toward me arms up and hands open as if to grab my arms, Zach yells, causing Probably-Jake's eyes to shift away for the briefest second. That is my cue to throw a hard shin kick to his groin and follow it with a hard elbow that connects on his right cheek with a crack as I yell, "Nice meeting you, Jake."

No-Neck hollers something as his buddy goes down on his knees, but my ears are a-buzz with adrenaline, so I can't make it out. Mouthing something at me, which I am positive is not charitable, he approaches me with menace. Keeping my hands up, I take a step back, feeling the wall fixtures at each elbow. No-Neck is so big, he pretty much takes up the entire corner, and his face is twisted in that angry man fashion. He would not go down from a blow from my fist, so I let him step in and slash at his eyes with my left hand straight like a blade. I know that won't stop him, but it gives him a millisecond of pause that allows my right hand to slip back and close around the handle of a cast iron skillet. I swiftly bring it around, and instinctively know I need to use both hands to swing it at his head. Pride looks unamused in my head as she says, *Time when you could do that one-handed.* Fuck Pride. No-

Neck falls like the proverbial ton of bricks. Which may be what he weighs. *Still worked,* I shoot back at Pride, who just rolls her eyes.

My eyes are wild and my breath is ragged as I scan the store for any further danger. With Jake and No-Neck down, that makes three I have bested this afternoon. The first one was dispatched too quickly to earn a nickname when I pulled the large apothecary cabinet over on top of him. But there were four in the group, I am sure of it. Where is Four?

I glance down and spot him. He is tending to the Apothecary Man (hey, he did earn a name!). Four has moved the heavy hutch and is half-carrying his compatriot out the door. "Where do you think you're going, asshole?" comes flying from my mouth as I jump up onto the low set of shelves that blocks me from my quarry. He looks back, and I am delighted to see fear in his eyes. He shoves past a stunned Zach and heads out into the snow.

I leap toward the door and am right behind him. I'll easily catch him since I'm not weighed down by a fallen comrade. Except as I reach the door, an arm goes about my waist, and I feel myself lifted off the ground. My feet continue their march for a moment until they realize they are airborne. Then I feel my body still as my brain prepares its plan to demolish whoever dares hold me back. I twist to begin the onslaught of headshots to my captor when I hear, "Enough, Kat! Let 'em go." It's Zach, and I have to downshift my fury quickly before I lay him out.

"Why'd you stop me?" I yell.

"I think you've done enough." While Zach isn't yelling back, his voice is certainly loud enough to penetrate my warrior haze.

I take a deep breath in. "Fine. Put me down, will you?"

I look around Brewster's General Store. It had been quite tidy when Zach and I walked in. Now, besides the large cabinet with its broken glass front and array of broken bottles on its side, a good portion of merchandise, once displayed on the shelves that run down the middle of the shop, are now topsy-turvy on the floor. Additionally, the display of mops and brooms is off-kilter, and a couple sport broken handles. There are several bolts of cloth tossed down haphazardly as well. And there're also two guys in white and gray moaning softly on the floor. Well, Jake is at least.

I walk back to where they both are prostrate on the wooden floor. I squat next to No-Neck and put my hand in front of his nose and mouth—a breath of air warms my palm. Good thing he is huge. That skillet might have ended a smaller man. I open both their collars to keep air moving for them and notice the deep blue shade of their undershirts. Fucking Bluies. Those politico-religious fanatics have not only sullied one of my favorite colors but have also truly taken over the status as the bane of my existence since Rob Abernathy is no longer around for me to parry with. Got to be honest, I did not anticipate seeing Bluies up here. But then there's a whole fucking lot I did not anticipate about this trip.

Rising, I catch Zach's incredulous stare. I shrug. "Part of the training."

"We need to leave now," he says, his words clipped and serious.

He has a point. "One sec." Smoothing my skirts, I reach into my sling bag and pull out a couple hundred markers, daintily stepping over the fragments of cabinet and merchandise. I lay them on the counter. Mr. Brewster, the balding, bespectacled owner of the shop, peeks out of the open door of the storeroom.

Then I look at Zach. "Did you get a razor?"

He doesn't answer even though his mouth is wide open.

"I'll take that one, Mr. B." I point to one under glass in a display on the main counter. Mr. Brewster makes no move, so I say, "I can get it myself if you'd prefer." His nod is close to imperceptible but present, so I present my most winning smile, open the case, and remove the razor. "Oh, and I'll take the strap for it too." I reach back into my bag, grab another hundred markers, and add them to the pile.

"Real sorry about the mess, Mr. B. That should cover it and then some. Have a good day." I wave, and he lifts his hand ever so slowly and wiggles his fingers, his face still a mask of fear and shock.

As we move out the door, Zach murmurs under his breath, "What the hell happened in there, Kat? I was only gone a few minutes."

All the post-fight happy chemicals have come flooding into my system, sharpening my wit and my tongue. "It wasn't my fault," I say with a saucy air. "You left me unsupervised." I am still laughing as we climb into the cab of Zach's truck.

Kat February 9 1545

The cab of the truck is quiet as Zach pushes hard down on the accelerator, but not the good kind of quiet, more the cut the tension with a meat cleaver kind. It is my assessment that Zach McKay is not used to afternoon brawls at the general store.

It had all started innocently enough. We had chatted for a couple of hours, mostly about my kids and his, and ate the soup I had made. That was when I reiterated the need to go into town to get a few provisions. The troopers and I had eaten quite a bit of what Zach had. Plus I felt I owed a debt since I had stolen Twilight's milk.

"Who's Twilight?"

"The gray cow."

"You mean Bossy? Is that why she be dry this morning?"

I looked at Zach with disgust. "Bossy?"

He returned the look. "Yes, Bossy. It be a perfectly good cow's name."

With a shake of my head, I explained the obvious to him. "She's the color of twilight over the lake in summer. Her name is Twilight."

Zach growled a bit and then stood and looked out the kitchen window toward the barn. Finally, he turned. "I learned early in life not to argue with Kat Wallace. Twilight, it be."

I preened in my victory for a moment, but Pride suffered a mild blow with Zach's next observation. "If we be going to town, you ought to put on something different that won't draw so much attention."

"What are you talking about? These are typical North Country clothes. I remembered how folks dress up here."

Now that his hair is cut, I was really able to see the extent his eyebrows went up. "That get-up you be wearing be for menfolk, and out of date to boot—by about twenty years."

"Really?" I was both dismayed and incredulous.

"There's some of Becca's old things up in my room. You should find something suitable so folks won't mark you as an outsider immediately." He then came closer and peered at me, moving his head from side to side. I realized he was inspecting my hair. "Can't for the life of me figure why you'd cut that beautiful hair of yours, Kat. The other pirates had longer hair."

I had no interest in discussing my hair length choice with him. What is it with men and hair? "If the other pirates jumped off a bridge, do you think I should as well?"

"What the hell does that mean?"

I sighed. "Nothing. You said the clothes were in your room?"

"Yep. You know the way."

Still shaking my head of short curls, I climbed the stairs. He was probably right about the clothes, though I was uncertain about fit since the last time I had seen Rebecca she was eighteen and as slender as the spring stalk of cotton grass. I had thought it was pretty odd that her things were still in Zach's room—the one she and Zach had stopped sharing fourteen years earlier and that he and I shared a decade-plus before that. Still, I made my way to the big room to dig through her left-behinds. Was it weird? Yes, it was. Did I consider what my life would be in an alternate reality? Abso-fucking-lutely.

I came back downstairs in a simple white top with a gray skirt that fell past my knees. I left the top button on the skirt undone and bloused the shirt over the waist. It allowed me to fit comfortably in it. I arrived back in the kitchen carrying my pistols, their holsters, and a soft rose-colored cardigan. "I need your help fastening these on, so they don't show under the sweater." I had tried a few ways upstairs, but my holsters were not designed to fit with this type of garment.

His expression was priceless. When he knew me, I was not only a terrible shot, but generally wanted nothing to do with weapons of any kind. He took up one of the Glock-147s and turned it over in his hands. "These be a real collector's item." His voice held admiration. "And you have a matched set?"

"I do. My adopted papa, Teddy Bosch, gave them to me. I treasure them."

Then he seemed to understand. "Ah, I see. I imagine they be sentimental. But be it wise to carry them with you?"

"Hard to use them for defense if they are not at hand." I grinned, realizing he thought I carried them as if they were showpieces.

"You have shot things with these?" His tone reminded me of RTT's as she looked at my knife.

I laughed. "I have shot things. And I have shot people. And…" I extended my right leg and drew up my skirt over the gray knit stockings I found in Becca's things all the way to my thigh, where my eight-inch bone-handled knife sits. "I have also used this to cut things. And people." I dropped my skirt. "Now help me get my holsters in the right place."

He said nothing more, and I wished I could help him understand, but our worlds diverged that awful fall day in the woods just south of here. Neither of us can fully understand how the other has suffered and was changed.

A bit later we headed into town to Brewster's General Store, the bright yellow building I had seen the previous day. "Are there two stores now? One on either end of town?"

Zach had shaken his head. "No, the old end be pretty rough. Even more so than when you be here. It consists of a shop that sells tobacco, whiskey, and beer—and where you can get your Glitter, just out the back door—the first three home-grown and south of mediocre, the last typically cut with some cheap filler; a couple run-down shacks that turn over residents quick; a place that sells coal and wood; a reasonably decent honky-tonk; and the old tavern."

I sneered at the mention of the place. Once we arrived in what passed for the new section of town here in Allanavik, I perused the goods in Brewster's General Store while Zach negotiated flour price with Mr. Brewster, then lifted the bag to his shoulder to take to his truck. A moment after he left, a foursome of militia walked in. They exchanged stiff pleasantries with Mr. Brewster. I heard one say to his mates, "Did you see shit-bag be in town?"—which evoked a braying laugh from the others.

I had moved to the soaps and lotions section and was focused on keeping my face away from them while still attempting to survey them surreptitiously. None were the same as yesterday's cohort, but I figured they talked to one another. I stood on my tiptoes to keep them in my sight as they moved around the store; three of them were now standing near the door.

"Ma'am? Can I help you reach something?" A voice behind me made me almost jump.

"I'm fine. Thank you."

"Ma'am, we don't see many women with chopped-off hair here. Where you be from?"

Fuck. I could feel the curtain about to rise on a shitshow. I tried to dodge away, but the man grabbed my arm and turned me to face him, lifting my chin with his hand.

"Hey," he hollered. "This is the short-haired one with the scar."

Realizing the jig was up, I jerked my arm from his grasp, and he countered with a hard slap across my face, which started my lip bleeding. Irritated, I reached around and toppled the large standing cabinet of small glass bottles and envelopes of powders onto him, at the same time landing a sharp kick on his right knee. I heard one of the other militia men yell out, and before you could say, "Kat Wallace is in the room," the fight was on.

CHAPTER 17

Flossie, February 9 1600

As they reached the ridge and then paused to regroup and review the plan to infiltrate the camp and extract Dr. Aung, Flossie took a few minutes to take in the view from the vista. A deep feeling of peace came over her as she looked out at the snow-capped mountains that surrounded her, their descent into rolling forest-covered hills, and in the center, the blue expanse of the lake. What had the MC called it? Tassy-Canner. Not a very melodious name for something so magnificent. She listened to the birdsong bubbling up from below and the sound of the wind as it eddied around the peaks. She took a deep inhale through her nose and smelled pine and cedar, along with a dry, salty fragrance she couldn't place. As she looked up at the clouds scudding by so close they seemed she could touch them, she saw some bird of prey wheeling about and coasting on the updrafts. Calling this place beautiful did not do it justice.

"You okay, hon?" Diamond's voice pulled her from her reverie.

Flossie's lips quivered a bit, but she gazed appreciatively at her friend. She had been such a support today when Flossie fell apart talking about her family. She hadn't realized how much the reunion of the MC and her former partner had affected her, but it had. Watching the MC's face as she looked at a man she thought had been dead made her wonder whether her mother would look on her with such affection. She didn't want to spend too much time plumbing that question. "I'm actually good, Di. Something about the unspoiled nature of this place really soothes me."

Diamond laughed. "Not me. I'm a city girl, through and through. I like to be clean and comfortable. But good for you, hon." Her tall friend came and stood next to Flossie. "Man, you can see forever up here, though." The two women stood in comfortable silence for a spell before Diamond spoke again. "Hon, my curiosity is just eating at me. What did you change your name from and how'd you pick Flossie?"

"I had a teacher in primary who accidentally called me Flossie. She felt badly about it, but I didn't mind, because she was so sweet. We decided she would call me Flossie sometimes, and I could call her Miss Jo instead of Miss Johanna." Flossie's face glowed at the memory. "So when I left, I decided to be Flossie."

Her friend looked fascinated. "That's a nice story. So, you went from what to Flossie?"

Flossie couldn't see how telling her best friend in the world her old name would hurt anything. "Farris. I used to be called Farris." She hadn't said or even thought of that name for so long; it was like speaking of a long-dead friend.

"Well, now, that's a pretty name as well, though Flossie does suit you. Farris Porter. Yep, I like Flossie better. Good choice." Diamond showed her approval, and Flossie felt as if she was transported to heaven in those eyes.

"Well, no. Not Farris Porter. It was Farris Abernathy. My last name used to be Abernathy." This name did not feel friendly in her mouth. It felt ugly and evil.

She glanced over at Diamond, sure she would see revulsion on her face. But Diamond's face looked just as serene and enchanting as it almost always did. Her friend reached out, lifted Flossie's hand, and gave it a squeeze. "I agree, Porter is better than Aber… What was it?"

"Abernathy."

The most beautiful woman in the world stood next to Flossie Porter in the most beautiful place in the world, holding her hand, and said, "Yeah, Porter is definitely better than Abernathy."

Kat, February 9 1600

The old truck bumps over the packed snow for several minutes before Zach finally breaks the silence. "When you three ladies said you got into it with the militia, I envisioned hair-pulling, slapping, and screaming."

Tipping my head from side to side, I say, "There was a bit of screaming early, mostly for effect. But none of the other things. Generally, with big guys, it's good to let them underestimate you. Then you can get the first few hits in before they figure out you're a real opponent." I demonstrate with my fists and elbows as I shadowbox from my seat. I stop to press the back of my hand to where my lip is still bleeding.

"I see." His eyes are on the road as he passes the entrance to the farm. "So, in two days, you be in two fistfights."

It's like the good old days. I feel a wicked grin, which I remove with haste as it won't help this conversation—and it really hurts. I opt for innocence. "Neither of which I started." I cringe a bit as I say this. "Okay, I sorta started yesterday's, but only so my team could get clear. Where are you going?"

"Going the back way onto the property. Built a hidden access road through the woods around the folks' old place. That way the gate stays locked, and there be no fresh tracks. I can let the dogs run. Figure holing up at Ma's place for the night will let things cool down."

It's odd to me. Can't imagine why a man living alone in Allanavik would need so much security. But then the militia did break into his house and bust up his radio, so he probably has a good bead on the situation.

I decide to focus on getting my lip to stop bleeding because, thus far, the process has not been going well. As I dig in the storage compartments for semi-clean clothes, he pulls out a handkerchief and then snaps, "So let me get this straight: You carry multiple weapons on you at all times, which you tell me you have used against what I assume are pirate enemies. In addition, you fight like a seasoned scrapper and can take down men more than twice your size. What other so-called talents have those pirates developed in you over the last quarter century?"

Given his tone, I refuse to tell him that every inch of my body hurts and these are the first fights I've been in for five years. The way he says *talents* doesn't sound as if he is paying me a compliment, and it gets under my skin, reminding me of the way my ex-husband used to demean my work as *soldier games*. I will not give him the satisfaction of hearing me complain.

I chew on that thought for a bit, then my annoyance breaks through my silence. "I'll tell you the talents I've developed. Every BPF recruit who graduates is adept at FFS: flying, fighting, and shooting. Because of the work I put in and the people that believed in me, I just so happened to excel at all three things, which is why I was the best at Glitter running and renowned throughout New Earth for my extraction work. Which in turn allowed me to get ahead, choose to attend officer training, then spearhead an anti-trafficking program that has freed close to three thousand souls and is close to dismantling the whole sordid trade worldwide. And if that weren't enough, the past leadership of Bosch appointed and approved *me* as the leader of both the entire Pirate Force and the nation of Bosch: because that's what being master commander means, Zach. So don't sit there and sound so priggish about my life choices. I was forced to be a thrall. I chose to escape. Good fortune landed me in Bosch. I did what I had to do, and I did it damn well. Still do as a matter of fact. Would you rather it had been me laid out on the floor of Brewster's? That way you could have come to my rescue. Would that have been more ladylike?"

Zach makes no comment.

I look out the window because I'm angry and don't want to look at him. Then the old McKay place where Zach's folks lived comes into view, and a flood of memories flows over me, pushing Anger toward the back of my mind. I remember that every year after I had turned ten, Dad rented me out to farms to help with the plowing, planting, household chores, and harvest. And every year, as I got stronger and more proficient, he collected more markers for my work. I landed on the McKay place the spring after I turned sixteen. Mr. McKay had been ill through the previous winter, so my help was needed. I'd been there about a month when their handsome, charming nineteen-year-old son came back from working the trawlers in Marpavik spinning tales of adventure. His name was Zach.

Now a much older Zach, scarred in body and spirit, parks the truck in the barn of the old place. He gets out of his seat and walks over to close the barn door, pausing there for a moment before he returns. I keep my seat with ferocious determination that has yet to be noticed. I am fed up with his silence and disapproval. Although it is overwhelming to be here, Anger has not fully left me, and I am still steaming and ready for another fight as I look at him.

Then he looks at the ground, and I see an actual smile develop on his face. Before my eyes, the gruff, crusty loner fades, and the affable, talkative boy who romanced me under the full moon stands looking at me. "Kat Wallace leads a nation of pirates, does she? Well, you always did chafe under the rule of the North, Kat. You truly be your Grandma Rina's granddaughter. Bosch was the fortunate one to have you come to their shores, and I am sure it has a strong leader in you.

"Let's go into the old place and we can talk about how we got to where we are."

The anger falls from me like the sliding snow of an avalanche. "Okay," I say softly.

Carisa, February 9 1600, Nyvik

"It's a good thing you got her here when you did. A few more hours and she would be beyond our help." The thin, blonde doctor wore a serious expression as she spoke with Carisa in the small waiting room of the bustling Nyvik University Hospital. Carisa thought that everyone there seemed pale with hair in various shades of blond and sporting light eyes—so vastly different from Bosch. "I'll be taking her back for surgery in a moment. Scans show internal bleeding, likely from her spleen, which I will remove. Once that is complete, Dr. Stefanson, the orthopedic surgeon, will repair the compound fractures of both of her femurs and the breaks along all three large bones of her right arm, as well as in her hand."

Carisa gave a sigh of relief. "Thank you so much, Dr. Mattiason."

"It is my job." Then the woman continued, "She sustained, oddly enough, given the extensive fall you described, only a mild concussion. For all her injuries, she is quite fortunate, and I am cautiously optimistic about her survival if there are no surprises in the theater." Then the doctor looked at Carisa as if actually seeing her for the first time. "The surgery will take several hours. You look in need of some care yourself." Her brows furrowed slightly, and she stepped over to the nurses' station and spoke for a moment to a woman with a friendly, open face who looked to be around the age Carisa's mother would be now if she had lived before returning. "Agnes will see to you. I will provide you with a status update when the surgery is complete." And with that she turned and disappeared behind a set of double doors that read *Operating Suites—no unauthorized admittance* in Dobarrian. Carisa stood staring at the words and spun her wishes out to the universe for the surgery to go smoothly and successfully with no surprises.

A warm voice broke into her ruminations. "I'm Agnes. And what's your name?"

Carisa looked up to see the older woman whom Dr. Mattiason had spoken with smiling at her and holding a cup of tea. "I'm Carisa. Carisa Morton."

"So then?" Agnes raised an eyebrow. "You're one of those Bosch pirates, huh?"

Carisa shook her head. "Well, no, I'm not a pirate. I was actually born here in Nyvik, though I haven't been back in years. My husband is one, though."

Agnes placed the cup in Carisa's hand and gave a wink. "Ohhhh, your husband, is it?" She leaned toward Carisa. "Is he a handsome devil? Did he steal you away from your home? I do love a good pirate tale. All that swashbuckling adventure."

Carisa couldn't help but laugh. "He is quite handsome, but he only stole my heart. And he does have adventures."

Agnes gave a delighted giggle. "As do you. Look at you, dragging your friend out of the woods in that extension of Niflheim they call the North Country. And you, not much bigger than my ten-year-old niece. And a pilot. You saved your friend. Those folks up there are still depending on poultices and teas to treat their ill and injured. You got her to a place that can piece her back together." She put a warm arm around Carisa's shoulder. "It's going to take them some time to do that, though, so, while you wait, let's give you our hero's treatment: one warm shower, one good meal, and one soft bed in the doctor's call room."

"Oh, Agnes," Carisa sighed, "that sounds amazing."

CHAPTER 18

KAT, FEBRUARY 9 1630

"So, where's your ma, now?" My voice is a bit muffled as Zach has provided me with a towel-wrapped snowball to press onto my face to deal with the cut lip and cheek bruise I sustained in the fight. I fondly recalled Mrs. McKay, who was kind to me and had lovely, dark brown hair and green eyes, as a traditional lady of the house. But she was also a doer, up early and always cleaning, or cooking, or sewing. She had been dismayed at first that Dad sent me to help. "Kat, a girl shouldn't be out in the sun and wind. It will ruin their complexion." Then she had added in a horrified whisper as she gestured to her lower abdomen, "and it can mess things up inside, so babies don't come."

I had been around enough to know that babies didn't come as long as I kept drinking Grandma Rina's tea, and after caring for my brothers and sisters, I was foursquare against the idea of kids. So, I had said, "I like being outside. And I don't want no babies anyhow."

This had scandalized Mrs. McKay, who made it her task that year to teach me how to be a lady, even if the lessons came after I finished a day of plowing. She never said anything bad about my mom or dad, but it was clear that she thought they had failed to raise me right. And she wasn't wrong. They were shit parents. But I liked the McKays, though I could see that death had marked Mr. McKay for a visit in the not-too-distant future.

In the now, Zach is building a small fire to warm the place as I sit on the sofa tending my injuries. We pulled the thick winter drapes for warmth and to avoid having a lamp signal our whereabouts. "She moved back to Jerglandsby up-mountain to live with my aunt a few years back. She could never really understand why Becca and the kids left, and then her brain started freezing a bit, and she slowly forgot… Well, she's forgot most everything now."

"I'm so sorry, Zach. That is worse than losing her to death."

He steps back to observe his fire. "That it is."

The moment feels right to ask my question again. "Zach, how did you survive? What happened after you were shot?"

He stands very still for a moment and then walks over and sits down in the chair nearest me. His eyes connect with mine, and then he grimaces, draws in a deep breath, closes his eyes, and leans his back to rest against the chair as he begins.

"I knew they were trouble when we first saw 'em. We both did. But I had heard the stories in town about traders coming into town looking for thralls. And those men… Well, it be clear they meant no good. Just the way they walked... So, I told you to run with Sean.

"As they come up, I tried to keep my voice neighborly, greeting them, and just as I be asking them what their business be, I saw one raise his shotgun. All I remember then was the noise and the pain.

"The bullet tore up my insides and nicked my backbone but didn't hit any big bleeder. Course, I didn't know any of that. Things went black pretty fast. Ma and Pa heard the gunshots and came running. They found me—the traders were long gone with you. Sean was dead. Ma got me home and sent for Rina. Them two saved my life. After I be stable, they took me over the mountains to Marpavik and had the medics fly me to the hospital in Dobarri." Now he sits up and opens his eyes. "They took out a good part of my gut." He unbuttons his flannel shirt and pulls up his base layer, exposing a long, ugly scar and a bag that hangs from a port in his lower left belly, partially filled with what must be stool.

He glances at me, and I know he's trying to gauge my reaction. I make sure not to look away from the scar too quickly, and when I do, I look straight at him. "I'm so grateful to those doctors and your ma and my grandma."

He drops his shirt and gives a scornful snort. "Grateful. In the early days, I be not very grateful. The pain wasn't just from the shot, you know. I wanted to die or kill, or both. But yeah, they let me have a life. And I s'pose I'm grateful too. Those early years with Lily and Max were real nice." He gives a small cough and looks toward the fire. "The doctors couldn't remove all of the shot. Some of it is lodged near my backbone, making my right leg a problem. They said it might never be anything more or it might move and split my spine, and then I'd never walk again. So far, I'm still walking, and it ain't a problem."

I reach over and grasp his hand. "Oh, Zach, that's an awful lot to live with."

He looks back at me and squeezes my hand. "Not nothing compared to what I live without, Kat."

We sit quietly for just a few moments, each lost in our own thoughts. Then the echo of the militia man's comment at the store comes to me. *Shit-bag*. They were calling him shit-bag. It makes me want to go back and use my knife. Anger wakes up and starts to swing its legs out of bed, but I sigh and tuck it back in. I can't change the North.

Zach stands and moves to peek out the curtains. "It's dark. I need to walk over and take care of the animals. I should be back in a couple hours."

I rise from the sofa. "Two people make the job go twice as fast. I'll come along. And I need to get the sponge if we're going to have bread."

He looks uncertain of the offer at first, then he points a finger at me and grins. "You just want to get at your Twilight again. I can see right through you still, Kat Wallace."

My hands go up in surrender. "Guilty as charged. Now, let's go."

Diamond, February 9 1700

The sun was setting as the two BI troopers looked down on the Chinese outpost where it lay in a cirque near a small lake just below the peak of the mountain they had scaled. They discussed its configuration in quiet tones, pointing to various places and creating a sketch of the design. Snow had been pushed aside and cleared to set up the encampment. Its layout was simple: six khaki-colored tents, two of which looked at if they could accommodate a dozen or more people, centrally located, and four smaller versions that likely housed four or so individuals. There also appeared to be a mid-sized tent-like structure open at the top, that was empty. Neither Diamond nor Flossie could discern its purpose. A large fire pit, with a fire a-blaze in it, lay between the two larger tents, and several men moved from fire to tent and back again. They counted eight people all dressed in civilian garb. Intelligence had indicated twelve souls at the encampment. No guards or weaponry were apparent, which was also in keeping with the intelligence that had been collected before the mission was ever put in the books, as well as the intel Diamond and Flossie, well, mostly Flossie, had gathered. The plan was to identify the tent Dr. Aung was kept in, establish where the essential research materials were housed, wait until the camp was fully asleep—around midnight—and then slip in and liberate both the good doctor and his gear and journals. Flossie would take the lead on communication as her Mandarin was far better than Diamond's. Once they had the prize, they would then head for the vessel.

A bell later, having positively ID'd the doctor's location,

Diamond and Flossie sat wrapped in their hot sheets, lightweight blankets that reflected their body heat back and allowed them to keep warm as they rested for a few hours before the extraction implementation. Diamond looked at her friend who leaned against a rock, head to the side, snoring ever so slightly.

So, Farris Abernathy had become Flossie Porter. Now, Diamond was not an authority on every world event that occurred in New Earth; sometimes it was all she could do to keep up with local issues, what with work and family and missions. But a person would have to be living in a hole, or up here in the back of beyond, not to have heard of Rob Abernathy—he had been the FA's vice president and one of the wealthiest businessmen on New Earth—and the mystery of his missing daughter had kept the conspiracy folk, mostly those blue-robed zealots, abuzz for months after his death.

Some additional research when she got back to Bosch would connect more of the dots, but one thing was certain, by befriending Flossie Porter, Diamond had struck paydirt. This mission had turned out to be more lucrative than Diamond could have imagined. She closed her eyes and settled into a dream of life on the beach.

Carisa, February 9 1830

"Your Dobarrian is really quite good. Most foreigners can't manage it so well," the nurse just coming on commented to Carisa. Carisa, on the other hand, had been sitting at the nurses' station for more than a few hours. She had eaten and showered, but sleep had eluded her, though she knew her body and mind were exhausted. The other nurses, who had been keeping Carisa distracted during the hours of Reeves' surgery, chuckled, since they had made essentially the same comment earlier.

Agnes spoke up. "This is no foreigner, Jon. Carisa was born right here in Nyvik and lived here until she was seventeen." Her face darkened. "And should have lived here after that if not for that Elka person."

The other nurses made tuts of disapproval, which warmed Carisa's heart. She hadn't intended to tell them her story, but while chatting with them and organizing their hand-out drawer as a thank you for their kindness, she had pushed up the sleeves on the clean shirt Agnes had found for her, exposing her thrall brand on the inside of her left arm—a puckered circle crossed with a "T." Carisa had forgotten that its presence might shock others, since there were now many freed thralls living in Bosch. When she told the story of its origin, the men and women who came to work every day to help the sick and injured were appalled.

"Excuse me for saying so about your kin, Carisa, but I don't see how anyone could be so monstrous to any child, much less one who just suffered the loss of her folks. The old gods would have something to say about that—that's all I'm saying." A ruddy-faced woman just a bit older than Carisa punctuated her remarks with a small fist pound on the desk, and there were several murmurs of agreement.

Agnes had gone to tend to one of her patients, but as she walked back, her face shifted, and she pointed behind Carisa. Carisa looked over her shoulder to see Dr. Mattiasson and a broad-shouldered, good-looking man approaching her.

"Mrs. Morton, this is Dr. Stefansson. I'll come straight to the point. Your friend, Zoya Reeves, has come through the surgeries well. She should, over time, make a full recovery. And while Dr. Stefanson and I have played a part in that, I believe the majority of the credit goes to you. I must say that if I am ever injured in the wilderness, I do hope that you, or someone with your good sense and courage, is there to aid me."

Carisa's hand had moved to cover her mouth before Dr. Mattiasson began talking, and it stayed there as she laughed and cried at the same time. She felt Agnes' arm go around her as Dr. Stefansson spoke in a deep voice, "She will need additional surgeries on her hand to stabilize the bones, but I did what I could, given the swelling. I will assess healing each day for the next week here in the hospital."

Carisa once again felt relief. "Thank you both so very much. When can I see her?"

Dr. Mattiasson checked her timepiece. "I would imagine she'll be somewhat awake in thirty minutes or so. I will have the recovery nurse come get you before giving her the next dose of pain control." And once again, she abruptly pivoted and disappeared back through the double doors.

Dr. Stefansson chuckled. "She is an excellent surgeon, but she is still developing her conversational skills. I do echo her sentiments. Both you and Zoya Reeves are remarkable women. May I...?" He held out a hand to Carisa, and she lifted hers to him. Instead of shaking her hand, he lifted it to his lips and kissed it, then looked at it appraisingly. "Such a delicate hand for a delicate, exquisite woman. I am most honored to meet you." His eyes danced their way into Carisa's as he said this, and she could see desire and attraction there.

She primly withdrew her hand. "You are very kind. You have both my appreciation and Zoya's, I am sure."

He gave a devil-may-care grin and turned to move toward the operating suite doors, looking over his shoulder and keeping her in his sight until the moment the doors closed. She turned and looked at Agnes, then at the group of nurses all poorly concealing their interest in the exchange. "You know, I don't think Aaron will ever want to move here."

The nurses erupted with laughter as Agnes shook her head and gave Carisa's shoulders a small squeeze. "That's Dr. Stefansson... He does have an eye for pretty ladies. Don't pay him any mind. We keep him in line. Now, maybe after you see your friend you can finally get some sleep?"

CHAPTER 19

Kat, February 9 1900

The night is not as cold as last night now that clouds have rolled in, and as we walk across the McKay fields I used to plow, Zach says, "You told me about your kids, but I expect there be a father to them in your life."

"Actually, there are two. My ex-husband, Takai, is Grey's and the twins' papa. He and I divorced several years ago. He was not exactly a one-woman man, and eventually, I lost patience with that behavior. Rini's daddy is my partner, Matty. Like me, he's a pilot in the Force. He is a good man. My very best friend. He wanted me to pass along his gratitude to you for all you did for me as a girl."

The Zach grunt returns. "I did what a man should do."

"Maybe so, but not all people do what they should. Most do what is easiest."

"True. Is this Matty a good husband?"

I laugh. "I wouldn't know. We aren't married. But he is an excellent partner in life."

Now Zach's voice is decidedly disapproving. "Why won't he marry you? Is that a pirate thing? How does he provide for you and your children if he ain't your husband?"

A good-natured scoff escapes my lips. There may be some modernization in Allanavik, but the thinking is still from the previous century. "Okay, first off, no, it isn't a pirate thing. It was a Matty and me thing, which recently has become just a me thing. And second, Bosch provides a basic income for all its citizens, but I put mine back in the pot because I've made enough markers over the years to take care of me and mine for a couple lifetimes." I look at Zach and wink as I say this and chuckle as his eyebrows go up, and he gives a low whistle. I continue, "And third, *we* never got married." I gesture between the two of us.

Zach groans. "You be speaking the truth. Of the regrets I have in this life, that be one of the biggest. I put off asking you, thinking I should wait until one more harvest when we could do it up right. But…well, we both know what happened."

I think about how much that statement would have meant to seventeen- and eighteen-year-old me, and I want to give that girl a hug and the reassurance that she would make it through the pain she would face in the next years.

We climb over the back fence that separates the two properties, and Zach gallantly assists me with my dismount. "So, this…" He runs his finger along his neck, mirroring where my old scar runs from my left ear to my right collarbone. "Be it from a pirate adventure?" His face holds the same excitement that my boys used to have when I'd tell them highly sanitized stories of my missions.

I shake my head as I run my own finger over my scar and say distantly, "Hazards of being a thrall." Zach's face darkens, but he does not ask any more questions.

The dogs, all of them big muscular animals, come trotting up to me when we get to Zach's place, tails wagging, and nuzzle my hands. I laugh, knowing what they are after, and I dig out the last of my dog treats from my bag, presenting one to each of them after giving a command to sit.

"So that's how you got past 'em. I was wondering," Zach comments, then addresses his three sentinels, all still sitting nicely and being very good dogs as I rub their ears. "You three... Some watchdogs you are." They look up at him, tongues out and wide dog-smiles on their faces. His voice remains genial. "You'd all give up the place for a few treats and some affection from a pretty face."

"While I appreciate the compliment, Zach, I think the treats carried the day. It was real dark when I first encountered them."

He grunts. "Mmm. I said what I said."

The barn is warm, and its delightful earthy smell engulfs me. After tending to the sheep and chickens, I move to take care of the cows. As I milk Twilight and her sister, Zach runs some recon and finds some fresh tire tracks on the far side of the gate but no sign of attempted entry. The militia boys are not exactly thorough investigators.

We are walking back to the McKay place with a bucket of fresh milk, a few eggs, my well-risen sponge, and a surprise loaf of bread and ramekin of butter from the outdoor freezer Zach rigged up next to the barn when Zach decides that now is the time to drop the million-marker question as we cut across the backfield. "Why be you here, Kat? I may not know much, but I gotta figure taxiing a couple...ladies—no, *troopers* is the word you use, right? Taxiing troopers to the far north isn't part of a pirate leader's job description."

I hoot a laugh, then drop my voice to match the quiet winter night. "You want to know what is on my job description? Meetings, meetings, budgets, justifying my existence to the council, followed by a couple more meetings, and paperwork to record all the previous meetings."

"Great Anguta! Do they ever let you outside?" Zach sounds horrified.

"Well, sure, if I'm willing to taxi a couple of troopers to the North Country."

We both laugh and continue toward the old place. Then Zach comes in with the redirect. "You almost got away with it, Kat. I applaud your distraction, but why did you come back?"

I sigh and look up at the stars, and the bank of clouds that signals new snow by morning. "Some new information has come to light that impels me to verify it. If it checks out, I'll be killing Cole Wallace."

We walk on in silence until we get to the old place. We enter and pull our boots off and hang our coats up, then silently wash our hands and faces. I pull out a bowl, crack four eggs in it, and add a few splashes of milk while Zach cuts thick slices of the loaf partially thawed under his shirt. From Mother McKay's spice shelf, I pull out some cinnamon and sprinkle it into the egg-milk mixture before plunging the bread in for a good minute soak. Zach looks at the bowl and then at me as I do this but says nothing. I can keep this up as long as he can—hell, longer. I live with three teenagers and a four-year-old; I never get to talk at home.

I melt a bit of the butter in the skillet over the fire, and when it sizzles just right, I add the lost bread, turning it when it is brown and crispy on the bottom. Zach comes over to the fire with two plates and stands wordlessly as I flip the pieces, hot and fragrant with the cinnamon and brown butter, out onto the plate. The skillet gets set back on the stove in the kitchen, and the two of us sit down at the table to eat by lantern light.

I am two bites from being done when Zach says, "I came real close to doing that myself a few times in the early days. What be the new information that you got?"

With a deep inhale, I say, "You're not going to like it."

"I don't much like Cole now, so can't see how that will be a problem."

So, I tell him.

Kat, February 9 2000

"So, Cole Jr. and Ollie jumped into the militia with both feet when it developed and decided to go to the camp on the coast.

Something about 'protecting our borders.' That was about three, four years ago."

I snort a laugh. "So they are still idiots. That fits." Zach had sat silent again as I told him about my suspicion that Dad sold me off. That was when he decided to bring me up to date on my family's history. I shake my head, not shocked, but dismayed. "What about Virgil?" Virgil was the only brother I much liked, mostly because he was a little boy—just eight—when I last saw him. It is Virgil I sometimes catch a glimpse of in my Macrae.

Zach shakes his head. "Virgil grew up wild. He was good-looking and charming, but always wanting things he couldn't have. When Old Man Weaver decided to buy the first vehicle we ever had in these parts, he decided he had to have it. He stole it, drove it real fast, then crashed into a tree and was killed. He was seventeen."

"Oh Virgil..." A pang of sadness flows through me as I remember the little boy with the messy hair and adventurous spirit. What a waste. Knowing his path makes me want to fly home, hold onto my boys, and keep them safe forever.

"And the girls?" I am sure this segue of his is leading somewhere.

Zach glances at me. "Your mom, she died about ten years back. The cause was never really clear."

Our eyes connect as I whisper, "That son of a bitch."

"Well, now. I'm not sure that be accurate." Zach's voice is placid.

I laugh, although my anger is still there. Peg Wallace was great at having babies, something I had thought, up until last year, I had inherited from her, but she was a distant and disinterested parent beyond the point of neglect. I guess I always was afraid Dad might kill her. His temper when he'd been drinking cheap whiskey and sparkling on Glitter was legendary. And without any kids around to spread the blows out, he finally did her in. I had no doubt. But Dad was not a son-of-a-bitch. His mother was, in fact, the only bright spot in my childhood.

"What are you not telling me about the girls, Zachariah Owen McKay? I know a sidestep when I see one."

He holds up a finger. "I be getting there. But full-naming me won't make me veer from the path. I be telling it in my own time. Was patience not part of your BPF training?"

Inwardly, I chuckle at the question. Outwardly, I pull a face at him. I never have been very patient, except with my kids and on missions. Otherwise, not so much. "Go on then."

"Your grandma was never the same after what happened. Her love for you was fierce," Zach starts.

My tears start with just the mention of her pain, and he pauses. "Need a sec?"

"No. Go on." The words come out in a squeak, muffled with a sob.

He continues but throws a concerned look at me. "When I got back from the Dobarri hospital, I heard her health had taken a turn. So I went over as soon as I was on my feet again, with plans to take care of her the way you would have wanted me to."

My tears give way to gratitude as I gaze at this man I had loved so long ago. "Thank you, Zach."

"I ain't done with the story. Now, hush and go back to crying." His voice carries the gentle tease he used with me so often, and I do as I am told and cry a bit more.

He continues, "When I got there, Becca be cooking for Rina. It was the first time we had really met. She and I started taking turns caring for her, which shifted into caring for her together, and she rallied. My ma said she probably gave me some love potion to get me and Becca together."

I sniff. "I wouldn't put it past her."

Zach chuckles. "She be real happy when we married and even came to the wedding, though she was frail. Lily be the apple of her eye, sort of like you. I expect her middle name helped with that. Did I tell you it was Katrina? She was thrilled with Max as well, but she was declining. We brought her to our place when Max was about a year old and set up a bed in the sitting room.

She passed real peaceful with all of us around her on the twelfth of July 2354 and…" Zach's voice is suddenly thick with emotion, and I look over to see tears on his face. "…before she went, she promised to look after Sean. We buried her next to him near the woods."

Something between a gasp and a moan escapes my lips, "Of course she did. Oh, Zach, I loved her so. Thank you, Becca, Lily, and Max for giving her the family she deserved." *July 12, 2354.* I repeat it in my head to memorize it, and from somewhere deep in me I feel a small nudge. Then a sense of awe washes over me as I realize that my Grey was conceived in the middle of July 2354. *Thanks, Grandma Rina. Leave it to you to direct the universe's gifts.*

Zach coughs and then stands up and walks to the fire to add some wood. He blows his nose and snuffles, then returns to his pa's favorite chair.

"Kat, the girls are gone." Zach lays this out without fanfare.

It's as if an enormous stop sign, red with flashing lights, has been thrown up in front of me. My tears cease as does my awe. Questions fall from my mouth in rapid succession. "Gone? All three? Even little Molly? What do you mean gone? Dead?"

Zach shrugs. "Gone. Disappeared. Violet, Bella, and Molly. All around fifteen, sixteen, seventeen years old. Cole made out that they had run off with men, but, uh…" He drops his chin and looks up at me with his eyebrows elevated. "…given what you said… I mean it seemed suspicious before, but now…." He trails off.

It is my turn to sit silent for several minutes as I watch the fire and think about my life's work to end enslavement. I say aloud, not necessarily to Zach, but to the whole of New Earth, "I have fought against the thrall trade for the past twenty-three years. Because of that trade, people I loved died. And in all that time I didn't realize, my own father was a trafficker."

Kat, February 9 2200

The bed I am tucked into in the room off the kitchen at the McKays is where I slept as a farmhand so long ago. Zach offered me his folks' bigger bed, but I had said it didn't seem right. I guess he felt the same because he went to his old room—up the stairs, first door on the left. I wonder whether the sixth step still has that loud creak that we learned to avoid as we snuck between floors that late summer and fall.

Sleep eludes me, so I pull out the SatComm. I listened on the ear comms at the designated check-in times. No report has come in from Porter or Miata, but I am unconcerned. They won't implement the extraction until after midnight tonight. And then only if conditions are ideal. I could try and roust the vessel since Reeves has ear comms, but it's late, and wearing the damn things while sleeping is annoying and only required on missions where the risk of attack is high. I create a picture of Reeves and Carisa fending off the militia as the dolts throw snowballs at the "big, shiny thing" and chuckle to myself. I wonder what it would be like to have the job of maintaining the vessel during missions. It sounds spectacularly tedious to me, but Reeves must be okay with it since flight engineers are usually the ones who get stuck babysitting, and Carisa is certainly cut out for that kind of prolonged routine.

Matty answers, "Yes, my most beautiful master commander?"

"How did you know it was me?"

"I didn't. I answer all comms that way. If it's you, then I win. If not, those folks generally don't comm back, and I still win."

I am back to giggling. "You are the only one who makes me laugh like I'm a giddy schoolgirl."

There is quiet on the other end. "Matty?" I frown, wondering if I've lost the connection.

"Oh, I'm here. I was just thinking about you as a giddy schoolgirl and got very distracted."

"That could be considered icky, old-man-who-turns-forty-this-summer." I am grinning as I say this.

"Well, let me remove the ick: Schoolgirls, in general, are just that, children who are to be revered and protected. No sexualization exists in my head for them. My future wife dressed as a schoolgirl—well, that's an entirely different story, isn't it?"

"Future wife? Congratulations! You should bring her around the to the house sometime," I tease.

A loud tapping sound comes through the comm, followed by Matty saying loudly, "Hello? Hello? Bad connection. Didn't hear your last."

I am back to laughing. "Okay, okay, you've made your point."

"Good. Hey, before I forget, Aaron hasn't heard from Carisa today. Is everything okay?"

"Oh, that's my fault. After the situation yesterday, I sent her back to the vessel, and this place is so isolated I'm the only one with a working longer-distance device—the one I'm talking to you on. Tell Aaron his sweet wife is sitting on a Whydah parked in a snowbank playing cards, maybe even a hand of White Bear, with Sergeant Reeves, waiting for me to get back and take her to Dobarri, where I plan to go in and smack that Ella or Elka person who was so horrible to her so 'Ris can get a bit of herself back."

"I'll never remember all that. I'll just say she's fine."

"Good enough."

"So, why'd you comm me?"

"To say I love you?" I say with as much innocence as I can muster.

Matty's voice is warm, but it's accompanied by a heavy dose of skepticism as well. "Yeah. I love you back. Now why else?"

A sigh. "Zach told me something about my sisters..."

DAY THREE

CHAPTER 20

FLOSSIE, FEBRUARY 10 MIDNIGHT

"Okay, let's go," Diamond whispered.

Flossie felt as if she had swallowed a thousand butterflies, although butterflies couldn't survive in this bone-chilling cold. Her brain gremlins had become increasingly loud over the last bell, reminding her that she was not a trained field operative, but a desk worker. If she couldn't break a code, which was seldom, she could always come back and look at it the next day. But this—the consequence of failing… She was sure she would screw this mission up and probably freeze to death. She wanted to answer Diamond, who had been so patient with her, but she thought if she opened her mouth, she might vomit. So, she simply felt her body unfold from where it was hunkered and began a crouched run, following the agile form of her slender, dark friend down the hillside into the Chinese camp.

It took them several minutes to reach the edge of the base, mostly because the snow had accumulated in drifts on the bowl-shaped plain, requiring them to actually dig a path with their hands at one point. At least getting out would be easier with a trail broken. The camp was dim and silent. The fire had been banked and gave off a soft glow, enough, combined with the sliver of moonlight, to see the tents' outlines. The two women both pointed to the scientist's tent, gave each other a thumbs-up, and then stood and walked with intention to the door of the indicated quarters. They pushed aside the door flap and stepped in.

It was very dark inside, and Flossie handed the night vision glasses the MC had issued her to Diamond. She trusted her to know what to do more than she did herself. She felt Diamond take her elbow and walk her to the corner of the tent.

"Let me get these glasses off," Diamond whispered, and Flossie stood in the dark hearing the tiniest rustle next to her. In a moment, her partner's small penlight came on, and after a couple of blinks to adjust her eyes, Flossie could see a dark-haired, West Continent man around fifty years old. His face matched the photo that had been distributed with the mission specs. Flossie laid a hand on his shoulder and leaned close as she whispered, "Dr. Aung? We are here to rescue you." She knew the word *rescue* was a bit of a stretch, since the good doctor did not seem to be imprisoned, although the reports were clear he had been taken unwillingly from his home. He made a small sound but did not wake. "Dr. Aung?" She gave him a gentle shake.

His eyes opened and widened as he asked in Mandarin, "Who are you?"

Flossie paused to translate in her head and replied in her own stilted Mandarin, "I call Porter. Here to take you safe place."

The man shook his head vigorously. "No, no. I have my experiment here and all my data. I cannot leave my work."

Flossie whispered back, "We will collect work. Take you to FA. Get family."

The word *family* made the doctor sit up. But still he shook his head.

Diamond broke in, speaking in Bosch, "Floss, get him up and let's go. I don't want to encounter some Chinese guy getting up to pee in the middle of the night."

Giving Diamond a thumbs-up, she kept eye contact with

Aung. "We need to go now," Flossie said, adding a tone of urgency to her voice.

"It's a bad time. The government official, Doctor Pan Qiu, her entourage, and her bodyguards arrived yesterday. Come back in one week." Dr. Aung's face was serious.

"Oh, fuck." Flossie breathed the curse out in Bosch. She hadn't caught all the words, but certainly got the gist. They couldn't wait a week.

"Floss, what's the hold-up?" Diamond pressed.

Flossie stood up and explained the dilemma. Diamond dropped her head back. "Ugh, we don't need this shit." She turned toward the tent door and stood very still for a moment, then turned back. "We have weapons, and there's no indication anyone else is awake. Let's go ahead and move."

It was at that moment that Flossie decided she did not like fieldwork and that, assuming she got back to Bosch and didn't freeze to death here in the North, she would avoid it at all costs and focus on codes and tech. They didn't carry any threat of physical harm. She looked at the woman she adored, took a breath, and said, "Okay. I'll tell him."

The doctor agreed, though his reluctance was clear. He stood up, revealing himself to be a slightly built man a couple of centimeters shorter than Flossie. It took only a few minutes for him to throw his journals and a few articles of clothes, along with a framed photo, into a small knapsack. He motioned for the women to turn around as he dressed. Flossie could feel the tension rising off of Diamond, and her own belly felt tight with anxiety.

Dr. Aung walked up and touched Flossie on the arm. "I am ready."

"Great. We too." Flossie let Diamond know they were ready.

With the small doctor in between them, the two women opened the tent flap and stepped into the center of four armed guards pointing serious weaponry directly at their heads.

Flossie, February 10 MN 30

"I told you," Dr. Aung said quietly as he looked at Flossie with soft, sad eyes, before stepping back into his tent. *Yes, you did,* Flossie thought, before wondering if this was it for her and Diamond.

The guards gestured to the women to put their hands up and spread their feet. They followed the instructions and were patted down and relieved of their pistols, ear comms, night vision goggles, compasses, and papers containing the coordinates of the camp and the sketch of it they had created. They also took their personal comms. *Good luck using those,* Flossie thought as she was marched past the firepit and up to one of the large tents.

One guard pulled open the door, and bright light came flooding out. Flossie blinked heavily and took a moment to glance over at Diamond, who was also slowly blinking at the sudden exposure of so much light. Her face was tight with tension. Flossie felt the rifle's barrel in the small of her back, urging her forward. Two thoughts repeated in her head: *Am I going to die? I'm so sorry, Di…*

As she walked in, though, she was stunned. Of the things Flossie knew from childhood, one certainly was what elegance looked like. This place looked like someone had taken some moneyed Chinese person's living room, complete with silken wall hangings and tasteful tchotchkes on the table, and dropped it into a tent in the North Country mountains. *Look on the bright side,* Flossie considered, *seems an unlikely place to be executed.*

The guards directed both women to remove their coats and boots and to stand at the edge of a low wooden table facing a wooden-framed sofa with a shiny black finish and red leather cushions. Flossie wiggled her stocking-covered toes on the intricately designed rug under her feet and glanced around the tent, looking for the mechanism that allowed such a large space to be kept so warm. *Who brings rugs and heaters on a scientific expedition?*

Diamond attempted to address one of the guards but was roughly hushed and directed to stand facing forward. Moments later, Flossie felt a cold breeze on her back, indicating the tent flap was open. She tried to turn to see the reason but met with the same response Diamond had.

There was the sound of movement, and a small woman, past fifty with coal-black hair pulled firmly back appeared before them. She walked back and forth, looking carefully up first at Flossie, then at Diamond, pulling her cream-colored satin wrap up around her neck as she did. Her two attaches, one carrying a notebook and pen, the other holding a small, black-faced dog, scurried behind her.

She finally paused in front of Diamond and in perfect, standard FA stated, "You are very tall. You wear excessive jewelry. And you are exquisitely beautiful. A questionable choice for a spy." She stepped over to Flossie. "You are far more suited to the task. Ever so plain, no one would recall seeing you."

Flossie stood still, a bit uncertain whether they had each been complimented or insulted. The tiny woman continued, "I am Doctor Pan Qiu, director of the Office of Science for China. Please have a seat, and we shall discuss your presence here and your attempt to remove our Dr. Aung." She motioned to the elegantly carved chairs placed at either end of the table as she made her way to the center of the sofa. The two young men took places behind the sofa to her right and left. Dr. Pan Qiu took the dog and settled in her lap, stroking its long, cream-colored fur. Flossie and Diamond looked at each other and moved to sit down in the straight-backed chairs on either side of the table closest to the sofa. Dr. Pan waved her hand, and the guards left the tent.

"Now then, please tell me why the Bosch are so interested in this project."

Diamond, February 10 0200

Diamond and Flossie walked out into the dark, escorted by a single guard to where a new tent had been set up. The guard pointed at it and said something in Mandarin to the effect of "Go to bed. I'll be right here." As the women opened the flap, Diamond expected to see two rough cots in a chilled, drafty tent, but was delighted to find two thick mattresses positioned on a soft rug similar to the one in the tent where they had just been… interrogated? Chatted with? She was still uncertain.

Diamond almost squealed as she moved to run her hands over the fur-lined, satin robes hanging on a wooden clothes tree. "If this is what being prisoners of the Chinese is, sign me up!" She looked over at Flossie who was frowning as her eyes flicked across the well-appointed tent. "What's wrong? You object to a little luxury while we figure this out?"

Flossie made a scoffing sound and crossed her arms like a stubborn child. "What's to figure out? They are trying to bribe us with extravagance, so we'll double-cross Bosch."

"Well, sure, that woman wants something from us, but she hasn't said anything about double-crossing Bosch," Diamond reasoned. Of course, she was loyal to Bosch, it was her home, but she had needs and wants that her paltry BPF paycheck was never going to cover. As she looked at all this elegance–here, in the middle of nowhere– she had an epiphany. She was aiming too low. Her post-Force retirement business of a gym for women in the posh section of District Two was fading, because if she played her cards right, she wouldn't need a retirement business.

Now she looked at her friend and recalled the pink she had seen in those pale cheeks in the truck. Prisoner or not, successful mission or not, she was alone with the heir to the Abernathy fortune. Flossie, aka Farris Abernathy, was more than a friend, she was an opportunity. And Diamond Miata was not someone to let opportunity pass by. It just might be the solution to all her woes.

"But she asked lots of questions about it. And you know the Chinese are always looking to increase their control of smaller nations. It's one of the major issues between them and the FA," Flossie protested, her brows clenched and her lips tight.

So very sanctimonious, Diamond thought, *it's kinda adorable, but I can get her to relax and enjoy what she has in front of her because it's something she really wants—me.* "Well, sure, but politics is so boring. I mean, we can't leave without Aung, but we might as well enjoy what we have," Diamond cajoled her friend as she walked to the small table between the beds that held a bowl of water, two washcloths, each embroidered with a black branch set off with red blossoms, and two small towels with matching embroidery. "C'mon, you can't say washing up a bit doesn't sound good."

She dipped her finger in the bowl. "Ooh, the water is nice and warm." Diamond kicked off her shoes and slowly, with careful intention, shed her parka and sweater, tossing them to the floor. She dipped one of the cloths into the water and squeezed it out. "Here." She walked over to her mission partner. "Hold still." And she began to slowly wipe Flossie's face and neck. She leaned close to her ear and murmured, "Lose the parka." Flossie unzipped and removed the thick coat and her sweater. Diamond bit her lip and gazed at her friend, lifting each of the woman's hands and wiping them clean, first the backs, then the fronts. She made sure to stay very close, keeping eye contact the entire time.

Flossie's breath began to quicken. "That does feel pretty nice." The words slipped from her in soft breaths that ended with a tiny moan.

"Mm-hmm, I bet it does," Diamond breathed. She walked back over to the bowl, took the second cloth, and dipped it in the water. She looked over at Flossie and gave a provocative little bite of her lip as she held the dripping cloth above her face; closing her eyes, she squeezed the water out, allowing it to rain down on her, droplets soaking into the thick rug at her feet. She opened her eyes and looked at Flossie, holding out the cloth. "You do me, now."

It took only a moment for Flossie to move to stand in front of her. She gently dabbed the droplets from Diamond's face, the cloth moving over her eyes and cheeks and down her long neck in soft strokes. "Wait," Diamond said, and Flossie, of course, did as she was told. Diamond pulled her base layer off exposing her breasts with her erect nipples sparkling with the diamond barbells that pierced each one. "Okay," she whispered. Flossie stood with wide eyes but slowly began to wipe down her friend's shoulders and collarbone. She paused at the soft curve of her bosom and looked up. "Go ahead." Diamond said, "I want you to."

Flossie passed the cloth along the contour of first one breast and then the other wiping downward. Diamond slipped her hands underneath each one and lifted them so Flossie could wipe underneath. Diamond let out a little purr of pleasure as Flossie dropped to her knees to continue the journey to Diamond's belly, "Hold on."

Flossie's hand froze in place at the command, and she looked up. Diamond saw shame on the plain face and knew an apology was about to slip from her lips. She stopped the words with a soft finger over them and gazed down at her friend. Then she reached for her hand and helped her to her feet.

Diamond took the cloth, re-wet it, and looked at Flossie. "Now you."

Flossie looked as if she might faint as she pressed her hands to her belly. Diamond gave a chuckle and then reached out and pulled at the hem of the sergeant's shirt as she looked into her eyes. "C'mon, Floss, don't be shy. We're friends, right? Really good friends."

She helped Flossie pull the base layer over her head, smoothing the woman's hair after. Then she turned her around and unhooked the heavy bra, sliding her hands slowly up the pale shoulders, underneath the straps until it slipped down in front. Flossie's arms were tense and glued to her side. Diamond leaned to her left ear and let her mouth touch the seashell curves of it. "Let it go." It dropped to the ground. Diamond kept her place as she breathed. "Now turn around, so I can see you."

Flossie turned, and Diamond gazed at her. Her body was actually quite lovely, and it triggered a familiar moist warmth and a tiny ache between Diamond's legs. Her sweet friend was ample, to be sure, but the curves were in all the right spots. Her breasts were large but stood firm, speaking to the bloom of her youth. Her BPF tattoo was emblazoned on her left breast, just above her heart, its dark ink a lovely contrast to skin that was even paler than her face and arms. Her nipples stood out from broad, pink areolas that tightened as Di watched and licked her lips in anticipation. Flossie's breath began to come in little gasps, and Diamond knew it was more from arousal than cold. She murmured softly as she began to stroke with the cloth, "Girl, you are a looker. How come you never said what you were hiding under all those clothes." As she wiped with one hand, she let the other explore, moving down from the broad shoulder to circle the body of one of those prodigious breasts until she came to the nipple, which she rolled between her fingers and pinched, first softly then with increasing pressure, pulling a groan of delight from Flossie Porter, aka Farris Abernathy, aka her wealthy, soon-to-be lover who would give Diamond the life she was meant to live. She carefully provided the same treatment on the other breast and then set the cloth down.

"We need to finish getting clean, don't you think?" Diamond breathed the words so close to Flossie their cheeks touched, but she held her lips at bay as she slid both hands onto the bountiful curve of Flossie's ass and squeezed.

There was only one word Flossie needed to say, and it slipped out immediately, "Yes." She even amplified it, "Yes, please." Her voice quivered with desire.

Diamond stepped back so Flossie could see her as she slipped her base layer leggings off, exposing the neatly trimmed dark hair on her mound where another diamond sparkled. She saw it catch Flossie's eye, and she said in a low voice, "There's even more treasure for you to find, if you're a good pirate." It was a line she had used many times before, and it had never failed her. A gasp slipped from her bountiful co-worker and Diamond felt the thrill of success.

She stepped toward her, slid her hands inside the waistband of Flossie's leggings, and moving as slowly as possible, she inched them down, moving to kneel in front of Flossie as she freed first one leg, then the other. She sat back and looked at the round belly and heavy thighs and felt her own wetness increase. Most of the Force trained their bodies until they were hard and muscular; this woman was soft and pliable, and Diamond found herself wanting to get lost in the secret curves of all that flesh. To bury her face in those beautiful, expansive breasts, explore the pink secrets that lay between those thighs, and smother herself as she tasted the sweetness. She took a breath and reminded herself to go slowly. She lifted one hand and let her fingers gently and reverently touch the wild expanse of hair on Flossie's mound before standing up.

She crooked her index finger under the chin of the woman who stood before her and lifted it to look into the deep green eyes as she whispered, "Flossie Porter, you are so very beautiful." She said it, knowing that it would please her friend but also knowing that it was so very true. *What a remarkable, delightful surprise,* she thought. Then Diamond Miata leaned in to taste her first kiss with her mission partner who returned the gesture with her warm lips and flicking tongue. *Who says you can't mix business and pleasure?* Diamond thought as the two women sank down onto the soft white-down comforter that covered the bed, kicking the bright quilts, unused, to the floor as hands and mouths explored each other with fierce, unleashed passion.

CHAPTER 21

Flossie, February 10 0900

Flossie opened her eyes as a howling wind pulled her into consciousness. She felt a heaviness in the soft mattress upon which she lay. She wasn't alone in the bed. Vague recollections began to solidify in her brilliant mind, and calculations were made producing the only reasonable explanation: *I'm asleep and this is the sweetest of dreams.* Some of the other troopers in the BI office she dutifully attended every weekday, and often one or two weekend days each week since coming to Bosch, liked to talk about lucid dreaming. She had not experienced one before, but now…she was positive that she was in a dream about waking after a night of sensual passion next to the most captivating woman in the world. She felt a deep appreciation for her imagination, which, after the events of yesterday, could have conjured a scenario placing her in a Chinese work camp locked away for life. This dream was infinitely better.

She hesitated to move her head, knowing how dreams could morph. Dammit. She shouldn't have thought about the work camp thing. Now when she looked over, she'd suddenly be out in the heat, breaking rocks or whatever it was one did in work camps. She was unclear on the details, beyond what she had seen in old films. *I just won't look. And I won't wake up. I'll stay in this perfect moment forever.*

A small breath, a tiny bit louder than a sigh, but not quite a moan, rose from the space next to her. Flossie held her breath and decided that perhaps she could just move her eyes without disturbing the illusion.

Diamond lay on her belly, asleep, beaded braids scattered across her back and the pillow. Flossie thought, *I may as well sink into the fantasy.* She pulled her arm from under the warm comforter and into the chill that the dream was providing. She reached one finger to stroke a braid. It was silky and felt so very real. She shifted her body onto her side to look at Diamond and held her breath. The image remained.

She moved her hand to brush the smooth, exposed skin of Diamond's shoulder, tracing the outline of the ship of her BPF tattoo and marveling at how the full moon it was silhouetted against took on a new moon look when applied to the palette of her silky, black skin. A purr came in response from the woman, and she stirred, stretched, and rolled over, her dark eyes open, gazing into Flossie's face. Her full, succulent lips created a tug in Flossie's middle that radiated south as she recalled their softness and amazing capabilities. Now, they blossomed into a teasing leer. "Hey there, you wanton woman." Diamond's voice was morning-thick, and her words came to Flossie in a throaty growl that created a thrill of desire in her. Diamond reached a finger over to stroke Flossie's cheek. "How'd you sleep?"

At first, Flossie wasn't sure her voice would work, still so convinced that she was floating in a dreamscape. But she figured she may as well try, so she swallowed and was delighted to hear herself say, "I think I slept the best I ever have in my life."

Diamond's eyebrows lifted, and she bit down slightly on her lower lip. "Well, we certainly earned our sleep. I wasn't expecting so much energy and passion from my little codebreaker." Her finger punctuated the remark with a soft tap on Flossie's nose.

"So, it wasn't a dream? We really made love last night?" Flossie thought her heart might leap out of her throat.

"Made love?" Diamond's chuckle was warm with a bawdy overtone. "Honey, you fucked me like nobody ever fucked me before. But I gotta say, I did love it. So, I guess *made love* works." Diamond's hand curled behind Flossie's head as it pulled her face in for a deep, languid kiss that ended with a soft bite on Flossie's lower lip. "Who knew that underneath that plain brown wrapper was a wanton, wild woman who knows her way around a pussy?"

The tug in her middle melded with the shift of her heart, and Flossie felt her whole being crack open with a joy she had never before felt. Gazing at this gorgeous woman, tears filled her eyes. "I am the luckiest woman on New Earth," she breathed with passionate intention.

Under the covers, Diamond's leg wrapped around hers, pulling her closer as she said with a giggle, "Girl, seems like that was more skill than luck." She pushed herself up on her elbow, and the curve of one perfect breast came into view as she stated, "I tell you something, though: It's damn cold in here, and I'm famished. Do you think they're going to feed us?"

The question her lover posed suddenly stirred the recollection in Flossie's brain that they were prisoners in a Chinese encampment in the North Country. *A damn, strange place to have the most magical night of my life,* she thought, but responded, "I'm sure they will. You stay here, all warm, sexy, and magnificent in our bed." *Our bed!* Flossie's brain exclaimed and she could hear her inner marching band preparing for a celebratory parade. "I'll get dressed, talk to the guard, and see if we can get some food and maybe one of those heaters from last night brought to us."

Diamond gave Flossie a coy look. "You taking care of your Diamond, honey?"

It was as if all the critical words and looks of disgust her father had bestowed on her over the years were suddenly washed away and replaced with an assurance that, yes, she would and could take care of her Diamond. In one swift move, she flipped Diamond onto her back, straddling her and pinning her wrists on either side of that gorgeous head, the covers tented above them. "Oh, I'll take care of you," she answered as she felt Diamond's breath quicken and saw desire in her eyes. "Now and forever." She leaned down and stole a kiss from this siren who had captured her very soul. "Food and heater first. Then, I'll have you."

Diamond purred, "Hurry back. I'll get a head start."

Flossie giggled and slipped out from under the warm covers. The chill of the February morning hit her bare skin as if someone had thrown ice water on her. She spied a pair of slippers tucked under the second bed that sat barely half a meter away, unused, on the other side of the tent and hustled to slide her feet into their cozy warmth as she wrapped herself in the lined, satin robe that hung on the clothes tree. It was better but she could feel the cold seeping in through the collar, the sleeves, and even through the fabric itself. Taking three steps, she pushed the tent flap open with one hand and stepped out into the frigid morning air.

Snow whirled and eddied about in the covered area directly in front of their tent door, and a guard stood directly in front of her, his coat collar turned up and the earflaps of his hat pulled down. He turned about and looked at her, snow packed in his eyebrows and the lock of hair that protruded from his cap, but his face was impassive. Flossie stomped her feet and wrapped her arms around herself as defense against the wind and chill, but she also blushed slightly, wondering if this guard had been there through the night listening to all that occurred in the soft bed in the small tent. But instead of shrinking back in embarrassment, Flossie felt a flush of warm confidence and bliss flow through her. She lifted her chin and in Mandarin asked, "We need food and warmth. Can you bring?"

The uniformed man pointed to the tent. "Go back inside. Breakfast trays will be brought soon."

"Good." Flossie began to turn back inside, but paused, unsure if a thank you was needed. *Don't be foolish, Floss, he's your prison guard.* She opted to give a small bow of acknowledgment. *Although,* she thought, *I really should thank Doctor Pan and the guards for providing such a wonderful opportunity.* The cold air had blown some common sense back into Flossie—she was no fool. She knew that the exquisite night she had just experienced was probably a one-off. One of those things that happens when circumstances conspire to provide forced proximity and a need to release tension and anxiety. *Once we are back in Bosch, assuming we ever get back, our friendship will go back to what it was, just with some special memories.* She sighed, thinking back to her delight at discovering the hidden diamonds among the brown and pink folds of the tantalizing Master Sergeant Miata. A tiny voice nudged, *You promised to take care of her—and she is getting a head start.* An eager flush poured through Flossie as she pictured her lover touching herself, and she stepped back into the tent.

Kat, February 10 1000

The snow, which started sometime in the deep dark, is still falling at sunrise, which is now around a quarter after ten bells. The wind is whistling down from the mountains, causing the snow to seem to come from all directions at once. Not exactly ideal circumstances to go visiting, but if people stopped doing things until the snow let up here in the North, nothing would get done until summer.

Zach had trudged over to his place around six bells to do morning chores, not bothering to wake me. I had slept poorly the first part of the night, troubled with the notion that the three little girls I once cared for had been condemned to a life of enslavement. Once I did fall asleep, I was pulled into a dream in which I was chased by the people I had killed over the years. I saw their faces, some distinct, some just shadows. I tried to run from them, but my legs could barely move, as if I was weighed down.

I was still in the midst of the dream when I heard a door open. Sitting bolt-upright and sure the militia had found us, I ran out of my room ready to add to the faces in my dream. Instead, there stood Zach holding a basket of eggs and some fresh milk for breakfast, ice driven into his beard and icicles hanging from his mustache as he stamped the snow from his boots. He had looked at me, standing in the close-fitted black leggings and long-sleeved black shirt that I wear for extractions and as the base layer for a cold mission like this, and in my bare feet, my curly hair untidy, and he had raised both his eyebrows and his hands.

He opened his eyes overly wide and pitched his voice high. "Please don't shoot me, Master Commander. I really don't want to deal with all that again."

Clicking on the safeties and holstering my weapons, I went to take the milk bucket from him and help him out of his coat. "Sweet New Earth, Zach. I thought we had been found out. Let a girl know when you are coming and going, and you won't take fire." I stepped on a pile of snow that he had tracked in and gave a little squeal. "I need some slippers. That is so cold!" I had hopped to the kitchen and stepped onto the rug in front of the sink, rubbing the insulted foot around to dry and warm it.

"Aw, it's just a bit of snow, Kat. Ain't nothing for us Northerners."

Now we are fed and dressed and getting ready to head to my old family place to confront my dad. "You know, I could find my own way there if you just loan me your truck," I point out.

The side-eye he gives me is enough to make me drop the subject.

Since blood had dripped on Becca's hand-me-downs yesterday, I head upstairs to explore Mrs. McKay's wardrobe. I return wearing a green skirt that fits decently. Underneath it is my base layer with the warm knit stockings pulled over them, my blade secure on my thigh. I don't put anything over my base layer top except my pistol holsters and pistols. I want to get to them quickly after I face down Dad and interrogate him about my sisters and me.

I keep chewing on something Matty said last night: "What's the line between justice and revenge, Kat? And what's the cost to you of dispensing either?" I really don't know how to answer either question anymore. But my philosophical deliberations are halted when I see Zach loading up not just his rifle, but a pistol as well. "What do you think you're doing?" I hope my blunt tone conveys the message that he isn't accompanying me to this meeting. "You know, your role is driver, only."

He looks at me with his patented Zach McKay equable look, as if there is no concern to be had heading off to kill some old man because a long-lost lover said it was a good idea. "You say you can shoot with them pistols you love, but since I ain't seen it and only know the way you shot a quarter century ago, I expect I should come along. Besides, ain't there supposed to be a second in a duel?"

It is all I can do not to pull my piece, call out one of the many ceramic dogs that Lily McKay collected, and shoot them off the shelf. But that would be both overkill and harsh. I note that I did not do it and file the note away to tell both Ruth and Matty and receive their praise. Good thing I don't have daddy issues. I scowl. "It's not a duel. No way I'd turn my back on Cole if he had a gun." Then I sigh. "But fine, bring your little toys. But remember, this is my fucking mission first and foremost, and I will not have you elbowing in before it is concluded to my satisfaction."

"Aye-aye, Master Commander, sir." He not only sing-songs this mockingly but gives a little eyebrow salute with his first two fingers that definitely has a flip-me-off quality. I'm sorta wishing he'd go back to a stone-faced recluse right now.

I go full MC. "Trooper McKay, it is *ma'am* to you, and this..." I click my heels together, stand up straight, look directly ahead, and snap up my right fist to the center of my chest where I hold it for a few seconds before dropping my arm back smartly to my side. "... is how you salute your master commander. Savvy?" I send a piercing stare into him that I have seen make lesser men wet themselves. He simply stands and grins. I relax and grin back. "Now don't be an asshole."

A chuckle rumbles in his chest as he straps on his holster and pulls on his coat. "No need. You have that covered."

Damn straight I do.

Carisa, February 10 1000

"So, we have an agreement? You will care for the Charlotte Isaksdottir memorial site and place flowers there and on the site of my father, Arthur Simonsson, as well each week, and I will pay you for your time and the flowers, of course."

The old man looked at Carisa with understanding. "It will be my pleasure. It never sat well with me that I was told to ignore Charlotte's resting place. But I've learned over time that families have their reasons for what they do. Now I won't charge you for flowers in the summer and fall, because my garden takes off then, and it would be my honor to use some of the ones I grow there."

"That sounds lovely. Thank you, Rolf." She reached out to grasp his hand in appreciation.

When she had arrived at the old Nyvik Memorial Park, chauffeured by Agnes, who had come in on her day off and said, "I won't take no for an answer, dear," she had been shocked at the state of her parents' memorials. Father's was well-tended, the snow brushed away. Fresh flowers sat next to a neat stone marker, and the area behind the markers held the traditional stacked circle of stones around a ground sconce, which was intended to hold a flaming torch on special holidays, its light ensuring the wandering spirit could find his way back to his resting place. Carisa could remember her parents taking her to her grandparents' sites on holiday nights and seeing the memorial park lit up with hundreds of torches. It was magical. She could not remember ever seeing her father's torch lit.

Her mother's stone, on the other hand, was not even visible when she first arrived, confusing Carisa. It was not until she began digging in the snow piled to the right of her father's site that her fingers found the stone. She then headed to the caretaker's home to request a shovel to clear the site. Rolf had been more than helpful as he pitched in to clear the memorial. Carisa and Agnes pulled off years of dead leaves and grasses. Carisa let her tears of anger and shame mix with her grief as she worked, and neither the nurse nor the caretaker suggested she do otherwise. Rolf pointed her to the stone pile, and she carefully selected several to make a small circle around her mother's sconce. Then Agnes and Rolf walked to the Rolfs' small house, leaving Carisa to chat with her parents and show them pictures of their grandchildren and son-in-law.

"I will bring them to see you both," she promised fervently, "at solstice for the next burning holiday. But you are both welcome to visit us in Bosch during your wanderings." She kissed her fingers and pressed them to each stone. Then she stood ready to claim the rest of her past.

CHAPTER 22

Diamond, February 10 1100

Diamond was usually an expert in keeping her emotions in check, but it took her more than a minute to remove the astonishment from her face when Doctor Pan Qiu, her attaches who Diamond and Flossie had begun to refer to as Thing One and Thing Two, and two guards, all of them well-bundled against the storm, walked the two troopers into the large, open-roofed, empty tent she and Flossie had observed from the ridge the day before.

It was not empty. Far from it. Spread out across an area of perhaps twenty to twenty-five meters in diameter were several clear domes set up on the ground with the snow pushed back from them. They each were connected to some sort of a box via tubing, and Diamond had to blink twice to believe that she could see some lush greenery in a few of the domes. Tables were placed near each dome with a variety of instrumentation that reminded Di of her secondary class's tour of the science department at Bosch's Central University, replete with beakers, burners, and gadgetry. Now, she watched as several people, whom she presumed to be part of the actual scientific expedition, based on the lab coats they wore over their outerwear, moved about the domes, some adjusting gauges, others peering into the bubbles and taking notes, and still others working industriously at tables. And notably, it wasn't snowing anywhere in the tent, although the sides did ripple with the wind that still blew beyond the canvas boundary.

Standing at her shoulder, Flossie slowly pulled her hood down and shook the snow from the crevices it had blown into as she exclaimed in a whisper, "What the fuck…?"

Dr. Pan had dropped her hood as well and was looking quite pleased by the activity occurring. She glanced at the two women. "This is Dr. Aung's work. Quite impressive, is it not?" She didn't wait for an answer, instead turning and saying, "Ahh, and here he is." The small, dark-haired scientist they had been sent to extract was approaching. "It is the man of the hour," Dr. Pan stated. "Porter, Miata, this is Dr. Aung. Though you all did have a chance to meet briefly last night, I doubt formal introductions occurred." There was a definite tone of amusement in the bureaucrat's voice.

Dr. Aung bowed formally before saying in Mandarin, "Dr. Pan Qiu, please, allow me to…"

Dr. Pan broke in, "Please, Dr. Aung, FA for our guests."

"Oh, yes, absolutely." He switched quickly to the standard Central Continent language, annoying Diamond as she thought about the communication challenges the night before. "Allow me to show you what we have accomplished here." He gestured for the group to follow him.

Diamond could not fathom why they, as prisoners who were presumed spies, were being included on this tour. She glanced at Flossie and couldn't help but glow as she recalled the impassioned night—and morning—they had shared. She eagerly looked forward to the next time they were alone. Okay, so she had initiated their lovemaking with, well, less than noble motives, but to her surprise, she discovered she felt…well, something. She couldn't place it quite, because it was different than anything she had felt before. Flossie made her feel safe and worthy. For now, she caught her friend's eye and attempted to subtly communicate her confusion at their presence here. Flossie shook her head, and

Diamond figured if the brilliant, young sergeant couldn't figure it out, she'd just have to patient and wait for more information to be provided.

But then she heard Flossie ask, "What is on top of this tent?" causing Diamond to glance up and see a sheen of something stretched across the roof. She could see the snow gust about through the air and the shape of the surrounding mountains off to the sides. What was it?

"That is a Chinese development for this project. We are calling it, fabric obscura. It allows sunlight in, when it is not storming, but sheds snow and rain immediately, protecting our experiments from precipitation. It also allows us to work without fear of being observed by the outside world." Dr. Aung replied.

"And what is your work?" Flossie queried.

"Come, I will explain at station one." The group approached the nearest dome, and the doctor began his lecture. "A short history review first: Humans have been altering their environment since the Stone Age with excellent results. And we continued quite successfully throughout history, allowing for our population to reach over ten billion individuals before human-created global warming reached a tipping point, resulting in cataclysmic melting and flooding of coastal areas, rampant wildfires, titanic storm systems, widespread crop failures, and rolling pandemics, which culminated in the start of the Climate Wars and resulted in the devastation of the human population."

Diamond knew all this, the history of the shift from Old Earth to New.

Dr. Aung continued with intent, "While on Old Earth science was able to manage cloud seeding to encourage precipitation and attempts at reducing hurricane intensity, we as a species have never been able to control the climate, and it resulted in our downfall almost to the point of extinction particularly near the equator and in the central areas of the larger continents." He reached over, lifted a small silver water bottle, and took a swallow from it before saying, "The question we asked ourselves was very simple: How can humans control the climate of the planet?"

Diamond and Flossie looked at each other. Dr. Aung had summed up a lot of Bosch Intelligence; the FA knew of this experiment. Anything new the scientist now mentioned needed to be memorized. Diamond knew Flossie was in her element with this and was unsurprised when she spoke up. "That is a question that has eluded scientists across the globe for generations."

A pleased, proud look crossed Dr. Aung's face. "Indeed, it *had* eluded science, until eighteen months ago when my research team at the University of Khumi City proposed the theory that by creating a closed system and inputting the correct amount of energy, we could control the system's climate."

"I'd have to imagine that 'the correct amount of energy' means massive amounts of it," Flossie said as she peered at the dome and the attached box.

It was Dr. Pan Qiu who answered. "It does seem to require large quantities, but our government has a plan to access a relatively unlimited supply very soon."

Well, that's a statement, Diamond thought. *Even I can see the need to follow up that up.*

But Dr. Aung cut off any further discussion on that topic. "The energy issue is not mine. My focus is the systems, like this first station." He gave a sweeping arm-wave as if presenting royalty. "The trials here in the North Country are the first in a series of experiments meant to test the soundness of our theory and apply its principles. We have created closed systems within the domes, powered them with the TF36 generator, and used step-down transformers and buffers to allot specific amounts of energy into each system. Each dome alters the ambient temperature of the below-zero permafrost in increments of five degrees with station one at 5°C. And these..." The man pointed to what Diamond could now see were high-quality cameras set up on tripods and then pointed into the domes. "...record the weather events, which often occur far too quickly to be observed by our eyes."

Now Diamond asked, "Weather events? Like what?" She watched as Dr. Pan Qiu observed the tiny bits of green growth scattered underneath the first station's dome.

"We have had cloud formation in most, rain in some, and even small thunderstorms in the higher-temperature domes."

They walked on to observe the 10°C dome, and then the 15°C station, where Diamond was astonished to see not only verdant plant growth, but also insects flying and crawling within the enclosure. Dr. Aung noted her expression and laughed gently. "We were surprised as well, but the ground contains larvae as well as seeds, all just waiting for the right temperatures. Which, we have supplied."

Flossie came up next to Diamond, but it was to Dr. Aung she expressed her question. "But it really isn't a fully closed system. It is exposed to sunlight."

"An excellent observation, Porter." The man was practically gleeful in his answer. "The sunlight does provide additional energy, but it is the same for each dome. Additionally, after we have collected the relevant data, this experiment will be replicated further north during the polar night."

Diamond could practically see the thoughts churning through her new lover's mind, and she found herself not just impressed, but aroused as they moved on to the 20°C dome, where a mass of blue and white wildflowers bloomed below it, insects buzzed about, and the leaves glistened with droplets of moisture. "Okay," Diamond commented, "this is remarkable."

"This station seems to be the optimal temperature based on preliminary findings," the small scientist agreed.

Dr. Pan Qiu added, "The results are most impressive," which garnered a small bow of appreciation from Dr. Aung.

Diamond looked up at Flossie with excitement and wonder. "Can you believe all these flowers up here in winter?"

"They are pretty, and their presence certainly makes for great optics when presenting the data to maintain funding, which I imagine is what is going on with your visit, Dr. Pan," Flossie commented. Diamond's surprise by her friend's frankness shifted into uneasiness as Flossie dug further for information. "But, doctors, what is the point? We certainly know that given access to fossil fuels, humanity would be able to drive up the overall temperature of the planet without using domes and generators. We have done it before and nearly destroyed ourselves in the process. Why recreate a mini-climate crisis, however attractive, in one of the few icy places left on the globe?"

As Dr. Aung listened to Flossie, his pleasant expression retracted, and he looked at Dr. Pan, caution written in his expression.

Dr. Pan, however, seemed relaxed. "I appreciate your reserve, Aung, but please, tell us about stage two of your experimental design."

Another small bow of acknowledgment, and Dr. Aung began, "Stage two is planned for this coming summer outside of Oraina in the Boiling Flats of Africa, where the average temperature is close to 45°C. We hope by reversing the energy flow, we can create decreases in temperature and increases in precipitation. In fact, I would very much like to achieve a small snowfall in one of the experimental domes."

Diamond was trying to imagine the appearance of snow in a place so long devoid of water and life when Dr. Pan interrupted her thoughts. "The tour is over," she said. "We will leave Dr. Aung to his work and retire to the meeting tent for lunch. Come. We have much to discuss."

Diamond exchanged a confused look with Flossie. What more was there to discuss than the grilling they received last night? Flossie turned to Dr. Aung. "Thank you, sir. If I have more questions, may I come and ask you?"

The doctor looked at the bureaucrat who looked curiously at Flossie, then signaled her approval.

"I would be happy to answer what I can," replied the scientist.

Carisa, February 10 1130

"Is this the one?" Agnes asked.

Carisa stood on the sidewalk, looking up the steps and at the white, wooden-sided house with the red roof. It was certainly similar to several others on the block, so Carisa checked the number not just once or twice, but three times. "The door and the stoop do look familiar," she replied. "Though everything looks so much smaller than in my memories."

"Well, dear, you were here as a child. The house must have seemed larger to you then," the nurse said gently.

Carisa glanced at this woman who was sacrificing her day off work to take a person she had only met the day before on two emotion-laden errands. The kindness bolstered her confidence, which had flagged when she first woke in the call room this morning with such intense pain in her legs, arms, and back that she was sure she was having a UN relapse.

Agnes had found her, curled in bed, and sobbing with pain. "Well, a relapse is one possibility, but I think the pain you are feeling is far more likely your muscles complaining about all the work you asked of them yesterday. Let's get you a cold plunge and some anti-inflammatories, plus a bit of coffee, and see where we are in half an hour."

Carisa agreed to try, though she was very skeptical of success, feeling resigned to several weeks of pain and disability. So, she was delighted when Agnes' treatment plan worked. Her muscles still complained, but far less, especially after some gentle stretches.

"You are right, yet again, Agnes." Carisa could feel anxiety building. "This is Elka's home." She slid out of the nurse's vehicle and peered back into the window,

"I'll park up the way and wait for you." Agnes gestured toward a small vehicle lot as she gazed encouragingly at Carisa.

She took a deep breath, steadied herself, put her hand on the stone rail of the steps, and slowly walked up the steps to the doorway, where she tapped the front door with the heavy wooden knocker.

Several moments passed, then Carisa heard footsteps, and the door opened. A young woman dressed in traditional maid garb stood at the door. "Yes, ma'am," she said politely. "May I help you, ma'am?"

Carissa could feel her nervousness come through her voice. "I believe this is the Simonsson residence. I'd like to see the lady of the house, Elka Simonsson."

"Very good, ma'am. May I inquire as to who is calling?" the young maid asked.

"I am an old friend of the family, Mrs. Morton. I have not been back for quite some time. Visiting here is part of my remembrance journey," Carissa said politely. "She may not know my name well, but I knew her when I was a child. I was just a bit older than her children, Rex, Naomi, and Elena."

"Yes, ma'am. One moment. Please step into the foyer. It's too chilly for you to stand outside." Carissa stepped in and waited patiently while the young woman scurried off through the house to announce the arrival of Mrs. Morton.

She used the time to look around the foyer. It was well-appointed and well-kept-up. Not an estate house to be sure, but the large, elaborate, gilded-framed mirror bookended by sconces, with the low spray of silk flowers in a vase set on the shiny, black-stained console table, spoke of a family a step or two beyond comfortable. Carisa put any thoughts of how much her parents' assets and the markers Elka received for Carisa may have contributed to this elegant lifestyle away in a tidy little box. That was in the past. The only thing Carisa wanted was to be seen and let the old woman know she hadn't destroyed her.

A gallery of photographs caught her eye. They ran up all along the staircase in frames of different sizes and shapes. She was captivated by them and recognized her father in many. She was not hopeful she would see her mother, but then two steps up found their wedding photo. She leaned in, gazing at the young, hopeful faces full of life and plans for the future. The image made her catch her breath. Now their future was to lie together in the memorial park.

"Excuse me… Mrs. Morton, is it?" a voice different from the maid's drew her from her thoughts as she turned to see a woman a few years younger than herself looking at her inquiringly. "Hello, I am Rachel, Rex's wife. I'm afraid you have me at a disadvantage. You see, I do not know Rex's distant kin."

Carissa stepped down from the staircase and approached the woman warmly. "I have not been back since Rex was, oh, twelve or thirteen. I was hoping to see Elka."

Rachel looked delighted. "Mother Elka is in the sitting room. We were having a cup of tea. Would you like to join us?"

"Yes, that would be lovely." Carissa walked as Rachel led the way to the sitting room.

Rachel asked kindly, "You are limping a bit. Have you hurt your leg?"

"It's nothing. I am applying tincture of time to it." Carisa recalled her midwife using the expression while she was laboring with Arthur and Carly.

Rachel laughed warmly. "Well, that is the way it is with women our age. Aches and pains happen, and we can't stop living, so we just wait for them to go away. Mother Elka says that I will someday reach a point in life where the aches and pains don't go away anymore."

With a little inward sigh, Carisa replied, "Yes, I've heard the same thing."

Rachel opened the doors to the sitting room, saying, "We keep the doors closed to keep this room warm for Mother Elka."

Memories flooded into Carisa's mind as she took in the room. She remembered the smell: fireplace ash and dust and rosewater. The furnishings had changed, but the windows, the fireplace, and the shelving holding knickknacks were in the same place. Carisa recalled chasing after her cousins who hid in there and then being scolded by her aunt for the messes they created. And she remembered standing near the fire as Elka explained the necessity of Carisa going to the thrall market. She had made it seem like it was something Carisa owed her. Anger that had been steeping for years began to boil up inside of her.

A blue velvet settee, a lace arm cover on either side and a cover neatly placed on the back, sat near the fireplace, which held a cheerfully crackling blaze. On it a tiny old woman sat nearest the fire, holding a teacup and saucer in one hand.

"Mother Elka," Rachel spoke with an elevated tone. "Mother Elka, this is Mrs. Morton." She carefully enunciated each word, then turned to Carissa. "Mother Elka is a bit hard of hearing now."

Carisa observed the woman who had tried to destroy her. She wore a long green dress with a high neck and a warm, fluffy, white sweater over her shoulders. Framed by the v-line of the sweater and nestled against the background of elegant green lay a gold pendant, inscribed with a stave of protection—the stave that had called to her from the book of Norse mythology. Carisa's hand rose to touch her own neck as the memory flooded back to her.

Her mother was laughing, full of life, her blue eyes sparkling, as a little Carisa reached out to touch the pendant. "It's so pretty, Mother!"

"That it is, my sweetest. It was my mother's. And someday you will wear it and your little ones will admire it."

Carisa felt her breath quicken as tears threatened.

"Please, sit down. I'll have Sharon bring another cup for the tea." Rachel indicated a chair across from Elka.

Carisa sat, blinking back the unshed tears of memory and pain. Elka greeted her with a tight bob of her head, and Carisa noted that her eyes were rheumy with the tiniest hint of white. Her vision was going. *Good,* the uncharitable part of Carisa exclaimed. Sharon brought a cup, and Rachel poured some tea into it and handed it to her.

"Thank you very much, Rachel." She accepted the cup politely, then focused on her aunt. "Hello, Elka," she said loudly and watched to see whether the woman would recognize her voice.

Elka paused as she sipped her tea. "Mrs. Morton, is it? I don't know any Mrs. Morton. Are you sure you have the right home?"

Rachel chuckled. "Now, Mother Elka, I am sure Mrs. Morton knows where she is supposed to be."

Carisa thought to herself, *In a different world, I might be the one inviting you in for tea.* But instead, she raised her voice slightly and spoke slowly and clearly so Elka would hear each word. "Oh, yes, this is the home I remember from when I was a young girl. You remember, Aunt Elka, I lived here after my parents died. I am your younger brother Arthur's daughter, Carisa."

The old woman fumbled her teacup, spilling tea onto the settee as the cup tumbled to the ground to land with a small plop on the soft carpet.

"Oh, dear, Mother Elka, are you alright? I don't think the tea was too hot. It didn't burn you, did it?" Rachel was quite solicitous of her mother-in-law.

Elka brushed off the concern. "Stop your damnable fussing, Rachel. I am fine." Elka's body was tense, and her face had tightened until she looked like one of those apple dolls Carisa had made in school in happier times. "My hearing is not good. What is your name again? I thought you said Carisa."

Even as the anger boiled over and coated every part of Carisa's being, a strange calm also came over her, and she impassively took a sip of her tea. Unsurprisingly, it was bitter.

"Oh, Elka, you heard me correctly. I am Carisa, your niece." She sharpened her look at the old woman. "The child you took in and turned into a servant after my parents' death. The young woman sent as a servant to your friends, and the young woman you sold into enslavement, so you could purchase the life that I was meant to live."

Rachel gasped. "Carisa? Arthur's daughter? But you died."

"I am sitting here talking to you, Rachel. Plainly not dead," Carisa said, spreading her hands.

Elka quickly snapped, "She is dead. Carisa is dead. She was an ungrateful little bitch who ran off with a man, and they were killed." The old woman looked at Rachel. "This woman is an imposter. A grifter. She is here to steal from us. She wants to try and take what's rightfully mine."

Carisa sat back. "I think you should be careful, Elka, in describing what you believe is rightfully yours." She looked over the younger woman, who was clearly distressed, looking from her mother-in-law to this new woman. "Rachel, you seem like a decent person, and I have no desire to upset you or disrupt your life. I simply want a chance to face this person..." She flicked her hand in a dismissive gesture. "...and let her know, that even with all the cruelty she subjected me to from the time I was an eight-year-old child who had just lost her mother and father until I was seventeen and she sold me into enslavement, where I was kept for almost half my life, that I survived despite her efforts. I am now free, and happy with a family of my own." Carisa inhaled.

"No, Carisa is dead. I tried my best for her, but she took after that slutty mother of hers and ran off with a man."

Carisa did not move, but said in a low and dangerous voice, "Elka, I would be very careful what you say about my mother."

Elka's eyes widened at the tone.

Rachel had both hands at her breast. Carisa couldn't help but think, *If only she had a strand of pearls, she could clutch them, but the old woman is likely holding onto those as well.*

"I'm sorry, Mrs. Morton, but you are upsetting Mother Elka. Cousin Carisa died years ago. I must ask you to leave." Rachel's words were firm, but her voice was tremulous.

Without standing, Carisa asked, "Does Rex still have that little scar on his upper left arm from where he jumped from the kitchen counter with a jam jar when he was five?"

She watched as the blood left Rachel's face. "Yes," she said, barely above a whisper, "he does."

Carisa gave a small chortle as she remembered. "Rex was always getting into things, and at that age was not a good listener.

I do hope he has improved in that respect. He wanted bread and jam, but Naomi was upset that Elena had cut the hair on one of her dolls, which was one of *my* dolls, given to her without my consent. But Rex wouldn't wait and jumped down from the kitchen counter just as I walked in. His foot caught in the drawer he had opened as a step, and he fell. I lunged and knocked the jar away, but it still broke and cut his arm deeply. It was hard to say what was jam and what was blood on the floor. I bandaged it and took him to the doctor, where he received eight stitches. I received twice that many lashings when Aunt Elka heard the story."

Rachel stood frozen where she had opened the door to show Carisa out. "That is exactly how he tells the story. Except he never mentioned you were punished. He does, however, say that if you hadn't knocked the jar away, it might have broken right under his neck."

Carisa demurred, "Who knows what might have happened."

"Rex and Naomi and Elena remember you. Rex said they were mean to you, and he is quite ashamed to this day."

"They were children. They did not have an example of kindness and empathy provided for them." A sigh escaped Carisa's lips as she said this.

Now Rachel left the doorway and approached her mother-in-law. "This is Cousin Carisa, Mother Elka. Why have you lied about her being dead for so long?"

The old woman ignored her daughter-in-law. She reached into a pocket, put on her glasses, and leaned to look at where Carisa sat. "You look just like your mother—a good-for-nothing gold-digger who spread her legs and got with child to trap my sweet Arthur. She fooled him, our parents, and the whole neighborhood with her wiles. But not me. I saw through her. When you all took sick, I went to church to pray that you and she would die, but the slut lured my brother to go with her even into death, leaving you with me."

Carisa stood up. "Thank you for the compliment. My mother was a beautiful woman." She walked over to the settee and stood in front of Elka, where she leaned into her, resting one hand on the settee's back until she was nose to nose with this who calculated her ruin. "But look closely, Elka, I have my father's eyes. Do you see him looking back at you? He despises you for what you did to his daughter." She watched the old woman's eyes widen and saw pain wash across them.

Carisa felt as if she was watching someone else—someone strong and sure of themselves, not scared-little-rabbit-Carisa certainly, as her hand moved up to the old woman's throat. Then she thought, *No, this is who I am and this is what I deserve.* And with that thought, Carisa grasped the pendant. "And this...was my mother's given to her by her mother." She gave a quick jerk and the chain broke. "And I am taking it with me." She stood and walked to the door and was pleased that the brace Reeves had made her allowed her to move with fluidity. "Rachel..." She looked at the woman who in a different reality could have been her friend and family. "...please accept my apologies for disrupting your tea. I will be taking the wedding photo of my parents from the hall. I will wire you markers to cover the cost of replacement when I return home to Bosch." The mention of the pirate island pulled a small gasp from Rachel. "Give Rex my best."

Carisa walked out the front door with her two prizes and toward Agnes' vehicle and wondered if this was what it meant to swagger.

CHAPTER 23

Kat, February 10 Noon

I stare at the old place from the warmth of the truck as the snow continues to fall. "I knew it was small, but holy shit, how did nine people ever fit in there?"

"Folk around here do with what they have," Zach says, but his brow is furrowed as well.

The main part of the cabin is made of chinked logs maybe four meters by five meters square with a peaked roof, a chimney, and two windows with shutters on either side of the front door. Three additions jut out from the sides that don't contain the door. They are constructed of flat boards that probably were scavenged over time. The one on the right was the boys' room. It had a window. The one at the back that we can't see was for Dad and Mom; it had a couple of windows. The one on the left was actually an extension of the front room without any windows. That was where the girls slept, on bedrolls that had to be stored each morning and curtains partitioning it off from the rest of the house at night. I can see a bit of light ooze through a couple of boards, and I remember how damn cold the place was for a good ten months out of the year.

Most of my emotions are in a tumult, and it's only through the strict discipline I've put in place over the years that they are not all on the surface and demanding attention. That and the fact that Revenge has stepped forward, and they tend to quiet the rabble and create focus.

I open the truck door against the wind and, while pulling my shoulders up in defense against the storm, I lumber through the drifted snow. A shadow appears at my side and slightly behind me, and I know Zach thinks he is safeguarding me. I pound on the door as I holler, "Cole Wallace. I want a word with you."

The door opens and an unsmiling woman, maybe my age, maybe younger—the years are hard up here—stands there. She has long, dirty-blonde hair pulled back in a sloppy braid. Her feet are bare, and she wears an apron over a shabby dress. "Who be you?" she asks, not unkindly, but she clearly has no love for strangers. She peers around me. "I know you. You be that McKay fellow—the radio-man."

"Yes, ma'am, that I be," Zach admits. I keep my expression neutral, but inside I am rolling my eyes. *Huh, her, he calls ma'am.*

"What do you want with Cole?" This is addressed to Zach, and I'm feeling testy. I don't like being invisible.

He starts to answer, but I lift my hand, gently striking him in the chest with the back of it. With the other, I point to my chest. "*I'm* looking for him."

Her eyes refocus on me. "What be your business?"

"I used to know him some years back. Here for work now and wanted to catch up." Not one fucking lie in that.

Her head and shoulders move in a *whatever* fashion. "Good luck with that. "He ain't here now. Off gatherin' up his cronies. They all be leavin' at dawn to go to Marpavik on the coast s'posedly to get some fish, but more likely to get better whiskey. Won't be home for some days, thank the Lord." She looks relieved, but also clocks my dismayed expression. "If you gotta see him, He'll be holding court down at the Burntback 'round supper time, as usual." She doesn't wait for a response, just closes the door.

We head back to the truck in silence as the cold wind whips at us.

"What do you wanna do, Kat?" Zach asks as we sit in the slowly warming vehicle.

I hunch my shoulders and throw up my hands a bit. "Burn some time until supper. Then go to Burntback." I look out into the storm. "I had forgotten that goddamn place's name."

Flossie, February 10 Noon

Lunch consisted of a bowl of hearty noodle soup, fragrant with garlic, sesame, and ginger, containing mushrooms, vegetables, and large pieces of chicken. The noodles were delicious, although as Flossie slurped them, spatters of oily broth spattered her front. Did the whole expedition eat like this or just the higher-ups like Pan?

As they ate, their Mandarin mandarin—Flossie giggled in her head at the play on words—kept up what amounted to a polite monologue about the differences between the North Country winter and the winters in northern China as well as postulating what the cook might be making for dinner that evening. Diamond added a few observations and spoke quite amiably with Dr. Pan. Flossie focused on her meal as she considered both the ramifications of Dr. Aung's work and their own captivity, however pleasant it was turning out to be.

After the bowls were cleared, Thing One and Thing Two brought warm cloths to each woman so they could wipe their hands and faces. The presentations of the cloths made Flossie recall the previous night and she flushed, glancing at Diamond, who lifted her cloth the smallest amount into the air as if toasting, making Flossie almost choke as she suppressed a giggle. When the cloths were taken back, small, fruit-scented jelly candies were placed out for dessert.

"The Bosch are a fascinating people," Dr. Pan Qiu said,

suddenly shifting the topic. "Even with little or no homogeneity in its populace, it has managed to create a forward-thinking and moving society. Would you both agree?"

"Bosch does stay current," Diamond said in response.

Flossie's eyes narrowed a bit and she replied, "Dr. Pan, you seem inordinately fascinated with the Bosch. You grilled us on who we were and what we were doing here in the North Country last night, but you also asked many questions about Bosch in general. I hope you know we gave answers that can also be easily found via devices on the interwebs once you are back in China, or at least somewhere with a signal." She tipped her head to the side as she thought. "So I wonder two things: one, why, after you accused us of being spies last night, are you showing us the details of and future plans for Dr. Aung's experiment? And two, what does China, a very large, wealthy, and powerful nation, want with Bosch? Is it Glitter? I am sure the negotiation teams would happily access the Chinese market."

Dr. Pan sat quietly for a moment, hands folded in front of herself, looking at Flossie. "You are a very intriguing woman, Porter. You behave somewhat gracelessly and present yourself as awkward, but you certainly are quite intelligent, and you have the mettle to break into a foreign camp to attempt to relieve us of our prize scientist."

"A scientist who you yourselves extracted by force from his home in Khumi City, if my research is correct." Flossie heard Diamond give a small choking cough, and when she looked at her sensual friend she saw that Diamond was staring back at her with wide eyes. Flossie wasn't sure where the confidence to push Dr. Pan was coming from but decided to roll with it. Every bit of information could be helpful.

Dr. Pan's eyes narrowed, and her face flushed. "Be careful, Porter. Your liberty in this camp is at my discretion." She took a breath in and seemed to compose herself. "Let me answer your second question first. As I am sure you know, our emperor, Xiang, has met with your master commander, a most auspicious privilege only bestowed on the most influential of world leaders, in hopes of creating some sort of mutually beneficial trade agreement. Now while we in China are not interested in Glitter as it is sold, as our people have no interest in its mind-altering effects, we believe that Glitter holds other intriguing possibilities—such as the fact it fuels your airships' fusion engines."

With that statement, Flossie drew a curtain over her face. She blinked and reached for a jelly, sneaking a glance at Diamond's face, which also had taken on a closed expression. The fusion engines that the Bosch Pirate Force used in their vessels, which allowed them to fly higher and faster than any other air-vessels on the planet, and also the fusion generator that manufactured power for the island, were closely guarded secrets. Troopers were instructed from their days as recruits to not discuss the topic at any time, and to neither confirm nor deny the technology's existence if questioned either on- or off-island. The secret was held so closely, in fact, that only a handful of specialized power engineers fully understood it, with flight engineers having the next level of clearance. For people in Flossie's and Diamond's place, they simply knew it existed.

"And what about my first question, Dr. Pan?" Flossie asked, pleased to hear her voice come out as cool and calm, revealing nothing.

Dr. Pan made a nonchalant movement with her head. "I see. I was told not to expect discussion of the fusion topic from you."

Who told her that? Flossie wondered.

"But I, instead," the refined politician continued, "will be very open with you. China plans to use Dr. Aung's findings to revitalize not only the old breadbasket in the northeast of our country, but also the plains on the Yakutian Plateau. We wish to become the source of wheat, millet, soy, and maize to the planet. And we will take the steps necessary to make that happen."

Flossie decided to gamble. "And would those steps include using the technology to devastate areas currently producing those crops?"

A tinkling, little laugh, like water over smooth pebbles, came from their hostess. "I repeat, you are quite intelligent. If removing a competitor allows us to more easily control the market, we will do as necessary." Dr. Pan waved her hand casually as she promoted what would amount to starvation for many thousands. "But let me answer your first question, finally." She sat back against the red sofa and looked first at Diamond and then at Flossie.

Dr. Pan began, "I wish for the two of you to return to Bosch and conduct your lives as you did before we met. And as a show of friendship, you will be given the means to communicate with me privately, passing on information about any variety of topics of interest to the emperor, the government council, and, of course, me. To be sure, Glitter's unique qualities will certainly be one of those topics."

"Why in the world would you think we would be willing to betray Bosch?" Flossie asked this with a small hoot of a laugh.

"That's not what we do in Bosch," Diamond confirmed without hesitation.

"Everyone has a price, Porter. For instance, Miata over there has a family, of, I believe, three brothers and a mother, on Bosch, all of whom weigh on her emotions and her pocketbook, but that she still wishes to keep safe. I expect an additional, hearty revenue stream from us could help her find some much-desired freedom. Perhaps even a little…power?"

Flossie glanced at Diamond's shocked face as details about her life fell from this Chinese bureaucrat's lips.

"And you, Porter," Dr. Pan continued, "a woman who simply appeared out of thin air on the planet six years ago. Your price may be different than Miata's. You wish to maintain your privacy and keep your past as the daughter of the late, disgraced vice president of the FA a secret. Your own mother doesn't know about you the way we do. You also have a brother, I believe?"

Flossie's stomach dropped.

"And let's not forget that most important of human connections, those we love both in body and spirit. Would either of you be willing to endanger your lover's life? Why Bosch would be so careless as to assign both of you to the same mission is beyond me. It makes it so easy to threaten to end one or the other of your lives." She made a small hand motion and Thing One and Thing Two swiftly appeared, each holding a sharp knife to Flossie's and Diamond's throats. Flossie's fear for her life flared but was replaced almost immediately with anger at Diamond's lovely neck being threatened. "And to be sure, it is not an idle threat. But not yet." Dr. Pan gestured again, and the Things pocketed their weapons and stood back.

The doctor did not wait for an answer. "We can guarantee all your loved ones' safety and your privacy and assure that you are comfortable and just a bit more for the rest of your lives, all for sharing a few select pieces of information that could advance science over time." Dr. Pan wore a pleasant, almost motherly, smile that Flossie wanted to slap off her face. Who did she think she was with her threats? *She's your captor, Floss,* she reminded herself. *But she is threatening my Diamond and Bosch.*

"Maybe you don't understand how it works on Bosch, Dr. Pan Qiu. We all have adequate markers. We are not a country with dramatic income inequality, such as you might find in Eternia, or dare I say, China. We cannot be bought," Flossie stated flatly.

The doctor looked unruffled by the flat refusal. "How foolish of me. I forgot to let you know what you will be giving up by accepting my offer. You see, normally foreign spies are taken to the homeland, where any useful information is extricated from them utilizing some of the most traditional and, I must say, painful persuasion techniques. That process usually takes place over several weeks, after which they are publicly executed."

"And what is to prevent us from agreeing to your bargain and then reneging and informing on you once we return to Bosch?" Flossie couldn't understand why this functionary wouldn't realize this gaping hole in her threats.

Dr. Pan raised her eyebrows. "We have three things. One, you are certainly not the first Bosch citizen we have made this offer to. Two, if you managed to remain safe on Bosch after betraying your agreement with me and the Chinese government, you would only be safe within Bosch's borders. We would take you the moment you left, effectively making your small island your prison—no more missions, no more visits to Truvale, only Bosch, Bosch, and more Bosch. Quite tedious if you ask me. And three, it is quite simple to leak the information to your government that you did indeed agree to serve as informants for us. In fact, we would be able to provide them with incontrovertible evidence and receipts of your disloyalty. Would they believe you when you said you were just saying it to get away? Possibly. But would they ever fully trust you again? Well, I think you know the answer as well as I do."

The motherly expression returned. She reached over and ran a small bell, calling in a guard. "Please escort Sergeant Porter to her tent to consider her choice. I wish to have a private word with Miata."

"No! We stay together." Flossie protested and struggled as the guard put a hand on either arm and led her less than gently out of the tent allowing only enough time for her to exchange a stricken look with Diamond.

Diamond February 10 1330

Pan began with preamble as Flossie was led away, "The daughter of the late Rob Abernathy will fetch a significant price at auction with those that were ruined by Abernathy Enterprise's ruthless practices. Those buying are almost as pitiless as he was purported to be."

Diamond felt her stomach drop but kept her expression blank. "And what do want me to do? Find this lost daughter?" She felt nervous sweat begin and also felt a protectiveness that stunned her both with its newness and its intensity.

Pan waved her hand, "This artifice does not become you. I am surprised that Bosch allows lovers to run missions together. But it is to my advantage. You will collect information for me, or I will open the market up on Farris Abernathy who shared your bed last night. Her life may or may not be cut short, but given the buyers, I think death might be preferable. If she chooses not to accept my offer, which I think is likely–she has the nature of one who holds to her standards no matter the cost to herself–then I will hold her with me, safely, as long as the information I request from you keeps flowing. You may see her again in several years. But she will be cared for."

Diamond had stood staring at the small woman as her heart began to race and a wave of nausea overtook her. Flossie....

"I need an answer, Miata." Pan's voice was sharp.

There was only one possible answer, "Of course, I will do as you say, as long as Flossie is safe."

Pan smiled a smile that was far more predatory that any Diamond had seen before. "Excellent. I look forward to a long and fruitful working relationship." She rang again for a guard.

As Diamond was escorted to the door, Pan said, "Oh, and Miata, let's keep this just between us."

CHAPTER 24

Kat, February 10 1400

"This is spectacular!" I exclaim as I take my first bite of the venison burger. The juices drip down my chin, and I savor the earthy flavor, rich with the taste of herbs and smelling of charcoal and pine. It's a bit chewy, but there's a bacon-like crunch to the bite, and the sweet red-berry sauce spread on the toasted buns complements it perfectly.

Zach laughs and swipes at my chin with his napkin from across the booth, before he takes a big bite of his own.

I swallow and say, "It has been literally decades since I have had one of these."

"I hear they mix in a bit of beef as well to get them juicy. I don't eat 'em much either. Having half as much gut tends to limit how much rich food I can eat." He sighs and looks longingly at the burger as he takes another bite. He pauses mid-chew. "Worth it."

I laugh, then frown and say with my own mouthful, "Damn, I hadn't thought about that aspect. That sucks. But honestly, we don't eat much real red meat at all, mostly the veggie or bean subs." I tip my beer up and am delighted at how it enhances the taste of the meat.

Zach is too busy delighting in his meal to comment.

The Polar Star is the newer honky-tonk—newer, as it has been around for about fifteen years. I have a skewed sense of North Country time—in the shitty section of Allanavik. There had been one when I was here called The Great Bear or something. I was never allowed there since Mom and Dad said only sluts go to honky-tonks. I take another bite of my burger and hear the band start to warm up and embrace my slut-hood.

As I eat, I decide to address a topic that perplexes me. "So, fifteen years ago Becca, Lily, and Max went off to fancy places. But you stayed in Allanavik with nothing but a radio. Zach, why are *you* still here in the frozen ass of the world?"

Zach slowly chews and swallows. "Well, I could say because Ma is still alive or because Sean's buried here, but truth?"

I grin; we used to play "Truth" all the time when we were young and in love. "Truth."

"I'm scared of what be out there. And how it may eat me up. Sure, in these parts lots of folk call me 'shit-bag' and whisper when I walk by and over their shoulders to protect themselves from the demons I may conjure. But maybe in Paris, it'd be worse. It ain't familiar. My life may be boring—least it was before yesterday—but at least I know what to expect."

The answer makes me sad. "Are you happy?"

"You only get the one answer," Zach says, sidestepping my follow-up. "Now you owe me a truth."

"Fair." It is part of the rules of the game.

"When you were telling me about your kids, you held back. I could see it in your face. Truth." He eyes me.

"I thought I controlled my tells better than that," I say, unamused I gave myself away.

Zach simply waits for my answer.

"Last year, Matty and I were trying for another baby after Rini. I had a couple of early losses, which was sad, but then I got pregnant, and it stayed. Until I got about halfway and the labor started. We had a tiny little boy that never breathed. He was perfect." I take a steadying breath and don't look at Zach. "We named him Warner and gave him my last name. That'd be hard enough, but about a half-hour after he was born, I was holding his sweet, wee body, and I said to Matty, 'I feel funny.' And that's the last thing I remember.

"Turns out I had started bleeding. And bleeding. Now, Matty and I have both been in combat, so we've seen blood. But he said it was more than he had ever seen, and it was everywhere as the nurses and doctors tried to stop it. They had to take me back to surgery. I got five units of blood, including one fresh from Matty, but I kept all my parts. They told me I was minutes from dying.

"After that, Matty put his foot down. He said he would not risk my life for a pregnancy when we already had great kids who still needed me. There was a bunch of other mushy stuff as well."

Zach's eyes are damp. "Damn. That's a big truth."

"Ain't it? Since then... Well, I can't abide a universe that would take not one, but two little boys from me." I take a deep breath. "So how 'bout that band." I point over to where the group is ready to go and focus my mind on it. Out of the corner of my eye, I see Zach give me a worried look.

The Sky Lights, playing to the daylight crowd, is set up with a double bass, a hand drum, an accordion, a banjo, and a fiddle. I see the fiddle player lay a harmonica out, and I spy a mandolin leaning on the wall near the dais. Matty would be drooling. I lean toward Zach. "Matty plays in a band. He would be all over all those instruments."

"Think he'd mind if we danced to a few of their songs?" he asks.

I know he is trying to distract me, and I appreciate it. So, I laugh and shake my head. "The guy is always playing on stage, so I'd never dance if I didn't dance with other folk."

And so, when the Sky Lights start to play the old "Dance of the Northern Lights," we abandon our half-eaten burgers and freestyle dance. The band shifts into "Dance the North Country," and we start to two-step, as the tenor sings:

"Dance the North Country, where the wild winds blow,
Stomp the boots on the wooden floor,
Fiddle plays high, banjo low,
Dance the North Country, land of snow."

We tumble back to our table after, laughing and out of breath, to take slugs of our beers and bites of our now cool burgers. Honestly, they aren't as good not piping-hot.

Zach twists his spine and massages his back on the right side, giving a little groan.

"You hurting?" I ask, concerned about his pain level.

He grimaces. "I'm always hurtin'." Then he grins and reaches out to cup my chin. "But having fun makes it slip away."

Before I can respond, he declares, "Oh, I love this one," and grabs my hand, dragging me back to the dance floor a moment later. I barely have time to set my beer down, as we start to stomp our feet to the "White Bear Stomp," another high-kicking classic of the region.

I am having the best time as the band transitions into "Whispered Dreams," a slow, romantic waltz. Zach looks at me, and I shrug and nod. His right arm slips around my waist and his left lifts my right hand. I grasp his shoulder, and we start to sway to the music. Zach begins to hum the tune, then pulls me close as he sings softly with the band:

"Hold me close, my darling, on this wild night,
Whispered dreams and tender sighs, the stars they burn so bright.
In your arms, I've found my home, where my heart flies free,
In this quiet moment, it's just you and me.
Let the world keep turning, let the storm roll by,
As long as I am in your arms, I know we'll reach the sky.
The night is ours to cherish the love we hold so tight,

Up here in the North Country, everything will turn out right."

Zach's cheek is against my head, and he nuzzles in, taking a deep breath of my hair. My head is almost touching his chest, but I keep it away. He doesn't see my eyes wide, my stricken expression. I can hear the song rumble in his chest, and he pulls me a few millimeters closer, his hand tightening on my waist. Apparently, I have ignored Matty's caution and inadvertently stumbled too far down memory lane. Now I have a situation to manage, and it means I have to break someone's heart. Again.

Diamond, February 10 1400

"We wouldn't do it forever, Floss. Just for a while. Take 'em for a pile or six of markers for a few months by feeding them trash." Diamond was holding her braids on her head with both hands as she stood on the soft rug that covered the small tent's floor. Diamond's stomach roiled as she said this. She had to make Flossie understand that they needed to comply with Pan's request. *She* needed to comply.

Flossie's beautiful green eyes sparked, "Are you kidding me? No! What did she say to you?"

"Nothing. She just said, it's not betrayal, just useless information." Diamond lied, "Nothing damaging to Bosch, only that science-y stuff dull researchers might find interesting." She looked at her friend and realized that she truly cared about her. In that moment, Diamond realized she would do whatever was necessary to keep Flossie–sweet, trusting Flossie– safe. Even if it meant losing her. Time to show her the ugly parts of the friend she thought she knew.

Flossie was glaring with her hands on her hips. "I can't believe you'd sell out Bosch for a few measly markers! Is that really who you are?

Diamond took a breath and snapped, "Oh, pretty easy for you to say—you don't know what it's like to do without! You come from one of the richest families on the planet!"

"What?" Flossie face dropped. "That was a long time ago."

Go all in with it girl. Do what has to be done. Diamond came over and grabbed Flossie by the shoulders. She kissed her hair and then her nose, before leaning her forehead against hers and looking into her eyes. "Baby, this could be big for… for you, for us. It could make me even with you. We could take your family markers and the ones we earn from old Pan-Face and use them to escape and start over. You did it once. We could do it again—this time together. Imagine it—you and me, on some tropical island in the Southern Sea, sipping on drinks, making love in the moonlight, no responsibilities." Diamond cringed as she saw the perfect dream evaporate.

Flossie wrinkled her brow as she shrugged off Diamond's hands and stepped back. "What the fuck are you talking about? There are no family markers. They were confiscated after the vice president died. Mother has money, but there isn't enough on the planet for me to go crawling back to her."

Even with everything else that was happening this information made Diamond's head spin. It made no sense. She stared at her friend and lover. That couldn't be true. "No markers? None? At all?"

"None. Anything I have, I've earned myself since enlistment." Flossie looked about to cry. "Is that why you suddenly thought I was worth fucking? Because I told you my dead-name, and it made you see marker-signs?"

Diamond stood for a moment, stunned. *No markers at all. Jokes on you, Diamond.* Her feelings careered about, first disappointment, then shame, the relief. But neither markers nor her confused feelings mattered now. She watched as pain and revulsion developed in her friend's eyes. *Turns out she was going hate you either way, Diamond. Figures. She's actually a good person.* Diamond stayed silent waiting for the final blow.

"And..." Now tears flowed freely down Flossie's face. "...did you forget, while we are off on that Southern Sea Island, spending markers that either don't exist or came from betrayal, our families would be picked up and likely murdered slowly and painfully because they can't tell the fucking Chinese brute squad where we went to sip our bloody cocktails?"

And then the only real friend Diamond ever had, and possibly the only person who she had ever loved, looked at her with disgust, slipped on her boots, grabbed her coat, and walked out of the tent.

Flossie, February 10 1430

Flossie pushed past the guard, who took a step toward her before she pivoted with her hand up. *Dammit, if they want to shoot me, they can just shoot me.* She decided to pretend she was somebody important, maybe the MC, as she lifted her chin and said in Mandarin, "I am going to speak to Dr. Aung. I have Dr. Pan Qiu's permission. Go ask her if you wish," before turning and marching across the compound. She heard the guard call to a comrade to watch the tent as he came scrabbling after her.

As she walked head down through the wind and snow, across the grounds, then along the path that yesterday had been packed and dirty with boot prints and now was drifted with the day's fresh snowfall, she let the tears flow unchecked, not caring if they froze in place. Her nose joined in, and she could feel the hot, thin, tear-mixed mucous coat her upper lip and ooze saltily into her mouth. Her face felt frozen from all the moisture, but she didn't care. Diamond didn't want her. She wanted her family's markers. *It's not the first time someone has pretended to be your friend,* Flossie thought. Secondary-school-Lana came first to mind; she had cozied up to Flossie and come over to study with her almost every night for a month. She thought Lana was a real friend until she had found her bent over her father's desk moaning as he fucked her. And what had her father said? "Honestly, Farris. You can't really think you are charming enough for a girl like that to be friends with. I took her on the first night she visited. That's the only reason she came back." Lana's waistline had started to expand soon, and she stopped coming to school and moved to Toronto. Flossie had stopped inviting people over after that.

Now she could hear her father laughing at her. *What did you expect? A woman as glorious as Diamond would actually want a lump like you? I'm not even alive and she wants what I could give her.* Actually, he would never think Diamond was glorious because she wasn't pale. Her thoughts returned to Diamond and her lips and kisses. She shook her head. *No!* She could not let herself get distracted. The fact was the only woman she loved was willing to turn traitor for the suggestion of a few markers. Would a goddess have done that? Did she even know who she had given herself to so eagerly the night before? A flush of shame flowed through her body, squeezing the last few tears loose from her eyes.

She wished she had never come on this mission. Why didn't she stay in Bosch, dreaming of the perfect woman with the flawless face and sparkling jewels, off on an adventure? But here she was, in the bowels of her shitty reality, which also turned out to be fucking cold, and she'd be damned if she would let some power-tripping bureaucrat systematically destroy the lives of so many others. It didn't matter whether Diamond would turn traitor. She had come on this mission to retrieve Aung and his data, and she was damn well going to do it. She would complete her first, last, and only field mission.

She came to Dr. Aung's tent and, using both hands, smeared the tears and snot aside, wiping her messy gloved hands on the sleeves of her parka before leaning in, lifting the tent flap slightly, and calling, "Dr. Aung? Are you in? I have a couple questions," leaving the guard outside in the cold.

CHAPTER 25

Kat, February 10 1600

I'm fifteen, and it's deep summer, past the solstice celebration, so the sun stays in the sky for twenty-four hours, blurring the days together. After supper, Grandma Rina and I walk deep into the woods behind her place picking berries—some to eat now, but most to put up in jams and jellies. The season isn't long, but it is filled with abundance if you know where to look. Grandma and I know.

We pick blueberries, strawberries, blackberries, bearberries, the low crowberries, cloudberries, and even some juniper berries; our hands and mouths are stained purple as we laugh and sing and talk. At one point I accidentally bite my lip near where it is split and swollen from Dad's most recent backhand. "Ow! Damn, that hurt," I complain, gingerly patting the puffy flesh that almost feels like it isn't part of my face.

Grandma Rina comes over and sets her basket down. "Let's take a look." She surveys my injury with a practiced eye, then says, "Well, watch how you chew, girl, and it won't happen again."

I am, after all, fifteen, so I grumble, "Wouldn't be an issue if the old bastard be keeping his hands to himself."

Rina looks at me with sharp, stern eyes. "He's no bastard. I'll have you know, I actually married your grandfather in that cross church over by the sea. Then I danced with him at Beltane and was handfasted. Your dad started growing soon after."

I am mortified thinking of Grandma Rina conceiving a child. "Oh, please, I don't want to think about that." I look offended and cover my ears.

She laughs her joyous laugh and takes one of my hands in hers. "My darling, being body-to-body and soul-to-soul with a person who be making your heart sing be the best feeling in the world."

My face and mood darken. "I don't find no pleasure in it. Cole says good women ain't s'pose to."

Rina wraps me in her arms and pulls me close, giving my long braid a gentle tug. "That's 'cause Cole's your dad and ain't got no business sticking it in you. But men will do as they do, and we women gotta work around the mistakes they make." She moves me away from her and holds my shoulders as she asks, "You taking your tea every morning?"

I nod.

"Same time, 'bout?" Her face, with eyes that mirror mine, is serious.

"Yes, ma'am."

I am pulled back into her embrace where I inhale her—her summer sweat; the powdery, floral scent of her linen dress; the tumultuous mix of all the hundreds of herbs she keeps; and the scent of woodfire. It is the best smell I know, and I sigh and relax into her. But my brain is still chewing on the rage I keep locked mostly down, and the words spill from me. "He's been doing it forever, and I hate letting him and I hate him. When I have enough markers, I be leaving, and I'll never do it again."

Grandma rocks me as we stand barefoot in the woods and shushes me. "There now, my strong Kat. It ain't meant to be so awful. It's only awful when it's wrong. Someday the universe will send you someone who will touch your heart and sing to your soul, and you won't hate it with them."

I don't contradict her, because my dad taught me with a stick to keep a respectful tongue in my mouth, but I think, *Nope, that'll never happen to me…*

"Kat?" Zach's voice rouses me. "Kat? Be you asleep?" An edge of concern shades his voice.

I shake my head to return to the present and turn to see him as a large shadow standing in the doorway of the dim, fragrant herb shack where I sit, lost in the echoes of the past. "What? Oh, Zach. Sorry, there's just so many memories here. I get lost in them."

He steps in and I hear him inhale. "This place holds one beautiful recollection for me."

"Oh? What is it?" I am still half-dreamy from the images and fragrances of long-ago.

A soft laugh and he says, "I never confessed it to you. Yet it be one of my best memories."

Now I am intrigued. "Tell me. Truth."

"Alright, Truth: After you moved in with me, I used to wonder what the two of you got up to on those nights you'd leave to visit her after supper but not come back until after dawn, exhausted and smelling of woodsmoke and herbs. I think I be a bit jealous of the time you took with her. When you were pregnant, I got worried and followed you. I snuck in here and hid, peering out this crack toward the firepit." He runs a finger on a small gap between the rough boards. "And I saw the most magnificent thing: You, with your belly round with our child, naked and dancing and chanting about the fire in the moonlight. Rina be naked as well, which probably should have shocked me more, but I be so entranced with you, I practically paid it no mind. I watched for a good long while, then got myself back home to wait for you to return."

He tells me this with such an air of reverence and awe that I am cast back to that night and can feel the fire on my bare skin. And the story stirs something far back in my own memories, and I hear Rina whisper, *Remember the chant?* I pause for only a moment, then let it tumble from my lips:

"Sing the gifts that the Mother gives
Triumphs, failures, joys, and sorrows.
Twisted braid that forms our lives.
Feel her in our earth's sweet motion,
Mountain streams wend to the sea
Drifting snows dress her curves
The lush of summer speaks of youth
Blood of life stains morning sky
Surging colors splice the heavens
Unite her with the sun and moon
Passion rises, Fury subsides,
Though sorrow deep
Joy still abides.
As through the Fire
We call to Mother
Make us whole,
Be our guide."

I take in another deep inhale of the dusty, pungent air and then let it out. "That was our chant as we paid homage to the Mother around the fire every solstice and equinox. But somehow, I had forgotten it until now."

Zach reaches out to touch my shoulder. "She be a wise old thing."

I laugh. "She was a witch, and we both know it." And Zach laughs with me, looking at me with love. *Oh, Rina,* I think, *help me know how to tell him. I hate that I have to hurt him.*

Once the realization of Zach's feelings came to me at the Polar Star, I knew we had to leave, so I asked him to take me out to where Rina's and Sean's graves lay.

"Sure," he had said. "Haven't been out there in a spell myself. It'll be good to go."

I wasn't sure *good* is the descriptor I would apply. More like necessary. "You said you buried her next to him. Where?"

His answer, "At Rina's old place," was simple, but the anticipation it evoked surged through me, and the pull of longing in my gut and chest intensified the closer we came to what was both home and holy place to the child, Kat Wallace.

He drove out past her house, which lay in ruins, beams charred and roof collapsed, with snow piled in and around it so deep one would barely know it was there. "Lightning strike a few years back," he said in a matter-of-fact tone as I gasped with dismay.

He parked the truck near the tree line and then walked me through the cedars to a small clearing where a low stone fence made a circle. A rough, steep open-walled lean-to stood inside. "I built that so the snow wouldn't fully cover them." He stepped in and his hands moved over the structure. "I fix it every few years. Looks like that'll be a job for me this spring." He offered me his hand as I too stepped into the circle. A small shovel hung from a hook on the roof, and Zach used it to push the snow away until two roundish stones were visible. The light was dim, but I could read them. The smaller one read "Sean Zachariah McKay: 8 months," and the larger one read "Katrina Clinton Wallace: Ageless." I kissed each stone and wept, but my heart was glad to have found them and to know they were together.

As we walked back, I said mournfully, "There is nothing left of either of them in the world. It breaks my heart."

Zach responded, "Not nothing. Look," and he pointed at the herb shack that stood intact with snow all around it. I practically ran to it. Zach helped me drag open the door where the snow held it shut and then said, "I'm going to walk a piece. Take your time."

Now as we stand in one of her sacred spaces, I know she is here. I entreat her aid and her whisper is in my heart, opening yet another memory. I turn to Zach. "Come with me. And grab the shovel." I head out the door.

"Sounds ominous. Should I be worried?" he calls to my back.

I just laugh as I make a lumbering beeline in the deep snow heading for the far edge of the woods, looking for the boulder that has a face. The sun has made a tardy appearance, hanging low in the sky, ready to exit as quickly as it entered from the grey-white snow clouds now pushed up around the mountains in thick drifts. My MC brain thinks of my troopers up there and creates a notation in my mind's calendar to connect with them tonight. But the rest of me is on the hunt as I peek between rough-barked trees and kick at snow-encrusted stones. Finally, I find the old familiar rock and run my hands over its brow, nose, and chin, whispering a hello to its rough surface.

Zach is only a few moments behind me, and he has the shovel, which he presents, his face awash with tenderness. *Don't put this off, Kat Wallace. It'll just get worse,* my better self intones. But the young Northern girl who only wanted to escape the outrages of her home is currently in charge and spots the twin pines, now much taller and broader, that stand in a straight line from my rock's stony nose and practically skips to them. I look over my shoulder, and it's as if I can feel the weight of my long-ago-severed braid on my back as I crow, "This is the spot!"

Zach takes a few steps and is next to me. "The spot for what?"

"You'll see." I start to dig. There's only a dusting of snow here as the trees are thick and provide a barrier, and the surface soil is firm, but not frozen, nestled in as it is near the roots of the pines. It only takes a few shovelfuls of dirt before I hear a scraping and drop to my knees and dig more gently with my hands. Finally, I feel its edge and use my index fingers to make a trench around it, then get under it and wiggle it free. I sit back on the cold, fresh-dug dirt and set the small box on my lap. Zach sits next to me, and his handsome face has curiosity written across it.

I open it and my childhood returns to me. I lift each item. "This is a jar of salve Grandma Rina gave me to use after the first really big beating Dad gave me when I fucked up the plowing at the Broberg place." The next item is barely there and ready to crumble, so I just point at it. "This is a butterfly wing I found the

August after I was eleven. I told Grandma that I want to be able to fly. She said if I wanted it bad enough, it would happen." Her prescience makes my heart feel warm and large. "These are violets that Violet gave me one spring because I took the blame and the beating for getting mud in Dad's boots."

I take out a dozen or so dull circles of metal. "These are coins that some of the womenfolk, your ma included, gave me at the farms I worked." I stir them in my hand. "I thought I was so rich to have this many." I chuckle at the girl's perspective. The last item I remove with utmost care, giving it the reverence it deserves in this moment. "And this is the bouquet of fireweed you gave me that August day we went for that picnic by the lake. You put your arm around me and told me about Marpavik, the coast, and how people from other parts of the world came there sometimes." I look over at him and know it is time. "I fell in love with you that day."

His eyes are tender, and his hand comes up to cup my cheek. "I'd been in love with you since I had walked back into the old place and saw my mother showing you 'the proper way to hold a teacup.'"

I give a small laugh and plumb the depths of his kind, deep blue eyes. "I never stopped loving you. Even when the memory of you was packed away deep in my brain, the love still was there."

He starts to lean in toward me, breathing, "Oh, my sweet Kat...thank the universe you came home."

I lean back, and I see his eyes squint as he is taken by surprise. I'm really bad at this shit. "But, Zach, my world and my life have moved on. I didn't come home. I came to revisit the past and seek justice or, more likely, revenge. And I always—always—intended to return to Bosch, because that is where my home and heart lie. I'm no longer the mistreated waif that I was in Dad's home, but I am also not the partner and mother I was in yours. Those will always be parts of me, but now I am whole. I am Kat Wallace. I am my joys and my agonies. I am my victories and my failures. I am master commander of the Bosch Pirate Force, and I am my

Matty's brightwork girl. You are my past and will always be beloved, but Matty is my present…and my future."

Zach sits back and looks away from me, then tips his head upward, looking into the trees. I sit very still to give him the space he needs. Finally, he speaks, his voice thick with emotion, "I guess I knew that all along, but at least we've had a wild couple days." He finally looks at me and doesn't try to hide the tears that roll down his cheeks into his beard. He stands and brushes himself off before offering me his hand. "You'll be taking the box back to Bosch?"

I shake my head and carefully put the top on it, then nestle it back in the ground; together, Zach and I bury the icons of my past. As we finish, I touch his arm and say with fervor, "Thank you." And there is so much encompassed in those two words—*thank you for rescuing me from the tavern and life with my dad. Thank you for the gift of love. Thank you for the child we both loved who was taken from us. Thank you for not dying, and thank you for letting me go.* I hope he heard each one.

CHAPTER 26

Kat, February 10 1900

I stand frozen at the entryway of Burntback with Anguish, Dread, and Disgust draped about my shoulders. Men's raucous laughter and loud conversations echo over the clinks of beer mugs and shot glasses, betting chips and coins. The place smells of old beer, sawdust, sweat, and ash. All combined, it makes me want to vomit on the floor and then take a torch to the place.

Zach's hand on my arm steadies me. "You ready?" I'm grateful that he doesn't give me any out.

"Yep, let's go." Revenge steps forward girded for battle and stands with their hand on their sword hilt.

Three steps and I am in. The old wood bar, with its many chips, scratches, and rickety high stools, is to my left. To my right are about five mid-sized tables. The place is so small. I could've sworn it was bigger… I don't want to look over by the fireplace at the beat-up armless sofa that was the main location of that gruesome night, but my eyes are pulled there anyway. There's no sofa, just a few stacked chairs with a red rag tossed on the uppermost seat. Somehow that rag catches in my brain, and I can hear my sobs as I begged for them to stop.

My plan is to get in, accomplish my task, and get out. But the past keeps folding itself over the present and confounding my intentions. Pull it together, Kat, I scold myself. This is just another mission. Save the goddamn emotions for Ruth's office. This thought garners insulted looks from several emotions brought to the forefront. I do a quick scan of the room—standard procedure —to locate the mark. As I do, I can hear his voice as I begged for him to make it stop. *It's your own fault. I made you, so you belong to me body and soul. Givin' it away is just like stealin' from your dear old dad. So, now you gotta pay what you owe me. With interest.* The memory of the smell of the local swill mixed with the putrid odor of his filthy mouth engulfs me and threatens to take me down. But my eyes are mission-focused and continue to flick about the room until they land on him. There at the head of the largest table in an oversized wooden armchair, which has been re-fashioned with a high back and flourishes of turned wood on either side so it resembles a throne, and surrounded by his motley court, sits Cole Wallace. Hi, Dad. Ready to die?

He is older, certainly, his face thinner. His hair is sparse; what is there is of it is gray and stringy. There's more of a hunch to his shoulders than I remember, and the arms inside the denim blue shirt seem punier, though it's hard to tell. Seeing his face allows Revenge to step in, though they glance behind themself several times as if listening to something. They push me forward.

I approach the table, and the men look up at me. One fellow comments, "Shit, a skirt and short hair. You a woman trying to look like a man? Or a man trying to look like a woman?"

Another man who is shuffling cards picks up the thread. "Either way, we ain't interested, so fuck off."

I unzip my coat as I say, "I ain't here to answer questions. I'm here to ask 'em."

The entire table erupts in jeering laughter. A third man leers. "It be a woman. Don't stop at the coat, honey. Keep going." The jeering laughter turns ribald.

"Good idea." I drop the jacket and pull both of my pistols in one smooth motion and hold them pointed to the floor, relaxed at my sides. "Now I said I had questions, and I'm gonna ask them of you, Cole Wallace."

The court goes silent, surprised to see a woman holding weapons. Cole, though, he just grins, showing a mouth that is missing half a dozen teeth, the remaining ones in various shades of brown. "Look at that, boys, a bitch that not only stands on her hind legs but does tricks too. Now, you be a good girl and let someone who knows how to handle those sorts of things take 'em." He juts his chin toward the man on his left, who stands to relieve me of my papa's pistols.

It takes only a second to raise and fire them exploding the wooden spindles on either side of the throne. "Thanks. I think I can manage." My hands are already back at my sides, both barrels still vibrating from my shots. The man who stood sits down. The rest of his court sits frozen with wide eyes that contain fear. Good. Cole's face has moved from initial shock to panicked fear to curious assessment.

There is a scrabble of movement behind me, and Zach barks at the bartender, "Put it down, Ruben. I been wanting to shoot you for years anyhow. Don't want to give me even more reason."

Zach's presence pulls Cole's attention for a moment, and he stares at him with contempt. "You taken up with a half-woman now, shit-bag? Guess that tracks."

I want to slap him for calling Zach by that vulgar name, but as he looks back at me, a vague sense of recognition crosses his face. He squints and lifts up the smallest amount from his chair to gaze at me. I keep my face open and expectant while he studies it. A dawning realization creeps over his loathsome features as the his brain slowly peels back the years. He drops back on his damaged throne, mouth agape, as he says in a stunned whisper, "It can't be....Kat?"

"Ding, ding, ding. We have a winner. Glad to see the years haven't robbed you of all your faculties, old man." I look at the round, red-faced man seated to my right who I'm pretty sure was an active participant that night and jerk my head and my right, still-holding-a-pistol hand to the side. "Get up." He does so and moves away, pretty quickly for a man of his age and size. Fear, after all, can be an excellent motivator. I pull the chair to me and spin it, so I can straddle it backward, and I sit with one arm draped over the back, the other still at my side. Every move I make is calculated to scream, *Power*.

Alarm has returned to the old man's eyes, and I am delighted. His skin is sallow, and the whites of his eyes carry a deep yellow cast. "Rotgut seems to be catching up with you," my voice carries a sneer.

He ignores my jab as his mind tries to make sense of the sudden appearance of this ghost. "But you can't be here… It ain't possible."

I scoff. "You worried the traders might ask for their money back, Cole?"

He freezes.

I wave the arm on the chair back, casually causing the men on that side of the table to scoot their chairs back from it and duck. I begin to speak loud enough for the whole busy tavern to hear. "Don't worry, Dad. I'm not holding a grudge. In fact, I'm here for three things and three things only. The first is to thank you. If it wasn't for you abusing me with your filthy fingers and your sad, little dick in my first memories as a little girl and then raping and beating me as I grew, culminating in you selling me to all your rapist buddies…" Now I gesture with my Glock meaningfully at a few of the faces I remember. "…right over there in public that November night, I might not have survived the beatings, rapes, and scarring…" Here I pull up my left sleeve and point first at the scarred circle with a "T" inside it, and then at my throat. "…that I endured as a thrall.

"Secondly, I want to congratulate you. You've tied with my enslaver for first place as the worst piece shit on the planet." I lean in a bit. "I'd suggest you share a congratulatory drink together, but he don't drink no more. Not since I killed him." Not strictly true but a small lie for performative effect seems acceptable.

Now Cole's eyes shift side to side; his face has taken on the look of a cornered beast. But the beast is now old and slow and likely dying from all the drink and Glitter he has poured down his gullet over the years. But even an old sick beast may still have a few tricks, though, so he bears watching. He sits up a little straighter and looks me in the eye, sneering. "You're welcome, Kat. How 'bout you and me share the drink, since he be out of the picture." He raises the small glass of amber liquid in front of him to me in a toast.

Keeping my Glock steady, I wrap the fourth and fifth fingers of my right hand around one of the full shots on the table, lift it, and throw it back without taking my eyes off of him. He follows suit and lets out an exaggerated exhale before gesturing to my left arm. "What's that you got by your brand?"

The question surprises me, probably because my tattoos are such a part of me, that I often forget they are there. But I know the one he means, and I raise my arm with pride. "That is the first tattoo I ever got, the night I graduated and became part of the Bosch Pirate Force."

"Bosch, like the ones that bring the Glitter?"

"Yep. Just like that."

He snorts. "Can't be much of a force if it got women."

"We manage." I will not be drawn into this distraction.

He stares at me and sneers. "And what be number three on your list, Kat? Something you want to do with those shiny pistols you be brandishing?"

"A good guess but incorrect. Killin' you—that'll be a bonus."

"I ain't got time for guessing games, girl. So you tell me the third or get on with it and shoot if that's what you came to do."

Not a bad maneuver to attempt to draw me into reaction. I come to the point. "I want to know, when you sold me to the traders, how much did you get for me?"

"Two hundred markers." He doesn't even try to hide it. Two hundred markers. I made three times that much during my first week out of recruitment. I probably have about that in small markers, crumpled up in the bottom of my black sling bag. Hell, I drop the same amount taking the kids out to lunch in the city.

"Did my sisters command the same price?" I keep my face inscrutable, but inside Fury is tearing up the place, and Revenge has drawn their sword.

Now he scoffs. "Stupid question—more, of course. I got better negotiating with each one. Got a full thousand for little Molly. 'Course, she be a fresh fifteen then, 'cause I ain't had her. They said when I sold Bella that fresh ones get a higher price, so I left her be." He grins a toothless leer and works his tongue around his empty gums.

I am repulsed and horrified, but I control my face and form it into an indifferent sneer. "I used to be so afraid of you. My fear was even bigger than my hate. Now look at you... You're pathetic and not even human enough to feel remorse for your atrocities."

"And why should I feel remorse?" he snaps. "You didn't have to be responsible for feeding and clothing seven brats and a woman. You didn't see your life narrow every time your woman's belly started to swell. All I ever did in this world be work for you kids. Every one of you belonged to me from the moment you be squeezed from your mom's cunt. So what if I used my belongings as I saw fit? That's my perog...pergog... My right." The pitch of his voice builds with his rant and spit flies from his mouth.

My brain nudges me. *What are you accomplishing here, Kat? Just shoot him and be done with it. He deserves to die.*

I flip my safeties off and raise my pistols, so both are pointed at him: one at the heart, and one at the head. I see his eyes widen as men's do when they realize they are about to die. And as they do, the years seem to fall away from him and I see how much he resembles Virgil, then, Sweet New Earth, my own darling Macrae. A tiny gasp escapes me and then my brain is flooded with Grandma Rina's voice: *Sweet Kitten, killing him don't change the past. It just be another burden on your shoulders. It's time to lay it down. Let the burden pass from you. Others can carry it.*

I blink. And just like that, my killing days are done. I see

Revenge sheathe their sword and remove their helmet, and Shame and Fury take a step back and both seem to shrink.

I drop my arms and flick the safeties back on the pistols, holstering them as I stand. I don't even look at Cole, who has not said a word. In fact, the entire fucking torture chamber that Burntback is has slipped into silence.

"You aren't worth it, Cole. Lookin' at you, it's clear you'll be dead before another winter comes. No sense in wasting ammo." Then a thought occurs to me. "But I tell you what. I am putting an embargo on Glitter to the North Country. You'll just have to die soaked in whiskey…without the sparkle."

I turn to leave, taking a few steps to where Zach stands with his rifle loose at his side. "What be you doing, Kat?"

The sigh that escapes my lips seems to encompass my whole being. "I've killed enough people in my life, Zach. It tatters my soul and burdens my shoulders, even if they deserved it. I'm done."

He shakes his head. "I can't say I understand what you are saying, Kat. I've never killed a man."

Lucky you, I think.

Behind me, a voice erupts in a furious whine, "You little slut won't keep me from my Glitter. I need it." The telltale click of a pistol cock makes me turn and start to reach for my own weapons. But my pivot is interrupted by a muzzle blast, and a sting sears into my shoulder. "Wha…?"

Even before I can look down to assess the damage, the brown-haired, bearded father of my first child raises his rifle and pulls the trigger, hitting Cole Wallace squarely in the heart. My eyes widen as he falls, and the pistol he held clatters to the ground.

Carisa, February 10 1900

"No, I will not just sit here for the next week. I am getting out right now!"

Carisa heard Zoya Reeves' raised voice echoing from her room at the very end of the hallway to the door to the unit. Agnes had dropped her off at close to nineteen bells after treating her to a celebration dinner with her husband and youngest child.

"Oh, honey," she had beamed at Carisa, "you did so good." Then she had gone to her room and found a gold chain. "Take this for the pendant. I'll get the broken one fixed, and we'll trade back when you come out with your family at solstice."

Carisa wanted to argue, but seeing her mother's pendant, its stave of protection shining, ready to wear, caused her to hold her tongue. "Thank you, Agnes. I am overwhelmed by your kindness." She fastened it on, then rubbed the surface as if it were a charm.

"It looks beautiful," Agnes said, then giggled and looked at her husband, Josef, who was an attractive man just a few years older than Agnes. "I just want to guarantee a chance to meet this handsome pirate of yours."

Carisa saw Josef roll his eyes with a grin. "You are incorrigible, Agnes. Whatever will I do with you?"

"Whatever you wish," Agnes teased.

With that, their daughter, Sigrid, stood. "It was nice meeting you, Carisa, but I go to my room when they start this talk."

Now Carisa hurried down the hallway toward Reeves' room. She pushed open the door without knocking. "What's going on?" She watched Reeves reaching with her one good arm to undo the ties that held her legs in small hammocks while the nurse and Dr. Mattiasson attempted to stop her.

"Reeves!" Carisa had to shout. "What are you doing?"

Reeves paused her struggles, which caused the doctor and nurse to pause as well. "I am not staying here for a week, Carisa. We need to get that vessel back to the North Country to pick up the MC and the team. I can't believe we can't even contact them."

"Ms. Reeves...," Dr. Mattiasson began.

"Sergeant Reeves," Zoya stated hotly.

"Sergeant Reeves, you just had several major surgeries. You cannot leave right now." The thin woman was taking her stand.

"I was in a wheelchair today for three hours getting scans," Reeves shot back. "I can make the flight to the North Country."

Carisa jumped in. Having accumulated years of experience dealing with Kat, this behavior was a known entity for her. "Reeves, you can't make the trip without me to fly, and I am not flying in the deep dark." She turned to the doctor. "What if I personally guarantee that I will escort Reeves to the Central City hospital in Bosch tomorrow after we retrieve our team members? Could we leave at first light?" Truth be told she was as eager as Reeves to get the team and get home. Having adventures was exhausting.

Dr. Mattiasson frowned. "I am clearly not good at negotiating with pirates. But your terms are reasonable. However, I will be contacting the hospital to be certain Sergeant Reeves arrives."

Reeves crossed her one good arm across her chest and curved her mouth in a skeptical expression. "First light?"

Carisa nodded. "First light."

"Fine." Reeves sat back with a huff. "But only because you're my guardian angel."

Carisa grinned. "Well, this angel needs some sleep."

"Then you should get some." Reeves sat back in her hospital bed still glaring at the doctor and nurse.

"I'll need her discharged just before dawn." Carisa heard her own voice, strong and commanding, and watched as Mattiasson nodded her assent. "'Night, Reeves. Get some sleep yourself."

"'Night, Carisa. See you before first light." Reeves called as Carisa stepped toward the door.

CHAPTER 27

Kat, February 10 1930

"Holy shit, Zach." Not the most erudite phrase to ever cross my lips, but it is all I can muster. One breath in, and I pull my pistols and say to him in a low tone, "Back to back. We need to be ready for retaliation." I glare at Ruben behind the bar, who raises his hands in a surrender motion.

Cole's court is mumbling amongst themselves until the man who sat on his right stands, and the table and tavern go quiet. I look at him, ruddy-faced and a good ten years younger than Cole; he does not evoke any memory of horror. He walks over and peers at the body of my recently departed dad, whose blood has formed a crimson blossom on his chest, and kicks the pistol away, then grunts. "Huh. He drew on a woman with her back turned." He turns his head to where Zach and I stand. "Seems to me it be a just shot, McKay. Man's gotta look out for his woman…" He peers at me as if he is looking at some aberration of nature. "…no matter how odd she be."

I want to protest that I do not need looking out for, nor am I "his woman," but now does not seem the time to parse the issues.

Zach asks, "So we be good, Jobe?"

Ruddy-Face passes his judgment. "Yep. Though I expect you oughta stick to the new place to drink for a spell."

"Understood."

Then Ruddy-Face Jobe turns, pulls out Cole's throne, and seats himself in it, scooting it back to the table and pulling his drink from its previous position. "Doug, Harry, take him back to his place." And Doug and Harry stand, get their coats, scoop up Cole Wallace by his arms and legs, and carry him out of Burntback as the conversation returns to its previous pitch.

The king is dead, long live the king.

Flossie, February 11 0100

She lay alone in the bed that had gone wanting the night before. She ached to wrap her arms around Diamond just once more. But if Flossie was to carry out her plan, she knew that putting her body against Diamond's warm and willing one would dissolve all her determination to move forward.

She had returned from Dr. Aung's tent having made plans for the extraction and found Diamond in tears on the bed. Her heart had leaped. Maybe her lover had reconsidered. Maybe Flossie had got it all wrong.

"I'm back," Flossie had said.

Diamond had looked over and Flossie thought for a moment that she saw joy on the beautiful features. But then Diamond pressed her own hand to that lovely face and when she removed it, her expression was unreadable as she responded, "So are we in then? You know, I was thinking, we can use the resources at BI to really look into your father's markers. Because markers don't just disappear. Someone has them, and you could put a claim on them…"

"No!" Flossie had stormed. "I don't care if there is a way to get all of them. Those markers are dirty, and I don't want them. I am no longer his daughter. I take care of myself, and I would have taken care of you, but you don't want me—I'm not rich, beautiful, or powerful. I am just Flossie Porter, a slightly overweight, plain as a glass of water, really smart tech wonk. But I'm also someone who actually loved you. I came on this mission because of you. Don't you have any interest in seeing it through?"

Diamond now looked past her, eyes cold and indifferent as she shook her head. "You rich folk. Always think you know what's best for the rest of us. Well, Pan is offering me a chance to get ahead and get rich. And it won't hurt anyone. What do I care if the Chinese figure out our fusion engines? Have you ever thought that Bosch is being miserly by not sharing its tech?"

"That's the stupidest thing I've ever heard," Flossie shot back. "You don't know who might get hurt. Look at what she said about Aung's research. Pan doesn't care who starves as long as it's not within China's borders." She threw up her hands. "Listen to yourself. How can you be so selfish?"

"So what if I'm being selfish? Somebody has to look out for me." Diamond's voice was low and fierce. "The mission is aborted. Period. I'm going in a different direction. You make your own choice."

"Believe me, I have," Flossie had spat, a little stunned at how furiously she had stood up to Diamond.

The rest of the day passed in stony silence. At dinner, Pan told them they would be outfitted with small tracking devices in the morning and given instructions for what information to collect and how to make their first communication before being escorted back down the mountain. They were instructed to tell their superiors that Dr. Aung had refused to leave and they had stayed an extra day to attempt to convince him to no avail. Diamond had responded, "That is a reasonable cover story. No one will question it." Flossie had simply nodded.

Now Flossie looked at her timepiece under the covers; it was almost one bell. Dr. Aung would be expecting her within the next thirty minutes.

He had been unsurprised to see her at his tent earlier in the day when she had appeared, tear-streaked but determined, and had hushed her with a hand before beginning to chat with her somewhat overly loud about some details of thermodynamics. He then motioned for her to walk with him toward the experimental tent. He told the guard to stay behind, saying, "You can see us from where you are posted. This way you are not in the wind." The guard gratefully tucked closer to the warm tent.

"I am recorded in my tent and at my workplace," he murmured as they walked through the blowing snow. "This walk is the only secure space."

Flossie spoke quietly, "Do you want to get out? If so, I will take you out tonight."

"I do," he said in a low tone, "but what about my family?"

"You get me the ear comms they confiscated from me and one of the weapons, and I'll get you free and communicate with Bosch to get your family out of Khumi City." She didn't tell him that his family's extraction was likely already underway, if not completed, as this was standard practice in Bosch missions that liberated highly valued assets.

"Done," he agreed. "I will slip you the ear comms at dinner and keep the weapon in my tent. Do not enter my tent, but simply cough twice at the entrance, and I will be ready. What time?"

"Between one and one and a half bells."

The small man looked confused.

"Between one and one-thirty in the morning, okay?"

"Okay."

She slipped out of bed as silently as a shadow and pulled on her coat and boots. She gazed at Diamond in the low lantern light, asleep with her back turned to Flossie, braids loose and scattered. *Maybe she didn't love me, but that doesn't mean I can't love her—warts and all.* She had a sad inward chuckle as she pictured how devastated Diamond would be at the idea of having warts. She reached out a finger to stroke one braid, then pulled her hand back. She pulled one ear comm out of her pocket and placed it on the small table between the beds with a small scrap of paper she had gotten from Dr. Aung on which she had scribbled, "It meant everything to me. Stay safe and stay alive." It was the first time she had used the Bosch saying that unit members used as an invocation to their teammates before going into danger. It felt right. As she settled her goodbye gifts, she saw the embroidered cloth from the night before, now casually draped over the basin. Lifting it to her face, she breathed in its fragrance– the floral of the soap and the traces of Diamond who smelled of strength and safety and friendship and what she had hoped was love, then let her fingers trace the black branch with its red blossoms. On impulse, she stuffed it into her pocket. It would be her talisman, keeping that perfect night sacred, no matter what came after.

Dropping low, she slithered on the frozen ground under the back side of the tent where she had cleared the drifted snow with her foot and kicked loose two pegs earlier. She placed the lone ear comm after standing, noting its empty static, an unsurprising sound here in the mountains where the steep rock walls blocked most signals.

She arrived at the good doctor's tent and coughed. He slipped out carrying a large knapsack. "It has all my notes," he whispered.

Flossie held out her hand. Dr. Aung placed a large semi-automatic pistol in it, and Flossie wrapped her fingers around the weapon. She wished she had asked him to get the IR glasses, but there were priorities. The slip of moonlight would have to suffice.

"Let's go," she breathed. "I know a place we can hide out before we make the vessel—the airship…" She translated the Boschian term for him.

And with that they slipped through the darkness of the sleeping camp and began to make their way up the slope of the mountain, the wind erasing their tracks as they went.

DAY FOUR

CHAPTER 28

DIAMOND, FEBRUARY 11 0730

"I'm telling you; I don't know where they are!" Diamond pleaded, bringing her arms up as far as their bindings would allow in an attempt to protect her head, as the heavy fist of a guard she had not seen on the grounds earlier struck her for the third time on the left side of her face. She let out a deep groan as pain shot through tissue that felt like chopped meat, and she tipped precariously off the chair, only to be caught and settled back, her head lolling on her neck as she tried to get her grounding. *Patience, Di. You can handle this. Wait for your chance. That's your only hope.*

Opening her eyes, she saw where Dr. Pan Qiu stood watching, her face impassive. "Your lover would not go off without your knowledge. We had a bargain. Now where is she?"

She's safe away from you. That's where. That knowledge fired a small spark of hope in Diamond. But surrounding that spark was her own recrimination as she wanted to shriek at her tormenter that she had made a terrible mistake and been cruel to the one human who had seen her as a person–beautiful, real, and flawed–and who still loved her, but she knew it wouldn't matter to Pan. She had managed to tuck the ear comm Floss had left away in a place unlikely to be searched. Not impossible, but unlikely. "I'm telling you, she left without me." Her words were getting thicker as her lips swelled with the punches. But the pain she felt as she said this radiated far deeper than the blows the man's fists had delivered.

Dr. Pan looked at her with a tired expression. "You will adhere to our bargain. We will retrieve Dr. Aung with or without your assistance. But you need more convincing to be open with me." She spoke to the guard, and Diamond had to focus to translate the Mandarin. *Flossie could have done it in a hot second,* she thought as she heard Dr. Pan say, "Guard quarters. Convince her to tell me what I wish. Use any means."

The guard leaned over and lifted her lanky form over his shoulder, but not before leering at her and repeating, "Any means." Looked like her ear comm just might be discovered after all.

Flossie, February 11 0730

"Just a little further, Aung," Flossie urged the scientist as they came out of the woods. "We just have to get to the road. The farm is just up the way." She didn't tell him it would be a three-bell trek.

"I am so tired," the small man moaned. "Just let me sit down."

"No!" She grasped his arm as he started to kneel in the snow and lifted him bodily to his feet, but he was close to frozen, and he responded by lashing out.

"Stop!" He shoved at her, shook his arm free, and began to run back to the woods, with Flossie in pursuit.

I am going to freeze to death out here. I am a really bad field agent. I should have done something else. Her thoughts went to the last time she was cold and tramping through the snow with the boy, Colm. *I should have been a teacher like Eliza.* And with that thought, the puzzle that her brain had been working on all by itself fit the pieces together: Radio-Man. Mr. Z. Cloudberry jam. Neighbor. It was Zach McKay. She felt a moment of triumph at solving the riddle, but that quickly faded back to despair. What did it matter? The next time Zach McKay saw her would be in spring when their bodies showed under the melted snow. Unless wolves ate them.

The idea of wolves sparked a tiny adrenaline rush, and she stumbled along, breaking yet another path in the drifted snow with her tired legs. She was exhausted. And she was starting to hallucinate as voices murmured around her. She stopped and slapped a hand to the side of her head. The murmuring got louder. It was her ear comm. The damned thing had slipped down from her ear, but her hat had kept it from falling into the snow. She jerked her hat off and stuffed the small communication device back into her ear.

"Mission 6412 members, come in. This is base. Report required. Position requested. Repeat, Mission 6412 mem…"

"I'm here. I'm here. Is that you, MC…? I mean, Rosie?" Flossie was breathless.

"Porter? Report please. Where the fuck are you?" It was definitely the MC.

"Almost where Zach dropped us."

"Hang on, we're not far from you. Head toward the farm." The voice ceased and Flossie turned to see Dr. Aung kneeling in the snow a meter from her. She ran and squatted in front of him. "They are coming for us. We will be warm in just a moment." He shivered without speaking, then they both stood and headed toward the road.

CHAPTER 29

Flossie, February 11 0900

"Go through it one more time, troop." The MC sat directly in front of Flossie, who was wrapped in a blanket warmed in the oven with her feet in a basin of steaming water and a half-drunk cup of hot broth in her hands. Somehow, she still felt cold. She looked at her master commander's face. She wasn't smiling but she didn't look mad either; she just looked…serious.

Under the blanket, Flossie fingered the cloth she had retrieved from her coat pocket. "We were captured, and they wanted us to turn traitor, so Diamond and I, —I mean Master Sergeant Miata and I, —came up with the plan to split up and have her pretend to accept their terms while I got Dr. Aung out." It was close enough to the truth, and Flossie just couldn't bring herself to say that the woman she loved actually was a traitor. She looked over to where the little man was bundled on the sofa, near the fire, now warm and blissfully asleep.

Glancing to the MC, she saw the barest hint of an eyebrow flick. "I see. Why didn't you report in?" The question was fired off rapidly.

"Our ear comms were confiscated. When I was able to retrieve a set, I left one for the master sergeant, but they don't work in the mountains—too much interference."

The MC folded her hands in front of her. "Understood, but I was ready to hike up and find you two myself, so figuring out communications needs to be a priority."

Flossie contritely answered, "Yes, ma'am."

"We need to get Miata and get to the vessel. They aren't answering either." Flossie had no idea why the vessel comms would be jammed.

"Kat?" Zach yelled from his radio room, "I got something."

The MC jumped up and took the ear comm from the bearded man. She put it in her ear and listened intently as she walked back toward the fire. Then she said her name and rank and began to speak in rapid and fluent Mandarin, and she did not sound happy. Flossie looked at Zach, who looked equally as surprised. She began to listen closely and caught a few phrases, including, "My trooper…better be intact…international incident... Don't speak to me that way… Your superiors will hear." There was a pause and then a sigh, then, "Big rock near lake…understood. Thirty minutes." She pulled the comm from her ear, and now she did look angry.

"They will exchange Miata for Aung and his materials. This is a total clusterfuck." The MC picked up a pillow and threw it across the room.

"Zach," she called to the man who stood peering out the kitchen window. "We need to get to my vessel, like, yesterday and see what's happening there. I got a hostage exchange to negotiate." She sounded fully disgusted.

Without turning around, Zach answered, "I expect that'll be a challenge. The militia is out front in full battle mode with reinforcements. I think I even see CJ and Ollie."

The MC stood still and then dropped her head back and, with her eyes closed, uttered, "Fuck."

Kat, February 11 0930

I am not happy with how this is playing out, but apparently, my happiness was not part of the mission specs. I will make a note and add it to all future mission specs.

Outside the farm are the dozen Allanavik militia members and about six others, including my two brothers who came from the coast. Chalk up one win for the landlines the North Country has installed. And one clear loss for Zach's fence. I am due any moment at a large boulder by Taseqarna to exchange the little climate scientist for one of my troopers who, according to the woman who had been making cow-eyes at her for the entire start of the mission, was "pretending" to turn traitor. And nobody is answering my comms on the fucking Whydah. I am truly about to lose my shit, but truth be told, this is a fuckload more fun than budget meetings.

Zach, Porter, and Dr. Aung have their coats and backpacks on. Zach holds his rifle, which I now know he is willing to use, and Flossie has her weapon. Zach also has a hunting knife, currently sheathed, strapped on the outside of his coat. They head for the back door. I am on diversion.

I walk out the door. As I step out, the sound of about twenty weapons being cocked and trained on me erupts. I am wearing a skirt with a kerchief around my head. *I'm just a fragile woman, boys, completely defenseless. Keep your eyes on me and don't look over at your vehicles.* I fold my hands in front of me, then reach up to coyly tuck a strand of hair under my kerchief. I wait until I know they're all looking at me. Then, I chirp, "Good morning…? Are you all here for me?" I am concerned that my decision not to kill anymore may have been premature, but here's to hoping.

Some murmurs pass through the group, and CJ and Ollie come forward—or at least I think that's who they are. I jump to get the first word in. "It's been a spell. I barely recognize y'all. CJ? Ollie? The two of you in town for the funeral?"

CJ glowers. "Where's McKay?"

Well, buddy, he's right over there, taking a knife to your tires.

"Don't look at me. Until three days ago, I thought the guy was dead. He doesn't exactly check in with me."

"We got a score to settle with him." This is from Ollie.

I frown. "Seriously?" I gesture to my shoulder. The bullet Cole shot barely grazed it, but it did bleed a fair bit. I kinda hope it leaves a scar. "He tried to shoot me in the back. Court called McKay's a 'just shot.' Besides, you both hated the old man. Maybe not as much as I did, but still plenty. You actually gonna hold it against Zach that he ended the man responsible for your nephew's murder and who sold your sisters into enslavement? Might want to step back from that stance."

The brothers look at each other and say nothing. I reach into my coat and hear some weapons being drawn, but I pull out two half-tin cans with a wick sticking out of each and light them with my lighter. The men all stare, wondering what's happening. I glance up and see the barn door open and the truck roll silently out.

"I'd love to stay, and catch up, but I have an appointment." I take a deep breath and toss my smoke bombs just as three more fly from the window on the driver's side of the truck. The smoke is distracting enough for me to serpentine to the truck, where I pull open the driver's side door. Zach looks at me in surprise. "Scoot over, McKay. I'm driving." He scoots.

I take off wishing it was summer and I could throw dust up in their faces. I think about the Old Days' song where the singer chased his pursuers "just once around the parking lot." Nope, no time. I hit the accelerator and yell, "Hold on!"

Flossie gives a little squeal, or it may have been Aung. Hard to tell. Zach just mumbles over and over, "Odin's Beard..."

A voice speaking Mandarin starts in my ear; I have to press my finger on it to hear over the wind and road noise as we bump along. It's that fucking bureaucrat. "We are waiting. Where is Dr. Aung?"

"Keep your pants on, Dr. Pan. We had a situation here, and we are on our way. Our ETA is less than ten minutes." As I say this, I see the militia trucks limping along behind us, but still in pursuit. I tap Zach's shoulder to get his attention, jabbing my thumb toward the blue-tips as he nods in acknowledgment and holds up his rifle.

"We will wait twelve minutes and then execute Master Sergeant Miata," the voice in my ear says.

I hit a large hillock of snow, and the truck goes airborne for the briefest second, evoking yells from all my passengers. I respond to Pan, "Yeah? Well, you better be bluffing because if she is harmed, I will personally hunt you and your family down. I've decided not to kill anyone, but I've got some tools in a cave I know that will make you beg me to reconsider my choice. Savvy? Don't fuck with me."

There is a pause, then, "We will expect you in fifteen minutes. Miata will be alive."

"Damn straight she will be."

I turn the truck down the water path. It is uneven, narrow, and not made for vehicles. I swerve in and around trees that brush the top and sides of the truck with branches dropping snow that obscures my view despite the wiping blades. I bring us to a sharp stop as the path narrows beyond what even I consider safe. "Gotta hoof it from here."

"Thanks be," Zach says and I roll my eyes. The four of us head down the path. We cannot run full out because Dr. Aung is in no shape for that, but we move steadily along. We come to the clearing ready to board the Whydah. Flossie and I stop in our tracks, as the two men continue down the path. My communication conundrum has been solved.

Zach turns and sees the two of us standing and staring. He jogs back while Dr. Aung stands on the path toward the lake looking back at us. "What's the holdup, Kat? We need to get to your vessel."

I look at him and point to the small clearing where snow and leaves are packed down, but the space is empty. "This is where I parked it. But it ain't here now."

CHAPTER 30

Carisa, February 11 1015

Kat's voice crackled over the vessel comm. "Carisa! Reeves! Where the fuck are you? Where's the Whydah? We have a situation here, and I kinda expected to find my vessel where I left it!"

Carisa looked over at Reeves, who sat in the electric wheelchair, both legs extended in stiff casts and her casted right arm elevated to shoulder height and bent at the elbow. "What do we do?" Carisa's voice held concern.

Reeves gestured at her body in a circular motion with her one good arm. "That's a damn good question. I'm at a bit of a disadvantage here. You're going to have to handle this. You may have to fire on the locals."

"Shoot them?"

"If you have to, you have to," Reeves reasoned.

Carisa didn't mention that while Aaron had taught her to fly, he had only shown her a demonstration of the railguns. When they flew together, it was for fun. They had flown over Bosch and played with the telescopic camera to look down on children playing and people on boats. The camera on these things was impressive; they had even seen a couple lovemaking on the deck of a small sailboat. Carisa remembered Aaron's bawdy laugh when the image appeared. She had slapped his shoulder good-naturedly as he zoomed in and insisted he turn it off. After an affable and spirited argument about the morality of voyeurism, she had offered up a bargaining chip he couldn't resist, and they had reenacted the scene on the flight deck soon after. She was pretty sure Arthur had been conceived that day.

Thinking about the camera spurred an idea. "Reeves, there's a loudspeaker, right?"

Reeves' worried look shifted to one of puzzlement, but she said, "Sure, we use it to communicate with locals on the ground sometimes. But from what you've told me, these folk are not inclined to negotiate with foreigners."

Carisa was biting her lower lip as she thought. "Nope. They are a bunch of conservative, dogmatic, superstitious provincials." Her quick mind began to review the reading and research she had done on the history of the North Country once she knew she was making the trip. This might just be an opportunity for her soft spot for the mythology and stories of different cultures to pay dividends. She considered her options. "I need to take us up far enough so we are barely visible. Can we use the speaker if we go up to the altitude limit?"

"FL15?" Reeves shook her head. "Not if we are moving, but if we put her on hover, we could drop the micro-speaker if I add a good length of stiff wire."

"How long would that take?"

The dark-haired woman scratched her head. "I'm one-handed here."

"I can help, if you tell me what to do."

"Okay, let me get supplies and I'll bring them up to the helm."

Reeves appeared with tools and wire in a matter of minutes and gave Carisa directions to hold pieces together while she attached them. "Okay, that should work. What are you planning?"

"I am planning to use their faults against them." Carisa hoped against hope this would work, "Get it ready to…ahhh, drop?"

"You mean deploy."

"Yeah, deploy."

Reeves saluted very gently with her only good limb. "Aye-aye, Mrs. Morton. Be aware, even with the high-speed winch, it will take a few minutes to get the speaker to operative level."

Carisa took a breath and began to increase the Whydah's altitude, watching the gauges. Most of the time the FL, or flight level, was about nine kilometers, though Aaron had told her the Whydah's could go up to fifteen kilometers. And the new 2070s could reach even higher. "I'm taking her to twelve and a half. That way we have wiggle room." As the vessel ascended, she reviewed her plan.

"Roger that." Reeves had wheeled herself back to the flight engineer's post.

Once Carisa hit her altitude, she shifted the Whydah into hover mode and pulled up the camera image. She could see the lake and a large object with a moving mass approaching the stationary one, but it was less clear than when she and Aaron had played with it. *You're up higher, 'Ris, make the corrections,* she reminded herself.

Zooming in and focusing, she saw the mass was a group of more than a twenty people—they couldn't be her folk. Another, smaller group of perhaps seven or eight moved from the right, coming out of the forest. Was that them? No, too many bodies. A slight motion behind the stationary object caught her eye, and she directed the camera in that direction. What came into view was a large boulder, dropped at the lake's edge by the ancient glaciers that used to cover the North Country. More zoom and a focus adjustment confirmed four figures pinned down behind the giant stone. Those had to be her people: Kat, Flossie, Diamond Miata, and the scientist the BI troopers had come to liberate. "Okay, drop—I mean, deploy—the speaker," she called to Reeves.

Carisa's knees bounced as she waited for Reeves to give the signal that the speaker had reached its operative level. She knew she couldn't use the comm to alert Kat and utilize the speaker at the same time, so she just had to hope that Kat would play along. "My turn, my friend," she whispered, fingering her pendant.

She cleared her throat and spoke into the microphone in her most melodious voice, "People of Allanavik, hear me." She paused, looking at the screen. The two larger groups had ceased moving and shifted about as if looking around. She sure hoped that superstition did indeed reign supreme down below.

"I am Ataksak, Goddess of the Sky. For too long, I have ignored my sweet earth-bound creatures. But no more. I have sent four emissaries, selected from all the peoples of the earth, to walk among you and see if you are worthy of my love, or if instead…" Here Carisa dropped her voice to use the reproachful tone she occasionally used with Arthur. "…you are to receive my wrath."

Carisa glanced back to the flight engineer. Reeves was staring at her wide eyes. She mouthed, "Are you kidding me?" Carisa shrugged.

She thought wildly of what a sky goddess's wrath would be. "If my emissaries are harmed, I will cover myself and my lover, the Sun, and the eternal ice will return to the world. It will not stop at the North Country. No, I will turn my lover's face away from the whole of New Earth, and there will be such cold and ice that no living thing will survive." Her voice boomed within the vessel, and she sure hoped it had the same impact below.

She was quite impressed by her goddess's cruelty. *Enough stick, now carrot,* she thought. Her voice softened. "But if my emissaries return to me and speak favorably of the North, I will ask the Sun to take the North Country as our third lover, and we shall bestow it with the heat of our passion, warming the earth, bringing the gentle rains, and providing for a bountiful harvest year upon year upon year until your children's children's children will be revered as the blessed of New Earth." She realized it was a bit of a reach to credit the harvest to the sky goddess, but she hoped the earth goddess would cut her some slack. She checked the camera; the dozen were milling about, and several had moved over to the smaller group, enfolding them, until both groups melded. But they had stopped closing in on her comrades. They were listening. A bit more push.

She considered that she had cast out her own demons this trip; she might as well try to cast out a few others. "Return to your village, people of Allanavik. Spread my word. Respect the old ways. Revere the color of the sky and its reflection in Tassy-Canner. Cast out those self-serving fools who would subvert my magnificent hue to bring hatred and evil among you. I do not wish to turn my lover's face from you. I wish for the North Country to join the virile Sun and I in our bed to bring a bountiful and teeming harvest to each one of you." She flicked off the microphone and turned back to Reeves, who was still staring open-mouthed. "Can you amplify this more?"

The flight engineer took a moment to respond, "Not without some significant reverb."

Carisa grinned. "Oh, that's perfect. Do it."

A few flicks of switches, and Reeves pointed her one good finger at Carisa. "Go."

"Obey Ataksak, Goddess of the Sky now, people of Allanavik! Or I shall call upon the creature that lurks in Tassy-Canner!" Carisa thought she just might like being Ataksak. She wondered whether there was a call for sky goddesses as a career.

The camera showed a few splintering off and heading back toward the village, but most still simply milled. Carisa took a breath. Time for a show of power. She had only one trick Aaron had shown her when they flew out over the ocean. She took a moment to remember the steps he had taken, then called up the weapons system and put in coordinates just off center in the lake. She pushed the button for the left railgun; it fired, and she watched with glee as a tremendous splash emanated up from the lake, raining water all along the shore. The large mass of people now splintered, and all the individuals save one began to run for the village. One ran straight for the rock, but Carisa knew Kat could deal with a single foe easily.

"Respect and revere me, people of Allanavik. I will speak to the Sun, and we will be watching to see if you are worthy of our love." *Nice closing, Ataksak,* Carisa thought and turned off the microphone. She directed Reeves to pull up the speaker.

The sergeant had started laughing the moment Carisa's finger had hit the off switch on the mic and now gasped out between convulsions of delight, "You mean, retract, oh, Ataksak, revered sky goddess?"

Carisa giggled. "Retract, then, oh, colleague of Ataksak." And she provided a circular flourish with her hand.

As soon as the crowd was completely out of sight, she circled the Whydah in a large loop, dropped her altitude, and landed neatly on the lake, taxiing to the shore where she dropped the ramp. Five dripping-wet individuals, all wearing astonished expressions, walked onto the Whydah. First came Flossie, holding a large knapsack and leading a small West Continent man who had to be Dr. Aung. Behind them came Diamond Miata, who stood apart from Flossie and kept her eyes cast down at the deck. She looked stricken, beaten, and disheveled. The last up the ramp was Kat, accompanied by a large, bearded man with brown hair and a hunting rifle who looked about the vessel with keen eyes and an expression of admiration. Kat did not seem concerned with the presence of an armed local, and he did not appear threatening.

"What the hell was that, Carisa? And where the fuck have you been, Sergeant Reeves?" Kat scolded. Then her face dropped as she took at Reeves' state and at Carisa's position at the helm. "What happened to you? And what are you doing there?"

Carisa beamed. "The sky goddess has had herself an adventure. I'll tell you all about it on the flight home."

CHAPTER 31

Kat, February 11 1100

I survey my people in the wake of our rescue.

Carisa is cleaning Diamond Miata's wounds, dabbing antiseptic where appropriate and generally ministering to the injured woman. Diamond is now only in name as all of the jewels that were outwardly visible—and almost all the others, according to the master sergeant—are gone, stripped from her by the guards who raped and tortured her. The emperor and I will have words about this, among other things.

I come close but not too close, and I don't touch Miata. I've been in her place: any touch after assault can re-invigorate the trauma. I recall Teddy instructing me in how to approach traumatized troopers: *Show 'em some respect, troop. Build 'em up a bit before you ask any questions.* "I saw your escape, master-sergeant– one guard down with a kick, another with those hammer-hands–quite effective, even though your arms were bound. Also, nice embrace of the opportunity as the water exploded. The Force is fortunate to have a trooper like you." Her nod of acknowledgement is weak. I kneel so I am level with her gaze, and my voice softens, "Diamond, you are safe now. Bosch takes care of its own." The abused master sergeant just glances at me with a far-away expression and then looks away.

It is notable to me that it is Carisa performing these tasks, not Sergeant Porter. In fact, Flossie Porter has said little to Miata, beyond an initial, panicked "Oh, Di, what did they do?" when Miata first stumbled over to us behind the boulder after her well timed run from the Chinese. Since then, Flossie has been either gazing out the vessel windows or speaking earnestly with Zach, who appears to have a willing ear.

Dr. Pan commed me soon after she was able to calm her guards, post the show of angry power from our resident "goddess." Get this—she still wanted to make the trade.

I spoke in pure FA, partly as a power play and partly so I could use all my vernaculars. "Maybe you don't understand how negotiation works, Doctor," I had said with a grin as I glanced over to where Dr. Aung was sound asleep. "Both parties need to bring something to the table, and I'm afraid your table is pretty fucking bare. Enjoy your position for the next few days. I'm taking my trooper's treatment real personal, and I expect you may be looking at some work camp time. But, hey, it'll be better than running into me at a state dinner since I have decided you are an exception to my no-kill policy." She isn't, but she doesn't know that.

I turned her off to chat with Reeves for a moment. She explained to me her fall, but has been closed-mouthed about what happened after.

"Carisa will explain it all," she said with a mischievous grin that I would not expect to see from a person with her injuries.

I take a breath and continue on my rounds, walking over to where Zach and Flossie are deep in conversation. It's going to be hard to say goodbye to him; I never got to the first time we parted. I look at Sergeant Porter. "I need you to take your post. We'll be leaving in a few minutes." The BI trooper looks at me and then at Zach, who appears to give her a silent nudge.

"What's going on?" I ask.

Nervous, the young woman's hands finger an embroidered cloth that she grips as she says, "I'm not leaving. I'm resigning my post and staying here."

"Excuse me, what?" I am flummoxed.

"Ma'am, I love Bosch, but Bosch doesn't need me." I watch as her eyes cut over for a split second to where Trooper Miata sits before she adds, "But here…ma'am, they don't let the girls go to school, and they barely school the boys. Eliza, she's Zach's neighbor that I helped out that first night. She's a schoolteacher. She and Zach had the idea of starting a secret school, and I want to help. I could maybe piece together another radio from the pieces Zach has and possibly even get a two-way radio built. That'd be great for the kids."

I look at Zach and his hands go up. "She has skills that are unique, and she seems real motivated. I could add a room at Eliza's… I need to go over and rebuild their chimney." He glances at Flossie as he says this, and she looks positively misty.

I look at Sergeant Flossie Porter, whom I truly admire, and say very quietly, "A broken heart can heal in Bosch just as easily."

Both her hands grasp that cloth she holds as if it were a lifeline. Her eyes blink quickly as she answers, "Yes, ma'am. But I think making a difference here is important."

I consider the proposal, and without saying anything I turn and, grabbing a bag, I move to chat with Reeves, who wheels over to those secret places flight engineers stash equipment and brings me what I requested. I stuff a couple more items in and return to where Flossie Porter sits. "No, Sergeant Porter, I do not accept your resignation from the Force. Bosch does need you. You are a valuable member of our Intelligence team and as such, we do not wish to part with you." She looks stricken, but I continue. "You are henceforth on special assignment as our North Country agent. I will leave you with the SatComm and chargers. Perhaps Mr. McKay can rig up some electrical options?" Zach nods and looks very happy with his assignment.

"Additionally, Sergeant Reeves has added in a couple two-way radios that you can use as prototypes and for parts. We also dropped in one of the older computing devices. Not much use without a signal, but I imagine that you are up for the challenge. I will expect quarterly reports on your progress as well as intelligence on any further Chinese incursions in the North Country. Good luck getting along with some of these troglodytes, and know that in a pinch, Mr. McKay is an excellent shot." In response, Zach snorts a small laugh.

Flossie probably stopped listening to my excellent patter at "special assignment." She says breathlessly as I hand her the bag, "Yes, ma'am. Thank you, MC."

I feel as if I am sending a little one off to boarding school. "You're welcome. Now go say goodbye to Carisa and your... friend?" I flash her a knowing look that causes her cheeks to grow pink.

She stands and takes a step, then turns and says in a low voice, "Ma'am, about the master sergeant..."

I cut her off. "Flossie, I have been around the block more than a few times, and I have pretty good instincts about whom to trust. Torture and abuse can be an excellent smokescreen for betrayal. I will not risk Bosch's security. But thank you for considering it first."

She presses her lips together. "Yes, ma'am. You're welcome, ma'am," she says, then moves off to say her farewells.

I look at Zach, and I am unsurprised to feel my eyes fill with tears. "What's going to happen with the militia?"

Zach raises his eyebrows. "You so emotional over the militia? They be after you, not me. And I can manage CJ and Ollie."

"Yeah? I expect you can." I pause and ask in a roguish tone, "But can you manage Eliza, Mr. Fix Her Chimney Man?"

He actually flushes. "Well, we'll see. Hopefully, I ain't fumbled it completely. And I have you to thank for it. You reminded me what it means to live, Kat. And what it means to love. I won't be forgetting that."

My heart swells with his words. "I hope it works out for you.

Maybe I could meet Eliza someday. And I have you to thank for giving me back my North Country memories of love and joy, not just of pain. And also for keeping me from getting shot...too badly." I ruefully rub my bandaged shoulder.

Zach looks at the deck. He takes in a deep breath and as he lets it out, reaches into his coat. "Speaking of memories, I thought you should take one of these with you." In his hand are two tiny, white, hand-knit baby socks.

I cannot speak at first, only softly keen "Oh, oh, oh" over and over as I reach with one finger to touch these garments I made for my son so long ago.

"I remember we put them on him the day he was born because it was such a cold day. I figured you could keep one, and so could I, and that way..." His voice breaks.

I take one of the wee stockings and hold it first to my lips, then to my heart. Then I fall into Zach's arms for an embrace, and we part as we met, remembering the boy who was stolen from our lives.

Flossie comes up with her kit and stops, unsure where to look.

Zach steps back from me, his fingers wiping the tears from my cheeks. "Goodbye, Kat Wallace, for now."

I take a breath and replicate the gesture on his cheeks. "Goodbye, Zach McKay, for now."

The trooper and my ghost-made-flesh walk off the ship, and I move to the helm, check they are a safe distance away, and then survey my abbreviated crew at their posts: behind me, a one-handed, triple casted flight engineer; on the left rail-gun, a bandaged, beaten gunner who can't seem to stop tears from running down her cheeks; and to my right, in the navigator's seat, a small, blonde civilian wearing a gold necklace and looking for all the world like a sky goddess.

"Ready to go home?" I ask, and start to move the Whydah across the water of Tassy-Canner as we prepare to lift off and return to Bosch.

ACKNOWLEDGMENTS

What a lovely journey it is to write a novel. What starts with a whisper and an idea, slowly develops into a full fledged story, complete with humor, drama, adventure and a chance to watch characters you love grow in unexpected ways.

My list of people that I am grateful to for their support during this book's development and birth continues to grow to include those who have lent their support since I first began my author journey and those who have stepped in to make *North Country* the treasure it is.

Martha Bullen, my book coach turned dear friend, has once again kept me on track and made sure I kept to my timeline, even if I did shift it by several months.

My cover guys, Alan Hebel and Ian Koviak, of The Book Designers have, as always, come through with a magnificent cover. Thanks to them for both their talents and their responsiveness.

My amazing regular editors, Dave Aretha and Andrea Vanryken, whose insights always improve my writing, were joined by a new editor, Rebecca Maizel, who did a magnificent job evaluating the *North Country* manuscript and making astute recommendations to create a more vibrant, readable story.

Kudos to Maggie McLaughlin who takes care of dealing with Amazon and Ingram uploading for me and is a deadeye markswoman when it comes to troubleshooting.

Special thanks to my readers, Cori and Darcie, who opened up to me about their personal experiences with MS and provided early reader feedback. Their invaluable input made Carisa's journey with UN authentic and relatable.

I also want to thank Paulette for providing guidance to show Diamond as a complex and complicated woman who is much more than her skin color and looks.

Sending out loads of gratitude to my author readers who graciously gave of their time to read and endorse *North Country*.

I cannot thank my early readers/street team enough for their commitment to spreading the word about *North Country* via word of mouth and social media. Your help is invaluable in a world where so many books appear on the horizon each day.

Thank you to those that have given me an opportunity to talk about my work whether via podcasts, classroom talks or book groups. (Yes, I can show up at your book group and answer question!! Just ask!)

Thanks to my children: David and Jana, Megan and Josh, Daniel and Jansu for all the love and support you all provide me. And love to my grands: Jude, Will, Ezra, Desmond, Julian, and Dilara–your love of story brings me joy.

And of course, all my love and appreciation to Rick, because he is the lodestar of my life.

ABOUT THE AUTHOR

Sarah Branson is the award-winning author of the four-book *Pirates of New Earth* series. She began conjuring stories of pirates at seven years old when her family hopped a freighter to Australia. Since then, she has grown up, traveling the globe, raising a family, and working as a certified nurse midwife.

Through these experiences, she has developed a deep appreciation for people's strength and endurance and believes that badass women will inherit the earth.

For more information and updates:

www.sarahbranson.com

ALSO BY SARAH BRANSON

Pirates of New Earth Series

Book One: A Merry Life

Book Two: Navigating the Storm

Book Three: Burn the Ship

Book Four: Blow the Man Down

The Legacy of Bosch

Unfurling the Sails: A Grey Shima Adventure

A Pirates' Pact: A Kik & Mac Adventure

Anthology

A Million Ways: Stories of Motherhood

WANT TO READ ABOUT HOW KAT'S ADVENTURE BEGAN?

A Merry Life: Book 1 of Pirates of New Earth

Kat Wallace is on a mission. After escaping tortuous enslavement, she sets her sights on ending the human trafficking that has flourished in 24th century Earth.

Adopted by the leader of the pirate nation of Bosch, Kat Wallace is determined to prove herself as a member of the Bosch Pirate Force and use her skills to avenge her enslavement and free other thralls.

But unexpected love and a test of loyalty threaten to rob her of what she wants most: a home.

A MERRY LIFE

CHAPTER 1: FREEDOM

Bellcoast Island: Late Spring, 2349

Dying is not an option. At least not today. Freedom is my only goal.

The sky is a brilliant blue. I half-hear the ever-present, plaintive cries from the seabirds. Sweat forms under my braid as the late afternoon tropical sun slants down on my bare neck. Earlier, the sun was more intense. Now it is dipping toward the horizon, and the sea breeze cools me a bit as we walk the dusty road away from our long day at the crowded marketplace. Carisa and I were sent, ostensibly, to buy landscaping supplies and seeds for the late spring garden. Carisa just arrived here a couple weeks ago in the most recent thrall coffle and was assigned to me. She's just a bit younger than me. She'll be twenty in the summer and nice enough. Petite and blonde, she is the closest thing to a friend I have found here. I take care of the gardens at the villa. My talent for caring for green, growing things was noticed a couple weeks after I arrived here in Bellcoast almost a year and a-half ago. Old Dorothy had told them about it because I had talked with her about her herbs. Working in the gardens kept me safe for several weeks. Until He noticed me.

Though we purchased seeds and mulch and tools that the guards hauled back to the villa for us, they certainly didn't have us dress like gardeners. No, given our filmy, sheer, and floaty attire, I suspect we had been sent to the marketplace to drum up another kind of business. I saw the guards handing out His card and talking price. But I don't plan to be around the villa tonight to receive any of His visitors. In fact, I don't plan to ever spend another night on this island.

I eye Carisa as we walk a distance behind Alexi, our guard. His laziness is to our advantage. I pull in a quick breath, and then I nod at her. Her face goes tight, and her eyes widen. She pulls in a breath as well, and her lips press together, probably mirroring the way mine look. She nods back. I pull the rock I had hidden away from my pocket and heave it toward the home to my right, shattering a window.

We run. I've watched Alexi enough to know it will take him a few moments to realize we're gone. He's big and strong but as slow and stupid as geese, so pulling his attention from the broken window and the ensuing chaos long enough to realize we aren't there will take a while. Dashing back to the marketplace, I try to get us lost among the people, but the crowds have headed home. Now, just a few people remain, mostly merchants checking out their competition. They won't help, being as terrified of Him and His guards as the thralls are.

"Is he following us?" Carisa pants. She's so petite, her blonde head only reaching just past my shoulder, so the words seem to bubble up from below me. I glance down and shrug, then grab her arm and hustle her with me.

"Hey, don't go away so fast...," some trader calls after us in a slurred voice. I dodge to the left into the nearest tent stall and drag Carisa with me into the darkened interior, putting a cautionary finger to my lips as we sink down and creep beneath the counter. The trader stumbles past, calling, "Girlies..." I hear him trip on something inanimate and swear, then apologize to the stick or the rock that tripped him up. He obviously had his rum with a side of Glitter. I hear him heave himself up and stumble farther away. Time to move.

I tug at Carisa's arm, but she pulls away, and I can just see her wide eyes through the dim light filtering in through the coarse cloth curtains of the stall. I reach out to touch her shoulder and realize she is stiff from…what? Fear? Resolve? No, it's fear; that's what her eyes say.

"C'mon." I breathe the words as quietly as possible. She shakes her head, her fine features rigid with terror.

"I'm staying." The words come from her at almost a regular volume, so they sound blaring given our previous whispers and silence.

"Shhhhhh," I caution and keep my voice as low as I can. "We have to get to the airfield."

"I can't run. I'm going to hide. Like a rabbit."

The image bothers me for some reason, and I shake my head vigorously. Not only to disagree but to clear the picture. "They'll find you." I tug once more at her. "They'll hurt you." She just shakes her head slowly.

I glare at her. How can she be a quitter? She came to me to escape, for New Earth's sake, not the other way round. Apparently just being willing to run counted me as an expert, no matter how often I was hauled back or how much the punishments escalated. I put my hand to the unhealed wound that runs from my left ear to my right collarbone. I can't get caught this time. I stand up and make for the next stall over, leaving Carisa huddled in her hiding place.

"Mary! Anne! Where the fuck are you two? Get your worthless asses out here, now!"

My breath draws in as I hear Alexi's voice, which is as big as he is, booming ever closer around the quickly emptying marketplace as he searches…for Carisa and for me. Of course, he uses our thrall names. They don't even know our real names. We aren't even allowed to use them with other thralls, though Carisa told me hers when she first arrived.

"Worthless," Alexi said of me. Maybe. I mean, certainly, my dad told me that often enough. "Worthless girl," he always said. It's likely true, but still, I can recognize an opportunity when one is presented, and this is an opportunity. Alexi has lost sight of me. Again. And of Carisa. I should go back. Convince her to run. I know they'll find her there. I tried hiding the first time, too. They find you and they make you pay.

I'm standing as still as I can next to the stucco wall, half-hidden in the afternoon shadows. The marketplace may be almost empty now, but the smell of old oil and herbs and the heavy, sugary stench from the various food vendors mixed with sweat and pee and the sour, dusty smell from the never-washed drapes of the stalls permeate the air. Over it all is the smell of the sea. Bellcoast isn't a big island, so the ocean is ever-present, and I can hear the surf on the rocks that border the town beach. The smell of fish hangs in the air. My heart is pounding, and my cheeks are getting warm even though the spring day is a bit chilly. *Slow your breathing. Keep quiet. Think. Which way to run this time?*

I put my hands over my chest and throat, trying to muffle my heavy breath and pounding heart. It is so loud to me. Can Alexi hear it as well? I imagine him moving among the stalls, lifting curtains and waiting to grab me and drag me back to the villa. I just have to be patient and quiet.

I won't be caught this time. I am going to live through this. I am getting away. I look cautiously around the wall and move quickly behind the nearest curtain.

I hear Alexi yell and then a scream. Carisa's scream, which after some scuffling is cut off with a sickening thud and then a grunt. I can almost see Alexi bodily tossing Carisa's unconscious form over his shoulder. He'll be back for me in a moment. Time to move.

I glance around and see that Morris, the lazy metalsmith, carelessly left a bag behind. His sloppiness is my good fortune. I spy a metal cup glinting in the bag and grab it. It's heavy, more like a club than a cup. Might come in handy, though. Maybe I could use it to bargain with traders. I drop it into my skirt pocket and feel the fabric sag with the weight of it. I slide quietly from Morris's stall over the cobbles to the next stall heading toward the gap between the marketplace and the landing area, where the airships are parked. The airships: They're my chance for freedom.

As I start to move to the next stall, I see Alexi, unexpectedly back and closer than I had imagined, peering into the stalls. I gasp a little and push myself backward, trying to become part of the wall.

The head of the guards, whom I have dubbed Henry the Bastard, must be beside himself. He hates me because of all the times I've run. I think it reflects badly on him. Boo-hoo. Henry would love to personally break my neck and would have if The Boss hadn't given specific instructions that He would dole out the punishments to me Himself. Maybe a broken neck wouldn't be so bad. I shut my eyes and drop my hands to my side. I feel the cup and draw it out. A sense of resolve rises in my chest, and I set my jaw. Well, if dying is back on the table, I won't go passively, like they would expect a thrall to. No, I'll go like the free woman I am meant to be. I slide behind the fabric of the stall.

Alexi is a big man, heavily muscled, but he has vulnerable points, and he won't be expecting me to attack. I make a little mantra in my head as I wait: his face, his balls, his face, his balls.

I see his feet come into view, and I pull in a deep breath as if I'm about to jump into the pool I used to swim in back in the North Country. How long ago was that? I see the fabric shift as he lifts it, exposing my hiding place.

"There you are, Mary!" He has a self-satisfied look on his face.

"My name's not Mary, asshole." I growl the words as I swing the cup as hard as possible at his temple and feel it make contact with a dull thump, while at the same time shoving my knee hard up and in between his legs. He groans a little and drops to his knees and falls forward on his face. For a moment I want to whoop a victory, then I turn and start to run, the cup clattering as it falls to the cobbles.

I hear someone running toward me from the direction I am headed, so I dodge into a stall closer to the edge of the market, on the airfield side. This is the herbalist's booth. The rough wooden walls have nails in them, and they smell pungent and bracing from the bunches of herbs that recently hung in there. It reminds me of my grandmother's place in the North Country. I hope she is in the air here and will protect me. I'm her namesake, after all. I duck down in the corner.

Footsteps, first quick then slowing. Henry and others are looking just for me by now. Get smaller. Keep your head down. Don't move. It's so dim in here, but sweat is accumulating under my hair, and I can feel it soaking my tunic in the front. A musty, dirt smell seeps into my nose, and there's a tickle, so I open my mouth to avoid a sneeze. The footsteps are getting farther away. Time to move.

I don't want to be seen, so I crawl to the next stall and feel the jerk as my hand catches on my braid that has fallen forward. Fucking hair. Blowing out a disgusted snort that I immediately try to silence, I grab the broad coil and stuff the end inside my tunic. The hard, packed earth of the marketplace is fairly even, but I feel some small rocks under my knee. I peer—nobody to the left. I shift my gaze. Nobody to the right. Go. I crawl forward.

Dammit. A sharp pain in the ball of my left hand. Oh, fuck. It's bleeding. There's a big shard of broken glass in the dirt. I grab it with my right hand and hold it up and away from the ground and dodge into the next stall. I kick at the dirt behind me to obliterate the blood smears. Leaning back against the stall corner, I drop the shard in my pocket and pull out the blue kerchief and wrap my hand. I pull the shard back out and stare at it. It's about as long as my palm and comes to a point, which is what punctured my palm. It's sort of a triangle shape with two thicker, smooth sides and one edge that is irregular and sharp. I turn my head, feeling my hair shift where it lies in my top. I look back at the glass blade in my hand. I hate my braid. It was the only part of me my ineffectual mother ever complimented. It's what He admired and would grasp during those horrible times. I shake my head to avoid remembering too much. But the anger is there, and it takes control of me.

I grab my thick braid with my wrapped left hand and pull it taut against the wooden beam of the stall. I raise the glass shard and start to saw at it, the tip of my tongue firmly in the left corner of my mouth as I concentrate. I get a rhythm going: "Fuck you, fuck you, fuck you," as I saw, my anger keeping me focused. The individual hairs release under the shard's edge as I work it deeper into the plait. My shoulders feel strained and awkward. My left shoulder is pushed down to make space to cut while my hand keeps pulling the braid a little farther as I reach the halfway point. My right shoulder keeps moving my right arm up and down, up and down.

The air is dry and dusty as I pant with my mouth open as I cut and sweat stings my eyes. I'm thinking of a plan. I feel the hair separate more, and I pull the remaining twisted hanks over my right shoulder and up to my face, sawing more furiously until the hair comes away in my hand, and my head tips backward now, unencumbered by the heavy weight. Free. I slice the bracelet from around my wrist and let it drop to the ground, then pull the green ribbon from the pocket I keep wrapped around my waist and drop it into the dust as well.

Peeking over the edge of the counter, I take my disembodied braid and pin it with the shard to the corner post at my head level. *Maybe. Might work.* Old Dorothy would be proud of the deception. The first day I arrived at the villa, she was in the kitchen garden walking backward in her footprints when she picked her special herbs: "It looks like I just flew away!"

I reach for the curtains of the stall. The blue fabric stops me for a moment as it pulls the image of the blue fabric that covered Old Dorothy's body yesterday. Then I remember Henry the Bastard pulling it off her as he threw a shovel at me, knocking me on my ass, saying, "The Boss says to get on with burying her." I pull the curtains around the braid. Good.

I turn ninety degrees from the path to the airships and run down the dusty corridor between stalls. Passing the last curtained stall and a couple of meters farther, I turn to a wall and pause, scraping the dust off my feet and smearing it on the wall, my breath coming heavily. *Control your breath.* Ever so carefully, I backtrack my footsteps just as Dorothy had done. These bits of deception might buy me the time I need. When I get to the stall that marks the edge of the marketplace, I look up and take another breath, jumping to grasp the beam that the long curtains of the stall hung from. I swing my feet hard but not hard enough, and I miss, but then I swing again harder and pull with arms that have gotten stronger over the last several months. Grave digging obviously has its advantages. My mouth forms a silent "Thank you" to the women I buried. I can feel the tightly pulled fabric of the roof of the stall under my body.

I spread my arms and legs out as wide as possible and crawl like a lizard, grasping the framework of the stalls over the length and width of the marketplace. I'm approaching the edge closest to the airships again, and I look at the tree line and toward the village. I see no one. Then there's a motion under the trees, and I hold my breath. It's a rabbit. I roll onto my back and take three deep breaths. *Fucking rabbits.* Either the other thralls thought they were good to eat, or the younger ones thought they were cute. I don't get it. They make me sick to my stomach. I flip back and rub both dry eyes with the heel of one hand, then drop to the ground. I flip back my chopped hair. It just skims my shoulders and feels heavy with grease and dirt. *Run. Now.* My legs start moving. The visiting airships are parked just a kilometer or two farther. One is bound to be unlocked.

Something in the brush makes a sound, and I stumble a bit. *What was that?* Maybe it's The Bastard in pursuit. Glancing over my shoulder as I run shows no one behind me, but as I look back, a tree root rises up and grabs my foot, and I fall forward. The balls of my hands catch my weight. Searing pain cuts through my left palm, and I feel the pebbles in the mud embedding themselves in my right palm as the side of my face lands heavily next to them, sliding to a halt. My cheekbone feels hot and cold at the same time. That's gonna leave a mark. *Keep going.* I scramble to get up from the slick sludge and wipe the dirt and scum from my left eye, smearing it down my face. I focus forward. *Get going, legs.* When I was in primary school, a teacher said the faster I pumped my arms, the faster I'd run. I work at pumping my arms back and forth, fast. Can someone's heart actually explode? Mine might. I can't hear anything over my own breathing and the blood pounding in my ears. A branch catches at my hair, jerking me back, but I simply jerk harder forward, pulling it loose, and keep on running. My scalp is burning now. Holy fuck, I've made the flight line at the landing field. I'm here.

I run up to the first airship. It's large and silver and has a shimmering F and A on it. The Federal Alliance. There are countries all over the world that are part of that. My dad hated them. *Too rich and too powerful,* he'd say as he took my pay and told me what to do. Hell, I'll go there; wherever *there* is. Why not? There's a pole with a keypad. I see the door's outline on the hull. Which buttons do I push to open it? Fuck. I don't know.

I plug in this year's date: 2349. Nothing. I run to the next ship and then the next, pounding the year into the keypads. Nothing.

Finally, I get to the small airships. The first has a green hull with a flying waterfowl etched in yellow and the numbers 2014 emblazoned on it. I try those and nothing happens. I try this year, and nothing happens.

Move on. A dark, black hull. I plug in the year and am finally rewarded by a grinding sound as the hull door slowly descends. I step back from it and look at the airship with its folded wings and double airscrews and realize this is one of those I have seen land on the water. I squint at the black hull and can just make out what looks like a sailing ship etched on it. That's odd. I glance behind me and then turn and run up the ramp.

My breath is rough and ragged as I stand in the doorway. I take a moment to lean on the wall and feel my chest expand and contract. *Slow your breath.* I pull air in through my nose to the count of four like my grandma said. I hold it for a bit and then blow it out of my mouth to the count of eight. *Thanks, Grandma Rina.* I feel my heartbeat slow.

I open my eyes. No people in the airship. But how the fuck do I shut the door? I turn to the wall and see another keypad. The buttons I push are random, and suddenly I hear another grinding, and the light in the airship starts to dim. Yes!

I feel my knees bend, and I slide to the floor. I give myself a moment of breathing to slow my heartbeat, and then I look at the fuselage. It's small with only five full seats and one smaller one folded up on the wall. The cockpit and the helm are essentially one and the same. Cargo netting is mounded behind the seat most remote from the helm. I see some rough pieces of fabric off to the side of the cargo netting. I snag one of those, moving in front of the helm and pull my makeshift blanket around me. When will the crew return? Tonight? Tomorrow? Next week? I try not to think about water and food. I'll deal with that tomorrow. I can go without for a while. I've been practicing with His help, though He doesn't know it. He holds onto water and food to get compliance. I've been pushing my needs for those things more and more. His face clouds with annoyance when I can go without, and that little bit of power delights me. I have paid for the delight in blows, but it meets Goal Two of my life: inconvenience and annoy Him. Goal One, of course, is to survive, so that sometimes requires I moderate Goal Two.

I lean my head against the helm. Could I sleep? I shouldn't. But I'll hear that grinding of the door, right? I feel the weight of the last few hours descend on me as the adrenaline subsides. I think about Carisa and my stomach hurts. Should I have gone back for her? But my eyelids are heavy. I close them for a moment, promising that I will open them to the count of ten. As I reach five, the emptiness of the airship starts to echo, and I feel my neck sink to the side and my head loll down to rest on the deck. I feel the sensation of the rough fabric on my face fade, and I slip willingly into a dreamless sleep.

Gasp. And then I hold my breath. The surface I am lying on starts to shake. What's happening? Where's the baby? What baby? Then I feel the cool metal under my hand and remember where I am and that it's an airship. It must be taking off. I hold my breath in an effort to maintain my hiding place. The longer I'm invisible, the better off I am.

"Hey, Teddy, looks like there's a refugee on the lee side of the helm." The language I hear is different from home and different from here, but still similar enough that I can understand most of it. Dammit. Is it too soon? Will they turn back and turn me over? I won't go easily.

"I saw," comes a gruff voice. "Let's get airborne before we suss out the details."

"Aye, aye."

Several minutes later, after I feel the curious drop in my body that comes when an airship goes aloft, I hear footsteps and then a grunt. I can feel someone's presence near my head. It's foolish but I try to stay still and imagine that I am invisible even though I know they obviously see me. I feel a tentative tug at the fabric I have pulled over myself, and I hold onto it more strongly. I hear a chuckle. Then the cloth is peeled back from my clinging hands, and even though I grasp and pull, eventually my face is exposed.

"Hey, it's okay." I hear a deep rumble from the brown face I am squinting at. It holds more than a few wrinkles, and the hair has more salt than pepper, but the eyes are kind and questioning, not dead and mocking like His.

"Whatcha found there, Teddy?" This is a woman's voice.

"Looks like one of the thralls from the villa. I hate that they use our Glitter to keep them docile." He shakes his head and looks toward the voices above me.

"Hey." He turns his focus back to me. "You got yourself here. You are safe. I'll take you to Miriam." He looks right at me, and his eyes dart over my face and the scar on my neck and down to my hastily wrapped hand. Surprisingly, they stop there. That is different and welcome. But I've been down that path, and I'm not going to be taken in that easily. Not any longer. Dammit, I am going to die free, and not even this old man will cage me with false kindness and manipulation. I lift my chin and pour all my resolve into my eyes.

There is a pause as he looks me in the eye and smiles.

"I get it," he says. "Don't worry. Nobody is touching you. I won't touch you. You're fuckin' strong. You got this far. Don't forget that. You are free. What's your name?"

He calls over his shoulder, "Can we get a better blanket, here?"

A soft, furry blanket is passed over, and he carefully lays it over me as he draws back the rough cloth.

I stroke the softness with my fingertips and look at the man sitting back on his heels, his hands entwined. He surely has passed half a century. It hard to tell his height as he crouches but he isn't particularly tall, but his shoulders are broad, and I get a sense of strength from him. He has a day's growth of beard, and his eyes are a deep brown. I try to read those eyes. There's no look of expectation. No lustful approach. No, if anything, he looks . . . impressed? Don't know why. I'm a thrall on the run. But still, something in my brain begins to wonder what it might look like to see pride for me in that face. I take two breaths as I look at the brown face, wrinkles carving the cheeks and eyes and forehead and into the soft brown eyes. My name? I haven't been allowed my real name for a year and a half. It's not fucking Mary.

"My name is Kat. Kat Wallace."

Made in the USA
Middletown, DE
20 January 2025